What readers have to say about

The Glittering Hour

'It's an **absolutely unputdownable** tale of great love, friendship, heartache and loss which I totally adored'

'A great love story, a well-researched historical background, a writer who is a **born storyteller**'

'There's a lot I could write about this **heart-wrenching and engaging page-turner** but to cut short a long story I would only say that this was an **epic reading experience** that moved me to tears more than once'

'This book was absolutely **everything I hoped it would be** – and then probably a little more'

'An **immensely powerful** and convincing love story, and one that fills you with absolute joy . . . but then goes on to shatter your heart into so many pieces'

'This book is beautifully written – the author is a very accomplished storyteller – and the sureness of her emotional touch **took my breath away** and made me ache inside. The characters are wonderfully drawn – satisfyingly complex, and there are those you grow to love quite desperately, as you watch their lives unfold before you'

'There are **moments of sheer joy,** but there are others of almost unbearable sadness; you might, like me, even need to put the book down from time to time. But you read on, wiping away the many tears, desperate to continue, and have the absolute joy of discovering an end that is so very uplifting, with real hope for the future'

'All drawn together in the most perfect way, and worth every moment of that long wait – **don't miss this one, whatever you do**'

'*The Glittering Hour* is a **truly spectacular** book that had me gripped from the very start'

'A **spellbinding story** of shocks and scandal, wonder and devotion, that shows us that where there is love, there is forgiveness'

'*The Glittering Hour* is **one of my favourite books of the year so far,** so well written, captivating, and one I can see making a wonderful TV or film adaptation. A must-read I can't recommend enough'

'This is a glorious feast of a book to be savoured. It is **gorgeously romantic and heartbreakingly tragic** by turns and goes straight into my top reads list for this year'

'Iona Grey wowed readers with her first book *Letters to the Lost*. I know that I am not the only one who has been eagerly waiting for her to write a new book. Here it is, *The Glittering Hour*; I can say without hesitation that it is a **complete triumph**'

'*The Glittering Hour* by Iona Grey had me sobbing by the last few pages. I was so invested in the characters and their lives that I felt a little lost when I reached the final page. *The Glittering Hour* has been more than worth the wait, I know that it is **a book I will visit again and again**'

'A **mesmerizing** read full of love, heartache, friendship, romance'

'The characters and their stories in this **exquisite** book will stay with me for a very long time'

'This is a **captivating, epic read**, with enthralling characters whose stories kept me fascinated and broke my heart in equal measure. I can't recommend this book enough'

'*The Glittering Hour* **totally blew me away** and exceeded all of my expectations'

'I adored this captivating, tender and poignant story. I loved absolutely everything about it . . . It had everything I most enjoy within its 400 pages and I give this novel a resounding 5★ award and the advice that it is totally **unmissable and truly magical**'

'I HAVE NO WORDS GUYS!
I have written and deleted the start of this review more

times than I care to remember. Please, someone, HELP ME! **I am completely and utterly speechless**, it has been days since I finished *The Glittering Hour* for the SECOND time in two days, seriously. I was so distraught at being forced to say goodbye that I couldn't face even looking at another book, let alone reading another one. So I did the only thing that made any sense, I picked it up again and went back to the story'

'How am I supposed to put into words how this story quite literally **stole my heart**, smashed it into a billion pieces and rebuilt it all in one day? How I cried so many tears of sadness and happiness that my eyes were swollen for three days straight? When Iona writes a book she uses witchcraft, I am sure of it, she captures your heart and it is **simply impossible to just put her books down**, for even a second! *The Glittering Hour* is of course no different, once you start, from that very first page, you are irrevocably hers until she has finished with you'

'*The Glittering Hour* is **breathtakingly beautiful**, but even that description doesn't give it the justice it truly deserves'

'I have waited for what seems a lifetime for *The Glittering Hour*; after loving *Letters to the Lost* so much I was worried it maybe wouldn't live up to expectations, that maybe Iona would never be able to top such perfection. But how wrong I was: ***The Glittering Hour* was EVERYTHING and MORE**. More than I could have ever hoped and prayed for. It has well and truly surpassed all my expectations and smashed them well and truly out the park'

Iona Grey has a degree in English Literature and Language from Manchester University, an obsession with history and an enduring fascination with the lives of women in the twentieth century. She lives in rural Cheshire with her husband and three daughters. She tweets @iona_grey.

Also by Iona Grey

Letters to the Lost

IONA GREY

The Glittering Hour

**SIMON &
SCHUSTER**

London · New York · Sydney · Toronto · New Delhi

A CBS COMPANY

First published in Great Britain by Simon & Schuster UK Ltd, 2019
A CBS COMPANY

This paperback edition published 2019

5 7 9 10 8 6 4

Simon & Schuster UK Ltd
1st Floor
222 Gray's Inn Road
London WC1X 8HB

Simon & Schuster Australia, Sydney
Simon & Schuster India, New Delhi

www.simonandschuster.co.uk
www.simonandschuster.com.au
www.simonandschuster.co.in

A CIP catalogue record for this book is available from the British Library

Paperback ISBN: 978-1-4711-4070-9
eBook ISBN: 978-1-4711-4071-6

Excerpt from *Four Quartets* by T.S. Eliot.
Published by Faber & Faber Ltd, 2001.
Reprinted by permission of Faber & Faber Ltd.

Typeset by M Rules
Printed and bound by CPI Group (UK) Ltd, Croydon, CR0 4YY

FSC
www.fsc.org

MIX
Paper from
responsible sources
FSC® C020471

For my mother, and hers

Footfalls echo in the memory
Down the passage we did not take,
Towards the door we never opened
Into the rose garden

– T.S. ELIOT

Prologue

The End

February 1926

The February dawn crept in slowly, apologetically, as if it sensed how unwelcome it was. The room came into focus in increments, like a photograph developing.

But the numerous images that had lined the walls were gone now, like everything else. The room – never lavishly furnished – had been stripped back to impersonal function-ality: a scarred table, a flimsy bentwood chair. A canvas kitbag was propped against the table leg. Her gaze flinched away from it.

She missed the faces on the walls. He photographed strangers: the poor and the dispossessed, the wounded and the mad, capturing dignity in their distress. Suffering gave people a natural nobility, he said, though she knew it was pointless to hope it might do the same for her. She had chosen the coward's way out. There would be no honour in her pain.

He lay behind her, the way they naturally fitted together, his chest against her back, his hard thighs tucked beneath her knees. She couldn't see his face but she knew he was awake and, like her, was watching the treacherous daylight gather. Across the city it would be stealing into another room, stretching out across an empty bed, touching the snowy silk folds of the wedding dress hanging on the wardrobe.

She had to go. Before the world woke up properly. Before her absence was discovered and the alarm was raised.

She turned to him for one last time.

PART I

1

Alice

January 1936

The winter sky was yellowish-grey and it sagged wearily over the frozen world. It had snowed last night, but disappointingly; a mean scattering of dirty white that had frozen into sharp crystals – nothing you could make a snowman from (would she be allowed anyway? Probably not). The cold slapped Alice's cheeks and burned deep into her bones as she trudged miserably after Miss Lovelock.

They had taken their usual route, along the west carriage drive and round the edge of the lake, where last autumn's leaves still lay in a mouldering rust-coloured carpet. The gardens at Blackwood Park were extensive and elaborate; once they had been the jewel in its crown, but now, with only elderly Patterson and a simple boy to maintain them they were overgrown and out of bounds. Alice's daily walk (non-negotiable: Miss Lovelock was a great believer in the benefits of Fresh Air) was over the rough parkland, past sheep that eyed her with hostility. After eleven days it had already taken on a familiarity that was oppressive rather than comforting.

Eleven days. *Was that all?*

The unsettled feeling in her tummy was back as she thought of all the days that yawned ahead until Mama came home. She stopped, focusing on the white swirl of her frozen breath and the poker-like plants at the edge of the water. Bulrushes, Miss Lovelock said. Alice had heard of them in the bible story of Moses, but had never seen them before she came to Blackwood – there certainly weren't any on the banks of the Serpentine or by the Round Pond in Kensington Gardens, or any of the other places she went for winter walks with Mama (sometimes followed by tea at Maison Lyons or Gunters, or – if they had got cold and wet – crumpets at home, toasted together in front of the parlour fire). She stared hard at them, making herself notice their compact shape and velvety texture, because noticing those things distracted her from the sick, hollow feeling in her tummy. She would have liked to break one off, to take back up to the house so she could sketch it with the beautiful set of pencils Mama had bought her for Christmas (twelve different colours, like a rainbow in a tin) but she suspected that wouldn't be allowed either. Grandmama had taken the pencils away when Alice had arrived, 'for safekeeping'. Drawing was not encouraged at Blackwood Park.

'Alice! Come along, child – quick march!'

Miss Lovelock's voice, bristling with impatience, carried back from the point far ahead to which her brisk pace had taken her ('quick march' was not so much an expression, but a command. She was extremely fond of marching.) Everything about Miss Lovelock was brisk and no-nonsense, from her lace-up shoes and mannish ties to her fondness for arithmetic and Latin verbs – subjects with exact answers and no room for 'what if?'

(Mama said that 'what if?' was always a good question to ask. She turned it into a game that they played on the top of the motorbus: what if you could be invisible for a day – what would you do? What if animals could talk? What if Parliament was filled with women instead of men?)

Alice left the bulrushes and began to trudge dutifully towards Miss Lovelock. The governess's arms were folded across her wide chest and, even at this distance, Alice could see that her brows were drawn down into a single black line of exasperation. Much as Miss Lovelock liked Fresh Air, Alice knew she was eager to get back to the house and hand over her charge so she could spend the afternoon listening to the wireless in the warmth of her room. Even so, passing the old boathouse Alice couldn't resist pausing to press her face close to the mossy window, peering in at the tangle of fishing rods in the corner, the pile of moth-eaten cushions, hoping to catch a glimpse of the ghosts that slumbered there dreaming of long-ago summers; of boating parties and picnics and swimming in the lake . . .

Blackwood Park was full of ghosts. Its empty corridors echoed with the whispers of lost voices and snatches of old laughter. It was a house where the past felt more vivid than the present, which was nothing more than a stretch of endless days fading into uniform blankness. It had been Mama's house when she was growing up, and she had told Alice how she, Aunt Miranda and Uncle Howard would play hopscotch on the marble floor in the entrance hall and French cricket on the nursery corridor with the footmen, in the days before the Great War when there had been footmen at Blackwood (and when there had been an Uncle Howard – though of course he hadn't been an Uncle then, and never would be a living one). Alice thought it might be their voices she heard. Their laughter, their footsteps.

'Alice Carew, will you please *get a move on!'*

Her sigh misted the greenish glass and she turned reluctantly away. The light was bleeding from the January sky and a pale smudge of moon had appeared above the trees. Behind Miss Lovelock the house loomed, dark and imposing, its windows blank, its secrets hidden. With a leaden heart Alice walked towards them both.

In the nursery corridor, high up at the top of the house, it was hardly much warmer than it had been outside. Alice's breath, instead of appearing in cavalier plumes, hung about her in a ghostly wreath. Her footsteps, as she followed Miss Lovelock to the day nursery, made no sound on the bald carpet, as if she were no more substantial than the childhood shadows of Mama, Aunt Miranda and Uncle Howard.

There had been no nanny or nursemaids at Blackwood for twenty years. The nursery corridor, on which the schoolroom was also situated, had been closed up for much of that time, the forgotten dolls and stuffed animals in the day nursery left to contemplate a more glorious past, the rocking horse to gallop, riderless, over the same patch of faded rug. The rooms must have been hastily cleaned and aired before Alice's arrival, but pockets of stillness remained where Ellen's careless duster hadn't quite reached, and the air had a stale quality, like in a museum.

There were no lessons after lunch at Blackwood, unlike at the girls' day school Alice went to in South Kensington. There the afternoons were spent in companionable industry, doing art or needlework or domestic science (Miss Ellwood, the principal, was a forward-thinking woman who was fully aware that even the most well-bred young ladies must be able to fend for themselves in a world where the Servant Problem was becoming increasingly acute). Miss Lovelock, having deposited Alice in the day nursery with the instruction to read something 'improving', retreated to her room with indecent haste and closed the door firmly. A moment later Alice heard the muted crackle of the wireless set.

She went across to the window and sank down onto its cushioned seat. As well as the strange feeling in her tummy there was a tight, painful lump in the base of her throat, which made it hard to swallow, hard to breathe.

She wondered if she might be coming down with some illness, and felt a tiny rush of hope. If she was poorly – really poorly – surely Mama would have to come back?

Outside the dusk was falling fast, swallowing up the bleak expanse of parkland. The frost lay thick in the folds and hollows that the sun's weak fingers hadn't touched, and it glowed palely in the gathering gloom. If you drew it like that it wouldn't look real, she thought, but she would have liked to try. She thought of the pencils again and the lump in her throat swelled.

She didn't know what she'd done to make Grandmama dislike her. While Grandfather, who was old and unwell, seemed merely indifferent, Alice felt Grandmama's disapproval curling around her like an icy draught, but one whose source remained a mystery. As far as she could remember she'd never disgraced herself in front of her; never been disagreeable or disobedient or shown off. In fact, before two weeks ago when she'd arrived at Blackwood she'd barely spent any time with her grandparents at all, which was why the news that she was to stay with them while Mama accompanied Papa on a business trip to the East had come as such a shock. They were strangers.

It wasn't *fair*.

The smell of toasting muffins drifted along the corridor from Miss Lovelock's room. Hunger pinched at Alice's hollow tummy and cold cramped her feet and fingers. There was a fire laid in the nursery grate, but she knew very well that she wasn't allowed to light it, and that Miss Lovelock would be cross if she knocked and asked her to (she would feel guilty that she had forgotten, which would make the crossness worse). There was a frayed tapestry cord by the fireplace which you could pull to ring a bell in the servants' hall downstairs, but it was Polly's half day, which meant it would be Ellen who would come. Ellen, who (Polly said) was seventeen, and had her head stuffed with the nonsense she and Ivy, the kitchen maid, read in magazines – film stars and hairstyles and all sorts of beautifying treatments that involved raiding the pantry for baking soda and honey to smear on their faces. Alice had almost smiled when Polly told her that, but she was still a bit afraid of Ellen. She looked at the cord, but she knew she wasn't brave enough to touch it.

She tucked her legs up against her chest and hugged them tightly. The nursery had subsided in shadow so she turned her face back to the window, but there was nothing to see now except the pale oval of her own reflection.

She should get up and switch on the lamp (she thought she was allowed to do that?) and choose a book from the shelf, but the minutes dragged by and she didn't move. Reading never brought her much pleasure because the words always seemed to shimmer and shift in front of her eyes, rearranging themselves until they made no sense. It wasn't just the cold that made her feel sluggish and numb, but the sense of being full to the brim of something that could spill over at any moment if she wasn't very still. So she stayed where she was, balled up against the cold, listening.

A door slammed far below. Distant voices swelled and retreated again – from Miss Lovelock's wireless, the servants' stairs or the vanished past she couldn't tell. Cold air shivered across her cheek, and strands of the rocking horse's tail fluttered as if touched by the fingers of invisible children. She squeezed her eyes shut. Her throat was burning now, and there was a pain in her jaw from clamping her teeth together to stop them chattering. The sudden, close-by sound of a door opening set her heart banging against her knees.

She edged back, trying to hide herself behind the curtain, aware of how silly Ellen would think her if she saw her crouching in the dark like this. She prayed for the footsteps to pass, but a figure loomed in the doorway and a second later the electric light flicked on.

'Oh my Lord—' Polly clamped a hand to her chest. 'You gave me the fright of my life! What are you doing, sitting all alone in the dark? Alice? Oh my lamb . . .'

The kindness was her undoing. Polly crossed the room with swift strides, opening her arms as the sobs that Alice had been holding back came spilling out. Polly held her, rocking and crooning until they had spent themselves, and then she gathered Alice more securely onto her knee and wiped her wet cheeks with a handkerchief.

'There, there, my pet . . . That's better . . . Polly's here now. It's just as well I came back early today – Lord alone knows how long you might have sat here in the dark otherwise. That useless Ellen, I could strangle her. Do you want to tell me about it, sweetheart? What's got you so upset?'

'N-n-nothing . . .' The lump in her throat had dissolved, but her head throbbed from crying. Her breath was coming in odd little gasps. 'It's just . . . I m-miss my mama.'

'Oh pet, *of course* you do . . . it's only natural that you would, and there's not much here to take your mind off it, is there?' Polly's hand rubbed a soothing circle on Alice's back. 'Especially not with the weather being so dreadful. Blackwood's a gloomy old place at this time of year, that's for sure. I tell you what—' The rubbing paused as she smoothed a strand of hair off Alice's cheek. 'Why don't I light the fire and get this place warm, and you can sit at the table there and write a nice long letter to your mama and tell her all about it. Not just about missing her, mind, because that would make her sad and we don't want that, but I'm sure if you try hard you can find some cheerful things to write. And thinking of cheerful things might even make you start feeling a bit more cheerful yourself.'

Alice shook her head. 'I'm not allowed. Miss Lovelock said. I'm to write one letter a week and make sure it's my best writing with no spelling mistakes because Grandmama will check it before it gets sent to Mama. I wrote on Sunday.'

It had been a miserable letter. Not outwardly, of course; the words on the page had been as bland and careful as she could make them, but the spaces between them had echoed with all the loneliness she wasn't allowed to express and the questions she couldn't ask. *Why can't Papa sort out the business with the mineworkers on his own? How far away is Burma? When will you come back?* Her tummy had felt very strange indeed by the time she'd signed her name beneath the few polite lines. She hated the thought of her mother reading it and thinking she was being cross and difficult.

'Well, that seems a shame to me.' Polly's voice was unusually curt. 'There's nothing nicer than getting a letter from home when you can't be there.'

'It's because it's so expensive. Grandmama said it costs a lot to send a letter all the way to Burma, and to the boat Mama and Papa are sailing there on.'

'Did she now?' Gently, Polly tipped Alice off her knee and went over to the fireplace. Her movements were jerky as she lit a match and held it to the paper in the grate. When the flame caught she turned back to Alice with a strange sort of smile. 'Well, I'm sure it can't be that much – and to my mind it'll be cheap at the price if it cheers you and your mama up. Look, why don't I go down and see if I can find some notepaper and you can write again, and say anything you like. I'll post it myself when I go into the village next.'

'Really?' Tremulous hope quivered in Alice's voice. 'You don't have to . . . I don't want you to get into trouble . . .'

'I'm not going to get into trouble, because no one's going to know except us two.' Polly went to the door, turning round to look back at Alice. 'And just between you and me, it won't be the first time I've risked my job to help your mama out.' There was something sad in her smile. 'Now, you wait here while I get that paper.'

2

The Game Begins

Alice knew that it would be a long time before a reply came to her letter. In her head she tried to keep track of the letter's progress, from the village post office to the sorting office in Salisbury and then to a Royal Mail Steamer at Southampton, but there her experience reached its limit. As her letter made its journey across the fathomless miles of ocean, the closeness she'd felt to Mama as she'd written it receded again.

A heaviness lay over the days, caused in part by the death of the old king at the end of January. Blackwood felt a long way away from London, but the news made everyone sombre and the world seemed altered in some significant way: less safe, in the careless hands of the dandy prince. If death could claim the King himself surely it could come for anyone, at any time?

The bitter cold continued, but still it didn't snow. The ground over which Alice trailed after Miss Lovelock each afternoon was frozen to flinty hardness, the grass brittle with frost. The hours between dawn and dusk were short and the sun barely managed to raise itself above the bare, black branches of the trees around the lake before the shadows on the nursery walls stretched and it slid downwards again, along with Alice's spirits. The days themselves might be short, but the empty hours dragged like weeks. Instead of her homesickness easing, it settled more solidly inside her, as if her heart was gradually freezing like the lake's murky waters.

But writing the letter had helped. There was the anticipation of a reply and, more importantly, the secret knowledge that she could write again which gave some small purpose to her days. She made it her business to look out for things to tell Mama; small details from her walks with Miss Lovelock, like the heron that they sometimes saw in the reeds by the lake, or the perfect pink sunset that, for a little while, had turned the hard, white world into a sugared confection of Turkish delight. Even the ordeal of Sunday lunch with The Grands (as Mama called them, though never to their faces) was made more bearable by knowing she could share it with Mama. She told her about the time Grandfather had caught her looking at one of the huge portraits on the dining room walls, and asked her if she recognized the young woman in the white dress. Alice had stared up at the painted peaches-and-cream complexion and piled-up, pale gold hair and felt her own face growing crimson with embarrassment as no answer presented itself. Grandmama's voice had been icy as she'd informed Alice that the girl in the painting was she, in the year of her Coming Out.

Did Grandmama really look like that, she wrote to Mama that night, *before she was cross all the time?*

In fact, Mama's reply came sooner than Alice had really dared hope. It wasn't quite two weeks after Polly had posted the letter, when Alice imagined it might still be making its epic journey, that Polly came into the day nursery with Alice's lunch tray and an air of suppressed excitement.

With a rustle of paper she slipped the letter out of her pocket and set it down on the table. There was only one word on the envelope, in Mama's familiar handwriting and trademark turquoise ink. *Alice.* She and Polly had agreed it was safer if Mama wrote to Polly, enclosing a letter for Alice, in case Grandmama decided to check her letters too.

'Well, aren't you going to open it? It feels lovely and thick.'

Alice's fingers itched to tear the letter open and let Mama's jewelled words come spilling out, but instead she picked up her fork. After waiting all this time she wanted to savour the anticipation a bit longer.

'I am, but later. After lunch.'

The oxtail and stewed prunes were rather less worth savouring than the anticipation, but she made herself eat slowly, sipping at her glass of water. When she had finished she stacked her plates onto the tray and took the letter to the window seat, settling an old, flattened needlepoint cushion with a pair of Noah's elephants on it behind her back and half-drawing the curtain to cloak herself in privacy.

Finally, carefully, she slid her finger beneath the flap of the envelope.

S.S. Eastern Star
The Suez Canal

28th January 1936

Darling, darling Alice,

I got your letter just now, and I didn't want to waste a moment before replying. It is the middle of the afternoon and fiercely hot, and we have just left Port Said where your letter was waiting for us. Papa has been terribly kind and said that he will try to get this letter sent back to England by airmail, which is as quick as the blink of an eye. Isn't that smart?

Sweetheart, I am so desperately sorry that you are feeling sad and lonely. I know how confusing all this must seem to you, and how sudden. Papa tries to shield us from all his business concerns but this trouble at the mine is something that he can't sort out from London and it will help tremendously to have a wife there to do the kind of social smoothing over that wives do, when the men have finished squabbling over their sheets of figures and legal small print. I would have simply adored to bring you with us, my darling — oh, the heaven of having your wonderful company — but it would have been extremely selfish. The heat is draining (hard for you to imagine, I know; how well

I remember that Blackwood feels like the coldest corner of Christendom in the winter) and, once we arrive in Burma the mine business is sure to take up every waking hour, which means you would have to be left alone anyway, and without darling Polly to look after you. There's no one in whose care I would rather leave you, sweetheart. Polly has kept many of my secrets over the years — I trust her with my life, and yours too, which is infinitely more precious. I know you will be safe with her, but I do so hope that we can sort things out quickly here and come home soon. Oh darling, I hope that with all my heart.

But for the moment we must both try to be brave and cheerful, because if we feel brave and cheerful the time will go much more quickly than if we are gloomy and despondent. So, I shall tell you about where I am sitting right now, because that will make me pay proper attention to how beautiful it all is rather than dwelling on how far away from you. I am on the little private deck of our cabin, sitting in the shade of a green and white striped awning and our dear steward Ahmed has just brought me some peppermint tea in a silver teapot, served in the daintiest little pink glass etched with gold. It's wonderful to be sailing again. In the harbour at Port Said the air was sweltering but out at sea the breeze is quite delicious. It carries the scent of spices out from the shore, which is just a dark blue line between the lighter blues of sea and sky. I swear I haven't seen a single cloud since we left Marseilles, though that was where we heard of the dear old King's death, so the blue skies felt all wrong. (Poor Grandmama – she danced with him in her youth, when he was the Duke of York and she a dazzling debutante. I expect she will be very saddened by the news.)

Papa managed to get us a rather lovely suite, which was jolly clever of him when the passage was booked at such short notice. My room is small, but very comfortable and modern, with lovely walnut panelling and the most sumptuous carpet and gold satin bedcover. There's a dear little lamp above the bed for reading, though for two entire days I could barely open my eyes or lift my head from the pillow because of the dreaded seasickness. I'm much better now. Papa, being so much more used to sailing than I am, has been perfectly well. His cabin is on the other side of our little sitting room, and is decorated all in green. (I'm glad I didn't have that one. I felt quite green enough.) The ship is terribly plush; there's a swimming pool and a gymnasium I believe (though I have no intention of seeking it out myself!) and a library – so you see, my darling, I have no excuse to be bored and gloomy.

How I wish you had all the lovely distractions that I do, but since you only have Blackwood Park, and The Grands and Miss Lovelock (who sounds terrifying – I must ask Papa where he found her) I've been trying to think how we might make things more fun for you. You have Polly too, of course – and she is the best accomplice for any adventure – and don't we always say that one can find treasure in the most unlikely places, if one looks carefully enough?

Blackwood Park might seem an unlikely place to find anything exciting. My darling, I know better than anyone that it can seem as still and silent as the sleeping castle in a fairy tale, and how time there seems to drag more slowly than anywhere else. But all old houses hold stories and Blackwood is no exception. It may be silent and empty, but it has its store of treasures to be discovered and secrets waiting to be revealed . . .

Please know, my dearest darling, how much I miss you – every moment – and how I'm longing to be back with you soon. Have courage, brave girl. In a world that is small enough for the same moon to hang over us both, we can't ever be too far apart.

With love from my heart to yours, and a lipstick kiss
Mama xxxxx

A lipstick kiss. There it was at the bottom of the page – the scarlet stamp of her mother's lips, just like she used to leave on the back of Alice's hand before school in the morning, or in the evening when she was going out with Papa. She lifted the paper to her face and breathed in a faint trace of Mama's scent, noticing as she did so that there was more writing on the other side of the paper.

She turned it over.

Where the sun's first rays
Turn lilies to gold,
There's a box in a drawer through a door.

Open it up
And the paper unfold,
And see if you want to know more.

'Well, was it a nice letter?'

Polly's voice behind her was soft and cautious. Alice turned and handed her the letter, curiosity quickening inside her. 'It's a poem, or a riddle. What do you think it means?'

Polly's eyes skimmed the paper. She was smiling as she handed it back. 'I'd say there's only one way of answering that. You'll just have to find this box, won't you?'

Alice would never have believed that she might actually look forward to her afternoon walk, but as they set off there was something very close to excitement beating beneath her tightly buttoned coat. Putting on her outdoor boots she had asked if they might vary the route today and go through the kitchen garden, and when Miss Lovelock asked why on earth she wanted to do that, she was able to say quite truthfully that she wanted to see what was growing there. Miss Lovelock had seemed surprised, but taking it as a sign of some fledgling interest in botany or horticulture, grudgingly acquiesced.

The drab park stretched away on all sides. Surely there were no lilies blooming at this time of year – had Mama forgotten what England was like in February? Alice thought of the wilderness that lay beyond the kitchen garden's walls, closed up and out of bounds, and the great orangery, with the overgrown plants inside pressing like prisoners against the clouded glass. Were there lilies inside its jungly tangle?

She remembered going in there once, with Mama, on a long-ago summer visit to Blackwood. She remembered the hot, damp air and the unfamiliar smell of earth and vegetation and something sweet and rotten. The plants looked like they'd been stolen from a giant's garden, towering above her with leaves as large as umbrellas. Little paths had wound between them and Alice remembered a fountain, tiled with tiny iridescent squares that shimmered beneath the splashing water like a mermaid's tail. She had said that to Mama, she remembered, but Mama had hardly seemed to hear. She had been distracted – it stuck in Alice's mind because it was so unlike her – as if she was listening to someone else. When she looked at Alice it felt as if it wasn't her she saw.

They didn't follow the carriage drive beneath the trees today, as they usually did, but turned under the archway into the stableyard. There used to be lots of horses at Blackwood, Alice remembered Mama telling her, but the stables were all empty now, with only the lingering horse smell and rows of saddles and harnesses – the leather now dull and cracked – to show that they had ever been there. Many of them had been taken by the army at the start of the war, Mama had said, and her voice had been flinty with blame and bitterness. There were no men to look after those that remained and so they were sold and the stables left empty.

The War. In Alice's head it always had capital letters. It

was barely spoken about at home, and never in front of Papa, but Alice felt that it had always been *there*, like a presence in the house, invisible and unwelcome. Sometimes she encountered it on the streets too, in men with missing limbs and rows of medals selling matches outside the underground, or shouting at nothing in the park. *It's The War, darling. Poor man. Don't stare.*

The kitchen garden was beyond the stables, reached through a door in a high wall of crumbling brick. Miss Lovelock led the way with her Sergeant Major march; she might not have instigated the change of routine but it appeared she certainly intended to take charge of it. She ushered Alice in, unnecessarily pointing out a large puddle in the path and speaking in a loud voice, as if she were marshalling a battalion instead of one small, quiet girl.

Alice hung back, looking around. The high walls were rosy in the weak winter sun and they enclosed its tentative warmth, hiding the bulk of the house and keeping the desolate expanse of parkland at bay. The earth beds were mostly brown and bare, she saw with a stab of disappointment. A row of glasshouses lined one wall, and beyond them, tucked into one corner was a neat cottage, as square and symmetrical as a picture in a storybook. A wisp of smoke curled out of the chimney and faded into the afternoon sky.

As Miss Lovelock lectured in a loud, know-it-all voice about the optimum conditions for seed germination a stooped figure emerged from one of the glasshouses. His clothes were worn to the same mossy colours as the walls and the soil and his face was creased like autumn leaves. Earth clung to his hands. Catching Alice's eye, he nodded.

'Afternoon.'

Miss Lovelock, who had been too preoccupied with airing her collection of horticultural facts to notice him, looked round in alarm, as if one of the winter cabbages had spoken. The gardener, coming over, gave Alice the ghost of a wink. 'You must be Miss Selina's girl. Heard you were staying.'

Miss Lovelock cleared her throat. 'Alice expressed an interest in seeing the gardens, Mr . . . ?'

'Patterson.'

'Very good.' Miss Lovelock spoke as if addressing a soldier of inferior rank. 'I did say there wouldn't be much to see at this time of year, but she insisted.' She turned to Alice. 'Perhaps now your curiosity has been satisfied, child, we can resume our walk.'

'Just because you can't see things in the garden, doesn't mean there's nothing going on,' Mr Patterson remarked, almost as if he was talking to himself. 'That's part of the magic, to my mind.'

Alice was intrigued, and emboldened enough to ask the question that had brought her here.

'Are there any lilies?'

'Lilies, child?' Miss Lovelock gave an incredulous laugh and rolled her eyes. 'Good heavens, I believe I could have told you that myself and saved us a wasted journey. Lilies don't grow in February! Not in England, anyway.'

'Well now, that's not quite true ...' The old gardener rummaged unhurriedly in the gaping pocket of his jacket, unearthing seed packets and lengths of twine before eventually pulling out a pipe. 'There are no lilies here now, but that's not to say I haven't had them blooming in winter before. Let me see – ' He peered thoughtfully into the bowl of the pipe, and gave it an experimental tap. 'It'll be eleven years ago, if I'm not mistaken. Your mama was a February bride, and I grew them for her wedding. It wasn't easy mind – I had to keep the fire burning behind that glasshouse wall day and night to make it warm enough, but it was worth it. The perfume in there was strong enough to make you swoon. And of course, she was a beautiful bride.'

Miss Lovelock gave a dubious sniff. 'Well, we mustn't take up any more of your time. I'm sure you have a lot to be getting on with.'

'You're welcome to come here anytime,' the old gardener said, looking at Alice. 'I'm sorry I can't show you any lilies, mind.'

As Alice followed Miss Lovelock back along the cinder path she peered through a pair of high iron gates that led to the rest of the garden. She caught a glimpse of tall hedges, dense and dark, and a pathway between them, twisting out of sight. She longed to linger, or to open the gates and follow the path into the abandoned kingdom beyond, but Miss Lovelock had already disappeared. Her voice swooped over the wall.

'Come along, Alice!'

She looked back. Mr Patterson, standing at the door of the glasshouse, raised his hand in a solemn salute, and she waved shyly back, thinking about what he'd said.

She'd known Mama had had a bouquet of lilies when she got married. There was a photograph in a silver frame in the drawing room at home, of her in her white satin dress with the long sheaf of pale blooms over one arm. Her other arm was hooked through Papa's, who looked as stern and distant as ever, as if he was going to a meeting at the bank rather than his own wedding. Alice loved looking at that snapshot of a moment before she existed, at Mama's luminous eyes gazing straight out at her, as if to say *'soon . . .'* and it made the back of her neck tingle to think that the flowers in the picture had been grown here, and that the old gardener had known Mama in that mysterious time. The Grands had the same photograph (beside a bigger one in a fancier frame, of Aunt Miranda and Uncle Lionel on their wedding day) on top of the piano in the drawing room, beneath the portrait of Uncle Howard in his soldier's khaki. (There would be no wedding photograph for him.)

Alice's heart gave an uneven thud. The lilies in the photograph – could they be the ones the clue referred to? Her mind raced, going over the lines again, trying to remember if the photograph was in a place where the morning sun might reach it, and if it was, where the door, the drawer and the box might fit in. The surge of excitement subsided as she realized how difficult it would be to go and check. Blackwood's stately downstairs rooms were not part of her

domain; she rarely ventured into them at all, except on
Sundays, and then she was always under the chilly gaze of
her grandparents and was forbidden from touching anything. Had Mama forgotten what it was like here?

She trailed along the carriage drive in Miss Lovelock's
brisk wake, listening to the shrill squabbling of the rooks
in the bare branches above her. She could feel the house
crouching at her back, its rows of windows like blank eyes,
watching, and she turned round to meet its gaze.

The nursery corridor ran along the back of the house, so
she couldn't see her own bedroom window from here. To
the right the shutters were closed behind all the windows on
the upper floors, where the rooms that had once been occupied by guests had been closed up on corridors that were
no longer used. To the left were the family rooms, and she
wondered which one might be Mama's old bedroom, trying
to remember if it faced out to the front. She had slept in it
once, with Mama, when she was quite small . . .

The memory began to emerge from the shadows at the
back of her mind, taking shape, gathering colour. Aunt
Miranda and Uncle Lionel had been at Blackwood too, with
Cousin Archie who had been a tiny baby. Alice remembered
the atmosphere, brittle with tension, and knew that somehow it had been her fault (she'd had a cough that had woken
Cousin Archie and made him cry? Something like that . . .)
Mama had come up to the nursery in the night and brought
her down to sleep in her bed.

The exact reason might elude her, but she vividly

remembered the delicious perfumed warmth after the hard little iron cot in the night nursery and the luxury of having Mama all to herself. She had woken up early the next morning and lain very still as the light glowed through the curtains, not wanting Mama to wake up and the ordinary day to begin.

The air left her lungs in a long, slow stream, making a pale garland around her head.

Of course.

Mama's bedroom, where the walls were pale green and the curtains were patterned with columns of ivory lilies, which got the full flood of golden morning sun, rising over the lake. Alice felt goosebumps rise on her arms, caused not by the February cold but by the delicious sense of having slotted the vital piece of the puzzle into place.

Behind her Miss Lovelock called her name crossly. Alice immediately turned and ran, propelled by a sudden burst of exuberant energy – much to the governess's obvious astonishment.

She knew she could have told Polly, but something held her back; a greedy impulse to keep the secret to herself perhaps. She drank her afternoon milk quickly, then tiptoed past Miss Lovelock's door and down the servants' stairs to the bedroom corridor below.

She immediately noticed how much warmer it was; how the thick carpet muffled the sound of her footsteps completely and made the thud of her heart seem louder. For a dizzying moment she couldn't think which room was Mama's, but some long-dormant memory resurfaced of a tall blue and white jar on a polished table, and she knew that the door opposite was the right one.

At least, she thought it was. She hesitated, her fingers clasping the handle, her courage faltering as her imagination tormented her with the image of Grandmama waiting on the other side of the door with an expression of thunderous rage. It was only the thought of Mama, who wasn't scared of anything – least of all rules – that stopped her from fleeing back to the Spartan safety of the nursery.

She turned the handle.

She had expected it to be dark inside, but it wasn't. The shutters and the lily-strewn curtains were open and the room was filled with the last dusky light of the winter afternoon; a melancholy glow, that seemed full of Mama's absence. The sadness that had retreated since the letter arrived curled its fingers around Alice's throat again. She tried to push it away, steering her mind back to the clue.

A box, in a drawer, through a door.

Did that mean the bedroom door? She turned round, uncertain, until she glimpsed her own ghostly reflection in the mirrored door of the wardrobe and another piece of the puzzle slotted into place. Inside, dresses still hung on the rails, their colours muddied by the fading day. As she ran her hand down them tears stung suddenly at the back of Alice's eyes. This was the closest she'd felt to her mother since she'd arrived in this cavernous, shadowy, silent house;

the most vivid and personal evidence she had to remind her that Mama had lived here. Caressing the velvet sleeve of an evening coat she wondered if that had been Mama's intention; if, knowing how much Alice was missing her, she had deliberately brought her to where comfort would be found amongst her things. It would be just like Mama to think of that.

She had intended to search out what she was looking for and leave as quickly as possible, but now she was here, surrounded by things that still carried a hint of Mama's perfume, she found she didn't want to go back up to the cold and comfortless nursery. Had Mama worn these dresses to parties and balls? Had young, beautiful Selina Lennox danced with Rupert Carew in those tissue-shrouded shoes and known he was the man she was going to marry? Had she loved him then?

The bedroom door opened in a sudden fan of electric light, catapulting Alice out of wistful imagining and into pure terror. She was hidden from view by the open door of the wardrobe, but that meant she couldn't see who had come in either and what they were doing. Dizzy with panic she shrank back between the folds of silk and tweed, drawing them around her in the hope of avoiding discovery, even though she knew it was futile. A second later a figure peered around the door. Alice gave a whimper of relief as she recognized Polly.

'I suppose I don't need to ask what you're doing in here . . .' Her arms were folded, but she didn't sound cross.

'There are lilies on the curtains.' Alice's voice was a breathless croak. 'I woke up in here with Mama once, and the sun came through . . . And look – drawers.' There was a row of them, beneath the shelves on which the shoes stood. 'The box in the clue must be in one of those.'

Polly grinned. 'Well, you'd better check quick then, before anyone notices that neither of us are where we're supposed to be.'

Alice started at the top, pulling the drawers open quickly. Handkerchiefs, stockings, a stack of neatly folded white blouses with girlish Peter Pan collars, stiff cotton night-dresses with frilled lace at the neck . . . And then, in the bottommost drawer, a box.

With Polly watching, she lifted it out and carried it over to the bed. It was made of cardboard, not heavy, and when she set it down on the lily-strewn counterpane she could just about make out a label on the lid in furling Art-Nouveau style.

'Maison D'Or,' Polly said softly, tracing a finger over the lettering. 'It was a dressmaking studio in London where your mama and Miss Miranda used to get a lot of their things made. The studio was all done out in ivory and gold – I only went there a couple of times to pick things up, but I was that nervous about trailing mud in off the street or making a mess. I wonder if it's still there now?'

'I didn't know you'd lived in London.' Somehow Polly, with her buttery west-country accent and wheat-coloured hair was part of Blackwood. It was impossible to imagine her amongst motorcars and trams and sooty streets.

'I didn't – not really. Sir Robert and Lady Lennox had a house there back then – in Chester Square it was – and I used to go up during the Season. They had separate household staff, but personal servants used to travel with the family. I went for a few years, from the time your mama had her Coming Out to when she married . . .' Polly became brisk again. 'Here, are you going to look inside this box or not?'

Alice lifted the lid and laid it aside. The first thing she saw was a piece of paper, folded in half. She opened it, tilting it to catch the words in the fading light.

21st MAY 1925

A not–quite MIDSUMMER NIGHT'S SCREAM

TO WHICH

ALL **FAERIE QUEENS, ASSES** AND **YOUNG LOVERS**

ARE INVITED

FOR A NIGHT OF **REVELRY** ON THE

STREETS OF LONDON

IN THE ETERNAL HUNT FOR **FUN** AND **TREASURE**

INNOCENCE MAY BE LOST BUT

PRIZES WILL BE FOUND

ASSEMBLE AT ADMIRALTY ARCH AT

MIDNIGHT FOR STIRRUP CUP BEFORE THE OFF

Alice read it through twice. There were words that were unfamiliar, but the message was clear. And thrilling. She looked up at Polly.

'A treasure hunt? A proper treasure hunt, for grown-ups?'

Polly laughed. Her hair gleamed palely in the dusk but her face was in deep shadow so Alice couldn't see her expression. 'I suppose they were grown-ups, though they didn't behave like them most of the time. If they'd been just a few years older the boys would have been through the war in France, but these were the ones who just missed it.'

'Papa went.'

'I know, pet.'

'Mama said that's why he's like he is.' It was The War's fault. Not Alice's. Never Alice's.

Polly sighed. 'I daresay she's right. It left its mark on all of those that went through it, but it had an effect on the ones who came after too.' The flimsy paper leaflet crackled softly as she smoothed it flat. 'It made them a bit giddy, I think, like they wanted to grab as many opportunities to enjoy themselves as they could, and never mind about rules and respectability – all the things that had mattered so much before. They were always doing madcap things – fancy dress parties and daft dares, pranks and practical jokes. Treasure hunts were quite the thing for a while – all of them tearing around the city at night in their motor-cars, making a terrific racket and getting themselves into the newspapers.'

'Did Mama get into the newspapers?'

'Oh yes – far too often, for your grandparents' liking. And your Aunt Miranda's. Your mama was part of a very glamorous set which lots of people disapproved of, but couldn't help being fascinated by too.'

'Do you think Mama is going to do a treasure hunt for me? Is this a clue?'

'I think it might very well be. Why don't you take this box up to the nursery and have a look through it? There might be some more clues in there.'

So she did, and while Polly went back downstairs Alice settled herself on the draughty window seat with Noah's elephants and lifted the flimsy cardboard lid. They had learned in school about Lord Carnarvon discovering the pharaoh's tomb in the Valley of the Kings, and she imagined this must have been what it felt like. She took things out, one at a time, examining them in the feeble light of the nursery lamp, marvelling over the mysteries they hinted at. A black silk bow tie. A navy blue spotted handkerchief. A tarnished brass key with a geometric pattern at the top. An invitation card, gold edged and elaborately lettered, to a costume ball – *Grosvenor Square, 24th July 1925 . . . Come as a Work of Art.* Questions rose and writhed like smoke inside her mind, dissipating as she came to an envelope with her name on the front.

Another clue?

She felt as if she had been running after Mama along winding passageways, trying to catch up with her, listening to the echo of her voice but unable to make out the words. And now she had appeared in front of her, and her voice was soft and clear.

Darling Alice,

If you're reading this it means you must have found the box — well done! It was the one my bridesmaid dress for Aunt Miranda's wedding was delivered in, which I swiped to stow away my treasures after the big day had passed.

I've been thinking a lot about that summer lately. (I suppose it's because I'm on a long and rather arduous journey, and journeys always make one look back at the places one has been before and view them with the clarity of perspective.) I can see now that it was a sort of turning point in all sorts of ways; a time of beginnings and of goodbyes. Of course, when I arrived in London in May it was with no clue that anything other than the usual parties and events of the Season lay ahead and no thought of doing anything but having as much fun as possible with darling Flick and Theo and the rest of our crowd (many of whom you know now as respectable married people and pillars of public life — how you would gasp to see them as they were then!)

To us, in that damp spring of 1925, it was just another Season, and we embarked on it with the casual arrogance of those blessed with money (though I was always notably less blessed in that department than my friends), privilege and time, and no sense that any of those things could be taken from us. We didn't know it, but the wild days of our youth were fast running out. By the time the next Season came round the following year, everything had changed in ways we could never have imagined.

Ah — but I'm getting ahead of myself, and if I'm to

tell you the story of that summer I need to begin at the beginning. You might be wondering why on earth I'm telling you this story at all, of people you don't know in a time before you were born, and thinking you'd rather have one about a singing fish or a box of wishes – or no story at all and another clue instead! But be patient, my darling. This journey is long, so the treasure hunt mustn't be rushed and the next clue will arrive in its own good time. One of the things I miss most on this endless voyage is sitting on your bed in the soft, sleepy evenings at home and making up stories for you. I can't promise that there will be beautiful princesses and grumpy talking camels (remember him?) in this one, but it's the story of how you came to be, and so it has the happiest ending of all.

But that bit is a long way off yet and there will be a lot of clues to discover before we get there! Let's go back to the beginning of that last Season, in the cool, blossom-strewn May of 1925. It all started with the treasure hunt . . .

3

The Hunters Assemble

May 1925

Flick Fanshawe sighed and slumped back in her chair, dispiritedly picking a transparent sliver of cucumber from a finger sandwich. The benevolent light of Claridge's silk-shaded lamps couldn't quite erase the shadows under her eyes (partly tiredness, partly the remains of last night's mascara) or warm some colour into her pallid cheeks. The Season itself hadn't got properly underway, but a string of parties had already left their mark on Flick's famous china doll beauty.

'The thing is, I'm really not sure I can be bothered. I'm simply exhausted, for one thing, and I'm not sure that any party of Aggie Montague's is going to be worth the effort of dressing. She invites everyone – no discernment at all. One spends the entire evening trying to avoid all the dull people.'

Selina looked at Flick fondly over the rim of her teacup.

In all other areas of her life, all her other relationships, Selina was cast as the feckless one; frivolous and flighty. Only with Flick did she feel remotely responsible. All things were relative.

'One simply has to look on it as a challenge,' she said soothingly. 'A sort of game. One can award oneself marks out of ten according to the dullness and persistence of the people one succeeds in avoiding. Last time I spent the entire evening successfully evading Margot Atherton, who kept trying to waylay me, like the Ancient Mariner from that frightful poem we had to learn in the schoolroom. I'd say she's definitely a nine.'

'Gosh yes, at least.' A note of indignation entered Flick's tone. 'What on earth could she possibly want to talk to you about?'

'Miranda's tedious wedding, I suppose – she's the other bridesmaid. As I hear about nothing else at home I absolutely refuse to talk about it when I'm supposed to be having fun.'

'Oh yes, of course.' Flick's memory was as short as her attention span. She frowned. 'Your sister is marrying her brother – so does that mean you and Margot will be sisters, of a sort?'

'There's a thought too gruesome to contemplate,' Selina said, putting her cup down and allowing herself a moment to admire the bright red mark her lips had left on its gold rim. (Her mother would be disgusted – she abhorred lipstick, which was undoubtedly part of its appeal as far as Selina was concerned.)

'Rupert Carew is back from Burma,' Flick said, shooting her a sideways glance. 'Isn't he going to be best man? Harry Lonsdale saw him at his father's club, looking terribly tanned and exotic, which is quite surprising considering he's spent the last year down a ruby mine. Apparently he's brought back the most enormous stone—'

'I don't think Rupert actually goes down the mine himself, just like Harry Lonsdale's father doesn't actually write everything in his newspapers,' Selina interrupted, with an edge of impatience. Rupert Carew's ruby had formed one of the chief topics of conversation at dinner last night, and Selina had sensed the change in atmosphere, the purposeful narrowing of her mother's eyes as Miranda had announced that he'd taken the stone to Asprey's to have it set into a ring. 'Talking of newspapers, where is Theo?' She twisted round in her chair, scanning the Grand Foyer, where the daily ritual of afternoon tea was coming to an end. A white-jacketed waiter immediately made his way over.

'More tea, Miss Lennox?'

'Thank you.'

'I imagine Aggie Montague will have invited him to her deathly party tonight,' Flick said morosely.

'Theo? Of course—'

'No, silly, Rupert Carew.' Flick peeled apart a meringue and scooped the cream out with her finger. 'What on earth is the point of having a party and inviting disapproving grown-up people who don't know how to have fun and are sneery about those of us who do? It's *too* frustrating – like being offered a giant box of chocolates and being told not to take any of the fondant centres.'

Selina wanted to say something positive and rallying; to remind Flick that Rupert was only a few years older than they were, but it would have been disingenuous. She knew exactly what she meant. Those few years had placed Rupert and his contemporaries on the other side of a great chasm. The war lay between them; an obscenity that the younger people were keen to forget and the older ones doomed to remember. Sucking her finger, Flick sandwiched the meringue together again and replaced it on the cake stand, then subsided onto the velvet banquette in picturesque despondency.

'And then, of course, there's the matter of what to wear. The things I had made by that little dressmaker on Brompton Road are all wrong – I mean, too, too hideous.' She sighed 'I suppose I must go and look at ready-to-wear in Harrods or Selfridges, but I'm not sure I can bear it, and I have simply nothing for tonight. I mean, really – not a *stitch* . . .'

Affection fought a niggle of impatience in Selina's chest. She would have adored to be able to afford Selfridges ready-to-wear, but had to make do with Miranda's cast-offs, cleverly remodelled by Polly. Really, Flick could be terribly tactless sometimes. They had come out in the same season, and the other girls had been wary of Flick, with her Parisian couture dresses, perfectly petite figure and porcelain beauty. 'Frightfully stand-offish,' was how they described her. 'She thinks she's heaps better than the rest of us,' one had said to

Selina, 'though her Papa is only the most minor Earl and her mother was one of the Irish Kilgannons and quite mad. She's jolly pretty, but that's no reason to be so superior.'

It hadn't taken Selina long to understand that it wasn't superiority that made Lady Felicity Fanshawe appear so aloof, but painful insecurity and desperate shyness. Her mother had died when she was small and she had been brought up in a rambling medieval manor in darkest Sussex by her elderly, bookish father and an Irish aunt – Aunt Constance – who had an instinctive mistrust of children, laughter, dirt, jazz, dancing, and anything that might loosely be described as fun. (Aunt Constant Killjoy, Theo called her.) Flick was simply unused to the company of other girls, and had practically never seen a male below the age of fifty in her life before that first season. Her lack of experience was coupled with an instinct for enjoyment that Selina found adorable but worrying. From the start she had taken on the role of Flick's protector.

'A nudist party,' she said lightly. 'Darling, how riveting. I don't think anyone's had one of those yet. Everyone would think you were frightfully *avant garde*.'

'Would they really? I'm sure I should just be frightfully chilly. Oh look – here's Theo.' Flick half got to her feet to wave, though they always sat at the same table and Theo was already making his way towards them, oblivious to the heads turning in his wake. In spite of the spring sunshine outside he was wearing a long, shabby fur coat and holding aloft a gold-tipped cigarette holder.

'Oh good – you didn't wait,' he began, when he was still three tables away. 'I called in to see Andrei at the theatre and quite lost track of the time, and then I dashed here and bumped into Lally Ross-Cunningham coming out of the ladies' cloakroom.' He flopped into the chair the blank-faced waiter pulled out for him. 'I begged her to go back in and see if my cigarette holder was still on top of the lavatory cistern where I left it last week at Bunny Hargreaves's party – remember, when I climbed over to rescue you from the stall next door, Flick darling? – and look!' He held it up triumphantly. 'The cigarette's still in it – isn't that a scream? A little damp, but I'm sure it'll be as good as new once it dries out.'

Theo Osborne was in his mid-twenties, but his angelic choir-boy looks made everyone want to mother him. (Everyone except his own mother, who despised his rackety lifestyle, extravagant tastes and aversion to manly pursuits, and regularly threatened to cut off his allowance.) Selina reached over to rub a carmine lip-print from his cheek and ruffle the patchy fur on his arm. 'Darling, what on earth are you wearing? Did it die of some fearful disease?'

He beamed. 'Isn't it gruesome? The costume department was throwing it out, so I took pity on it and staged a rescue. I might take it to Harrods to have it gift-wrapped and give it to my mother for Christmas.' Shrugging it off he dropped it onto the spare chair and helped himself to a salmon sandwich. 'So, what news on the Rialto?'

'Aggie Montague's party,' Flick said, ignoring the

Shakespeare and pulling a face. Andrei, Theo's current obsession, was costume director at the Savoy Theatre, which meant he spent a lot of time in the company of theatrical types and his conversation was peppered with borrowed lines. It was slightly less alarming than when he'd been in love with an opera singer and kept bursting into song.

'Ah, yes.' Theo wiped his fingers fastidiously on his napkin. 'Everyone's going.'

'I know,' Flick moaned. 'Isn't it a bore? It's all right for you – it's black tie, so you don't have to bother deciding what to wear.'

'More's the pity. You know I'd far rather slip into a delicious confection of silk and feathers.'

'It would be entirely wasted on Aggie Montague's crowd—'

Selina broke off as Theo gave a stifled cry and lunged towards the discarded fur. 'Heavens – how could I forget? Lally gave me this.' Scrambling in the mangy pocket he pulled out a piece of paper and dropped it onto the table.

Flick picked up the leaflet. '*A Midsummer Night's Scream,*' she read slowly, '*To which all faeries, asses and young lovers are invited* . . . Oh how super, it's a treasure hunt! Such ages since we've had one of those – I thought all the clever people had got fed up of thinking up clues. Whose motorcar shall we commandeer?'

'I vote Harry Lonsdale's. He's yawn-makingly clever and he owes me plenty of favours after all the beastly things his papa's newspapers have printed about me lately – they've been utterly savage.'

'The problem with treasure hunts is that one gets so terribly chilly in one's evening clothes . . .' Tapping ash into her teacup Flick hunched her shoulders against the anticipated cold, her blue gaze lighting on the fur coat. 'I rather think I might borrow your friend here to keep me warm.'

'You'll need to spend a month in quarantine if you do,' Selina remarked. As they'd talked half her mind had also been occupied with the question of what to wear, which was nothing new. Whereas for Flick the problem was created by an excess of choice, for Selina it was quite the reverse, and there were only so many times she could rotate the same three dresses, only so many alterations Polly could make to them, before people began to make cutting comments. She often joked that it was a shame Flick's generous heart was housed in the most delicate little ribcage beneath a barely-there bosom, which meant that her own ample chest could not be contained in Flick's beautiful couture cast-offs, no matter how tightly she bound it. She narrowed her eyes, exhaling a plume of smoke. 'Theo darling, how many dinner jackets do you have in your possession?'

'Too many, alas; though several are of highly dubious origin, collected like scalps, my dear. Why do you ask? Are you planning something naughty?'

'Not at all.' Selina adopted an expression of studied innocence. 'I'm on the strictest instructions to behave myself. Mama doesn't want my name to appear in the newspapers between now and my sister's big day for fear that clan

Atherton will be whispering about me behind their hands instead of ahhhing over Miranda as she walks down the aisle. Which is why I'm planning on being excessively obedient. Flick dearest, if an invitation specifies 'Black Tie' don't you think it would be a gesture of supreme courtesy to go along with the hostess's wishes?'

Flick frowned in confusion. 'You mean . . . you and me? At Aggie's?'

'Why not?' Selina shrugged. 'Smart, correct, and marvellously practical. I'm game if you are.'

She knew that Flick would probably look far better in a man's suit than she would, but she was used to that; resigned to it. The contrast between Flick's dark and delicate beauty and her own golden voluptuousness (as Theo loyally framed it) was one reason why the press photographers pursued them so relentlessly. Admittedly, the other was that they could usually be relied upon to do something scandalously newsworthy. It had reached the stage where Selina almost felt a responsibility not to disappoint.

She slipped the Treasure Hunt leaflet into her handbag. If it was left lying around the press would be onto them before they'd even started, and part of the fun was keeping them guessing.

'Problem solved,' said Theo approvingly. 'Genius girl. Now – I do believe it must be almost six o'clock . . .'

'The glittering hour!' Flick announced joyfully. 'Let's have cocktails.'

*

Aggie Montague's narrow house in Bruton Street was far too small for parties of the size she insisted on throwing. However, the crowd of people crammed into its rooms and thronging its hallway always gave a great impression of popularity and conviviality, as if simply *everyone* was there. (Which, as Flick had pointed out, wasn't far from the truth.)

The cocktails at Claridge's had been followed by sherry (smuggled up from the terrifying Mrs Osborne's drawing room drinks tray) as they dressed at Theo's house, but in spite of the pleasant alcohol haze Selina was aware, as they shouldered their way to the stairs, of eyes on her; some gazes admiring, others disapproving. She and Flick had made free with Theo's hair oil and tried to be as authentically masculine as possible in their costume, though had allowed themselves some leeway when it came to shoes. Red satin toes peeked out from the pinned-up hems of Flick's evening trousers, gold glacé kid from Selina's.

It was crucial not to look back, not to notice the stares, or else one lost one's nerve. One childhood Christmas, in that golden age before the war, a circus show had come to Salisbury and Howard had taken her and Miranda. She remembered watching a man walk a tightrope strung high above their heads, and being awed and desperate to know how he achieved this seemingly superhuman feat. *He didn't look down*, Howard said afterwards, *not once. That's the secret.*

She had never forgotten it.

'"Hell is empty and all the devils are here",' Theo yelled above the noise as they went up the stairs. 'It rather reminds me of Regent's Park Zoo. I'm not sure whether it's Aggie's interior décor, or the reek of pheromones.'

'*Telephones?*' squealed Flick. She was a different person from the bruised, fragile creature who had picked at tea in Claridge's a few hours earlier. The first cocktail of the day had revived her, like water on a parched plant, and each successive drink had made her stronger and more certain, dissolving her ennui and the existential doubts that beset her during the sober hours of the afternoon. Above the starched collar and black silk bow tie her elfin face was animated, the dark circles beneath her eyes disguised with face powder. She sparkled, once more the aristocratic beauty who so bewitched the newspapers and dominated their society columns.

Heat softened and smudged everything, so that the champagne was the only thing that was cold and sharp. The noise level was such that it was necessary to stare at the mouth of whoever one was talking to in order to have any hope of working out what they were saying, which seemed like a lot of effort for such banal conversation. Selina, drifting from one group to the next, knew that tomorrow she would have no recollection of most of what was said. Fingers brushed her slicked-back hair and tugged her bow tie undone, and the faces behind the lipsticked mouths talking at her slid out of focus as her glass was filled and filled again. She lost Flick and Theo, and going in search of them to suggest dinner she bumped into Harry Lonsdale, who caught hold of her waist and brushed his mouth across her bare nape. 'Dressed like that you remind me of a boy I knew at school,' he groaned. 'God, the agony of first love.'

'Poor Harry. Any idea where Flick is?'

'Last seen powdering her nose upstairs. High as a kite, bless her.'

Selina wriggled out of his embrace to go and find her. It was a fine balance, a thin line between the state of exhilarating intoxication where reality was brighter and more beautiful and one felt magnificently invincible, and the tumble into oblivion. As she wove her way through the dancers and stepped over the legs of people sprawled on the floor, Selina thought of the tightrope walker again, and the ruthless focus and control that kept him steady. At the same circus there had been a trapeze artist: a dainty girl in a sequinned costume who had sailed through the air, twisting and spinning and turning somersaults, then releasing her hold on the trapeze and hanging suspended for a breathless moment before plunging downwards. Now, all these years later, Selina couldn't remember what the girl had looked like, but when she thought of her it was always Flick she saw.

The champagne in her glass had turned warm and acidic. Going out onto the landing she tipped it into a vase of spiky gladioli and was heading for the stairs when she had the uncomfortable sensation of being watched. She looked round. Rupert Carew was standing a little distance away with Margot Atherton (which explained why she hadn't been stalking Selina all evening).

Oh God, she should go and talk to him. Say hello. She

had known him since she was a child, when he had often come to stay with Howard at Blackwood in the school holidays, seeming oddly adult even then, and too serious a companion for her laughing, teasing brother. He was one of those sorts who was good at everything, Howard had explained cheerfully; sport and music and schoolroom study – the kind of chap one wanted on one's team. They had joined the army together in the autumn of 1914, straight from the OTC at Cambridge, and served together in France and Belgium. Rupert had been in the same push in which Howard was wounded. He had been with him in the shell hole at the end.

Selina didn't want to think about the shell hole. Or the end.

At that moment there was a high-pitched whoop from the top of the stairs and Flick swung her leg over the banister and shot down. A cheer went up as Selina caught her, and Flick, playing to the crowd, kissed her extravagantly on the mouth.

When she looked again Rupert had gone.

4

The Thrill of the Chase

The spring night was chilly when they spilled out of the restaurant and piled into the sleek motorcar that Harry Lonsdale had secretly 'borrowed' from his father. As he drove, Harry peeled off his spectacles and handed them to Theo to polish, as if smeared lenses rather than cocktails and champagne were the reason he couldn't see straight.

The motorcar's canvas hood was folded down. Selina and Flick sat in the back, their legs awkwardly positioned around a crate of champagne they'd discovered tucked behind the front seats ('Pa always keeps one in the car, for emergencies,' Harry explained). Flick had also swiped an unfinished bottle of wine from dinner, and they passed this between them as they spun through the streets. At Admiralty Arch they discovered about thirty motorcars, circling like thoroughbreds waiting to go into the stalls. No one wanted to lose time having to restart their engines when the first clue was released, but passengers ran between the vehicles, fanning away the exhaust fumes as they exchanged greetings of lighthearted rivalry. Theo vaulted out of the passenger seat to be ready to collect the clue while Selina and Flick lit cigarettes for them all and assessed the competition.

'Bother. There's Georgie Stanhope, talking to Hillary,' Harry said, crossly (they often teased him that his fearful competitiveness was a sign of his middle class roots). 'What's the betting she's pumping him for information? She's with Clarence Seaton too, who's infuriatingly good at working out cryptic clues. He'll be able to pay off his father's death duties on treasure hunt winnings alone soon; we don't stand a chance of beating them.'

'Darling, who really cares about winning?' Selina drawled, looking out into the blue London night. In spite of the relative warmth of her clothes she felt shivery; restless and keyed up, as if she was waiting for something more significant to start than another night-time treasure hunt (fun, but hardly momentous). Another motorcar swooped past them in a cacophony of hooting and, recognizing Lally Ross-Cunningham, she raised the bottle she was holding in salute. 'I can't think why she's with Aubrey Hastings,' she remarked. 'See how desperate he is for us to notice his new motorcar. Oh look – the clues are being handed out. Are we ready for the off?'

She and Flick leaned into the front as Theo leapt back in, tearing open the envelope. Harry had his cigarette lighter at the ready to illuminate the page.

'*The banks of the River Irwell are an unlikely place to find the well-earned spoils of a kilted rebel,*' he read quickly, then repeated it more slowly, placing the emphasis on different words as Harry joined the procession of vehicles roaring under the archway.

'Where are we going?' Flick asked, gripping the back of Harry's seat hard to avoid being flung out.

'I'm waiting for you to tell me,' Harry yelled back, swerving around the flashy blue motor with Lally's gleaming dark head in the front seat. 'Any ideas? Let's get away from the field so blasted Hastings doesn't just tag along behind us all night.'

'It sounds quite simple,' Theo said. 'Where's the River Irwell?'

'Well, that's rather the question,' snapped Harry.

'Oh, I do hope it's not going to be one of *those* nights,' Flick moaned. 'I remember now why I'd got so tired of treasure hunts. Selina, remember that time we were with Clarence and Lally and we ran out of petrol somewhere near Maidenhead? It was gruesome. I'd always thought that Maidenhead sounded marvellously romantic, but it absolutely wasn't. The man at that hotel we stopped at was utterly beastly.'

'We did wake him up at four o'clock in the morning,' Selina remarked absently, her mind spinning back to the schoolroom, and a particular geography-obsessed governess. 'I have a feeling the River Irwell is up north somewhere, you know: Nottingham or Leeds or somewhere like that.'

Flick wailed. Theo looked aghast. Harry, speeding along

the Strand, suddenly hauled on the steering wheel and swung round in a U-turn, so for a moment it felt like being on a fairground carousel. A couple coming out of Savoy Passage stepped back in alarm, the man raising his fist in fury as the motorcar mounted the kerb and bounced off again. Flick's wail turned into a scream.

'Manchester!' Harry yelled triumphantly as they hurtled back down the Strand.

'But that'll take *hours* . . .'

'And be *deathly* . . . Isn't it all factories and dirt?'

It wouldn't be the first time that they had made an impromptu night-time trip out of London, but after the last one, when Selina had decided it would be fun to get the sleeper train to Scotland and have breakfast in Fort William, their reluctance was understandable. The idea had been romantic, but the reality of the long journey, made in evening dress, had been chilly, uncomfortable and expensive. Harry laughed.

'Manchester *Square*, you dullards. The kilted rebel is William Wallace – the Wallace Collection is in Hertford House. Five minutes away and not a cotton mill in sight.'

With relieved laughter they passed around the wine bottle again. It was exhilarating, hurtling through the early summer dark. On nights like this the venerable old city belonged to them – the Bright Young People, as the newspapers called them – its streets and squares were their playground, its stately public monuments their toys. Tomorrow the more populist newspapers would carry excited reports of the evening's events, fed to them by treacherous insiders (Theo came up with a new list of prime suspects after every event) while snide summaries would appear in the broadsheets, and consequently a thick fog of chilly disappointment would hang over the Lennox luncheon table in Chester Square, muffling conversation.

But tomorrow was a whole lifetime away. Tonight stretched ahead, glittering with fun and possibility, ringing with the whoops and shrieks of their fellow hunters as they converged on Manchester Square. Harry had worked out where the clue would be hidden ('*Well-earned* – pound to a penny there's a decorative stone urn somewhere') but as it turned out so many other teams were there that it was simply a matter of joining the jostle around the gatepost to read the words chalked on the stone pilaster on which the urn in question stood. It was always like this at the start of the hunt, especially when the clue was so straightforward; later the cars would spread out as the trail got harder and intelligence and tactics began to tell. Theo leapt out to join the crush, gaining a crucial few seconds' advantage by hearing someone else shout it out. He raced back to repeat it.

'*The principal of judgement.*'

'What?'

'That's it. *The principal of judgement* – nothing else. Everyone seems to be a bit stumped.' He took a swig from the bottle and wiped his chin on his sleeve. 'It must be something to do with the law, so what do you say – shall we head to the Old Bailey? Lincolns Inn?'

'Anywhere!' Selina cried, flinging her arms out. 'We need to lose the others. For God's sake Harry, just *drive!*'

The night's edges blurred. Points of light – streetlamps and the bright squares of windows – became a continuous golden stream as the car hurtled through the streets. High above a half moon floated indolently on her back and the stars circled and spun. They lost Flick at the Criterion ('*principle* of judgement, not principal,' Harry had grumbled, bafflingly) where they'd stopped for special Treasure Hunter cocktails that had appeared on the menu (gin, framboise and grenadine – marbled pink like the sunrise that was only a couple of hours away – with the next clue wrapped around a cocktail stick) and she'd been bundled into Aubrey Hastings's car amid much squealing and laughter. Selina had glimpsed her again as they raced away from collecting the next clue, but Harry's blood was well and truly up by then and he refused to slow down, so all they could do was stand up in their seats and blow extravagant kisses as they flew past each other.

After that the field thinned, so it was impossible to know where they were in the race. Every now and again distant whoops and horn blasts reached them on the warm night air as other teams encountered each other. Screeching out of Baker Street (straight after finding a clue in the windowbox of number 221: *We don't want to lose our marbles*) Theo let out a blood-curdling view halloo as he spotted a police car and Harry, with the best part of a bottle of champagne and the Criterion's extremely potent cocktail sloshing through his system, roared down Euston Road as if it were the track at Brooklands.

On the surface the rivalry between their set and the city's police force was good natured enough, though spiked with mutual distrust. Police officers tolerated a certain amount of high spirited fun from young people, many of whose fathers were responsible for making the laws they were charged with enforcing, but they had an unpleasant habit of mentioning to newspapermen whenever one of the Bright Young People ended up spending the night in the cells. It was best to elude them wherever possible.

Selina turned round and kneeled on the seat to watch them give chase. Having put some distance between them, Harry swung right and plunged into the shuttered, sleeping streets of Bloomsbury.

'Are we shaking off our constable friends, or heading to the next clue?' Theo asked, gripping the sides of his seat.

'Both,' Harry grinned. 'It's the Elgin marbles, isn't it? The great big ugly things Sandy Bruce's ancestor swiped from the Greeks and sold to the British Museum. Too bally easy if you ask me.'

It was darker here; too dark to see whatever it was they hit. Afterwards, when the moment replayed itself in Selina's mind, she would fancy that she glimpsed a streak of dark fur, a flash of white, the fleeting gleam of eyes, but at the time the thud and jolt came from nowhere and were all the more shocking for it. The car swerved crazily, the wheels losing traction on the cobbled road, bumping and skidding sideways until it hit the kerb. The engine cut out suddenly.

For a second the world seemed absolutely silent, and then, slowly, the sound returned: a gentle hiss from somewhere beneath the bonnet, the frenzied yapping of a little dog in a nearby house, the distant hum of a speeding engine, getting closer. Perhaps it was this that galvanized Harry. He swore and looked around.

'No harm done. Let's be off. Someone start her up.'

In the front seat Theo moaned. His hand was clamped to the side of his head. 'No harm done? For Christ's sake, Lonsdale, I think I may have fractured my skull. What was it?'

'I don't know – a damned cat, I imagine. Nothing important. Come on, crank her up and let's get moving before our friends from the Met arrive.'

'Everything's blurred. I think I might have a concussion.'

'That's the booze, you ape,' Harry snapped. 'Ye gods – Selina, you'll have to do it.'

She climbed unsteadily out of the car and went round to the front. As she bent to turn the starting handle she saw a shadow in the gutter, beyond the dim beam of the headlamp bulbs, like something spilled. The world tipped and swung, as if she was on a fairground swing boat. She yanked the handle round, but there was no strength in her arm and her hand slipped on the metal. When she tried again, harder, the engine coughed into life and Harry gave a triumphant shout from the driver's seat.

'That's my girl! In you get!'

She couldn't leave, not without looking. Checking, just in case ... Reaching out, her hand encountered fur, soft and warm and silken. When she lifted it up it was heavy and supple, for all the world like a fox fur stole.

'It's a cat.'

'Thought so. Thank God that's all.' From the darkness beyond the dazzle of headlamps Harry's voice was clipped with impatience. 'Dear God, Selina – it's probably hoaching with all kinds of vermin and diseases.'

The champagne rush had retreated and there was a sour taste in her mouth. The cold breath of reality had blown away the evening's glitter, and a shadow had fallen across it, dulling its dazzle.

'We can't leave it. I don't know if it's—'

The word stuck in her dry throat.

'Darling, if it isn't dead now it soon will be.' Harry gunned the engine, impatience simmering into irritation. 'It's just a feral thing, for God's sake. Put it down and get in the car, like a good girl.' His head whipped round. 'The police were only a minute behind us—'

In spite of the dinner suit she was shivering. Only her hands were warm, buried in the animal's fur. If it was warm did that mean it was alive? The car shot backwards as Harry straightened it up, and the headlamp beams swung over her. 'Theo, tell her, would you? We haven't got time to moon about giving the last rites to a bloody alley cat. If my father hears about this it's the last time I'll be given free rein with the motor. Selina – *get in*.'

Theo giggled. 'Bring it along, darling. It can be our mascot.'

Along the street the windows above the shuttered shops had all been in darkness, but by now lights showed behind a few of them, and curtains stirred. Someone lifted a sash and shouted something in an accent so purely Cockney it was as unintelligible as a foreign language. They were a long way from South Kensington.

'On our way, old chap,' Harry muttered through gritted teeth. 'Selina—'

The cat's head was heavy in the crook of her arm. She had no idea what to do with it, but she knew that she couldn't drop it back into the gutter. 'We should take it somewhere. To someone who—'

Harry gave a slightly wild laugh. 'Are you out of your mind? I'd say for once we're in with a good chance of winning this thing. You do *know* that the prize pot is one hundred guineas tonight? Added to the fact that the police will be here any second and I have the tiniest suspicion they might think I'm not sober enough to drive. For God's sake put down that unsavoury creature and *get in now*, or I'll leave without you.'

For a second she didn't move. And then she stepped back, onto the pavement.

Harry threw up his hands then rammed the gearstick forwards. 'Very well, have it your way. We'll see you at the British Museum. If we've already left, one of the other teams will be along soon, I'm sure.'

The car shot forwards. She saw Theo's face, his eyes wide and his mouth opening, though if he spoke the words were lost beneath the engine's angry growl. And then he was gone, and there was nothing but the glow of red lights, briefly visible through the cloud of exhaust smoke before the car turned the corner.

5

A Door Opens

Left alone, Selina looked around.

She imagined that during the day this would be a lively street, busy with vans and carts and shoppers on pavements cluttered with crates of fruit and vegetables, tin baths and dolly tubs. Now it was eerily still, though not quite silent: the city never was. She suddenly felt very sober and rather shaky. In an instant the shiny surface of the evening had cracked, exposing the void that was always there, just out of sight. She clutched the cat, her fingers stroking its soft fur, and tried to quell the old panic. Tried to think.

She was unfamiliar with the streets of Bloomsbury that lay beyond the smarter squares and the British Museum, but knew that neither could be very far away. If she walked to somewhere civilized she might just be able to flag down a late taxi and be back in Kensington in no time. Polly would know what to do. Her people were farmers. She was bound to have lots of experience with injured animals.

She glanced at the cat in her arms and, catching the glisten of something wet in the dark fur by its ear, looked away sharply. *Don't look down. Never look down.* She started to walk in the direction she guessed might take her somewhere more familiar – Russell Square perhaps, where years ago she'd attended Italian lessons with an exiled Contessa – but her footsteps faltered as a pair of headlamps appeared at the far end of the street. Oh God – was this the police? Part of her longed to surrender herself, and the cat, to their charge, but Mama's warning to stay out of trouble rang loud in her head. She was fairly sure that being caught by the police wearing men's clothing and carrying a bleeding cat was precisely the sort of thing she was supposed to avoid; the sort of thing the newspapers would adore. Oh God, the lights were approaching rapidly. She looked round in desperation for a doorway to duck into.

Nowhere. There was nothing. And then directly behind her a door opened and a figure appeared, silhouetted against the light behind.

'Are you all right?'

A male voice; gruff, slightly wary, but not hostile. She held out her arms to show him the cat, unaware until that moment that there were tears streaming down her face. 'I'm afraid I . . . I don't know what to do. The police—'

He glanced in the direction of the headlamps and swiftly stood back, indicating for her to go past him into the hallway beyond, shutting the door just as the police car shot by.

'Oh – thank you.'

It was only afterwards that she was struck by the rashness of her behaviour. If she'd been sober and thinking straight, she would never have gone into the house of a stranger in this less-than-smart part of town. In truth, the less-than-smartness didn't fully hit her until it was too late, and she looked around.

It was one of those mean, communal spaces, with a grimy tiled floor and scuffed dark green Lincrusta on the walls. A gas sconce on the wall spat dirty yellow light over a cheap table on which stood an aspidistra in a pot full of cigarette ends. The man who had let her in pushed it aside and motioned for her to put the cat down.

'Is it alive?'

'I don't know.'

Her arms felt weightless without it, and cold. She folded them across her chest, noticing that there was blood on her shirtfront. She couldn't quite bring herself to look at the body on the table, so instead she looked at the man who had come to her aid. Not wealthy, but civilized-looking, thank goodness – collarless shirt, clean and open at the neck. A little older than her, she guessed, though young enough not to have been in France, which was how one automatically categorized people. Slight build. Dark hair, thick and badly in need of a cut, falling over his face as he bent over the cat. Dark eyes, which sent a jolt through her as he looked up at her suddenly and gave a brief shake of his head.

'Sorry.'

A sob rose in her throat, catching her off guard. She turned away, pressing the back of her hand to her mouth and struggling to compose herself. 'Oh gosh, how shaming. I'm so sorry. You're very kind to help.'

'I saw what happened from the window.'

'It came from nowhere. I didn't even see it – none of us did. There was no way Harry could have missed it—' She stopped, choking on the glaring truth that he could if he hadn't been going so fast, and wondering why she felt the need to explain herself to this stranger. She summoned a practised smile, at odds with the tears that were still sliding down her cheeks. 'I suppose cats must be hit by motorcars all the time these days. Even so . . . it's wretched.'

'But not a hanging offence.' His smile was grave. 'I don't think the police would have taken you in.'

There was a stillness about him. A watchful reserve. She wondered why he was still up at this hour.

'No,' she said ruefully. 'But I could do without the . . . attention, Mr . . . ?'

'Weston.' The yellow light gilded one cheekbone and carved a deep hollow beneath it. The other half of his face was in shadow. 'Lawrence Weston.'

'Selina Lennox.'

The smile widened a fraction. 'I know.'

'Exactly.'

She laughed, swiping at her cheeks again. He had been standing with his hands in his pockets and he withdrew one now, producing a crumpled dark blue spotted handkerchief which he held out to her.

'Thank you.' Her eyes flickered in the direction of the table. 'I'm not quite sure what to do with it now.'

'Leave it with me. I'll . . . dispose of it.'

'In a dustbin?'

He rubbed a hand over his forehead. 'I'm afraid I can't afford a plot in Brookwood cemetery,' he said, and she got the feeling that he was teasing her a little.

'Poor cat. It doesn't seem right.'

She pictured herself wrapping it in her jacket and taking it home in a taxi, but her courage quailed a little at what she would do with it at Chester Square. She could hardly leave it on the table in the hallway for Fenton to deal with in the morning, or in the scullery where Mrs Barnes hung rabbits and pheasant. But to be dumped in a dustbin, amongst rotting peelings and tealeaves . . . The rats would pick it apart in no time; she knew that from what Howard had told her. They would take its eyes first.

She took a breath.

'Mr Weston, I don't suppose you might have such a thing as a shovel?'

Obviously, there was no question of him letting her do it alone. No matter what she said.

Just as she, rightly or wrongly, felt a responsibility for the cat, he, rightly or wrongly, felt a responsibility for her, and the streets of Bloomsbury at almost three o'clock in the morning were no place for a less-than-sober society girl dressed in a man's dinner suit. Her extraordinary appearance made her too conspicuous; her casual confidence – ironically – made her vulnerable. The small hours belonged to the city's misfits and outsiders, the disturbed and dispossessed. Many of them were gentle souls. Some of them were not. Sanity was a fragile thing these days.

She had waited in the hall while he'd gone back up to the flat to collect the things they needed, taking care not to disturb Sam, who shared the scruffy set of rooms at the top of the house: he wrote acerbic, socialist pieces for the *Daily Herald* and would have swooped on the story like a pigeon on a bun. Lawrence had half-expected her to have disappeared when he came down again, having changed her mind, dried her tears and decided that a stray cat wasn't worth such a fuss after all, or for the whole thing to have turned out to be the latest prank by her silly, thrill-seeking set.

But she was there. He'd wished fervently that he could have brought his camera down and captured her like that, leaning against the wall with her hands in the pockets of her belted-in trousers, her slicked-back hair the colour of tarnished gold in the lamplight, the opulent sheen of her beauty incongruous in the shabby hallway. He suspected she would have disappeared pretty rapidly if he had.

Neither of them spoke as they walked along the sleeping street, Lawrence carrying the cat (now shrouded in a pillowcase) and the coal shovel, which was the most suitable grave-digging tool he could supply. The night carried distant sounds of revelry – the blast of motorcar horns and faint shrieks – but if she heard them she gave no sign. As she walked beside him she kept herself very upright, though every now and again her arm or her hip bumped softly against his; evidence, like the glitter of her eyes in the hall-way and the careful clipping of her well-bred words, that she (like he) had had a substantial amount to drink.

'Where are we going?'

'There's a garden in front of the crescent up here. Not as smart as Russell Square, but we're less likely to be caught climbing over the fence.'

They passed beneath a streetlamp and he saw her swift smile. 'You say that like a man who knows from experience.'

'The doormen at the Russell Square hotels are very keen to keep undesirables off their patch.'

'And you're an undesirable?' Her voice was low, with a husky quality that made up for her posh-girl accent, and her laugh was as deep and rich as expensive port.

'I'm an artist,' he said dryly. 'I think it amounts to the same thing.'

They had reached the junction where Tavistock Place crossed over Marchmont Street and the crescent stood before them, its garden dark and shadowy against the row of houses that curved behind it. He led her to the place near the apex of the semi-circle, beyond the pool of light cast by the streetlamps, where the trees and shrubbery were thickest. Two large stones had been placed on the other side of the waist-height railings, to provide a sort of step.

'Here. I'll go first and help you. If you stand on here it's easy enough to climb over.'

He lowered the pillowcase over and slid the shovel through the railings, then stood on the stones and swung himself over. It was a move he'd done many times, on summer nights when the walls of the flat seemed too close, on autumn evenings when the leaves rained silently down around him, or any time when too much booze and too many cigarettes had pushed him far beyond sleep. He'd never brought a girl here, though he knew Sam had (no doubt regaling them with his favourite speech about how property is theft and access to green spaces was a right for all). It was his space, where he came to be alone. Until now, anyway.

'That's it, put your foot there and lever yourself up.'

He watched her stand on the step and grip the metal spikes, his arms ready to catch her if she slipped. Perhaps intoxication made her less aware of the danger, but she moved with the assurance of someone who was used to climbing and skilled at it. He had a sudden vision of a vast estate somewhere, brothers perhaps; a childhood of climbing trees and riding horses. He wondered why she wasn't afraid. If being alone in the dark with a stranger – a lower class one too – didn't frighten her, did anything?

'Men's clothes are much more practical than women's. I'd hate to attempt this in a dress.'

She swung herself over and dropped to the ground beside him, staggering slightly. He caught her arms to steady her.

For a moment they were only inches apart and he saw the liquid gleam of her eyes, the glisten of her lips. He let her go as if she was red hot and stepped away, going over to retrieve the shovel.

They found a place inside the spread of a large shrub with leathery leaves where the ground was soft, but even so, slicing into it with an implement designed for a very different purpose was hard going. The handle of the coal shovel was so short that Lawrence had to kneel, half-digging, half-scraping the earth and its tangle of roots. By the time he'd gone down a foot he was breathing hard and his shirt was sticking to the small of his back.

A motorcar passed on the road a few feet away, its head-lamps sending a broken beam of light flickering through the leaves. Instinctively they stilled, their eyes finding each other's and holding fast until it was gone. Then she picked up the pillowcase and lowered it into the shallow hole, tucking it in tenderly.

She surprised him. He knew about her, of course; you'd have to be an illiterate hermit living on a remote island not to have heard of Selina Lennox, baronet's daughter, fully paid up member of the set the newspapers called the Bright Young People. They played out their charmed and privileged lives in the beam of public attention, attracting amusement and disapproval in roughly equal measure. Sam Evans – a miner's son who'd grown up in the gnawing poverty of a Welsh pit town – virtually frothed at the mouth at each front page photograph of outlandish fancy dress costumes and every report of flamboyant excess. In theory Lawrence shared his indignation about *parasites living off the sweat of the working man*, but he couldn't help being drawn to their glamour, admiring their innate elegance. He recognized Selina Lennox's face, but the newspaper photographs hadn't prepared him for her extraordinary colouring; the old-gold hair and the creamy vellum texture of her skin. The astonishing aquamarine eyes.

She took a handful of earth and scattered it on top of the bloodstained pillowcase.

'Do you think it had a name?' she asked softly.

'I doubt it.'

'We should give it one.' She looked around. 'What's the name of this place?'

'Cartwright Gardens.'

She considered it. 'Not pretty, but distinguished. Very well. Cartwright ... may you rest in peace, and your soul roam freely in a heaven with no motorcars and an abundant supply of mice.' She paused. 'I'm trying to remember how the burial service goes, but my mind's gone blank.'

'Something about us coming into the world with nothing, and leaving with nothing?' In Lawrence's case, that was a state of affairs that seemed likely to persist through the intervening years too. 'And a bit about the resurrection and the life. *He who believeth in me will live, even though he dies.*'

'Yes, of course. What rot.' In the deep blue shadow he saw her take something from the pocket of her jacket – a silver cigarette case – and snap it open. 'Damn. Only one left. I hope you don't mind sharing.'

She put the cigarette between her lips and he held up his lighter. For a moment her face was bathed in the glow of the flame and he watched her cheeks hollow and the cigarette tip glow as she breathed in. Her eyes glittered gold through her lowered lashes. And then she was veiled in shadows again.

'You don't believe in the afterlife, Miss Lennox?'

'I'm afraid not.' She settled herself back against a broad branch. 'I think it's just another story we're told to make us more accepting of life's cruelty, don't you?'

She held out the cigarette and he took it, putting his lips where hers had been. He thought of Cassie and his mother, dead within a week of each other, and everyone saying at the funeral how it was good that they were together.

'Yes,' he said, and an echo of the fury he'd felt then, in the churchyard with the tattered remnants of his family – his father, ashen and helpless, and Stephen, glassy-eyed and silent (always silent) standing beside the obscene hole where his mother and sister were to be left – came back to him, souring the taste of the rich tobacco on his tongue. It wasn't *good* that they were together. They weren't happily living a parallel family life somewhere else, the two of them, his mother doing the wash on Mondays and calling Cassie in from playing out for bread and dripping. The fact that the Spanish influenza had taken them both in one savage swipe was just brutal and unfair.

His hand shook a little as he passed her the cigarette.

In spite of all the wine he'd drunk earlier his senses were painfully sharp and he heard the tiny kissing sound her lips made as she took a drag.

'So ... you said you're an artist. Too glamorously bohemian. What do you paint?'

For a split second he considered telling her that he didn't paint; that he was actually a photographer and the reason he was still up was that he'd been taking advantage of the dark and Sam being asleep to develop prints in the flat's tiny kitchen area. But then she would ask what he did with his photographs, who bought them, and the answer to that was nothing, and no one. He decided to be honest. 'I paint portraits for grieving parents from photographs of their dead sons.' His voice held the bite of self-mockery. 'Neither glamorous nor bohemian. Very pedestrian, in fact.'

There was a pause as she took another pull on the cigarette. Her head was tipped back, her face pearly pale in the blue gloom. She'd pulled the collar off the man's shirt she was wearing and removed the top two studs from its starched front, so it parted a little across her generous chest. Her black silk bow tie hung loose around her neck and a strand of gleaming hair, heavy with oil, had fallen forward over her cheek. She exhaled a plume of smoke and he breathed it in. The intimacy of it stirred something inside him.

'Important though.'

'I'm hardly setting the art world on fire.'

She made a dismissive sound. 'Who cares about the art world? I sometimes go to the Royal Academy Private View and most of the work is either screamingly dull or hilariously dreadful. Last year I actually wondered if someone was playing a rather good practical joke.' Their fingertips touched as he took the cigarette and he wondered if she felt the same little jolt as he did. 'My parents got my brother to sit for a portrait in the first year of the war, before he went over to France. It's my mother's most treasured possession. She loves it more than she loves my sister and me.'

Her tone was light, but he sensed that it was a brittle veneer.

'He didn't come back? From the war?'

She answered with an abrupt shake of her head, almost imperceptible in the darkness.

'I'm sorry.'

'That's how I know there's nothing else,' she said softly. 'No jolly afterlife in heaven. I went to a séance once; just for fun. Just to see . . .'

He took a long drag of the cigarette as she faltered, then prompted her gently as he handed it back. 'And?'

'I gave them my maid's name at the door, so they wouldn't know who I was and cheat. The medium was a ghastly little man with painted-on eyebrows and long fingernails.' There was only an inch left of the cigarette and she consumed it in one hard pull, then tipped her head back to exhale. 'When the lights went off he rubbed his leg against mine under the table. He made a big drama about seeing a young man dressed in khaki smoking a pipe, which safely encompassed every officer in the British army. Luckily for him Howard's spirit was obviously absent or it would have strangled the odious little fraud with his greasy cravat. Anyway—' Brusquely, without giving him the chance to say anything, she ground out the cigarette and got to her feet. 'I suppose we'd better finish the job. Poor Cartwright. It hasn't been much of a send-off.'

'Oh, I don't know . . .' He picked up the shovel and began to scoop earth back into the hole. 'That was the best cigarette I've had in a long time.'

Her laugh was a husky ripple in the damp night air. 'Stolen from my father. My parents hate me smoking. In fact, my parents hate everything I do. Daddy didn't speak to me for ten days when I shingled my hair. At dinner every night he asked Mama who the strange young man was.'

Lawrence straightened up and dropped the shovel. He felt warm from the exertion, light headed from booze and being near her – this girl whose face had appeared in a hundred newspaper photographs, none of which had done her beauty justice. In a minute they would leave their tent of leafy shadows and climb over the fence again to return to their separate worlds, and this strange and surreal encounter would be over. Tomorrow he would struggle to convince himself he hadn't dreamt it. The realization made him bold. Reaching out he took hold of the ends of the bow tie and slid his fingers down its length.

'To be honest,' he said gravely, 'I can see his point . . .'

He was close enough to smell her warm skin beneath the fragrant cigarette smoke and the masculine, sandalwood scent of hair oil. She didn't step away and her gaze didn't waver from his. Mesmerized, he pulled gently on the ends of the bow tie, drawing her towards him.

The roar of an engine. Voices, echoing through the quiet night. He heard them, but it was only when he felt her flinch and saw her head snap round that he realized they were calling her name.

'Damn.'

'They're looking for you.'

'Yes.' Her eyes, luminous in the gloom, found his again. 'I should probably go . . .'

It sounded uncertain, like a question. He answered it for her, letting go of her silk tie and stepping back. 'Yes. Go.'

She walked unsteadily to the railings. The ground was higher on this side, making it easier to climb out than it had been to climb in. She had managed it without difficulty before, but now she struggled to lever herself up, as if the strength had gone out of her.

He knew the feeling.

He went forward to help, crouching down on the earth so she could step on his knee and spring over, holding her hand to steady her as she dropped down on the other side. The shouts and catcalls were getting closer and the sudden glare of headlamps cut a slice through the darkness as the motorcar squealed into the crescent. Lawrence shrank into the shadows. He saw her turn back towards him and for a moment he thought she might be going to hide herself too, and wait until the car had gone past. But then the shouts

turned into shrieks of delighted recognition as the headlamps found her and the motorcar – the same dark blue
Crossley that he'd seen from the window, though packed
with more people now – screeched to a halt in the road.

'Selina darling! Where the devil were you?'

'Thank God we've found you! Poor Harry's been beside
himself with guilt. Get in, angel.'

'Wicked girl – you gave us the most frightful scare. We've
spent more time looking for you than for clues, but we can
join the others for breakfast.' A rear door opened and she was
pulled onto the lap of a young man that Lawrence instinctively wanted to punch. 'Heavens darling, there's blood all
over your shirt! Are you all right?'

'The cat—'

There was a chorus of protesting groans. 'God Selina, not
the bloody cat again!' The car shot forwards with a grating
of gears and skidding tyres, and the girl perched on the
folded-down hood squealed as she was catapulted backwards
then grabbed and dragged onto the crush of bodies on the
back seat. But Selina Lennox stood up and, as the car passed
beneath a streetlamp, Lawrence saw her turn back towards
the garden, one hand raking her hair from her face, her eyes
scanning the undergrowth.

And then she was gone; pulled down again just before
the car turned the corner, and all that was left was a cloud
of exhaust fumes, the echo of voices floating through the
spring night, and the too-fast beat of his heart.

S.S Eastern Star
  Bombay

February 18th 1936

Darling Alice,
  How lovely it was to get your letter. I knew you'd be clever enough to work out the clue eventually, without Polly's help. I want to make them a little bit hard to give you something to think about; treasure hunts are never any good if the clues are too easy and one knows where to find them straight away, because part of the fun is searching, and discovering other interesting things in the process. I'm glad you met Patterson. He's been at Blackwood for ever, and is the kindest man. When the weather warms up he might show you some of the gardens, if you ask him nicely. They're all neglected and overgrown now, which is terribly sad, but they used to be quite magnificent. I know you'd like to explore them.
  You asked about the other things in the box. The bow tie you mentioned was the one that I wore that night, to go to Aggie's party. Later it became quite the rage for girls to dress up in men's clothing and it seemed that everyone

*was doing it for a while, but back then it was still rather
shocking. (That was the first time I saw Papa after his
return from Burma, and I know that he was not impressed!)
The handkerchief belonged to the stranger who opened the
door to help me that night. How differently things would
have turned out if he hadn't done that . . . (I might have
been arrested!) You'll have to be patient to find out about
the other things as you discover more clues. The next one
will be arriving soon.*

*We're nearing the end of this outward voyage now. We
have crossed the Arabian Sea – which sounds so romantic,
but was hot and sticky – and two days ago we docked in
Bombay. Papa and I went ashore for a few hours. Oh
Alice, how I wish I could have had you there, to see it all,
and taste and smell and hear it! Do you remember that
time we went to the market in Berwick Street, and how the
traders shouted their wares? It's like that, times a thousand,
with people selling lemonade and chai tea and nuts and
pastries from trays and baskets on their heads (Papa said I
mustn't buy anything to eat, for fear of the dreaded tummy
trouble, but I was sorely tempted by the pastries . . .)*

*Bombay is so beautiful. I wonder if London would look
as lovely if the sun was as bright and the colours as vivid?
The native men wear loose white robes and the women
are swathed in jewel-coloured silk saris, so much more
colourful than the drab tweeds and twills and gaberdines
that crowd English pavements. I kept thinking how you
would have loved to sketch it all – I can just imagine the*

79

marvellous drawings you would have done of the majestic Gateway of India, the street vendors and their exotic wares, the rickshaws and dear little donkeys patiently pulling carts laden with people and goods. Papa took me to the Taj Mahal Hotel for tea, which was terribly smart and luxurious, but rather British – a bit like going to The Ritz. (Of course, it made me miss you even more too, since you are my usual – and favourite! – companion for afternoon tea.) I rather longed to spend the time exploring the streets and markets as we were there for such a little while, but it was very kind of Papa to treat me to such a lovely tea.

This evening we are back on our dear old ship, and a delicious breeze is blowing across the water as we get ready to leave Bombay harbour and all its glorious chaos. In ten days we will dock in Rangoon and begin the journey to Mandalay, which will be our base while Papa gets on with what he came to do. I count the days until we can be home again, but for now the sun is going down and the heat is easing a little (blissful) and it will soon be time to change for dinner. I am sitting here thinking of you, and not even trying to pretend that I'm not missing you painfully. How hard it is, this separation! But we must remind ourselves that we are never truly apart from those we love very much. We might not be able to see them or speak to them or hold them in our arms, but we carry them always in our hearts.

Remember that, darling Alice, and know how much I love you. I'm blowing a flurry of kisses into the breeze, hoping it will carry them all the way back to England, and you will catch them tomorrow when you're out on your walk with Miss Lovelock. And here is another one, captured for safekeeping.

With love from my heart to yours

Mama xxxxx

P.S. Don't forget to look out for the next clue!

6

Lady Lennox

March 1936

Spring came slowly to Blackwood Park.

Each day, on Alice's afternoon walk there were tiny changes, little signs that winter's grip was loosening. The parkland began to lose its bleak, barren look as the blackthorn blossomed and lambs appeared in the fields, beneath a sky that turned gradually from bleached bone white to soft blue. When Alice went to the drawing room for her weekly interview with Grandmama one Sunday afternoon in early March, there was a bowl of paperwhite daffodils on the table by her armchair. Their delicate perfume was fresh in a room that smelled of stopped clocks and old paper.

There was nothing warm about Lady Lennox. The spring hadn't melted the ice in her eyes or softened her voice. She was wearing a steel-blue dress and her hair was set over her ears in rigid iron waves, which matched her rigid iron expression. Noticing that she was holding a piece of paper, Alice felt pins and needles all over at the horrifying thought that she had somehow found out about her secret correspondence with Mama.

'Miss Lovelock passed on your letter . . .' As Lady Lennox unfolded it her tone gave nothing away, beyond a general resigned disappointment. 'If one can call it that, when one side of the paper is taken up with a drawing. You're old enough to undertake a proper correspondence now, Alice. Also, I noticed that you had addressed it to your Mama only.' She looked up, with an expression of cool enquiry. 'That seems rather unfair on your Papa, do you not think?'

Relief washed through Alice's body; a hot tide that made her feel weak all over, and glad that she'd gone to the WC when she'd come in from her walk. The letter in Grandmama's hands was the one she'd written with Miss Lovelock, not Polly. It took a moment to remember that Grandmama had asked a question, and appeared to be waiting for an answer.

She struggled to think of how to give one without sounding rude. Without contradicting Grandmama and saying it *was* fair, because Papa hadn't written to her, like Mama had. She hadn't expected him to. Even at home he barely spoke to her, except to reprimand or rebuke, never to tell her interesting news or ask about her day, her life. Grandmama, apparently tired of waiting, folded Alice's pen and ink drawing of a clump of primroses and put it down beside the daffodils. 'Now. I'll get a new sheet of writing paper from the library and you can write a proper letter.'

Left alone, Alice allowed herself a private smile. Grandmama didn't know that she had written a proper letter only two days ago; three luxurious pages in reply to the wonderful letter Mama had sent from Bombay. (Polly never fussed about correct spelling, or making the writing neat and keeping it brief because of the cost of sending it abroad.) She had told her about the new lambs in the fields and grumbled about having tapioca for lunch. It all seemed very dreary compared to the sights and sounds of India, but she knew that Mama would sympathize about that. Once, when Alice was quite small, Mama had come into the nursery at Onslow Square and found her sitting at the table with a bowl of cold tapioca that Nanny had said she must finish. Mama had tipped it out of the window and taken Alice out for an ice in Kensington Gardens.

Her gaze found its way to the grand piano, on top of which a collection of photographs stood in silver frames. The largest of these was a studio portrait of Aunt Miranda looking regal and triumphant in her wedding dress. Beautiful too, though dislike and loyalty made Alice reluctant to admit this; to her, Mama was a thousand times lovelier. Her eyes moved to the next frame, which held a photograph of the day itself, of Aunt Miranda and Uncle Lionel standing in a drift of confetti outside a London church (Alice didn't recognize it), arms linked, smiles fixed. Mama stood a little behind Aunt Miranda, not looking at the camera, but somewhere just to the right, her face a little blurred but her smile luminous. Her hair had swung across her cheek, giving the impression that she had just turned her head.

Alice stepped closer, looking harder, wondering what she had seen to make her smile like that; what, or whom. It couldn't be Papa because he was standing beside Uncle Lionel, his face grave as he looked directly into the camera. Alice gave an involuntary shiver as her eyes met his, and she looked away quickly.

Their wedding photograph – his and Mama's – was further back, behind one of Cousin Archie as a baby in layers of frilly lace. She looked past him, finding Mama, feeling a tiny jolt as she registered the contrast between the first photograph and the second. The broad, bright smile was gone and Mama was thinner, but it wasn't just that. Alice had seen the photograph lots of times before, but for the first time she noticed that Mama's eyes, gazing out of the frame, were heavy-lidded and puffy and there were dark smudges beneath them. Not enough to notice ordinarily, but next to the other picture . . .

By the time another Season rolled around everything had changed, in ways we couldn't have imagined.

'Don't touch the piano, Alice. Now, let's try again.'

Alice hadn't heard Grandmama come in and her voice made her jump. She followed her over to the bureau in the window's bay and sat obediently, picking up the fountain pen and examining its inky nib, silently willing Grandmama to move away. It made her nervous, knowing she was watching. She pressed her pen to the paper too hard, making a puddle of ink. Blotting it quickly, she tried again.

Dear Mama

'And Papa,' Grandmama said smoothly. 'Don't forget.' She leaned over Alice's shoulder to make sure she wrote it. 'Never forget, Alice, how good your Papa has been to you. And to your Mama.'

The clock ticked on. Grandmama went back to her chair beside the fire. Alice's knuckles were white as she gripped the pen too hard, making the words spiky with anger.

I hope you are well

Grandmama was wrong. Papa wasn't good to Mama, not really, no matter what Mama said about how lucky they were to have the beautiful house in Onslow Square and all their lovely servants; how kind he was to give her such expensive jewels, such a generous allowance, and to pay for Alice to go to Miss Ellwood's school. Alice saw how things were, even if no one else did. She saw how cold he was, when Mama was so warm and loving, how disapproving when she tried to make things interesting and fun. At Christmas they had gone to a party at Lady Londonderry's and Mama had worn a red satin dress and Grandmother Carew's ruby choker, fixed across her forehead as a headband. She had been dazzling, but Papa had frowned and said she looked like a circus showgirl. He told her to take the choker off and wear it properly.

That night, much, much later, Alice had woken and heard Mama crying –

Grandmama's voice was as sharp as a ruler across her knuckles. 'Staring out of the window isn't going to get your letter written.'

Alice blinked. She hadn't been aware that she was staring out of the window. The ghost of Uncle Howard in his soldier's khaki hung in front of her, reflected palely in the glass.

'I don't know what to say.'

'Then you must think. Correspondence requires consideration, thinking of others before oneself. The art of letter writing lies in putting oneself in the position of the recipient and knowing what he or she would be interested to hear, whether they might want to be informed or amused or diverted. So. Your Mama and Papa will receive your letter when the ship docks in Bombay. What do you think they might like to read about home?'

Bombay? The lines of Mama's last letter leapt across Alice's mind; images of the street vendors and donkey carts flickering vividly to life. For a moment she was confused, but then realization dawned. *Of course.* Grandmama didn't know about the secret correspondence between her and Mama. She didn't know that the ship had already docked in Bombay and was now on the final stretch of the voyage, because Mama must have written to Alice more recently. Alice hugged the special insight to her, congratulating herself for not giving it away.

In the glass in front of her Uncle Howard's faint smile was conspiratorial. She bent her head and began, laboriously, to write.

*

The second letter was hardly an improvement on the first. It began with *Dear Mama and Papa* at least, but the writing was still an abomination and its few lines were littered with spelling mistakes. They snagged Lady Lennox's attention. as her eyes skimmed over the page, like little thorns in her flesh.

How apt.

The child's intelligence was clearly limited. Selina had said that she struggled with writing and spelling, but was bright as a button. Lady Lennox was of the opinion that the first statement rather disproved the second. Salt in the wound for Rupert, who had been such a distinguished scholar at both Eton and Cambridge (Howard had joked about bribing him to write papers. At least she thought he had been joking . . .) Thank goodness the child was a girl – which wasn't a sentiment Lady Lennox had ever expected to feel about one of her own grandchildren – and Rupert would be spared the expense and embarrassment of putting her through a proper school.

Small mercies.

If one tried to be dispassionate about it (and she did try, for the sake of her own sanity) one could see that she was pretty enough, though not in any way that Lady Lennox recognized. Alone in the drawing room after she had sent Alice back to the nursery, she went over to the piano (wiping the child's fingerprints off its polished lid with her hand-kerchief) and looked at the photographs that she had caught her studying. She wondered if the contrast was as marked to

Selina's dark, gypsy-eyed daughter as it was to everyone else. Even in black and white, the golden Anglo-Saxon colouring of the Lennoxes was striking.

Her hand went to her own hair, faded now to silver, as her gaze moved over the images of her children, and came to rest – uneasily – on Selina. Hesitantly she reached out and picked up the photograph of her as bridesmaid on Miranda's wedding day, frozen in that moment when she'd turned her head and smiled.

Her fingers tightened on the frame. Time had taught her that anger was an easier emotion to manage than sorrow, and she reached instinctively for it now. The bobbed hair, swinging across Selina's face ... Such a silly fashion, and so unbecoming – unlike the elegant waves pinned beneath Miranda's veil. There was something shameless about the exposed curve of Selina's neck and shoulder that Lady Lennox found provoking, even all these years later.

That was Selina all over. Shameless. Defiant. It was how she had been from the start, as a wild little tomboy in the nursery who had far more in common with her brother than her sister, but had never grasped that qualities that were admirable in a boy were quite the opposite in a girl. Lady Lennox had wondered whether Selina might grow up to be one of those sexless women who enjoyed gardening and bred spaniels: confirmed spinsters. The reality had turned out to be far worse. A predilection for dahlias and dogs wouldn't have resulted in the ignominy of the changeling grandchild or the burden of looking after her.

Robert said she should have been firmer with their youngest daughter. She'd tried, of course ... but Selina had always been dismissive of rules and disdainful of discipline. Howard's death had snuffed out any sense of propriety she might once have had, as if she was thumbing her nose at the figures of authority whom she held responsible. She had always behaved as if his loss had hurt her more than anyone else – more even than it had hurt his mother.

They had both loved him so very much. In the aftermath of his death grief should have united them, but instead it had driven them further apart. Lady Lennox sensed the unspoken accusation behind Selina's casual defiance, the implication that it was *her fault*. She had failed as a mother because she had let him go – encouraged him, even. As if she'd had any choice but to offer her fine, strong, healthy son up to serve.

The fact that she blamed herself didn't make her daughter's censure any easier to bear. It widened the cracks between them into a chasm. It made it difficult to view Selina's behaviour – the drinking and partying and getting up to high jinks – as anything other than acts of personal revenge, of which the child had apparently been the ultimate.

With a sigh Lady Lennox set the photograph back amongst the others, but her eyes stayed fixed to her daughter's face. Things had come to a head that summer, the year that Miranda had got married. It was a long time after Howard's death, years after the end of the war but, covered up and hidden from view the wound of their mutual grief had festered rather than healed. Looking back she remembered how tired she had been in the run up to the wedding, how exhausted by the preparations and the pressure for perfection, by the need to keep going and hold back the great weight of her sadness. She had lacked the energy to deal with her wayward daughter and the patience to understand her.

Time had given her perspective and made her able to be kinder to herself. Her fingers went to her throat now, fumbling for the gold cross that hung there; banished to the depths of her jewellery box when Howard died but unearthed again a few years ago, when the asphyxiating cloud of grief began to lift. Those had been dark and difficult years, but gradually her belief in a God of mercy rather than cruelty had begun to reassert itself. Surely the failings of a grieving mother might be forgiven?

It was unfortunate that her granddaughter's presence — her very existence, in fact — meant they could never quite be forgotten.

7

Worlds Apart

June 1925

Selina stood beside Miranda in front of the huge mirror in the salon of Maison D'Or and concentrated hard on not fainting, or being sick. Eau de nil wasn't her favourite colour at the best of times, but this morning, after a rather lively night, the shade Miranda had chosen for her bridesmaids was regrettably similar to Selina's complexion.

Outside the day was muggy and overcast, with clouds like bundles of dirty linen heaped in the sky. Inside it was sticky and uncomfortable too, with an atmosphere one could slice with a knife. No one spoke much, which was a blessing in one way (Selina didn't feel up to making conversation herself) but, on top of a monumental headache, the simmering tension was extremely unpleasant. If there was music to be faced, she'd rather just get it over with.

And of course, there was music to be faced.

Last night had started off as a perfectly ordinary party; rather on the dull side, if anything, which was why they'd spilled out of the house in Queens Gate in the early hours and continued their own revels, complete with stolen booze and a 'borrowed' gramophone, in Kensington Gardens. How was she to know that a photographer was lurking when she decided to climb onto the Albert Memorial and watch the sun come up over the city from beneath its arches? The morning papers had carried a photograph of her (unmistakably) reclining on the Prince's lap and kissing him on the lips, a bottle of champagne dangling from her hand. Miranda and Lady Lennox had taken a very Victorian attitude to this, and were decidedly Not Amused.

'Yes.' Lady Lennox broke the silence, her eyes sliding over Selina to linger on Miranda's far more pleasing reflection in the looking glass. 'Yes. I believe that's just right. Good.'

Selina felt a stab of relief. She was going on to the Royal Academy Private View and had told Harry Lonsdale to pick her up here at midday. A little silver carriage clock on the bureau began to announce the hour in a tinkle of musical chimes. Her head throbbed. She opened her mouth to make her excuses, but was beaten by Miranda, who was surveying her own reflection with cool detachment.

'Too simple, do you think? Dull?'

The dress was a narrow column of white silk – double layered and drop-waisted – ending six inches above Miranda's elegant ankles. The neckline was simple and square, the perfect showcase for her delicate collarbones and long neck, unadorned by beads or ornaments, because – as everyone would understand – the real jewel was Miranda herself. She twisted around, this way and that, making the skirt swish around her calves. 'I know everyone wears a higher hemline these days but . . .'

'Understated,' pronounced Lady Lennox.

Understatement, being the opposite of vulgarity, was a quality to be admired and aspired to. Miranda seemed mollified. Selina seized her chance and stepped down from the dais.

'It's perfect. Now, if we're finished, I simply must dash—'

'We're not,' Miranda snapped. 'What about your dress?'

'Oh – it's fine. Don't worry about me.'

'I'm not. I'm worrying about me. It's my wedding and I don't want to be shamed.' She turned, fixing Selina with her pointy icicle glare. 'It looks too tight across the bust – don't you think, Mama? It was perfectly all right at the last fitting. You must have put on weight. Hardly surprising, given that you're always gorging on cake and sticky buns at Claridge's or vast dinners at the Eiffel. I suppose it's too late to let out the seams, so you'll just have to exercise some restraint between now and the wedding.'

If it hadn't been for the nausea swimming in her head Selina wouldn't have been able to stop herself from responding to this unexpected round of sniper fire. As it was she gritted her teeth and retreated to the dressing room, waving away the offer of assistance from a young modiste.

She slipped her chemise over her head and reluctantly examined her image in the looking glass. When she had come to London for her first season she had realized that the body she had taken for granted – that had served her well for riding and running and climbing trees – was all wrong. Desperate to alter it, she had sent away for a vicious rubber bandeau that promised in the newspaper advertisement to 'melt away fat and flatten the fullest of figures.' Dishonestly, as it turned out. The extreme discomfort had not justified the minimal change it made to her figure and Polly, in a rare display of indignation, had thrown it away. 'You're perfect as you are,' she'd protested. 'Never you mind the pictures in the fashion papers. None of them can hold a candle to you.'

Darling Polly, whose judgement was clouded by loyalty but whose kindness was without equal. She was the only one who knew about Selina's insecurity and understood her hidden shame. It had been Polly who noticed when not eating pudding had led to missing mealtimes altogether and telling fibs to hide it. It was Polly who had helped her back from the edge, with her combination of common sense, patience and loving persistence. She felt like more of a sister than Miranda had ever been, and there was nothing Selina couldn't share with her.

Almost nothing.

A sudden memory of damp earth and dark eyes jarred in her head. The soft, secret sound of shared breathing, the knowledge of nearness and the intoxicating mix of intimacy and unfamiliarity. She hadn't told Polly about that, knowing it would alarm her. The recklessness of going into the shabby house of a stranger, the danger of following him into the darkness. (*Anything might have happened!*) She couldn't reassure Polly that she wouldn't do it again because she would, in a heartbeat. If only she had the chance.

As she emerged from the dressing room she heard the trumpet of a motor horn in the street below. Miranda, being helped down from the dais, gave a disdainful sniff.

'Your barbarian friends appear to have arrived. I can't think why you're going to the Royal Academy since none of you are remotely interested in art.'

Selina went across to the window. 'It was Theo's idea. We're looking for inspiration for the Napiers' party – you know, *Come as a Work of Art.*'

It was almost the truth. That had been Theo's grudging reason for acquiescence when Selina herself had suggested going to the Private View. None of them usually bothered since it was one of the season's more staid events, but it was her one tenuous connection with her artist; her best and only hope of bumping into him again, short of turning up on the doorstep of the house in Marchmont Street. Which she had actually considered, during the wakeful hours of the night when desperation got the better of discretion . . . Thankfully her daytime self had a little more self-control.

So far.

She couldn't stop thinking about him.

Harry's motor (or his father's) had pulled up in the street below, with Theo and Flick slumped together on the back seat. They both wore dark glasses, suggesting that they too were suffering the after effects of the previous evening. As she watched, Harry squeezed the horn again, causing a pair of pigeons pecking in the gutter to take off in a flurry of feathers.

'I must go. Sorry, Mama.'

Her mother's cheek was as cool as marble as she bent to kiss it.

'Be careful, Selina.'

'Of what, Mama?'

Lady Lennox touched her fingers to her temple, frowning faintly. 'I hardly need to remind you. The war has narrowed the field of eligible men. You'd be very foolish indeed to miss your chance when one shows an interest in you. Especially one like Rupert Carew.'

Selina felt the quick beat of blood in her wrists and saw colours flash behind her eyes. A bubble of wholly inappropriate laughter rose in her throat – a ridiculous reaction to the pain. She wanted, so badly, to say that she couldn't give a tinker's toss what Rupert Carew thought of her, and what the war had done to her marriage prospects was nothing – *nothing* – compared to what it had done to her brother. But she didn't. The loss that had scored those lines around her mother's mouth and taken the light from her eyes must never be mentioned. Howard's name must never be spoken. The subject of his death was forbidden.

'He's hardly shown an interest, Mama; it's just because he's an old friend of the family. That doesn't mean—'

Her mother cut her off with an impatient sound. 'It's time to grow up, Selina.' Her lips were tight, as if moving them was an effort. 'It's been three years since your Season. Your father and I have been patient and made allowances, but this behaviour – this *cavorting* – cannot continue. Your reputation, once lost, cannot be regained. Rupert understands ... how things are, but his understanding is not without limit.' She paused, one finger circling on her temple. 'Look on it as one of your treasure hunts. Don't get so caught up in the exhilaration of chasing around with your friends that you take your eyes off the prize. Because if you do ... someone cleverer will get there before you, and you'll regret your foolishness when you have to take what's left. Remember that.'

Desperate for air, Selina clattered down the narrow staircase, ignoring the receptionist's polite goodbye. A muted cheer rose from the occupants of the motorcar as she emerged onto the street. Flick moved over to make space as she climbed into the back, curling into her side like a kitten.

'We're never drinking again,' she whimpered.

'Not until at least lunchtime anyway,' Theo added.

They all lapsed into silence as Harry swung the motor through the midday traffic. Behind his dark glasses Theo's face was the same ash grey as the clouds. The pain in Selina's head settled to a steady pulse as her mother's words richocheted around it like a bagatelle ball. She stroked Flick's hair, breathing deeply in rhythm with the strokes in an attempt to calm her anger, gazing out at the people walking along the pavements. The car slowed as they drew alongside an ex-serviceman sitting against the railings outside Burlington House selling matches, and for a moment her eyes met his. He tipped his hat, and they began to move again.

Seven years on from the armistice and the scars of the war were still visible everywhere. One got adept at looking past them, or through them, or pretending they weren't there at all. One got on with things in the best way one could; there was always someone worse off, like the man selling matches, or Lady Renshaw, who had lost all three of her boys, or Harry's cousin Roland who had lost his left hand and his entire right arm. One could never complain about one's own loss. Selina understood why her mother had buried hers in the deepest recesses of her heart and hardened her face against the world. It was her way of coping, of Getting On. But it was a sad legacy for a boy whose smile could light up a room.

Howard had been twenty when he died; a year younger than she was now. She remembered him, coming into the nursery at Blackwood Park in his uniform, his Sam Browne belt creaking as he scooped her up to hug her goodbye. He had seemed so old to her eleven-year-old self – though he must only have been eighteen then – and when he came back at Christmas he seemed older still, and Mama had issued strict instructions that she must be quiet around him, and not silly. It had only taken him a day to notice and to seek her out to ask if she was all right. He had sighed when she'd told him what Mama had said, and the new lines around his eyes had softened a little. *Oh Selina . . . don't ever stop having fun or finding the joy in life. Please, promise me. I actually don't think I can bear it if that's lost, on top of everything else.*

She had promised.

Mama and Miranda were shiveringly censorious about the way she lived, as if it was all an elaborate and extended act of disrespect to Howard and the brave young men who'd died alongside him. She saw it differently. She was living for both of them; breathing the air he couldn't breathe, drinking the champagne he couldn't taste, cramming her days and nights with all the exhilarating experiences that had been stolen from him by the same old men who puffed out their moustaches in disapproval at the newspaper reports in which her name appeared.

She closed her eyes briefly and tried to usher the thoughts from her mind. The anger lay just beneath the surface, like a constant itch under her skin and the only way to deal with it was not to think about it. Not to think about anything much at all. Miranda sneered at her for being silly and superficial, but it was all part of the strategy. Think about today, not tomorrow. Dance over the cracks so you don't fall into them. Drink champagne in the afternoons and invent ridiculous cocktails to make the ruined world glitter again. Keep going, one foot in front of the other. *Don't look down.*

Flick raised her head and groaned as Harry swung around a motorbus outside The Ritz. Her lips were white.

'I feel most awfully peaky . . .'

Harry glanced over his shoulder and rolled his eyes.

'For God's sake, don't you dare be sick. We're nearly there.'

'Jesus Christ, Weston, you pick your moments. One small favour, what – four years ago? – and you reappear now to demand repayment. God – hurry up, would you. If we get caught down here, we'll both be thrown out, only I'll lose my job as well.'

Lawrence, who had slowed down to look at a dust-furred bronze cast of an outstretched hand, picked up his pace again, following his erstwhile friend through the vaults beneath the Royal Academy. George Holdsworth had been a fellow student at the Slade; a talented enough painter, but one whose commitment had been sorely tested by the hours of rigorous anatomical study the course demanded, and who had opted to spend more of his time in the Sir John Russell than the Life Room. After two grinding years he'd only been allowed to graduate onto a third because Lawrence had given him a sheaf of his own (plentiful) studies to submit.

'Small favour?' he said dryly.

Holdsworth had the grace not to argue. 'Yes well, fat lot of good it did me. Here I am, in the Royal Academy – as a sodding porter.' Pushing through a set of swing doors he threw a glance at Lawrence over his shoulder. 'Don't know what your excuse is though. You want an invitation to these swanky parties, you should submit your bloody work.'

Lawrence thought of the canvas he'd left on his easel

in the studio. It was the early stages of another quiet, conventional portrait, of Captain John Markham, Royal Highland Fusiliers, who had died at Messines Ridge in 1917. It certainly didn't push any artistic boundaries or subvert any rules, but then Captain Markham's parents weren't asking for Lawrence's vision and they didn't want to be challenged or shocked. They wanted their boy, safe and recognizable.

Lawrence simply needed to be paid. Artistic integrity was a luxury he couldn't afford.

'When the Royal Academy start accepting photography, maybe I'll start submitting,' he said, following Holdsworth up an echoing staircase.

Holdsworth's laughter bounced off the tiled walls. 'Still messing around with that camera, then? Well, I hope you're prepared for a long wait – not really art, is it?' Reaching the top of the staircase he paused outside a set of giant double doors and lowered his voice. 'Right – in here.' For the first time since he'd met Lawrence at a side door and ushered him into the service corridors, Holdsworth looked at him properly. 'Christ, Weston, you might have smartened yourself up a bit. You do know what these people are like, don't you? You're going to stick out like a sore bloody thumb.'

Lawrence dragged a hand through his hair. There was probably no point in saying that he had smartened himself up. Holdsworth opened the door a crack, admitting a wave of noise, peering through for a moment before turning back to Lawrence. 'Right. You're on your own. If anyone says anything, I don't know you, that clear?' He opened the door wider, muttering 'I hope you know what you're bloody doing ...'

Lawrence wasn't sure that he did. In truth, he hadn't really thought it through. He and Edith, who owned the studio he shared in Gower Street, sometimes came to the Summer Exhibition to see what the selection committee had chosen that year, what they had hung in the best positions and who had been relegated to the rafters, but that was usually in the dog days of August, just before it was dismantled. He'd never felt the need to go in the opening week, never mind try to get in to the Private View, for God's sake. This was the preserve of the wealthy and the well-connected; a high profile opportunity for them to congregate and buy paintings they barely glanced at for houses they scarcely lived in. It certainly wasn't about art, but it was just about the closest the orbit of his world was ever likely to come to that of Selina Lennox.

And he wanted to see her again.

The noise level in the room was incredible. Posh people, it seemed, had voices that could carry over grouse moors and down twenty-foot dining tables, and no facility to moderate the volume. As he moved around the room he caught snatches of different conversations. *'I've bought that Munnings. Same as all the other damn horse daubs we've got, but I daresay we'll find a space for it somewhere . . .' 'I'm not inviting her again this summer. Last year she ruined the pillowcases with panstick and propositioned one of the footmen. Genuinely. Mummy was livid.'*

He sifted the sound, trying to pick out the husky note of her voice. Not finding it, he kept moving.

It was warm. The great glass lantern roof of the main gallery showed a murky sky, but the room had a hothouse humidity, heavy with expensive scent and hair oil. Paintings in heavy gilt frames crowded the high walls, from skirting to cornice, but no one was paying much attention to them. Lawrence wasn't surprised, it was derivative, conservative, predictable stuff, for the most part – Captain Markham would have been quite at home here. The one notable exception was a large and startlingly modern female nude, prominently hung in the first gallery. The artist had used blocks of vivid colour: a glaring egg yolk yellow for her hair, undulating swirls of purple and green shadowing the stylized features of her face and the contours of her body. Lawrence paused in front of it, drinking it in. 'Bally hideous,' a braying voice behind him scoffed. 'Damned cheek to call it art.'

He ran his finger around the collar of his shirt. His fingers twitched with the urge to light a cigarette but he knew that in here the smell of cheap tobacco would draw attention to him like a distress flare on a dark ocean. He moved on.

There were three galleries. He circulated around each of them twice, his eyes sliding over the canvases on the walls and combing the faces in the room instead, his hope of finding hers amongst them dwindling as his sense of foolishness grew.

What was he doing here?

What was he *doing*?

It had been a long shot. A ridiculous, romantic notion. A test of fate, almost, and of the irrational feeling he'd had since the night that he'd let her into his hallway that there was meant to be more. That it wasn't the end.

Well, fate had answered.

He shouldered his way past bespoke-tailored backs, heading for the door. There was no need to leave via the same furtive route by which he'd entered, but he noticed the doorman's frown as he passed, and felt his suspicious eyes on his back as he went out into the courtyard.

The zoo-like squawk of voices faded, overlaid by the everyday noise of the city. He tugged at his tie, pulling it loose. As he went through the archway out onto Piccadilly a motorcar swung past him in a screech of tyres, so close that he had to step back against the wall to avoid being hit.

He swore under his breath, staring after it as it came to a haphazard halt in the courtyard. The doors opened and its passengers spilled out, their voices carrying across the elegant square.

In the shadow of the archway Lawrence groaned and swore again. He hesitated for a moment, his hands balled into impotent fists, then forced himself to turn away and walk on.

It was too late.

'Your driving is worse than going on a ferris wheel,' Theo complained, helping Flick out of the car. 'It would serve you right if we were sick all over your splendid upholstery. Are you all right, Selina darling?'

She had got to her feet and was standing in the back of the car looking towards the archway. Her chest was tight, her heart kicking hard against it.

'Selina?'

'Hmm?'

'Are you feeling perfectly gruesome? I say, you're not going to faint, are you? You're awfully pale . . .'

'No. No, I'm fine. Perfectly well.'

'Of course she is,' Harry said briskly, slamming the car door. 'Now do stop beefing or I shall make you all get a taxi home. Come along, boys and girls – Lord knows why I brought you, since none of you know a Picasso from a Pisarro – but we're here now, so we may as well go in.'

'How rude,' Theo scolded, rearranging his trailing silk scarf and taking Flick's arm. 'I'll have you know I have an exceptionally good eye for pretty pictures, though today we're hunting for inspiration, remember? *Come as a work of Art . . .*'

He tucked Flick's arm through his and began to walk towards the entrance to Burlington House. Selina hung back, smoothing her ruffled hair away from her face with a shaking hand. In the two weeks since the treasure hunt she had seen Lawrence Weston a dozen times in the most unlikely places – on the pavement in the Strand, in the stalls below their box at the theatre, dancing in the Blue Lantern, disappearing just ahead of her through the revolving doors at Claridge's – and when she looked again, heart racing, she always found that she had been mistaken and it had been another dark head; neater than his, more ordinary. This was just another of those times, she told herself wearily, trailing across the courtyard after Theo and Flick. Wishful thinking, that was all.

But still . . .

She stopped at the top of the steps and looked back, unwilling to quite relinquish hope or snuff out the flicker of longing that had flared back to life in the pit of her stomach. In the sticky afternoon the courtyard was empty except for a respectable couple getting out of a taxi, and a cluster of debs hurrying out, fanning themselves with exhibition programmes.

Swallowing her disappointment, she went in.

The Strand Hotel
  Rangoon
  Burma

12th March 1936

Darling Alice,

So, here we are — in Burma at last.

I must admit, it was quite a wrench leaving the ship that has come to feel like home during these past few weeks, and it feels jolly strange to be back on dry land. We docked two days ago but I still have the strangest sensation of the earth moving beneath my feet. How peculiar to feel seasick when one is no longer at sea!

The hotel is wonderfully smart — if it weren't for the heat and the big ceiling fans that whirr constantly one could easily believe one was in London within its elegant walls. (No Burmese guests are allowed.) Our room is large and airy, with a view over the river — I'm writing this at a little table by the window and looking out over the water now. I'm longing to go and explore the city, but Papa is looking after me terribly carefully and insists that I rest from the journey.

The Glittering Hour

Earlier we had luncheon in the restaurant downstairs and I watched the people coming and going on the street outside. It's less busy than Bombay, but still fascinating. The women are delicate and beautiful, with shining dark hair, heavy as silk. As we ate, a procession of men filed past, dressed in yellow robes with their heads shaved. Buddhist monks, Papa said, perhaps on their way to the great Shwe Dagon Pagoda that dominates the Rangoon skyline, much like St Paul's rises above London. (Except the Shwe Dagon is gold and glittering, rather than leaden grey – can you imagine?) I would love to visit the temple and hope to be allowed, though Papa says there are complicated rules and customs that must be observed, and that European people scarcely venture there. I believe that one has to remove one's shoes before entering, but I shouldn't mind that at all. I can't think of anything more lovely than to walk with bare feet on ancient floors where millions have walked before. I do hope it might be possible to go.

It's very warm. The other colonial wives have beautiful silk parasols, so my first task, when I venture out, will be to buy one. We had coffee with a Scottish couple – a Colonel and Mrs Muir – after luncheon, and the wife informed me that I simply must visit Rowe & Co., which is apparently 'the Harrods of the East' and is stuffed with treats and treasures from home, as well as everything one needs for this climate. I can't help thinking I'd rather make my purchases in the little streets and alleys where the local women shop, but when I mentioned this Mrs Muir nearly spat out her coffee. Poor Papa was mortified. I suppose I shall have to do my shopping in the respectable halls of the Harrods of the East after all.

Oh — I've just glanced out of the window and you won't believe what I can see . . . ELEPHANTS! Oh Alice — they're too sweet — I wish you could see them! There are three of them, with men crouched high up on their necks on strange wooden platforms, and they've guided them into the river, I think perhaps to cool them down or something. They certainly seem to be enjoying the water (the elephants, not the men, who look rather cross — flapping and kicking their legs). I wish I had a camera, or was as good at drawing as you are. I could share with you how magical and majestic they are.

Tonight we are going across town to have dinner with some more English people, at a place called the Pegu Club. Papa goes there often when he's here; I believe it's quite the place to be in Burma, and it apparently has its own famous cocktail. I'm not sure I'm recovered enough from my seasickness to sample one though.

It feels like time is going particularly slowly just now and the days seem very long. I'm finding it quite a struggle to keep smiling and talking to all these new people — friends of Papa's, important government officials and businessmen and their wives — when I'm feeling off colour and missing you so much. I want to talk about you all the time. Lots of them have children who they send back to school in England. I'm not sure how they bear it. (Papa says I mustn't ask.)

My darling, I'll finish now, and lie down for a little while before it's time to bathe and dress for the evening. Papa says that the time here is hours ahead of England, so as I'm writing in the afternoon, you're probably still in the schoolroom and working hard at your lessons. Oh, how clearly I can see you there, and how much I wish I could reach out and touch you. In a few days we'll be making the journey north to where Papa's mines are, and once we're there I hope he might conclude his business quickly so we can return home. It can't be soon enough for me.

Write back, my darling. Your letters bring me such joy.

All my love (and a lipstick kiss)

Mama

Xxxx

8

Miss Lovelock

April 1936

Dust motes swirled in the shafts of light filtering through the schoolroom window. Squinting through them, Vera Lovelock chalked algebra equations onto the blackboard, copying them from a faded sheet that had seen her through many a slow morning in various schoolrooms over the years.

In her last position (two girls and a boy in Peterborough) even the youngest had been able to complete these sums, but she suspected she was being optimistic in giving them to Alice Carew. The child spent more time gazing out of the window or at the map on the schoolroom wall than she did writing anything, never mind correct answers. The old saying about horses and water came to mind.

It was all the same to her. Any illusions the young Vera Lovelock may once have had about firing up young minds and filling them with knowledge had long since been abandoned. Age had made her cynical and taught her to look out for her own interests, because there was no one else to look out for them. Experience had shown her that teaching itself was a thankless task, but having a roof over one's head, a room to oneself with meals provided made it a practical option. Especially when one's charge was as quiet as Alice, leaving one plenty of time to pursue one's own interests.

She finished chalking and looked at the clock on the wall. 'Three quarters of an hour until lunchtime,' she said, in a cheery, encouraging tone. 'Let's see how many of these you can do before then.'

The child jumped a little, as if she was surprised to see the algebra equations, or to realize that they were any business of hers. Miss Lovelock saw her slide a scrap of paper off the desk and shove it into her pocket. The younger, keener version of herself would have swooped down and performed a confiscation, followed by a sharp reprimand about disrespect and underhandedness, but these days she lacked the will. She doubted that little Alice Carew would be writing notes to herself poking fun at the governess (*Miss Lovelock has teeth like tombstones* was one that she had come across several times. Ten-year-olds were an unoriginal lot when it came to similes.) Another bonus of having a solitary pupil.

She was a funny little thing. Sweet-natured, certainly, but not quite all there as far as Miss Lovelock could tell. One had to make allowances, of course; circumstances were certainly ... testing. Sitting down behind her own desk she felt a moment of pity for the forlorn little figure staring blankly at the blackboard, but it was quickly forgotten as she slid out the publication she had concealed beneath her papers, the arrival of which she had been eagerly anticipating for days.

The Blackshirt was a weekly newspaper to which Miss Lovelock was an enthusiastic subscriber. The latest edition carried an article written by Adeline Pugh, a great friend from her suffragette days, entitled *Women Answer The Call to Fascism!* in which she reported on the number of women swelling the ranks of the British Union of Fascists, and the variety of roles they were undertaking. Miss Lovelock knew all of this because she and Adeline had exchanged much correspondence during the writing of the piece. Adeline had sent her the final draft, so she felt no particular urgency to find the printed article now, and took her time turning the pages, enjoying the many photographs of Sir Oswald Mosley instead.

Miss Lovelock removed her spectacles and gave them a polish on the edge of her cardigan, the better to study one of these. In it, Sir Oswald stood, champagne glass in hand, beside an elegant blonde woman in a neat black suit. Diana Guinness, whose passionate affair with Sir Oswald was the whispered talk of the B.U.F., had been a member of that privileged set of partygoers the papers used to call 'The Bright Young People'. As had Selina Lennox. This tenuous connection had been the primary reason Miss Lovelock had overlooked the drawbacks of the position at Blackwood Park – the house's isolation and distance from London – and decided to apply for the post. One never knew. Packing her things in the dingy room she had rented in Clerkenwell she had let her imagination carry her a few months into the future, to the time when Mrs Carew would return to Blackwood to be reunited with her daughter. *Miss Lovelock,* she would say, taking her hands, *I can't thank you enough – my daughter has spoken so warmly of you. It so happens that I have a friend who is looking for a governess for her young sons . . .*

That would put her one up on Adeline for a change.

Remembering this fantasy rekindled a flicker of professional enthusiasm in Miss Lovelock's breast. She glanced up from Lady Guinness to look at the solitary figure in front of her. Dark curls obscured Alice's face as she bent over the desk with a focus that was unusual and rather gratifying. The imagined scenario gathered substance.

'How are you getting on? Any questions?'

The child lifted her head, frowning slightly. 'What does *interred* mean?'

Alice had expected to be told off for her lack of progress on the equations, but instead Miss Lovelock – exasperated rather than cross – dismissed her early for lunch. 'Spring fever, I expect,' she said as she gathered up the papers on her desk. 'Difficult to concentrate when the sun is shining outside. We'll try again tomorrow.'

It was difficult to concentrate on equations whatever the

weather, but Alice wasn't going to admit that the real reason for her distraction was the clue that she had discovered that morning, just before lessons started. It had been slipped inside the folds of her flannel on the edge of the bathroom basin; she would have discovered it earlier and had all of breakfast to ponder it if she hadn't tried to get away with just splashing her face with cold water instead of washing it properly, which – as Polly teased – just went to show it didn't pay to cut corners.

With twenty minutes still to go until Polly would be bringing the lunch trays up, Alice crept along the corridor and slipped through the door to the servants' staircase. She had discovered a place on the turn of the stairs where she could sit, out of sight of anyone passing by in the passageway below, but close enough to be able to hear snatches of conversation in the kitchen (particularly from Ellen, whose voice was the most strident). It was draughty, but then so was the nursery, which was also a lot more dull and lonely without the diversion of listening to Ellen and Ivy plan a trip into Salisbury to look for dress fabric on their half day, or talk about a film they'd seen at the picture house. ('I don't know what she was making such a fuss about – I'd have been his in a trice.' 'Ellen, you wouldn't!' 'You bet I would. Maurice Chevalier? You'd have to be wrong in the head to say no to him.')

Settling herself down on the wide step at the staircase's turn, Alice took the slip of paper from her pocket and smoothed it out on her knee. The hairs lifted on the nape of her neck as she ran her eyes over the mysterious lines.

A Roman Queen, a circus clown
Mrs Andrews's pale blue gown.
French dancing girls, a Cavalier,
All interred together here.

Questions buzzed in her brain like bees around a hive. Miss Lovelock, clearly caught off guard, had explained 'interred' ('It means buried, in a grave or a tomb, though I can't think why you need to know. I mean – I can't think what it has to do with algebra'), but that only made things more puzzling. Why would those people be buried together . . . and who was Mrs Andrews?

There was a chapel at Blackwood, at the end of the carriage drive near the boundary to the park. That was where Cousin Archie's distantly recalled Christening had taken place, though from what Alice could remember it wasn't a very grand resting place for a Roman Queen. Perhaps Miss Lovelock would agree to walk down there this afternoon. The chapel itself would probably be locked, but it was the graveyard that Alice was interested in and she was confident that Miss Lovelock would think that a suitably serious subject for study.

The smell of frying onions and roasting meat drifted up from the kitchen, along with the echo of voices. Alice tried to pick out Polly's, but as usual it was Ellen's that was the clearest. 'She's a piece of work, if you ask me . . .' she was saying. 'Nice looking, I'll give her that, and some lovely clothes, but she can be a right cow.'

Alice folded the clue and slipped it back into her pocket, settling herself in to listen. She had never heard anyone express opinions as freely as Ellen did (Mama and Miss Ellwood were united in the view that in the absence of anything nice to say it was best to keep quiet) and found it both shocking and fascinating. Ivy's reply came from further away, at the far end of the kitchen, and was lost to Alice amid a clatter of saucepans. Ellen's laugh was loud and sharp-edged.

'Just you wait – you won't be saying that when they've been here for a few days. They're bringing a nanny for the kid, but I don't suppose she'll bring a maid. It'll be muggins here who gets lumbered with all *her* fetching and carrying, but you'll end up spending all your time preparing food for the nursery.'

There was a loose thread on the hem of her dress and Alice pulled absently at it as she tried to work out who they might be talking about. Visitors to Blackwood? It seemed unlikely. Ivy's voice was distant and indistinct, but Alice caught the word 'nursery' again, before the rest of the sentence was drowned in a rush of water.

'Well she's no bother, is she? Poor kid don't say boo to a goose; you hardly know she's here. It'll be a different matter with Master Archie, you mark my words. You'd think he was bloody royalty the way they treat him – he's got to have a fire lit in his room, fresh eggs for breakfast, complete quiet in the house when he's having his nap. It amazes me that her Ladyship puts up with it – she's all for children being neither seen nor heard where the other one's concerned, but with little lord Archie . . .'

Alice's cheeks tingled with sudden heat, as if they'd been slapped. They were talking about *them* – the family: Grandmama and Aunt Miranda and Cousin Archie. About *her*. She was rigid with embarrassment, and though part of her wanted to get up and go back up the stairs, she didn't move.

Neither did she hear the door open high above her, or the sound of footsteps on the stairs. It was only when they stopped, and Polly cleared her throat loudly that Alice looked up and saw her there, leaning over the banister.

'And what are you doing, young lady?'

'Oh – nothing! Waiting for lunch, that's all. Miss Lovelock finished lessons early.'

She stood up, noticing with dismay that a long stretch of her hem was now sagging down, feeling disorientated and caught out. Polly began to clatter down the stairs, and Alice watched her hand (the only part of her that was visible) slide along the banisters, getting closer, and wondered what she was doing up there in the attics instead of being down in the kitchen.

'Seems like it's your lucky day today then,' Polly grinned, appearing round the corner. 'Come on; run along and wash your hands – properly this time – and I'll go down and get your lunch.'

The child's request to walk down to the chapel was a surprise, but not an unpleasant one. It was a bright day, almost warm in the sunshine, and a change was as good as a rest, as the saying went. (Miss Lovelock, whose life as a governess had been ruled by routine, could attest to this.)

Blackwood Park looked a little less gloomy with the weak spring sun on its face and a thin swathe of daffodils straggling along the line of the ha-ha, like a jaunty yellow scarf. Miss Lovelock had a firmly held belief in the health benefits of fresh air whatever the season, but she was convinced these were increased tenfold when combined with warmth and sunlight. As she walked her mind turned towards the summer. How wonderful it would be to travel to Italy, or Germany perhaps, and see the Blackshirt cause already in effect. Her funds, swelled by Mr Carew's generous rate of pay, could probably stretch to a trip, though the indefinite nature of her contract was irksome. One didn't want to be insensitive, but surely it wasn't unreasonable to ask for some idea of when her services were likely to be no longer required? She resolved to raise the matter with Lady Lennox at the next opportunity.

The chapel was a simple, low rectangular building made of the same grey stone as the main house. The row of arched windows that stretched along its wall were plainly glazed, and the only nod to ornamentation came from the little gabled bellcote in the middle of the roof and the carved coat of arms above the porch door. As a girl, Miss Lovelock had experienced a phase of quite devout religious belief, during which visiting churches (as well as copying out the Bible's more dramatic verses in her best handwriting) was one of her favourite pastimes. The phase had waned when she'd discovered the suffrage cause (in which women were not merely supporting players to the starring roles, like in the Bible) but her knowledge of ecclesiastical architecture remained. 'Victorian, I should say,' she declared, going through the rusted gate. 'With a nod to the Norman. Plain, but certainly not unattractive . . .'

Alice Carew looked distinctly unimpressed. As Miss Lovelock went up the path she hovered at the gate, looking around at the unkempt grass, the straggling tentacles of brambles and ivy beneath the obligatory yew tree, in obvious disappointment.

'But – there are no gravestones!'

'No.' To Miss Lovelock's surprise the church door was very slightly ajar and creaked open easily at her tentative push. 'It was never a parish church – just a convenient place of Sunday worship for the family and staff.'

'I thought Uncle Howard was buried here?'

'Well, I believe there is a family vault, but I doubt Captain Lennox will be in it, having been killed in—'

She stopped. Lady Lennox was seated in the front pew, her head bent. Miss Lovelock experienced a moment of agonizing uncertainty. Should she grab the child and retreat? Pause and apologize? Continue, in respectful quiet? She had just decided on the first course of action when Lady Lennox raised her head and turned round. Miss Lovelock cleared her throat nervously.

'Lady Lennox. I do apologize for disturbing you.

The child asked if we might come down here on our walk and I—'

'Please, Miss Lovelock – there's no need to apologize.'

Her tone suggested otherwise. She stood up, her cool blue gaze finding Miss Lovelock like a searchlight, exposing her darns and patches, the cheap fabric of her coat and the frayed edges of her collar. It came to rest momentarily on the circular silver brooch with its lightning strike emblem, then moved down to the child.

'Hello, Alice. You wanted to see the chapel?'

'Y-yes, Grandmama.'

'I heard your question.' The heels of Lady Lennox's patent shoes (very impractical for outdoor wear, to Miss Lovelock's mind) rang on the floor as she went across to a brass plaque on the wall, near the altar. 'Miss Lovelock is correct. Your Uncle Howard died in Belgium, in the war. It wasn't possible to bring him home, but we remember him here.' A curt movement of her head invited the child to come closer and examine the plaque. 'Can you read what it says?'

Miss Lovelock squirmed as Alice began to stammer her way through the brief inscription, although the child's inability to read certainly wasn't due to any failing on her part. She just about managed '*In loving memory of*' and obviously remembered her uncle's full name – '*Howard Robert Kinross Lennox*', but then she ground to a halt. After a frozen pause Lady Lennox took over.

'*Captain, 19th Royal Hussars,*' she read. '*Only son of Sir*

*Robert and Emilia, Lady Lennox, of Blackwood Park. Killed in
action at Passchendaele, 26th October 1917. Aged 20 years.'*

The words died away into the chapel's echoing silence,
like stones falling into a pool, spreading ripples. At length,
just as Miss Lovelock was wondering how to extricate herself and the child, Lady Lennox spoke again. 'Was there
anything else you wanted to ask?'

'Is anyone buried here?'

'Not buried exactly,' Lady Lennox said. 'Interred, in
the vault.'

'Where is the vault?'

'Beneath the floor.'

'Can I see?'

Dear God, what the dickens had come over the girl? One
could never usually get a word out of her. Miss Lovelock
would have quite liked the vault to open up and swallow
her at that moment, as Lady Lennox cast her an accusing
look, as if she was responsible for the child's interest in
burial rites.

'No. No one goes down there, except for during an interment, of course, and we hope that it'll be a very long time
before we have one of those.'

She spoke firmly, drawing the subject to a close. Yet still
the child persisted.

'Is anyone called Mrs Andrews . . . *interred* there?'

'Of course not. The vault is for family members only.'
Lady Lennox collected the gloves she had left on the altar
rail and began to walk back up the aisle. 'The only Mrs

Andrews I know is from the Gainsborough painting – wasn't that the name, Miss Lovelock?'

'Oh – yes.' Miss Lovelock's mind was blank. For the life of her, in that moment the only painting she could think of was the nude that Mary Richardson had taken an axe to in the National Gallery (the glory days of the Suffrage campaign) and she was sure she wasn't Mrs anything. Miss Lovelock had never had much time for art.

Lady Lennox stopped at the door to put on her gloves. 'I only remember it because Miranda copied the dress for a costume ball. Blue satin. A long time ago.' She deployed her chilly smile and was about to leave when she appeared to remember something. 'Oh – that reminds me. Miss Lovelock, you might like to know that you won't be required here over Easter. My elder daughter and her family will be visiting, so you may take four days' holiday, beginning on the Thursday evening. Alice can have a break from lessons to play with her cousin. Won't that be nice, Alice?'

Miss Lovelock's thanks were rather more enthusiastic than the child's agreement. Four days wasn't much, but it was long enough for a trip to London, where some Party activity was bound to be going on. She would write and ask Adeline, and hopefully secure an invitation to stay into the bargain.

The subject of holidays reminded her of her unresolved plans for the summer and the matter of her contract. She almost opened her mouth to ask, but changed her mind at the last minute. She didn't want to push her luck. And besides, if there had been further news Lady Lennox was unlikely to divulge it in front of the child. Especially if . . .

Well, anyway. Four days was enough, for now.

In the night nursery Alice, still wearing her coat, slid the Maison D'Or box out from beneath her bed and lifted the lid. Her thoughts shimmered and swirled, like dust in the sunlight of the little chapel. All the items were familiar now, so she didn't linger over the handkerchief or the bow tie, but went straight to the gold-edged invitation card. *Come as a work of art.*

So Mrs Andrews's pale blue gown had been worn by Aunt Miranda, to the party in Grosvenor Square in July 1925. Alice recited the clue in her head again, her excitement mounting as the pieces slotted together. Putting the lid back on the box she shoved it under the bed and raced out into the corridor, straight into Polly.

'Where are you going in such a hurry?'

'I've worked it out! When Miss Lovelock told me what interred means I thought there might be graves of a Roman Queen and dancing girls at the church, but we went to look and there are no graves at all.' She didn't want to think about the vault. 'But we saw Grandmama there, and she said that Mrs Andrews is from a painting, and Aunt Miranda once went to a party as her, and so I think they're all fancy dress costumes! You said that costume parties were all the rage—'

Polly smiled. 'Very clever. So where do you think you're going to find all these costumes?'

'The attics!'

That's why Polly had been up there earlier. Alice had been too preoccupied with what Ellen had said to think much about it at the time, but it made sense now.

Polly's smile widened to a grin. 'You'd give Sherlock Holmes himself a run for his money. Off you go, then. Give me a shout if you need help.'

It was colder up in the attic. The air had a damp, mossy quality, as if it had thickened with age and neglect. At the top of the stairs she found herself on a dingy landing with doors opening off it. The ceiling was much lower here than downstairs, and everything was on a smaller scale, so it felt as if she'd climbed into a doll's house. Looking over the banister she saw the stairs spiralling down to the familiar world she had left behind, and if she listened hard she could just about hear the distant rise and fall of voices in the kitchen. Reassured, she went forward and saw that the first door was half open.

The room was small, with a sloping ceiling and a tiny fireplace. The walls were covered with sprigged wallpaper, across which sepia patches of damp stretched like a map, and sooty cobwebs quivered in the corners. The light from the little window fell on the confusion of tea chests and suitcases, stacks of paintings, their faces turned to the walls, and a jumble of furniture. There were tennis racquets, Alice saw with a rush of excitement, before noticing how the damp had twisted them and remembering that she had no one to play with anyway.

If the fancy dress costumes were here they were likely to be in a trunk, she thought, edging tentatively through the clutter. She could see one on top of an old chest of drawers by the fireplace and made her way towards it, shutting her mind to the thought of scuttling spiders and scrabbling mice (she didn't mind mice, actually, with their bright little eyes and tiny pink hands, but spiders were a different matter). The trunk was khaki-coloured canvas, banded with brown leather, and had the initials HRKL stamped upon its top. She lifted the lid and found herself looking at a khaki tunic, folded flat, and breathing in the smell of wool and mildewed earth and something rank and rotten that made her recoil, dropping the lid with a shudder.

Unnerved, she retreated, tripping over a tapestry fire-screen on a spindly stand. Back at the door she rubbed her palms on her skirt and thought about going downstairs to find Polly. As she weighed up the comfort of having her there against the undeniable defeat of enlisting help she realized that she was looking straight at another trunk. And that from beneath its heavy black lid a corner of pale blue satin was visible.

In an instant she was in front of it, opening it up and pulling out the dress. Its slippery skirts were huge: Alice held it against herself and was swamped by folds of satin. She bundled it up and laid it aside, eager to see what else the trunk contained. It was easy to spot Cleopatra's gold headdress (cleverly made from papier-mâché and collapsing a little now) and some rummaging amongst the jumble-sale tangle of tweeds, mothy velvets and fragile silks revealed the white ruffled collar from a clown's suit. And a thick cream envelope.

Hastily she shoved everything back into the trunk and let the lid fall with a puff of ancient dust. The broken chairs and unloved paintings settled back into stillness and silence as her footsteps echoed down the stairs.

Darling Alice,

Another clue solved — well done! You must have found your way up to the attics and had a look around, which is very brave! I hope you found the fancy dress trunk easily — dear Polly said she would make sure you didn't have to search too deeply through all the junk. When I was your age that part of the attic was where the maids slept. It was only after the war, when the staff was so much smaller and lots of rooms in the house were closed off that they moved down to the old footmen's rooms in the servants' basement, and the attic filled up with all those odds and ends. The Grands should have a giant bonfire one day and clear it all out; I can't think that anyone in the future would be interested in a broken clothes horse or twenty cracked chamber pots, can you?!

It's been a long time since I opened the fancy dress trunk myself, and I had to think hard to remember what was in there. I believe it began life as Grandfather's school trunk, but when Aunt Miranda and I were quite young for a brief time we had a governess (none of them ever stayed very

long, mostly because I was so naughty) who was very keen
on theatricals, and used to make us learn endless scenes and
speeches from Shakespeare. I think we decided that reciting
these would be more fun if we could dress up, and that was
how the fancy dress trunk came into being. At first it was
filled with whatever cast-offs we could swipe – petticoats
and tea gowns from Grandmama, Howard's school shirts
and cricketing whites, and a rather lovely silk dressing gown
of Grandfather's that I think was probably taken without
his say so, but made a marvellous robe for stately roles – but
later, when we had long left the schoolroom, it came into its
own again as the craze for costume parties got underway.

I'm not sure how it started, or whose idea it was, but we
thought it was frightfully good fun – mostly because people
of our parents' generation found it intolerably childish and
infuriating. Their disapproval only encouraged us, I'm
afraid. At first the costumes were rather low key – the sort
of thing that might easily be dragged out of the nursery
fancy dress trunk and completed with a smudge of burnt
cork for a moustache or a bit of panstick – but as time
went on they got more elaborate and more expensive, until
it got to the stage where people would contact their clever
little Knightsbridge dressmakers the moment an invitation
card arrived.

That's what Aunt Miranda did, with the blue gown.
Did you look at it? Isn't it quite something? It was an old
dress of Grandmama's from her Season (in 1889!) which
Aunt Miranda dragged out of mothballs when word got out

about the Napiers' party. The theme was 'Come as a Work of Art' (perhaps you found the card? I think it might have been in my box of treasures) and it was typical of Miranda to be so well organized, and organize Lionel too. The party was just a week before their wedding, so she had lots of other things to think about, but they certainly attracted lots of attention.

I was far less well prepared, as always. I cheated a tiny bit on the clue I gave you because, although I mentioned the French dancing girls, you wouldn't have found the costumes in the trunk. My friends and I left it terribly late to decide what to go as, but luckily Theo was chums with someone who worked at the Savoy Theatre, and he pleaded with him to let us raid their wardrobe department. What fun that was! We weren't allowed to borrow any of the main character costumes, so we decked ourselves out in chorus line corsets and frilled petticoats with wide skirts over the top and – with the addition of thick black stockings and long black satin evening gloves – went as a trio of Toulouse-Lautrec's Moulin Rouge girls. (I showed you one of his paintings in the Tate once, though maybe you were too young to remember.)

The party was held by the Napier twins, Eva and Lucille. You might hear Lucille's name sometimes; she married an American millionaire and went to New York for a time, but she came back – with a large collection of vulgar jewellery, but not the American millionaire – just before the Wall Street Crash. (Eva fared less well, and I believe is in a sanatorium somewhere suffering with fragile health.) Their father, Josiah Napier, was a mill owner who made an awful lot of money during the war manufacturing webbing used by the army, and he was happy to spend whatever it took for his daughters to be accepted in society.

The Napiers' parties were always right at the end of the Season, which meant they were still being talked about weeks later in chilly Scottish castles, on country house lawns and sun-baked terraces overlooking the Mediterranean. Perhaps because they came from a slightly different background, their guest lists were always a little more adventurous than those of the more established hostesses. They knew all sorts of people — actresses and businessmen, artists and music hall singers — and weren't afraid to mix them all up, which was another thing that set their parties apart from the others. One never quite knew who one was going to meet. They were always absolutely spectacular too; designed to be remembered long after the sun had risen and the last guest had left.

That party, in July 1925, was certainly no exception.

9

Worlds Collide

July 1925

Captain John Markham was almost finished. Only the eyes remained to be painted in. The most important part, always.

In the studio photographs Lawrence was given, the eyes of the young men came only in shades of sepia and were often fixed at some point just past the camera, as if they were looking into the far distance towards the destination that awaited them (more distant even than France). It was his job to make them blue again, or green or hazel or chocolate-brown; luminous with life. It was in his power to enable them to look directly once more into the eyes of those who loved and missed and mourned them, and re-establish the bond that the war had broken. A tiny point of light here, a shadow there could entirely alter the mood of the face, and over the course of four years and countless portraits he had perfected the skill of distilling the essence of the man in the photograph, capturing his character in those painted eyes. It was the most delicate part of the process.

He studied the photograph clipped to the side of his easel, tilting it up to the light that filtered through the grimy skylight above. Over a stultifying tea in the parlour of their gloomy red brick villa in Guildford, Markham's parents had told Lawrence of a studious boy who had excelled at mathematics and been head of his house in the minor public school he had attended (the name had meant nothing to Lawrence) before going up to Cambridge. He had not been much of a sportsman, but had enjoyed birdwatching and music and had been a good pianist. (His mother's eyes – that English blue, Lawrence noted carefully, touched with grey – had moved to the upright piano behind the door when she'd said that, as if for a moment she could hear her boy playing again.) He had come away with the photograph, a down payment of five guineas on the commission, and an insight into John Markham's quiet, diffident character. The light in his eyes would be gentle; no sparks of patriotic pride or the thrill of adventure – *let's get over there and show them, lads* – that Lawrence often saw in his subjects.

He mixed china white with lamp black and added a touch of Prussian blue. In the second that his brush hovered over the canvas the slam of the front door downstairs reverberated up through the building like a gunshot, jolting his hand. Voices carried up the stairwell – Edith's bark, and a familiar

Welsh baritone, which got suddenly louder as the door at the bottom of the attic steps was pulled open.

'Guess who I found on the doorstep,' Edith said as she appeared at the top of the stairs. She was wearing a voluminous shepherd's smock and red espadrilles and had a bundle of cloth and a plaster reproduction of the head of Michelangelo's David clasped in her arms.

'Goliath?' Lawrence muttered. 'John the Baptist?'

Edith glanced down at the head, almost as if she'd forgotten she was carrying it. 'Oh – Berwick Street market. Couldn't resist. I need a new subject now the Napiers are finished. No – chap from your lodgings. At least I hope that's who he is, and I haven't been taken for a fool again by someone to whom you owe money.'

'He does owe me money, as a matter of fact. Rent day was Monday – two days ago. That's partly why I'm here.' Emerging from the stairwell, Sam looked around. 'Jesus – this place is even more untidy than the flat.'

The studio took up the entire top floor of the house in Gower Street, where rooms had been knocked together and poky windows replaced with skylights to create one large, airy space. It was owned by Edith, and shared with a shifting population of painters, sculptors, students and artist's models, who drifted in and out like stray cats, often sleeping on the divan in the corner (or posing for Edith on it). One thing they all had in common was a lack of domestic skill or interest and the space was cluttered with unwashed plates, smeared glasses, books, dead flowers, empty bottles, paint-encrusted brushes, and cups in which mould flourished in fascinating patterns on long-abandoned coffee.

'I'll pay you,' Lawrence muttered, turning back to the easel to avoid Edith's eye. He owed her rent on the studio too, though she was kind enough (and well-off enough – her wayward Bohemianism was built on privileged foundations) not to mention it very often.

'You always say that, boyo. Sometimes you even get round to doing it,' Sam said cheerfully, leaning against the table and folding his arms across the straining buttons of his shirt. He was bred for wielding a pick and hauling coal rather than bashing out words on a typewriter, and London life had softened him physically, if not in temperament. 'Today's your lucky day. I'm giving you the chance to write off the debt.'

Lawrence put down his brush with a sigh. 'How?'

'No need to sound so suspicious. Nothing illegal, nothing dangerous and you'd get to play with that fancy camera of yours. There's a Miners' Federation meeting tonight, speakers coming from all over to discuss strike action. Word has it that the police are going to start a bit of trouble, make it look like our fault. A tame photographer would be a useful thing to have on our side.'

Lawrence's heart sank. He'd been dragged into photographing Sam's political rallies before, and the results were as dull as the meetings themselves; a waste of film, which would probably end up costing twice the rent money he owed. He had tried to explain that it wasn't his sort of photography, but as far as Sam was concerned one camera was much the same as another, and the same went for photographers.

'Can't you get someone from the newspaper?'

'I've already tried – I know you're a total prima donna about not dirtying your pretty artist's hands on such ordinary stuff. Thing is, the chaps we use are all taken up chasing the toffs tonight. The end of the Season, isn't it? The Bright Young People . . .' – he said the words as if they tasted bitter on his tongue – 'will all be out to play before they bugger off to Biarritz and Baden-bloody-Baden for the summer. There's some big fancy party in Grosvenor Square, and that's what the public want to see, apparently. The idle rich in their ridiculous costumes.'

While he'd been speaking, Edith had cleared a space in the clutter on the floor (piling most of it onto the sagging divan) and she was now kneeling in front of a linen sheet she had spread out. She looked up at Sam with an arch smile. 'Not just the idle rich in their ridiculous costumes, Mr Evans.' She looked down at the sheet. 'I've left it rather late to make mine. Too busy faffing about putting the final touches on the portrait – I've never known anyone worse for interfering, but there we are. I certainly can't accuse Josiah Napier of being miserly. He paid three times the going rate.'

Colour had crept into Sam's florid cheeks, so they were almost as red as his hair. Wrong-footed, he gave a scornful snort. 'Easy to be generous when you're as rich as that, Miss Linde.'

'I daresay . . .' She leaned forward and began to sketch an

outline on the sheet. 'Easy to overlook the eccentric and disreputable lady artist who painted your daughters' portrait and not invite her to the unveiling party too, but he didn't, so for that reason I rather like Mr Napier.'

Lawrence could tell Sam was struggling to know which of his clearly defined headings to file Edith under. The shepherd's smock made it hard to argue with the 'eccentric' bit, but Edith's plummy voice made 'disreputable' something of a stretch. Sam Evans was a man's man; a pint and pub and politics man, who thought women came in two varieties only, neither of which had any business having opinions. Clearing his throat he turned back to Lawrence.

'So then boyo, you'll come to the meeting? Not going to let me down on this, are you?'

'Well, since he can't be in two places at once it looks like he'll have to let one of us down,' Edith said mildly, not looking up from her sketching.

For a moment Lawrence was caught off-guard. She'd teasingly pleaded with him for weeks to go with her to the party, but he'd refused, in spite of the fact that Selina Lennox was likely to be there. *Because* Selina Lennox was likely to be there. It had taken him enough time to get her out of his head after the Royal Academy fiasco and he wasn't going to humiliate himself again. But Edith, he realized, was throwing him a lifeline. A ready-made excuse.

'What?' Sam scowled. 'You're going to this posh bastard party?'

Edith dropped her pencil and rocked back on her heels,

mustering a tremulous smile. 'Of course, you don't have to,' she said bravely, the picture of dejected disappointment. 'I'm sure I can go alone. It won't be as much fun, but I daresay I'll find someone to talk to.'

Lawrence had never realized she was such a good actress. She pitched it perfectly. Looking at Sam, he raised his shoulders in a gesture of helplessness.

'Sorry, but I did promise.'

'You kept bloody quiet about it,' Sam growled. 'Anyone would think you were ashamed of yourself, fraternizing with the enemy.' He levered himself up from the table and stepped awkwardly over Edith's sheet on the floor. 'Oh well, I'd best let you get on with it then. Enjoy your evening. Miss Linde.' He nodded at Edith, and shot Lawrence a narrow look, which suggested the things he would have said if it hadn't been for the presence of a lady. 'I won't wait up, boyo.'

Lawrence waited until the heavy tread of his boots had died away on the stairs and the front door had slammed before turning to her.

'Edith . . .'

'Now, don't be cross. I was trying to help, that's all. When I realized it was the same chap who made you take photographs for his *Communist Worker* article on low wages and didn't pay you, I couldn't sit here and say nothing. We artists need to eat just as much as miners do.'

'He's going to find out.' Exasperation fought with gratitude. 'I live with him, for Christ's sake. He's going to know I didn't go to the party.'

'Not necessarily.' Edith beamed at him from under her sharp, square-cut fringe. Her severely bobbed hair had made Joan of Arc an obvious costume choice, though after fruitlessly scouring junk shops and antiques stalls for armour she had been forced to compromise with chain mail (knitted) and a linen tunic. 'Not if you *do* go . . .'

'Edith . . .'

'I know, I know – you've said you don't want to, but I really don't understand why – you're not usually such a stick in the mud. It'll be a hoot. Free champagne and a ringside seat at the greatest show in town. Come on, Lawrence – where's your spirit of adventure? How often does fate present ordinary folk like us with the chance to experience glamour and extravagance on this scale? It'll be a feast for the senses, a glimpse into another world . . .'

'Exactly.' His voice was flat. 'A world in which I don't belong.'

There was a kind of relief in speaking aloud the truth that taunted him whenever his thoughts turned to Selina Lennox. It was good to put it out there, so that the harsh glare of reality could expose the preposterousness of those thoughts, make them wither like blighted fruit. It was all right for Edith. She might describe herself as ordinary, but that was only in comparison to those who commanded dukedoms or business empires. Everything was relative. There was only so far aspiration, ambition and artistic talent could take you, and from the damp, cramped streets of a small seaside town to the glitter of Grosvenor Square was pushing it.

But that was what he always did. Pushed too hard, too far. Overreached himself. Wanted too much. Bohemian Bloomsbury and the company of artists was more than he'd dared dream of in his father's workshop in Hastings, but here he was, mesmerized by the memory of a girl who was so far beyond his reach she may as well be on the moon.

'Don't be so parochial,' Edith snapped. 'It's very disappointing of you. These people are young, beautiful and rich, and you, my darling, can move amongst them as an equal on two of those counts – don't undervalue the privilege of that. I don't fit in on any, but I'm not going to let that spoil my fun. One thing I've learned is that one must grab at the chances life offers – taste the fruit, drink the wine.' She sat back on her heels and fixed him with a stern look. 'At the hour of one's death there will be no solace in knowing that one has known one's place or lived safely. Just ask the young man in front of you.'

Captain John Markham gazed out of the canvas with his blank, dead eyes, agreeing with her.

'I haven't got a costume ...'

Edith grinned, sensing victory.

'My dear, we are *artists*. This is not a problem ... It is a *pleasure*.'

In the evening the clouds that had blanketed the sky all day grew blacker and heavier, turning the fading daylight purple. As the time of the party approached, as if to prove that there were some things that even filthy rich industrialists couldn't buy, the heavens opened.

It was a deluge of biblical proportions. The doorman at Claridge's, where Theo had taken a room in which they could dress in their borrowed finery, had held his vast umbrella over them as they hurried into a taxi to travel the short distance to the party. Grosvenor Square was jammed with vehicles – other taxicabs and smart cars, some of them driven by chauffeurs, some more erratically piloted by exotically dressed partygoers – all waiting to deposit their occupants as close to the front steps of the house as possible, where a canopy had been erected over the pavement. Theo lowered the window an inch and they heard music from the party, and the shriek of voices calling to each other from rain-stranded cars.

'"*Frame your mind to mirth and merriment*,"' sighed Theo, tugging at black satin cutting into his waist. 'Dear God, this corset pinches. You've laced it far too tightly, Selina, you beast.'

'It's supposed to be tight – that's rather the point of a corset,' Selina replied, looking out of the window through sheets of rain. She was shivering, partly from the cool air on her bare skin and partly from a sort of jittery restlessness, which meant she had to clamp her teeth together to stop them chattering. Theo had ordered champagne while they were getting ready, and two glasses drunk too quickly had left her feeling both hyped-up and somehow achingly weary at the same time. The Napiers were famous for the originality of their parties, but she felt as if she could see every detail of the evening that stretched ahead, as if she had somehow lived it already, and the predictability of it all made her want to weep.

Beside her, Flick wriggled irritably. 'How on earth did women endure wearing corsets every day? I simply can't breathe.'

'My mother still wears them,' Theo said, raising his flounced skirt to take out the silver hipflask he'd tucked under his garter. 'I'm beginning to understand why she's always in such a vile temper.'

He handed the flask to Selina, who took it and swigged. 'I rather like it. At least it keeps my ridiculous chest in check. Oh God, I promised my mother I wouldn't get tight. Don't let me, will you? Less than a week to the wedding and the atmosphere at home can only be described as fraught.'

'All the more reason why you absolutely need to be tight,' Theo said, sounding horrified at the idea of a sober evening. 'Parents simply don't have the first idea, do they?'

'I have plenty of happy dust, darling,' Flick said vaguely, rubbing a porthole on the steamed-up window with one gloved finger. 'High isn't the same as tight, is it? Oh look – how thrilling – ' She pointed to a row of four green sports cars, parked haphazardly alongside each other at the edge of the Square. 'This is where the Bentley Boys live, isn't it? I do hope they'll be at the party. If not, maybe we should knock on their door and introduce ourselves. I wonder why we don't know them?'

'Because we only ever meet the same people,' Selina said and her laugh jangled with despair. 'Different parties, different costumes, but the same old crowd. People like us.'

The Season had passed in a blur of cocktails and jazz and

late night stumbles through dark streets. She had been to the Henley Regatta and Royal Ascot, though cried off the Chelsea Flower Show and the Eton and Harrow match at Lord's (pleading tiredness; more acceptable than the truth, which was that she was bored and frustrated and simply couldn't be bothered). She had attended debutante dances and sat through numerous plays and musical revues, all of which blended confusingly into each other. She had danced and smiled and made the smallest of talk. She had been pleasant to Rupert Carew whenever the occasion unavoidably demanded it. And all the time she had been aware of that growing restlessness. A sort of hunger. A sense of floating above herself, watching. Searching.

The taxi drew up behind a silver Rolls Royce, out of which Georgie Stanhope was emerging, shrieking as she tried to hold trailing bits of muslin from her Botticelli robe out of the puddles. 'At least the rain has foiled the photographers,' Theo said, swiping Flick's compact ('careful darling, that's rather good stuff') and peering into its tiny mirror. He pressed his painted lips together and brushed a flake of mascara from his cheek, then snapped it shut again, striking a dramatic pose. 'My dears, are we ready for our entrance?'

Josiah Napier was a pragmatic man as well as a rich one. He wasn't foolish enough to expose his own immaculate home in Carlton House Terrace to a plague of careless partygoers, and so the Grosvenor Square house had been hired, with staff, for the evening, and decorated in keeping with the theme. Empty frames had been hung on the walls around the entrance hall and up the sweeping staircase, and suspended on long wires from the ceiling. This created the impression that the figures that thronged the space in flowing Pre-Raphaelite dresses, Renaissance drapes and Renoir frills had been brought to life by some enchantment, and stepped down into the real world.

They joined the tide of people flowing upstairs. 'It's like Campaign Headquarters in the Peninsular War,' murmured Theo, looking over the banisters. 'I must be the only male who hasn't come as the Duke of Wellington.' They followed the scent of Mitsouko to where Lally and Harry stood at the gallery rail, overlooking the hall. Lally was a striking Klimt in a long evening coat of shimmering gold and jewel-like embroidery and Harry sported an impressive false moustache as the Laughing Cavalier.

'I don't feel much like laughing,' he moaned, sliding his fingers beneath his flounced lace collar and pulling it away from his neck. 'Far too bloody hot. I intend to start shedding layers as soon as things get going properly. I assume we were ordered to get here so bloody early because the Napiers are planning some stunt in there.' He nodded to a set of grand double doors, firmly closed, and rolled his eyes. 'I prepare to be thrilled.'

Lally leaned over and kissed his cheek indulgently. 'Poor baby. Overtiredness has made you grumpy. Don't worry – any day now you'll be let out to pasture on a grouse moor, dressed in your tweeds and clutching a gun.'

It was a reminder that the hectic rhythm they'd all grown accustomed to over the past weeks was about to change when the Season ended and London emptied. 'Rather you than me,' Theo said with a shudder. 'I shall be in Italy, replete with red wine and Renaissance art . . .'

The conversation turned to plans for the summer. Flick was being dispatched to the continent to stay with her glamorous and rather louche godmother (or godless-mother, as she called her) in Cap Ferrat. Lally was joining a group heading to the Isle of Wight for Cowes week, and Harry and Selina would both be going to Scotland for the shooting – in different parties, and with very different attitudes. Selina had tried not to think about it, but being forced to confront it now made despair weigh her down like damp Highland plaid. She and Miranda had little in common, but their low-level combat usually provided a diversion of sorts. This year, with Miranda on her honeymoon, she wouldn't even have that to pass the time. The pulse of restlessness quickened.

Draining her glass, she looked around for a waiter to supply another one. The crush behind them was building, the noise level rising to drown out the insipid band. 'I say, Selina, your sister is quite the centre of attention,' Lally remarked, looking over the gallery rail into the hallway below. 'Splendid frock, but look – her chap can't get anywhere near her with that skirt. Poor thing.'

They all crowded along the rail to look down. Josiah Napier was there, dressed as Holbein's Henry VIII, his booming Yorkshire voice rising above everyone else's.

Miranda and Lionel had come as the sour-faced couple from the Gainsborough painting, and the wide panniers of her blue satin skirt created a space around her that automatically made her the focus of attention. Lionel hovered uncertainly, looking surprisingly dashing in his waisted coat and knee britches, though the effect was somewhat marred when he removed his hat to reveal the thinning hair on his crown. After the barbed comments in Maison D'Or, Selina was pleased to see that Miranda's bosom, viewed from above, looked surprisingly fulsome. She fished the cherry out of her glass.

'Bet you sixpence I can get this down the front of my sister's dress . . .'

They all leaned forward to watch as she took aim, but just as the cherry left her hand another figure moved into view directly below the balcony and looked up.

Time stalled. The cherry completed its arc in slow motion, taking an age to make its inevitable contact with Rupert Carew's forehead.

'Oh God, oh God—'

They all drew back sharply, clutching at each other, snorts of barely stifled laughter ringing out over the hallway. Selina was torn between horror and hilarity. 'Oh God, why did it have to be him?' she gasped when she'd stopped laughing enough to speak. 'I suppose I'll have to go and apologize. My life won't be worth living once Miranda tells Mama if I don't.'

The band came to the end of the number with a flourish

of strings, and then – quietly at first, but building in a rapid crescendo – a drum beat grabbed everyone's attention. The clamour of voices dropped away as people looked round to see what was happening.

'Too late,' Flick whispered, clutching her arm. 'You can't go now.'

The double doors swung open. A cheer went up as people recognized the figure that stepped through them as JC Carmelo, leader of the best Negro jazz band in London. He held his hands up in a fruitless attempt to quell the noise, and in the end simply yelled above it.

'Ladies and gentlemen – nymphs and goddesses, generals and dancing girls.' He flashed a grin at Theo, Flick and Selina. 'Allow me to welcome you all here this evening, and to introduce your beautiful hostesses, the Misses Eva and Lucille Napier!'

'Oh, for pity's sake,' groaned Theo as a vast gilded frame containing a portrait of the Napiers was rolled forward on a specially constructed trolley. The people on the first floor gallery stepped aside to clear a path while those in the hall below pressed back and craned their necks to see what was happening. In the ballroom JC's band launched into 'Five Foot Two and Eyes of Blue' in a triumphant blast of trumpets.

'Don't tell me – yes, I thought so,' Theo sighed as the surface of the portrait was suddenly rent apart and the Napier sisters burst through, throwing their arms wide and simpering madly as they jumped down and began to dance a skilled Charleston, beckoning their guests into the ballroom.

'Do you suppose we've seen it all now?' Lally said faintly. '*Do* say we have. Do say parties simply cannot get more vulgar than this . . .'

'Too, too ridiculous,' Flick beamed, 'but thank goodness there's a decent band after all. Come *on* – let's dance!'

She grabbed Selina's wrist and began to pull her towards the ballroom, where lights blazed and trumpets screeched. Selina looked over her shoulder, down into the hall below. She was thinking of Rupert. She should find him, apologize quickly, to limit the damage, but something in the crowd caught her eye and drove him instantly from her head.

She stopped, jerking her hand from Flick's, her eyes raking the press of people coming up the stairs to recapture the glimpse of dark hair, the slash of a cheekbone . . .

Him.

It was different from the hundred other times she'd found herself chasing some elusive glimpse of a dark-haired stranger. This time there was no uncertainty. Her body recognized him while her mind was still trying to catch up, and she could feel her heartbeat at the base of her throat; too fast, too hard. She was suddenly very hot; lightheaded, so that the air seemed to liquefy for a moment and swirl around her. She grasped the gallery rail, searching for him again.

People were still surging up the staircase, a bizarre procession of saints and soldiers, courtiers and courtesans. Noise rose up around her – discordant jazz and shrieking, over-excited voices. The effect of the cocktails seemed to hit her in a rush, making everything seem too bright, too fluid, just a little out of sync. Suddenly Miranda loomed in front of her, Margot beside her, arranging her ridiculous wide skirts like a natural bridesmaid.

'Oh look – my insufferable sister.'

Her tone was light but Selina knew her well enough to feel the grit beneath it and see the daggers in her blue gaze, even through the haze of cocktails and adrenaline.

'I was just – ' Her eyes slid past her sister, searching.

'Waiting to apologize, I hope,' Miranda hissed. 'Honestly, Selina, grown-ups don't find your schoolroom japes in the slightest bit amusing.'

Beside her Margot tilted her head, regarding Selina archly. 'Is something wrong?'

No.

Yes.

Both.

Because he was there, coming up the stairs. As the people around him moved she could see that his chest was bare and his skin had been painted with swirls of deep indigo and Catherine wheel stars in silver and gold. Van Gogh, she thought dazedly. He was a starry night made flesh.

'Selina?' Miranda's voice was sharp. '*Selina?*'

'Oh—' she was breathless. 'No. No, nothing's wrong.'

He was looking at her.

Straight at her.

'Good.' Miranda seized her hand, her fingernails pressing

crescents of pain into her skin. 'Here's Rupert now so you can say sorry.'

'Ye Gods, it's hot,' Edith grumbled above the music, looking round the seething ballroom. 'You don't know how fortunate you are to be so unfettered by clothing. Chain mail really isn't the most practical choice for parties.'

'Just as well you didn't find a suit of armour.'

'Good Lord, yes – can you imagine? Though ...' she dropped her voice and leaned closer. 'I'm beginning to get the impression you might be in need of one as things get going. My dear, you're creating quite a stir. Such looks ...'

Lawrence looked. Two girls in powdered Rococo wigs and plunging dresses (Marie Antoinette? Madame de Pompadour?) were staring at him with open interest, whispering behind their hands.

'Admiring your artwork.' His eyes slid past them.

'Admiring the canvas,' Edith corrected, swiping two glasses from a passing waiter. 'Almost as blatantly as those naughty Napiers did. I have a feeling that's Pamela Fitzsimmons, though it's hard to tell with the wig. If it is, you're being ogled by the most sought-after deb of the Season.'

He couldn't have cared less. Selina Lennox was standing at the opposite side of the room, with a tall man in a red cutaway military coat festooned with gold braid. There were a dozen Duke of Wellingtons at the party, but this was the same one that had moved in on her before Lawrence could reach her at the top of the stairs. She had her back half turned, but he could tell from the rigid set of her shoulders that she was tense. Was that a good sign or a bad one? It had been impossible to tell what she was thinking earlier, when their eyes had met. All he knew was that she remembered him.

That was something, at least.

He seemed to have finished the champagne Edith had handed him without tasting it; posh people drank out of ridiculously small glasses. His gaze moved impatiently around the room and his mind raced ahead, calculating how he might approach her. If he should approach her.

'Do you know her?'

Edith's voice – dry and slightly mocking – interrupted his thoughts.

'Who?'

'The Toulouse-Lautrec girl you can't stop looking at. The one you exchanged a rather electrifying eye-meet with as we came up the stairs.'

'Yes.' There was no point in lying. 'Her name's Selina Lennox.'

'I know that. I must say I'm surprised you do, though.'

The statement hid a question, which he chose not to answer. 'Who's he?'

'The Duke of Wellington, I imagine – like every other chap here. Criminally predictable.'

Lawrence dragged his eyes away from the back of Selina's neck and gave Edith a grudging smile. 'Very funny. Who is he really?'

'Rupert Carew.' Edith leaned on her sword and plucked

at the neck of her chain mail vest, fanning cooler air against her skin. 'Second son of the Earl of Ashbourne. Big family pile in Lincolnshire, I think – King's Aston. Ruby mines in Burma.'

'No one important then. Good.'

She grinned. 'Anything else you'd like to know?'

'Thanks. I think I've got the picture.'

'Quite a crowd, isn't it?' Edith squinted into the melee on the dancefloor. 'Good heavens, is that little Bunny Hargreaves? Over there, in the angel wings? Her people are neighbours of ours in Sussex – her coming out portrait was my first commission. Dearest, I'm going to say hello, and I suggest you do the same with the lovely Miss Lennox. Carew has monopolized her for far too long.'

Lawrence watched her launch herself into the chaos of flailing limbs, brandishing her sword like a gentleman's walking cane. She made it sound simple. But then perhaps it was to people of her class: start with hello, and five minutes later you've discovered you're second cousins on your mother's side and your brothers rowed together at Oxford. His connection with Selina Lennox extended only as far as a dead cat and a cigarette shared in a scrubby communal garden. Not exactly Debrett. Hello was really all he had.

In the midst of the crowd on the dancefloor Edith was talking animatedly to a rather lumpen girl dressed as a Renaissance angel with a pair of impressive feathered wings. He had to admit the costumes were incredible. No detail had been spared, which he supposed was what happened when you had infinite resources of time, money and professional help. As well as the proliferation of Iron Dukes, Pre-Raphaelites were predictably popular, but he could also see an inventive Picasso and Vermeer's pearl-wearing girl, who was furtively inhaling cocaine from a silver salver.

Jesus – if he had his camera he could be a rich man by morning. Newspaper editors would climb over each other to be first in line for this kind of look behind the closed doors of Mayfair. Gainsborough's Mr and Mrs Andrews were stranded at the side of the room, the woman's wide satin skirt making dancing impossible. Her face was sour as she watched the other two dancers from Selina's Toulouse-Lautrec trio improvise a stylish can-can/Charleston cross-over, amid much amused and admiring attention.

Lawrence watched them too. Flick Fanshawe was the darling of the press; the girl the newspapers always focused on, because her collection of attributes – fashionably delicate beauty, vast personal fortune, attitude of total self-absorbed indifference – made her a perfect figurehead for the Bright Young People. Theo Osborne, with his flamboyant homosexuality and eccentric, extravagant clothing, also claimed a large number of more disapproving column inches, carefully framed by gleeful newspaper editors to provoke disgust and outrage in the common working man. Watching him now Lawrence felt neither of those things. Just a kick of sharp, old-fashioned jealousy at his glamorous insouciance, and the fact that he was Selina's friend.

Inevitably, his eyes went back to her. She was still talking to Carew, and an earnest, colourless Pre-Raphaelite with curtains of long hair. Impatience swelled inside him. He had thought obsessively about seeing her again, but hadn't got beyond that; hadn't considered the eventuality of seeing her but not being able to reach her. Why didn't she turn round? Did she know he was there? Was she wishing he would leave?

The possibility skewered him with anguish. He couldn't stay where he was anyway, standing on his own like the last wallflower. The Season's most sought-after deb was looking at him again, in a way that suggested she was about to come over. Edith was right – even without a shirt it was boiling; he was in danger of sweating off her masterpiece. He began to thread his way through the crowd towards the door in search of air. And more alcohol.

Out of the corner of her eye Selina saw him move. Panic spiralled through her.

She had been aware of him all the time she had been standing there. Her back was towards him but some sort of shivering sixth sense had made her conscious of his eyes on her. The minutes had stretched. She had apologized to Rupert for the cherry incident, but then felt duty bound to stay and talk to him, and to Margot who hovered at his elbow. While she appeared fascinated by every word he spoke, Selina was struggling to focus on anything other than how to extract herself. It required constant effort to keep from looking round. Rupert, watching her (always watching) was obviously aware of her agitation as her gaze flitted over the dancefloor, her body twitching instinctively to the pulse of the music.

'You still like dancing,' he remarked. A statement rather than a question, and a reference to the times he had come to Blackwood with Howard and she had insisted that they roll back the rug in the billiard room after dinner and dance to ragtime on the gramophone. Somehow the reminder felt like a rebuke.

'Yes.' It was evident that he still didn't. She remembered those evenings, and her vague irritation at his presence. He never joined in as Howard two-stepped her around the room. *Carew's got two left feet,* he used to laugh. *Just as well — one wouldn't want a chap to be too good at everything . . .*

At a loss for anything else to say, she risked a quick look round. That was when she saw it: a flicker of blue at the corner of her eye. Turning her head she saw him disappear through the wide double doors that led out onto the gallery. Margot was fanning herself with her dance card, complaining about the heat. Selina seized her chance.

'Beastly, isn't it? I simply must go and get some air . . .' She stepped backwards. 'This corset . . .'

She turned and pushed her way quickly through the dancers to the door, not looking back, not caring what they might think or say about her once she'd gone. It was no less crowded out on the gallery: people had spilled out of the ballroom to talk and laugh and dance there too. Selina slipped through them, taking care not to catch anyone's eye, not wanting to be waylaid. She heard someone call her name but didn't look round.

He was there, ahead of her, walking away down the corridor, where the crowd thinned out by the dining room and the stairs to the upper floors.

'*Lawrence.*'

She didn't raise her voice – she didn't dare – but he must have heard because he stopped. Turned.

It was the most extraordinary feeling, going towards him. After the long weeks of thinking about him, imagining him, it was hard to believe that it was real and he was there, looking back at her. She felt the blood rush to her cheeks and throb in her temples, at the base of her throat. Her mouth spread into a smile.

'Hello.'

She was breathless, as if she'd sprinted through the streets to catch up with him, instead of just crossing a room choked with people. She stopped, a little distance from where he stood.

'Hello.'

'It really is you. I . . .' She shook her head a little, still smiling. 'I had to check.'

A lie. She had known, without doubt.

'It really is.' His smile was guarded. 'I came with a friend. She painted the portrait. Of Eva and Lucille.'

Selina nodded. She didn't care who he'd come with or why. Explanations were wasting precious time, and she was afraid that any moment someone she knew would appear and try to drag her back to dance, or talk to her about inane, unimportant things, not realizing that they were interrupting the moment for which she had been waiting for weeks. A lifetime. Around them the party was getting more raucous. One of the Napiers had climbed up to sit in one of the empty frames that hung from the ceiling high over the gallery, while the group of people watching whooped. There was a muffled explosion as someone on the balcony uncorked a shaken champagne bottle and sprayed it over people in the hall below. Selina winced.

'It's very noisy—'

'And very hot—'

'And very full of people I don't want to talk to.'

Their eyes were locked together, searching, questioning. Her heart was beating so hard she was sure he must see it, pulsing beneath her corset. She felt like she had the summer when Howard had taught her to jump into the lake from the rope swing – how much she'd wanted to do it, but how terrified she'd been. How much courage it had taken to let go.

'We could go somewhere—' Her voice had dried to a croak. 'Away from here . . .'

'Could we?' His eyes searched hers. 'Where?'

'Who cares? We do it all the time – life's too short for dull parties. We can be back before the end. No one will notice.'

'I'll go upstairs and borrow some coats, then let's get out of here.'

10

Starry Night

The relief of finding each other, of escaping, made them reckless, and they ran.

She knew where to find the back stairs, and they clattered down them in coats 'borrowed' from the pile left by guests in an upstairs bedroom; through the steamed-up kitchen, past harassed staff who shouted angrily after them. He reached for her hand. A lightning bolt shot up his arm as her fingers closed around his.

He wondered, briefly, if he was dreaming.

Outside, beneath the area steps, there were bottles of champagne cooling in zinc tubs of ice. Selina grabbed one and slipped it beneath the frock-coat she was wearing and they scrambled up the stairs to the street.

He felt drunk already, though he hadn't had much. He was intoxicated with potent audacity, swaggeringly invincible. It had stopped raining, but the pavements were puddled and shining wet. He pulled her close into his body and they walked quickly, resisting the powerful urge to run again before they'd left the square because that would draw attention to themselves, and their bizarre clothing was bad enough. Hot bursts of adrenaline fizzed through his veins. As soon as they turned the corner into Duke Street, where the shadows were thicker, they broke apart and, clasping hands, began to run again, jumping over puddles or splashing through them. By some unspoken understanding they veered off down the first side street they came to and, breathless with laughter and exertion, fell against the wall and kissed.

He'd imagined it a thousand times. Dreamt about it. Nothing prepared him for the luminous reality.

She was hampered by the champagne bottle, so he took it from her and tore the foil off. Shaken up during their escape (Lawrence knew the feeling) it frothed copiously over his hand when he opened it, and she lifted his fingers to her lips and sucked the bubbles from his skin. Leaning against the wall they passed the bottle between them, swigging recklessly, taking it from each other's mouths, until the stars above them reeled like the ones painted on his chest.

'Will they notice you're missing? Your friends?'

'Not for ages. It's such a bear pit in there. Flick and Theo will assume I'm with Rupert.'

'Who's Rupert?'

He wasn't going to admit he'd already cross-examined Edith on that subject. Her lips closed around the neck of the bottle as she took another mouthful. He had kissed off all her lipstick and now he couldn't take his eyes off her mouth.

'The man they want me to marry.'

Jesus. Edith hadn't prepared him for that. Primitive jealousy kicked him under the ribs.

'Do you want to marry him?'

'God, no. I don't even want to talk about him. Come on, let's go.'

'Where?'

'I don't know . . .' She was already moving away from him with dancing steps, looking teasingly back over her shoulder. 'That's up to you.'

Afterwards he would remember how quickly, how casually she had dismissed the subject of Rupert Carew, and how easily he was reassured by that. And he would feel pity for the naïve fool that he was then, on that night when the stars swam in puddles of molten silver and they danced in the empty streets and anything seemed possible.

As they reached Oxford Street they slowed to a more leisurely pace, swinging their clasped hands and talking, breathing in the peculiarly piercing scent of summer rain on city pavements.

She couldn't stop looking at him; stealing swift glances, letting her eyes linger on his bare, blue-painted chest beneath the jacket he had swiped. She felt a stab of jealousy when she discovered that it had been painted by a woman. He admired her costume, moving in front of her and walking backwards for a few paces as he pulled open the coat to appreciate it properly, and the look on his face made something flare and smoulder deep in her pelvis. He had been to the Moulin Rouge in Paris, he told her, and seen the dancing girls for himself.

'What were they like?' she asked. 'Were they beautiful?'

He shrugged. 'Compared to you? They were ordinary.'

The lighted windows of Selfridges department store drew them like a beacon. The displays had been created to celebrate the Season, with each window depicting an event. They stood in front of Royal Ascot, where mannequins wearing rictus smiles and dresses of lemon and forget-me-not and strawberry-ice pink stood on greengrocer's grass, eyes fixed glassily on a point in the distance.

'Surprisingly realistic,' Selina remarked. 'Though they need a touch more blue in their cheeks. This year it was arctic.'

Lawrence pulled a packet of Chesterfield out of his dinner jacket's pocket, with a nod of appreciation. 'Did you enjoy it?'

Watching him light a cigarette, she considered the question. The day had been exactly as she'd expected – the same people doing the same things; getting tipsy, making amusing, bitchy small talk, putting money on horses with the silliest names or the prettiest colours. She had been drunk and bored enough to consider taking up Harry's dare of riding his father's horse into the winner's enclosure, naked like Lady Godiva. The cold had deterred her in the end, but it had briefly seemed like a good way of livening things up.

'No,' she said, removing the cigarette from his mouth so she could kiss him again. 'Because I knew there was little chance of seeing you there.'

They walked on, sharing the cigarette. It was stronger than she was used to and made her head spin; though that could have been the champagne they were drinking in great indelicate gulps, or just the effect of being with him. Perhaps he felt her movements slow, her body grow heavier because when a motorbus rumbled along and slowed down outside Evans & Co. he pulled her up onto the back step and held her against him as it swayed on its way again.

'Where are we going?'

'Somewhere where we can sit down.' He brushed his lips against her ear. 'Somewhere dark where I can hold your hand. Somewhere we can talk.'

She leaned against him and felt the warmth of his breath in her hair. An unfamiliar pulse was beating at the top of her thighs. The conductor's feet appeared on the stairs above them and she wondered if Lawrence had any money, but it seemed tactless to ask. She kept an emergency half crown tucked under the insole of her shoe, but she couldn't very well recover it now, and anyway, this was hardly an emergency. The bus slowed and she seized his hand and pulled him down into the road.

'Jesus, Selina—'

They almost fell, but righted themselves just in time and, clinging together, stumbled into a side street. She was breathless and laughing. He caught her mouth and kissed her hard, almost angrily as the adrenaline of the fall pulsed through them both.

When they eventually pulled apart she felt jolted into sobriety. They were both breathing fast, and his eyes had a dark glitter that thrilled and unnerved her. She glanced around, realizing that the street they were in was narrow and unlit and was suddenly aware of the risk she was taking. Shaking him off, she stepped away, out of the shadows and into the road.

'Selina? What's wrong?'

'Nothing.'

'It's not nothing.' He made to follow her, but stopped as she flinched away. 'Tell me.'

She shook her head, trying to clear it. 'It's just – why does it feel like I know you when I don't? I *really* don't . . . not at all . . .'

'What do you mean?'

'Sorry. I've just realized how . . . foolish I'm being.' She tried to laugh, but it splintered into sharp pieces. 'I've never been very good at obeying rules, but this is *madness*, even by my standards. I've been drunk before and I've absconded from plenty of parties, but never with . . . a *stranger* . . .'

A motorcar came round the corner, headlamps swinging in a wide arc. He moved quickly, pulling her onto the pavement, then immediately let her go. Thrusting his hands into his pockets, he half-turned away. The noise of the motor receded. She wondered if he was going to be angry and felt defensive indignation rising within her.

'And that's what we are. Strangers.'

The softness of his voice caught her off-guard. He turned back to her. His head was lowered, that heavy lock of hair falling forward again. He pushed it away and sighed.

'You're right. God, I'm so sorry. Do you want to go back?'

'Back?'

'To the party.'

She pictured the Grosvenor Square house she had left without a second thought or backward glance; the brightly lit rooms, the oppressive heat, the band and the drunken high spirits that by now would be tipping into disorder – an obligatory food-fight, someone removing their clothes or having them removed, ostentatious same-sex kissing and scandalously provocative dancing.

'No.'

'Then what?'

'I want to get to know you.'

'Get to know me? How?'

'I don't know ...'

'Shall I call at your house tomorrow afternoon? Take you out for tea? Bring my friend Sam along to vouch for my good character?'

He was teasing, but serious. She got the impression that he would do all of those things if she said they were necessary. His earnestness made the panic ebb away a little and she laughed.

'No.'

'Good. Because much as I would love to take you out for

tea, I wouldn't like to risk Sam in anywhere smart and I'm not sure he'd vouch for my good character. Edith might be a better bet.'

'Who's Edith?'

'My artist friend.' He pulled the edges of his jacket apart to flash his painted chest. 'She did the Napiers' portrait and she owns the studio where I work.'

'How did you meet her?'

'At the Slade. We were students there together, though she's older than I am. And far wiser and more respectable. What else do you want to know?'

'Everything.' They had come together again and she seized the lapels of his stolen coat. 'Who you are, where you come from—' It sounded so trite that she laughed again. 'And much more than that. Let me see – did you have a pet when you were growing up? What did your father do, what was your mother's name? Do you have any brothers and sisters? What food do you love, what do you hate, what's your favourite place in the world? What's your earliest memory, your happiest one—'

She was drunker than she'd thought. The champagne they'd stolen and swigged so fast was hitting her bloodstream, making her talk too quickly, too wildly, and all the things she'd wondered about him in the past maddening weeks spill out into the inky-blue dark. He pulled her towards him, pressing his mouth to hers to capture her words.

'Elizabeth,' he said, against her lips. 'My mother's name was Elizabeth. My father was a signwriter.' He paused to kiss her properly. 'No pets, but a brother – older – and a sister – younger. I hate sardines. I love—' he kissed the corner of her mouth, her jaw, her earlobe. 'Oranges. Strawberries. Buttered toast. Earliest memory . . .' He pulled away, still holding her hands. 'My mother, pouring me a glass of milk in the kitchen. I must have been two or three, I suppose.'

Her lips tingled from the graze of his stubble. Her head reeled as she processed this feast of information. She was delighted and dazzled by it, and distracted by the idea of him as a tiny boy of two or three. She could picture him; dark, serious eyes and soft lips. 'A glass of milk. Why do you remember that?'

'Because it was beautiful. In that moment *she* was beautiful. It was morning, and the sun was coming through the window and making everything glow, like a Vermeer painting.' His tone was wry. 'Though I don't suppose I made that connection at the time. I remember how white the milk was. My mother was . . . expecting a baby. Her stomach was round and tight. It was . . . frightening and fascinating.'

'The baby was your sister?'

They were walking again, a little way apart, their steps distracted and directionless.

'No. A boy. He died soon after he was born. Too soon to have a name.'

'Oh—'

'I was ten when my sister was born. My mother lost another one in the years between. She was besotted with Cassie from the start. We all were.'

There was something in his tone that made her look across at him, but the street was too dark to see his face.

'Is she terribly spoiled?'

'I wish.' He kicked a loose stone, hard, so it clattered across the road and ricocheted off the opposite kerb. 'She and my mother both died, in the influenza outbreak after the war. She was eight.'

'Oh, Lawrence . . .'

It had been a game until then, but suddenly it wasn't anymore. She went to him, sliding her arms around his waist beneath his jacket, holding him tightly and feeling the movement of his lithe body as he walked, the bump of his hip against hers. He kissed the top of her head.

'There was another question, but I've forgotten what it was.'

'So have I.'

'Tell me about you, then.'

'You know about me. You know where I come from and what my father does.'

'That's not who you are.' He pulled away a little, enough to look down at her. A streetlamp threw his face into sharp relief, with deep hollows of shadow beneath his cheek-bones. 'If it was you wouldn't have run away from that party with me.'

They walked on, his arm around her shoulders, his body warm against hers. They were in the heart of Soho, passing pubs from which the sound of raucous laughter and the smell of beer spilled out, and groups of swaggering men who would have intimidated her at any other time. She moved amongst them unnoticed now, protected by his proximity.

'When I was a child I always wanted to run away,' she said, resting her cheek against his shoulder. 'From Blackwood Park — our house in Wiltshire, which looks lovely but felt like a prison. Everyone else in my family was always going to more interesting places — up to town or to stay with friends or to school, and I was stuck there on my own, up on the nursery floor with Nanny and the governess of the day. Once I got as far as the station, but the stationmaster spotted me hiding amongst the milk churns and stopped me getting on the train.'

'Where were you going to go?'

'Cambridge, I think, to ask my brother if I could live in his rooms. I didn't have any money, so I wouldn't have got far. Did you ever want to run away?'

'Not when I was a kid.' They came to a junction, where an inky puddle of water in the gutter reflected the stars. He took her hand as they jumped it, her frilled petticoats bouncing. 'I suppose I had a lot of freedom, compared to you. I used to go down to the beach and wander for miles, or spend time with the fairground people when they were there.'

'The fairground people?' She was instantly intrigued. 'That sounds fun.'

'I knew them. My father painted their signs and they used to put me to work touching up the paintwork on the carousel horses. I slept there quite often, under a tarpaulin on the carousel.'

'How romantic. Didn't you want to join them? To live that life?'

He shook his head. 'It was romantic, in a way, but it was hard. Poor and basic. I wanted bright lights of a different kind.' He spread his arm wide, taking in the layers of life around them on all sides. 'I wanted to read books and learn things.'

'I spent all my time trying to avoid learning anything, mostly by thinking up ways to torment the governesses and make them leave. I didn't realize that the person who would end up losing out was me. I'm woefully ignorant, and it serves me right.'

He pulled her into the shelter of a doorway and kissed her lightly on the lips.

'What did you do to the poor governesses?'

In between kisses she confessed about apple pie beds, earwigs slipped under eiderdowns and dramatically faked illnesses. His eyes gleamed with amusement as she told him about the elaborate hoaxes she'd set up to convince the more nervously disposed that the nursery floor was haunted. 'That was my most successful tactic, I'm ashamed to say. Two of them left within the first three days, poor things. My only defence is that I was bored. Bored and frustrated and resentful, which is no defence at all.'

'What were you resentful of?'

She looked past him, to the glistening street and the slice of sky above. The moon was just visible between the chimneypots; a watery smudge behind a veil of clouds. She took a deep breath and let it out in a sigh. 'This is going to sound appallingly crass but I resented my own privilege, I suppose. That's what it amounts to, anyway. I resented the rules and restrictions and the rigidness ... The hypocrisy and control ...' She met his eye with a self-mocking grimace. *Poor Little Rich Girl*. It was the musical hit of the year – the song one heard everywhere. 'Their favourite punishment was to withhold food, and I resented being sent to bed hungry while downstairs seven courses were being served in the dining room and people were only picking at each of them. And the more resentful I was the naughtier I became and the more I was punished ...' She laughed. 'I spent my childhood feeling permanently ravenous.'

It had been Polly who pointed out that she was punishing herself in the same way, years later.

'And now?' He came towards her, his jacket falling open to reveal the ridged contours of his chest with its galaxy of swirling stars. 'Are you still hungry?'

'Yes. Always.'

'Come on then.' He took her hand. 'Let's go and eat.'

He took her to a tiny restaurant on Old Compton Street, hidden behind an unassuming façade that looked like an ordinary house.

La Normandie was owned by a French couple, Monsieur and Madame Aucourt, whose sons had grown up and returned to their homeland (one of them permanently, since he was buried in a cemetery near Verdun). It was simply furnished, with scrubbed pine tables and chairs that clattered noisily on the terracotta floor. The walls were covered with playbills, posters and gaudy paintings in a variety of styles and stages of competence, alongside charcoal sketches, pen-and-ink cartoons and caricatures (mostly of Madame) produced by the artists who made up a large proportion of the clientele. Monsieur cooked in the tiny kitchen at the back – vats of soup and fragrant stews, fillets of pork sautéed in the cream and apples of his native Normandy – while Madame presided over the front of house. She was particularly fond of Lawrence, a fact he was aware of exploiting in turning up after midnight and asking for a table.

The kitchen was closed, though diners still lingered at smoke-wreathed tables littered with bottles and smeared glasses. Madame, once she'd kissed him resoundingly on both cheeks, told him off for arriving so late and rolled her eyes at what he was (or wasn't) wearing, ushered them through to a room at the back where the tables were all empty and bustled off to see what her husband could heat up for them. Before she went she swiped a stubby candle from one of the other tables and ordered Lawrence to light it.

As the candleflame leapt Selina arched an eyebrow at him. 'I consider myself to be something of a favoured guest at Claridge's and the Savoy Grill, but I don't for a moment think they'd open the kitchen for me at this hour.'

'This isn't exactly Claridge's, but Madame has a soft spot for undernourished artists.'

171

'I can see that.' She looked around the crowded walls. 'Are any of these yours?'

'Yes, actually . . .' He nodded in the direction of the frame in the centre of the wall.

'The photograph?' She frowned. 'I thought you were an artist – a portrait painter.'

'I am.' He lit another stolen cigarette, inhaling the rich smoke as he watched her face. 'But that's by necessity, to make a living. Photography is what I'm most interested in. What I'd like to do.'

She grimaced, shrugging off her borrowed jacket and dropping it over the back of the chair. 'You don't want to be one of those dreadful little men who sneak into parties and lurk outside nightclubs to snap unflattering pictures for the newspapers, do you?'

'No, not that sort of photographer. And not one that does studio portraits either, flattering debutantes to simper against painted backdrops and trying to get bored children in sailor suits to stand still.'

'I wouldn't have known there were any other kinds.'

She got up, and went over to examine the photograph. He had taken it one lunchtime, sitting at a table by the window at the front, and it showed Madame, smiling and wreathed in steam, serving customers with bowls of stew. The light had been difficult and most of the frames he'd taken were far too dark, but he'd caught one lucky moment, when her face had been turned towards the window and the steam had made a halo around her, turning her into a plump Madonna. For all her protests that her hair was a mess and he'd showed her double chin, the photograph had been framed and hung in a prominent position, beneath the arc of light from the wall sconce.

He took a deep drag on the cigarette, waiting for Selina to say something, unwilling to acknowledge how much he wanted her to like it. After what seemed like an age she looked round at him.

'It's extraordinary, Lawrence. As beautiful as a painting, but better, because it's real.' She turned back to it. 'What else do you photograph?'

He shrugged, tapping ash into the little tin ashtray on the table. 'Just . . . people. In cafés and pubs and on the street. Their faces. Hands. I like capturing a moment . . . a fleeting moment in an ordinary day. Stopping time.'

'Do you sell them? To magazines and newspapers? Exhibit them somewhere?'

'If only it were that easy. I don't have the right names in my address book, which is why I'm still painting portraits.'

Madame came bustling back, bearing a tray laden with bowls of fragrant *pot au feu* and a bottle of red wine, setting them down onto the table and making a great show of leaving them in peace to eat. Lawrence noticed the covert glances she threw in Selina's direction and knew that she was bursting with curiosity. On a good day Madame could have given the Grand Inquisitor a run for his money, and usually made it her business to vet all guests brought by her regulars. On this occasion he was grateful for her restraint, and her uncharacteristic tact.

As she took the first mouthful Selina gave a groan of pleasure.

'Oh God, it's delicious . . .'

He sipped the smoky wine and watched her. La Normandie was not the kind of place he would have imagined bringing a girl like Selina Lennox, until he'd discovered that Selina Lennox wasn't actually the kind of girl he'd assumed she was. The flickering light of the candle brushed her exposed shoulders, the swell of her breasts spilling out of the corset, with gold. He barely tasted the food he swallowed, and even as his bowl emptied his stomach remained hollow with desire.

They talked in fits and starts, their voices overlapping, words tangling, just like their eyes across the table. Answering her questions, he found himself telling her about his family; about Stephen, who had seen action at Loos and the Somme, but no one knew what kind of action, because he hadn't spoken a word since he'd been invalided home in 1916. About Cassie too, talking about her in a way he hadn't for years so that things that were buried and forgotten came back with piercing, poignant clarity. Her love of elephants (Lawrence used to draw them for her to colour in), her infuriating habit of waking up ridiculously early and waking him too. He would take her out sometimes, to let his mother sleep on, and they would walk down to the beach to watch the fishermen come in. She was desperate for him to teach her how to skim stones across the surface of the water.

'For ages she just couldn't get the hang of it, but by that

winter her persistence had almost paid off – she was so nearly there.' He took another mouthful of wine. 'I couldn't stop thinking about that, after she died. About how unfair it was. She'd been so determined to do it, and now she'd never get the chance to—'

His voice cracked, and the sudden emotion took him by surprise. Selina reached across and took his hand, her fingers entwining with his. She had peeled off her satin gloves, and the feel of her bare skin skewered him with want. That took him by surprise too.

'Tell me something happy about her. A good memory.'

He took a breath. It wasn't difficult to think of a happy memory of his little sister, though focusing on her just now, with Selina's thumb gently stroking the back of his hand, was harder. 'Just after the Armistice there was a firework display in Eastbourne. She'd heard about it somehow and was desperate to go, though she knew that because of Stephen it was ... difficult. So I took her – just the two of us.'

'Did she love it?'

He smiled. 'Oh yes ... I didn't watch the fireworks, I watched her face, tipped up to the sky, all the colours reflected on her happiness. That was the moment I knew I wanted to be a photographer, because I remember thinking if I'd had a camera I could keep that image for ever.'

Her fingers tightened around his. Across the table her aquamarine eyes reflected candlelight, shimmering with tears. She stood up and cupped his cheek with her free hand as she leaned across to kiss him.

'*Alors* . . .'

It was Madame, tactfully announcing her arrival by speaking particularly loudly. They broke apart as she appeared, cheerfully brisk, to clear the table, brushing aside Selina's compliments and Lawrence's thanks. With a stab of regret he realized how late it was; the restaurant was quiet now, and the bottle of wine almost empty. Monsieur had emerged from the kitchen to tidy the bar and move chairs aside to sweep the floor. Behind her wide smile, Madame's face was tired. He followed her through to the bar to settle the bill, but she waved the suggestion away with a flick of her hand.

'Next time. It's late now.' She winked encouragingly. 'And you'll be wanting to get your young lady home . . .'

If only, Lawrence thought as they went out into the dark street again. It had rained some more while they'd been inside. Water dripped from doorways into streaming gutters and the air had a saturated smell. Above the Soho rooftops the stars had been washed away and the sky was like wet, black ink. Even here, in the part of the city that paid least heed to conventional hours, the streets were quiet. They wove their way through the puddles, in the direction of Shaftesbury Avenue to find a taxi, her body folded into his, warm and heavy with wine and drowsiness.

'Thank you,' she murmured. 'Thank you for taking me there.'

'My pleasure. I think you made quite an impression on Madame.'

'It was the most wonderful food I've ever tasted.' She

laughed, that husky, throaty laugh. 'What a cruel stroke of fate that tonight of all nights I should be wearing a corset.'

He wanted to make a joke about unlacing it, but knew it was too close to the bone to be amusing. His hand was round her waist, resting on the curve of her hip, and only heroic amounts of willpower made him able to keep walking straight. He wondered if she knew how intoxicatingly desirable she was?

'My sister will be furious,' she sighed. 'She's getting married this week and I'm chief bridesmaid. For months she's been nagging me to slim down so I don't embarrass her and spoil the photographs.'

He stopped walking. 'Did she say that?'

'Yes!' Laughing, she pulled him onwards. 'Too late now. Yesterday she instructed me to hang well back and stay out of the way. She's expecting quite a crowd of photographers from all the newspapers and the illustrated magazines and is desperate to snatch the dazzlingly pointless accolade of 'society wedding of the year' from Baba Curzon. She thinks I'll ruin her chances.'

They emerged onto Shaftesbury Avenue, where it was noisier, busier, rougher. His arm tightened around her. 'And when is this wedding, exactly?'

'Thursday. St Margaret's, Westminster.'

'Excellent.' He kept his tone perfectly bland as he stuck his hand out to flag down the taxi that had appeared in the distance. 'I'll make a note in my diary. I'd hate to miss a chance to see the society wedding of the year.'

PS Siam
  The Irrawaddy River
  Burma

2nd April 1936

Darling Alice,

   *I'm so sorry it has been such an age since I last wrote.
It's too frustrating – your wonderful letter arrived at the
hotel just after we left to begin our journey north, so it took
several more days for it to catch up with us again. But of
course, it made receiving it even more of a joy. I can't believe
you found the clue so easily! I thought I'd been terribly
wicked and made it far too hard. Polly said you didn't need
to ask for help at all.*

   *I'm glad your first idea was the chapel, and you got to
walk down there and see Uncle Howard's memorial plaque.
It's rather lovely that Grandmama still visits – I didn't
know that, but I suppose I'm not surprised; she simply
adored Howard. It doesn't get much use these days, though
you and Archie Atherton were both Christened there. Papa
would have liked you to be Christened at King's Aston, or
in London at the Guards Chapel where we were married,*

but I rather put my foot down. I always used to say that I didn't believe in God or heaven or life after death, but when you were born that changed somehow (how can one not believe in miracles when one holds the evidence in one's own arms?) I knew with great certainty that I wanted you to be connected with that place, where some tiny essence of my darling brother might be found, even though he's not actually interred there. His grave is in a place called Tyne Cot in Belgium, but I like to think of his bright spirit at rest there in our peaceful little church.

If I close my eyes I can almost imagine that I'm there. I can feel the coolness inside, and the quiet, and picture the way the light comes through the windows and makes shimmering patterns on the floor. You've no idea how wonderfully soothing it is to think of that just now, in the place where I am.

We left Rangoon two days ago. I'm afraid I didn't get to do any of the things I would have liked because after I wrote to you I came down with some wretched fever and felt absolutely ghastly for days. Perfectly horrid. Anyway, I'm right as rain again now and we're on the next part of the journey, inland to Mandalay. The roads are very rough and the only vehicles one sees are little carts pulled by oxen or donkeys, but thankfully we're not travelling on one of those! We are on another boat – a paddle steamer – sailing up the Irrawaddy River, which winds its way through dense, jungly forests and wide fields of rice. Women work with their babies tucked in brightly coloured shawls against their backs.

*It's all terribly beautiful. Everything is very flat, except for
the smoky blue silhouette of steep, jagged mountains in the
distance, and there are temples and pagodas dotted about,
clinging to the slopes, their domes and turrets peeping out
through the foliage. The colours are marvellously intense,
especially the sunsets, which are scarlet and orange and turn
the river blood red (doesn't that sound dramatic?) Oh, but
the heat! The air is thick with it. My skin feels permanently
sticky and my hair is damp, and there is no comfortable cabin
with a darling little bathroom on this boat. Papa bought me a
parasol in Rangoon, and a fan (made of thick paper, painted
with beautiful birds and flowers – you would adore it) but
even moving it feels like the most frightful effort.*

*Sometimes we pass other vessels – paddle steamers like
ours, or flat barges carrying cargo. Earlier today I saw one
with a huge stone Buddha lashed to its deck. I wonder
where it was going?*

*Tonight we will be staying at one of the hotels along
the river. They are mostly old government circuit houses –
beautiful, in a faded and crumbling sort of way (like
Blackwood!) but not at all smart or luxurious, and one feels
that one day soon they might just collapse into the water.
The people here are wonderfully polite and wherever we stay
the staff are attentive and efficient, so I'll leave this letter
with them to post. Oh darling, I do hope it reaches you
soon. I wish it could cross all the miles between us as swiftly
and invisibly as my heart does, and my thoughts. They are
with you all the time, every hour of every day.*

The Glittering Hour

We are due to reach Mandalay in another three days, I think. Tomorrow I will occupy my time in thinking up the next clue in your treasure hunt, if you're not bored of it? I've been so terribly slow, so I wouldn't blame you in the least if you were. It's awfully selfish of me I know, but I like doing it. I like letting my mind travel back to Blackwood and wander through its rooms, along its passageways. I like conjuring the lushness of the parkland, green and gold beneath the gentle English sun, and remembering that summer.

More very soon darling, I promise. But for now, know that I'm thinking of you and loving you, always.

Mama xxxxx

(No lipstick kiss because I'm not wearing any, but I'm blowing kisses to you and sending them across the seas.)

11

Aunt Miranda

April 1936

By the time the Athertons' Easter visit to Blackwood came round the daffodils had withered to unsightly brown husks and the newly rampant grass, too wet for Patterson to mow, was littered with dandelions.

'Good Heavens, the place looks shabbier than ever,' Lionel remarked as Fairley steered the Rolls Royce carefully around the potholes in the drive. Miranda's lips tightened. She might have been thinking the same thing, but coming from Lionel it felt like a personal criticism: a snide reminder that she was, by birth and by blood, a Lennox, and an Atherton only by association. She brushed a smut from her skirt and bit her tongue. The visit was going to be draining enough, and she didn't want to be at odds with her husband before they'd even stepped out of the car.

They had made most of the journey by train, but Fairley had picked them up from Salisbury to drive them the last ten miles or so. There was something comforting about his familiar, solid neck and the fringe of grey hair beneath his cap, and she was glad that she had made the decision to bring him – or rather, for him to bring Archie and Nanny and all the luggage while they travelled separately by rail. Lionel had raised his eyebrows when she'd put the plan to him, but it saved such a lot of bother: finding porters at Waterloo and Salisbury, having to wait in the rather basic tea-room there for the branch line connection, and suffering the ignominy of being collected from Hindbury station by Patterson the gardener, because there was no chauffeur kept at Blackwood anymore.

It also spared her the trial of travelling with Archie, though she hadn't said that to Lionel, who always hid behind his newspaper and left her to intervene when boredom made Archie more demanding than usual. ('Determined' was her preferred euphemism for her son's character.) She had been sure he would have outgrown his tendency to be sick in the car, and felt mildly guilty that this had turned out not to be the case. Wafting her handkerchief beneath her nose, she leaned forward to breathe in the thin stream of fresh air coming through the open window, and relief that she had not had to deal with any of it overwhelmed the guilt. Nanny Bell was wonderfully proficient at such things. Archie had been 'right as rain, full of beans again' by the time they'd arrived at Blackwood an hour ago, Fairley reported. If there was a hint of acid in his tone, Miranda chose to ignore it.

They emerged from the tunnel of trees along the drive and the house loomed in front of them. Lionel was right; it looked half derelict. She twitched her skirt over her knees and snapped open her handbag, more for the reassurance of its contents – Cartier compact and Elizabeth Arden lipstick, silver Aspreys notebook – than because she needed anything. Coming back to Blackwood always made her feel like this; resentful and insecure, just as she so often had when she was a child and Howard had reigned over their nursery kingdom, adored by all.

But that was in the past. As Fairley pulled up on the (weed-choked) gravel beneath the front steps she reminded herself that she was Mrs Lionel Atherton now, no longer invisible and powerless. She commanded a beautiful home in Egerton Crescent, and staff who were efficient, loyal and discreet. She sat on committees of the most respectable charities and had the most prestigious invitations on her chimneypiece. She had proved herself more than equal to the task of running Cranleigh, Lionel's vast ancestral home, when the time came, and she had provided him (albeit not as quickly she would have wished) with an heir. Stepping out of the car as Fairley opened the door she summoned a smile. She had put plenty of distance between herself and the challenges of her childhood. She had risen above the petty injustices, the frustrations of financial and sibling embarrassment . . .

Almost unconsciously she looked up, her eyes going to the window of Selina's room. For a fleeting second she glimpsed a face but it was gone so quickly that she almost thought it was a ghost. She shivered, in spite of the mink wrap around her shoulders.

It must have been the child. Alice. The realization didn't make her feel any less uncomfortable as she went up the steps where Denham waited, stooped and ancient, with his lugubrious welcome to Blackwood Park.

Alice watched the Rolls Royce make its painstaking way up the drive. It was a dark, shiny red, and something about the polished grille at the front and the position of the head-lamps gave it the suggestion of a face. As it navigated the puddle hollows she imagined that its expression was set in a grimace of distaste.

It had first appeared about an hour ago, bearing Cousin Archie and his Nanny, and so many bags and trunks and items of equipment that Polly had been summoned from the nursery to assist with carrying them inside. Before she'd gone down she'd reminded Alice to give Cousin Archie the picture she'd drawn for him (of rabbits, which had seemed appropriately Easter-themed, though regrettably not coloured-in because of the missing pencils) and to be nice and friendly.

She had tried. She had got up from the window seat when she heard them all coming up the stairs, and been ready to put on the smile she had practised in the bathroom mirror that morning. When Cousin Archie had come in, sobbing dejectedly, she had stepped forward to give him the picture, but Nanny Bell had rounded on her, hissing:

'Not now, child! Master Archie has had a long journey – can't you see he's feeling unwell? Run along and leave us in peace. You may talk to him later, if he's feeling up to it.'

She hadn't known where she should run along to. Nanny Bell obviously didn't know the rules at Blackwood, and that she wasn't really permitted anywhere other than the nursery. Stiff with awkwardness she had walked along the corridor and headed down the back stairs to the sanctuary of Mama's room, where she stood at the window and watched the car trundle back up the drive, on the way to meet Aunt Miranda and Uncle Lionel at the railway station in Salisbury. When it had disappeared she wandered around the room, opening the wardrobe to bury her face in Mama's clothes, touching the silver-backed brushes on the dressing table and the tortoiseshell pot with Mama's initials on it. Then she had curled up on the lily-patterned counterpane and taken Mama's last letter out of her pocket.

She still hadn't got over the relief of its arrival. Waiting for it, as the days slipped into weeks, she had gone through frustration to anguished imaginings involving fire, kidnap, fever. Polly had stroked her cheek when she'd confessed that, and said it was the postal service, more likely. Another letter would arrive soon. Alice just had to be patient.

She was right about that, though Alice's fear about fever had turned out to be well founded. Poor Mama. Alice took the letter out of her pocket and unfolded it, smoothing it against the counterpane. She'd read it so often that she almost knew the lines by heart, but that didn't matter. It was like listening to Mama's voice. It lulled her, so that by the time she finished reading (always easier in her head than out loud) her eyes were heavy, and her mind was full of strange and exotic images, like pictures in a storybook, of jungles and temples and a wide red river.

She might have slipped into sleep had it not been for the sound of the motorcar engine, which jolted her back into full consciousness and sent her scampering to the window to watch its approach. Uncle Lionel got out first, though from her vantage point Alice couldn't see much of him other than his hat and his overcoat, straining a little at the buttons. His gloveless hands, emerging from the sleeves, looked oddly small and pale.

Aunt Miranda followed him. She was wearing a pale green two-piece suit, and shoes of glossy black patent leather. Beneath the brim of her hat Alice could see the gleam of blonde hair, curling neatly over her collar. Out of the two sisters Aunt Miranda was supposed to be the beautiful one, though Alice had always thought that was stupid. It was like at Miss Ellwood's: the girls who tried conspicuously hard to please the teachers weren't necessarily the cleverest ones. Aunt Miranda might have a fashion plate figure and perfectly styled hair, but she could never be half as beautiful as Mama.

At the very moment she thought that, Aunt Miranda looked up, straight at the window. Her eyes were narrowed, her expression faintly accusing, as if she had read Alice's mind. Alice darted back, ducking out of sight, sinking down onto the floor by the bed.

She was still there when Polly peered round the door a few moments later.

'I thought I'd find you here,' she said, coming in and shutting the door. 'Nanny Bell told me she'd sent you away. I'll be falling out with her before very long if she carries on like that.' She rolled her eyes. 'Anyway, Mr and Mrs Atherton have just arrived and everyone's having tea in the drawing room.' She held out her hand to help Alice to her feet. 'We'd better smarten you up a bit before you go down.'

Alice looked down at herself. She was wearing her Sunday dress – navy blue velvet with a white peter pan collar – but the skirt was creased into stiff folds and bits of fluff had mysteriously attached themselves to the fabric. Polly tugged and rubbed at it with lick-dampened fingers before steering her towards the dressing table.

In the mirror Alice's face looked small and pinched, her eyes too large and too dark. Beneath Mama's silver brush her curls crackled with static, only seeming to get wilder with Polly's swift strokes. Her hair – its colour and thickness and refusal to lie flat; its lack of resemblance to Mama's (or Papa's for that matter) – had always been a source of misery to her, and looking at it in the mirror that had once reflected Mama's image made her more aware than ever of its wrongness. She averted her eyes as Polly retied the bow at her temple.

'There now. Pretty as a picture,' Polly grinned. 'Though it would be an even prettier picture if you could manage a smile too. Come on – I'll come down with you so you don't have to walk in on your own. Sometimes there's nothing so frightening as a closed door.'

They went down the main staircase and across the marble hall. From the other side of the drawing room door the murmur of voices was just discernible. Polly knocked, giving Alice a rallying smile before turning the handle and ushering her in.

'. . . dear Rupert – no expense spared to make her comfortable.'

Alice was used to being invisible at Blackwood, her presence largely ignored, but Aunt Miranda stopped speaking immediately, and all heads turned towards her. They had been talking about Mama, Alice realized. Saying how kind Papa was to arrange the very best accommodation on their trip, when really it was the least he could do. She hadn't even wanted to go.

'Come in then, child – don't hover at the door.' Grandmama held out an imperious, heavily ringed hand. 'Come and say hello to your aunt and uncle.'

Alice went forward. Aunt Miranda was perched on the edge of the sofa nearest the fireplace, her legs arranged at an elegant (but uncomfortable-looking) angle. She turned towards Alice with a frosty smile but didn't quite meet her eye. It was Uncle Lionel who spoke, his voice too loud and falsely hearty.

'Good heavens, young lady, you've grown! Must be all this good country air, eh? Having a splendid time staying with your grandparents, are you, hmm?'

'Yes, Uncle Lionel.'

It was the only appropriate answer, but once she had dutifully delivered it the conversation stalled. Fortunately, distraction came in the form of rapid footsteps crossing the hall, followed a second later by the door flying open. Archie charged in, flapping a piece of paper.

'Look, Mummy – I did a picture!'

At five years old Archibald Atherton was sturdy of limb and rosy of cheek. He had clearly made a complete recovery after the unfortunate incident in the car, and had the sort of ruddy, energetic health displayed by children in magazine advertisements for vitamin tonic drinks. He rushed over to where Aunt Miranda sat, thrusting the paper at her. Nanny Bell's voice could be heard in the hallway, calling his name, and she appeared in a flustered rustle of starched apron, pushing past Alice.

'Master Archie – you know better than to run around like that! I *am* sorry, madam. He's excited to be here – not that that's any excuse for poor manners . . .'

'Don't worry, Nanny Bell,' Aunt Miranda said smoothly. Alice looked at Grandmama, expecting to see quite a different attitude expressed on her face, and was surprised to see a smile there too. Not a broad one, but a smile nonetheless.

'Feeling better, old chap?' Uncle Lionel's voice was full of genuine warmth now. 'That's the ticket. Let's see this work of art, then. My word!' He took it from Aunt Miranda and laughed indulgently. 'I'd say you could give that Picasso charlatan a run for his money. Very colourful. Not sure I've ever seen a purple bird before, old boy . . .'

'I wanted to use *all* the colours.'

'Did you indeed? And which colours might these be?' Uncle Lionel looked around the other grown-ups, as if sharing a private joke. 'There certainly seem to be quite a number of them.'

Aware that all eyes were on him, Archie was hopping on one leg. Showing off, Alice thought disapprovingly. 'The colours in the tin. The *pencil* tin.'

'I found it in the schoolroom cupboard,' Nanny Bell said 'On the top shelf. I was sure it would be all right for Master Archie to use them.'

Alice felt as if her heart was being squeezed. The air burned the back of her throat.

'Yes, Nanny Bell. Perfectly all right,' Grandmama said blandly.

'There's some writing here,' Uncle Lionel said, stooping to point out a scribble in the top corner of the picture. 'What does that say?'

Archie's blue eyes slid towards Alice.

'It says *To Alice.*'

Uncle Lionel laughed again. 'Well in that case I'd better hand it back. Aren't you going to give it to her?'

'No.' Archie's smile was sly as he went to Aunt Miranda's side. 'I only put it because Nanny Bell said I had to. I want

Mummy to have it.' He twisted his solid body against his mother, his voice turning babyish and petulant. 'Is it tea-time yet? I'm *starving*.'

Miranda had forgotten how heavily the time hung at Blackwood. On the first full day of their visit they had woken to leaden skies and a cold wind that found its way through the gaps in the windowframes, making the silk blouses she had brought pitifully inadequate. By lunch-eon time rain was falling in steady sheets across the park. Good Friday? Too ironic. There was nothing remotely good about it.

In London one never paid much attention to the weather, beyond glancing outside to see if one should wear the fur coat or the light wool. (Not that it mattered much, since one was only exposed to the elements as one went from front door to motorcar, and there was always a butler or a door-man to hold an umbrella.) At Cranleigh one didn't mind it either. There was an army of staff there to keep fires banked and bring trays of tea, and Miranda's mother-in-law took all the weekly illustrated newspapers and upmarket monthly magazines, so a rainy day was an opportunity to catch up on society gossip and fashions for the upcoming season, or both in one fell swoop if there had been any sightings of the new King's American divorcee. (Miranda couldn't help being fascinated by the story, partly because she found the King's devotion so incomprehensible. Mrs Simpson wasn't even pretty – how had she managed to get such a hold over him?) At Blackwood Lady Lennox passed the time by doing endless tapestries, which ended up on ugly cushions and footstools, and the only magazine she took was *Country Life*. To Miranda's mind life in the country was so tiresome that the last thing one wanted to do when one was forced to be there was read about it as well.

On Saturday afternoon she re-painted her fingernails and wrote an overdue letter to a friend. Then, in the absence of anything else to do, she went up to the nursery. There she found Archie, his cheeks scarlet, galloping poor Trojan hard enough to make the floorboards shake, letting out blood-curdling whoops while Nanny Bell stood by, imploring him to be careful. Selina's girl sat at the table colouring a picture she had drawn. It was of the orangery, and (Miranda acknowledged grudgingly) surprisingly good.

There was something extremely provoking about her quiet, self-contained industry, her dark head bent over the page. It felt like a rebuke; a veiled criticism of Archie's boisterousness, which of course was just perfectly normal high spirits. Archie was a boy (thank heaven) and boys were given to being noisy and playing lively games. She was sure Howard had been just the same.

A sudden memory came back to her. Not of Howard riding Trojan, but Selina, a wild-haired urchin dressed in some outlandish get-up from the dressing up trunk, brandishing a wooden sword while Howard stood on the window seat, on the lookout for invading armies. Miranda had never been part of their games. She had always preferred

Iona Grey

creating domestic order and harmony in the doll's house, pretending she was the pretty matriarch presiding over home and hearth, loved and admired by all.

She looked around the room, taking in the faded wallpaper (sagging and stained in the corner where damp had seeped through) and the peeling frieze of Noah's animals; the lumpen sofa and Nanny's old armchair beside the fireplace fender where they used to dry damp woollen leggings after winter walks.

Old Nanny Cole might have ruled over the nursery kingdom, but Howard had been its Crown Prince. Its golden boy. Miranda had accepted the special treatment he'd received; he was the prized son and heir, after all, and the significance of this favoured position was implicit. It never occurred to her to question his privilege, or to mind that she was largely invisible to him. Beneath his notice.

Until Selina was born.

He had doted on the new arrival from the start. Miranda recalled how he used to ask to be allowed to hold the baby, to give her a bottle. Selina had been his special pet, and – as she got older, and bolder – his partner in crime. In the long school holidays he had taught her the kind of silly things that held no interest for Miranda: overarm bowling with a cricket ball, climbing the giant cedar of Lebanon on the lawn, jumping into the lake from a rope swing he had fashioned in the oak tree. But then, of course, the war had come, and their bond had been severed.

Blackwood had lost its heir, but Howard's death also left a

194

vacancy for a favoured child and it was Miranda who filled it. She didn't like to think of herself as a spiteful person and had always been ashamed of the tiny voice in her head that whispered it served Selina right to find herself without her ally. In the years that followed she had done her best to make overtures of friendship towards her sister, but it was as if Selina was determined to be contrary. As if she had made a conscious decision to punish them all for Howard's death and make life as difficult as possible for everyone . . .

She pressed the back of her hand to her mouth, to stop the sharp gasp of her indrawn breath. Even so, Alice looked up from her drawing. Their eyes met.

Miranda turned and left the room.

Downstairs, she found her mother in the drawing room, bent over the inevitable tapestry. She barely glanced up as Miranda came in.

'Have you been to the nursery?'

'Yes.' Miranda forced a laugh to cover her agitation. 'Archie is giving dear old Trojan some exercise.'

'I imagine Alice must be rather enjoying the company.'

'Not so one would notice.' Miranda wandered over to the bookcase and bent to look at the lowest shelf, where the photograph albums were kept. 'She's doing her best to ignore him and completely monopolizing that tin of colouring pencils.'

'Poor Archie. I hoped as they're cousins they might get along.'

Miranda was about to point out what a foolish hope that was, since she and Selina were sisters and they'd never got along, but she saw the direction in which her mother was trying to steer the conversation and thought it wiser to divert it. 'Did you see the prospectus for St Winifred's? I left it there, beside your chair.'

Spotting the cream-coloured box for her wedding album she eased it out of the pile and took it over to the sofa. She thought wistfully of the warm fires and attentive servants of Cranleigh and wondered if she dared ring for more coal to add to the ashy smoulder in the grate. Deciding against it, she pulled her cardigan a little more closely around her.

'A trip down memory lane?' her mother said, looking at the wedding album over her spectacles.

'Oh – hardly. On the way here yesterday Lionel and I were talking about a hotel we stayed in on our honeymoon. In Florence, I thought, though he swears it was Rome, and neither of us could remember the name. I'm sure there must be a postcard or something in here.' She opened the cover and folded back a leaf of protective tissue. 'We thought we might go back for our wedding anniversary in July . . . Just the two of us.'

Her mother said nothing, but pointedly picked up the printed pamphlet sent by the Headmistress of St Winifred's. The temperature seemed to drop another couple of degrees.

Miranda looked down at the album, the memories of that day faded and pressed flat, like flowers. There she was, leaving the house in Chester Square, Papa handing her into the car (gosh, how he had aged since then – quite shocking) and stepping out again at St Margaret's, veiled and solemn. A funny little chap from Bassano's had taken the photographs; the same studio that the Duke and Duchess of York had used for their wedding a year or two before. She came to the photograph of her standing at the church door, and smiled as she remembered him ordering the bridesmaids to spread out her long lace veil then to get out of the way so he could photograph her alone. Of course, the dress looked frightfully dated now – shapeless and dowdy, with that dropped waist and high hem – but it had been a great success at the time. *The Sketch* had called it the 'Wedding of the Season'.

Mama turned a page in the school pamphlet. '*A rigorous academic curriculum*,' she read out loud. 'I don't think that's going to be very suitable. The child can barely read and her handwriting is shocking too – that's why Selina doesn't want to send her away. I'm not sure the school would accept her, anyway.'

There was a faint throbbing at Miranda's temples, the result of one too many gin-and-Its before luncheon, but she was distracted from it for a moment by this rather satisfying revelation.

'Well, perhaps St Winifred's isn't the right place for her,' she said, kindly. 'We must look for somewhere more suited to less able children. I'm sure such places must exist ...' She hoped her mother had picked up the inference that Archie's precocious intellect meant that if they did, hitherto she hadn't needed to know about them. 'We must all work together to find the best solution for everyone. You've said yourself that it's far from ideal having her here, with Papa's health being so fragile, and you must see that it's quite impossible for us to have her.'

Lady Lennox's silence suggested she might not actually see the latter at all, but Miranda refused to be swayed. Or to feel guilty. Indignation bubbled inside her, like milk coming to the boil. Miranda had done her best to guide her sister, and to keep her from the path of self-destruction she seemed determined to pursue, but Selina had always been ungovernable. To Miranda's mind, all of her current misfortunes were the result of her past waywardness (and even if one didn't subscribe to that opinion, it was impossible to deny that her daughter was, at least). It was too bad that they must all bear the consequences.

Turning the last page of the photograph album, she found herself looking at a copy of *The Sketch* tucked into the back: the edition in which her wedding had featured, obviously kept by Mama as a souvenir. In a rush, the old resentment came back. The memory of how excited she'd been to open the copy Mama had forwarded to Paris, the first stop on their honeymoon; how her hands had shaken as she turned the pages ... only to come across *a full-page photograph of her sister.*

And, in the pages that followed, several more. Not exclusively of Selina admittedly, but she featured in all of them, with the token exception of a not-particularly-flattering photograph of Miranda and Lionel alone. And that was what had hurt the most; what had, if she was honest, genuinely shaken her. *She* was the pretty sister. Selina was the plainer one – Nanny Cole had always said it – but no one flicking through *The Sketch* would have seen it that way. In those photographs, taken not by the loyal Bassano's man, but one of the anonymous hacks who had crowded onto the pavements with the other onlookers, Selina had looked . . . well, *radiant*. Even Lionel had commented on it. Miranda had stamped around Notre Dame afterwards in the blackest mood.

The ormolu clock on the chimneypiece began to chime its silvery note, announcing that it was teatime. Relieved to reach this comforting milestone in the seemingly endless day, Miranda shut the album and put it back in its box.

The ungainly housemaid (Ellen?) appeared with the tea tray. In the ensuing diversion of positioning the table and setting out cups and so on, Miranda took the magazine she had removed from the box and dropped it quietly into the wastepaper basket to the side of the sofa. And felt much more cheerful.

Blackwood felt different with more people in it. The ghosts had retreated from Archie's strident voice and stamping feet, and Alice suspected that the most fearless phantom footman wouldn't dare to play French cricket beneath the superior nose of Nanny Bell. She never thought that she would find herself thinking fondly of Miss Lovelock, but as the days passed she began to look forward to her return (if only because it would mean the departure of the Athertons).

Admittedly, the visit did have its compensations. There were eggs for breakfast, and bread and jam with their mid-morning milk. Nanny Bell refused to expose Archie to the danger of open water, so walks were not taken around the lake, but in the stretch of garden directly behind the house, beside the orangery. Alice liked to peer through the mist of condensation to the wilderness within, and think of the lush forests Mama described in Burma. There was the return of the pencils too, although this was a very bittersweet blessing since it caused her physical discomfort to watch Archie chew the ends and scribble so hard the leads snapped. Fortunately his attention span was astonishingly short and he had little patience for colouring.

Time passed more quickly with Archie around, though not necessarily more pleasantly. He was exhausting company, given to sudden loud outbursts of excitement, frustration or rage. Even Nanny Bell, for all her strictness and her coolness towards Alice, seemed fearful of his temper, and was at obvious pains to avert another tantrum like the one Alice had witnessed on the first evening of their stay, when it emerged that a particular stuffed rabbit had not been included in the vast supply of toys that accompanied him.

Alice noticed that his behaviour was particularly horrible after one of his parents made a rare appearance in the nursery. Aunt Miranda came up on Friday afternoon, but only to stand in the doorway looking vaguely around, barely noticing Archie's attention-seeking bravado on the rocking horse. After her abrupt departure Archie began to bellow, at ear-splitting volume, about a bang to the knee that Alice strongly suspected was made-up. The following day Aunt Miranda got their chauffeur to take her into Salisbury for shopping, and it was Uncle Lionel's turn to spend time with his son.

To Alice, listening to their conversation as she finished her picture, it seemed like Uncle Lionel was discharging a duty. He set out the legions of toy soldiers from the nursery cupboard in battalions, and Alice could hear the exasperation in his voice as he tried to encourage Archie to think of a battle plan instead of just smashing them all into disarray. He excused himself after half an hour and retreated downstairs, leaving Archie hurling tiny lead figures across the room in a fever of thwarted energy.

On Easter Sunday they joined the grown-ups in the dining room for luncheon, and Archie was in a particularly excitable mood. If he was a good boy and sat nicely at the table using his best manners there was to be an Easter egg hunt afterwards, Nanny Bell had announced. Mistakenly, in Alice's view, since it dramatically increased his agitation.

It was easy to see why he was so given to showing off. Ignored by his parents for long stretches of time, he suddenly became the centre of their attention when he was with them. Watching him across the dining table, Alice was reminded of a dog she and Mama had seen in a show on Brighton Pier once, on one of their impulsive trips. It had worn a silly clown's ruff around its neck and its tongue had lolled from its mouth as it panted eagerly and waited for the next command to perform a trick. At the end of the show a girl sitting in the front row had gone up to pet the dog, and Alice had seen her snatch her hand back from its vicious snap.

Annoying though it was listening to Uncle Lionel boast about how clever Archie was, and recount the amusing things he'd said (all of which Alice knew would earn her a sharp ticking off) it was better than the oppressive silence that usually reigned over the table at Sunday luncheon, and Alice was relieved to evade everyone's notice. The attention seemed to go to Archie's head, like the wine Denham kept pouring into the grown-ups' glasses. As the meal wore on her cousin's cheeks grew more hectically flushed and he became increasingly excitable, until Aunt Miranda rose abruptly and rang for Nanny Bell. It seemed that, despite Archie not having behaved that well, the egg hunt was to go ahead anyway.

Outside a brisk wind had blown the clouds away, but it was jarringly cold. Alice had never done an Easter egg hunt before. She imagined that it might be a bit like a treasure hunt, and hoped that here at last might be an opportunity for her to take the lead and help Archie. Nanny took them through the servants' yard into the lawned garden, and she saw straight away that Archie wouldn't be in need of any help at all. The small, shiny-wrapped eggs had hardly been hidden, just placed beneath bushes or perched on the edge of ornamental urns.

Archie charged around like a crazed bull, whooping with triumph every time he found one, pausing only to tear the silvered paper off and shove the chocolate into his mouth before rushing on again.

'Now, Master Archie, that's enough,' Nanny Bell scolded, 'you'll make yourself poorly if you eat them like that. You give them to me when you find them, and I'll look after them for later.'

Alice fought back disappointment. She wished the eggs had been hidden better; it only took a few minutes for Archie to cover the whole terrace, snatching up his spoils. She couldn't quite bring herself to employ his tactic of run and grab. For her it wasn't just about the chocolate (though her mouth watered at the thought of the small clutch of eggs in her pocket) but the challenge of finding them. Half an hour after they had put on their coats they were taking them off again, and Nanny Bell was delivering them back to the drawing room.

Once again Alice got the impression of a conversation cut off. As Nanny withdrew again there was a moment of awkwardness, but Archie, oblivious to atmosphere, bounded forwards. 'I found eggs! Chocolate eggs, in the garden!'

There was much exaggerated surprise and effusive delight. Even Grandfather levered himself slightly upright in his chair and adjusted his spectacles. Grandmama put down her coffee cup and managed an indulgent smile. Uncle Lionel, sitting on the sofa beside Aunt Miranda, hoisted himself forward and slapped his knees heartily.

'Well, come on then – empty your pockets! Show us the loot!'

Nanny had scrubbed the chocolate from Archie's face with the corner of her handkerchief outside the drawing room door. He produced the two eggs – one from each pocket – that she had allowed him to keep, while she took the rest away for later. Alice laid her handful of eggs down on the ottoman in front of the sofa.

'Good heavens, young lady – what a lot you've got! Let's see – six eggs? My word, what a hoard.'

'It's not fair! She's got more than me!'

'Steady on, old chap,' Uncle Lionel soothed. 'I'm sure Alice won't mind sharing, will you Alice? Here, let's divide them up. Two for Alice, two for Archie, and one each for Mummy and Granny – what do you say?'

Alice wanted to say that Archie had already eaten numerous eggs and had more waiting for him upstairs, but she didn't know how to without sounding spiteful. A sneak. And besides, it was too late. As soon as Uncle Lionel had spoken Archie was grabbing his share, tearing the paper off one and cramming it into his mouth.

'Darling, no need to devour it quite so ferociously.' Aunt Miranda gave a tight little laugh. 'It's not a race. Here – why don't you come and sit between Daddy and me? You can tell us where you found those eggs.'

Alice picked up one of her eggs and sidled away. She didn't want to see Archie being fussed over by his parents, cuddled and cosseted; it gave her a cold, spiky feeling inside.

Everyone was watching him, listening to him as he told them about the hunt (in the silly, babyish voice he used sometimes when he knew he was the centre of attention). She would have liked to slip out and go and find Polly, but she didn't dare. Instead she settled herself on the floor behind the sofa, out of sight, and began very carefully peeling the shiny paper from her egg.

There was a wastepaper basket at the end of the sofa, with a magazine in it. She could just see the title – *The Sketch* – which she recognized as one Mama took. She nibbled her egg, scraping thin slivers of chocolate off with her teeth and letting them melt on her tongue, to make the pleasure last as long as possible. Tentatively, as the voices on the other side of the sofa rose and fell ('My, weren't you clever to think of looking inside the flower pot?') she reached across and lifted the magazine out of the wastepaper basket.

It was an old one, its pages slightly yellowed at the edges. Alice felt a little tingle of interest as she noticed the date at the top. *July 30th 1925*. She wondered if she might have inadvertently stumbled across the next clue, and checked to see if there was a letter in the bottom of the wastepaper basket. Nothing – only an empty cigarette packet. Disappointed, she began to flick through the magazine's pages.

There were lots of photographs, mostly of society events – top-hatted men with ladies in droopy, old-fashioned dresses at Goodwood, in straw boaters and blazers at Cowes. She studied them, wondering if Mama or Aunt Miranda might appear in any, and had just about given up hope when she turned the page and found herself looking straight into Mama's eyes.

The Wedding of Miss Miranda Lennox to Lionel Atherton.

And there they were, Aunt Miranda and Uncle Lionel, looking slightly tense as they stood together outside the church. It was almost the same picture as Grandmama had on top of the piano, but taken a few seconds earlier perhaps? Behind them, Mama was smiling, looking straight into the camera.

Alice sucked in a little breath as she understood. Not taken earlier, but at the same time, by someone else. The person Mama was looking at. The person who had made her turn her head and smile.

And there were more photographs. Mama crouching at Miranda's feet to smooth out her train. Mama sitting in the back of a motorcar, beside the other bridesmaid (Alice recognized Aunt Margòt, looking oddly the same as she did now, but with more hair, wrapped in cumbersome coils at the nape of her neck). In this one Mama's face was a pale oval through the glass, her smile softer. She looked beautiful.

Behind her, on the other side of the sofa Archie said plaintively, 'I feel sick.'

There was an ominous gurgling sound. Aunt Miranda shrieked and Uncle Lionel said a word that Alice knew was forbidden as Archie regurgitated chocolate all over Grandmama's damask sofa. Safely out of the way, happily forgotten, Alice finished her egg and turned back to the beginning to look at the photographs again.

12

An Impulsive Invitation

July 1925

The wedding had been a success.

No one knew what particular combination of luck, efficient organization, extravagance and taste was required to produce such an outcome, but somehow Lady Lennox had achieved it. The heavy clouds that had staled the city air for weeks rolled back, bringing a shimmering blue day and an atmosphere of a festival. Miranda had looked beautiful, and the crowd that gathered outside St Margaret's to catch a glimpse of the wedding party had been gratifyingly large, with a satisfying number of photographers jostling to take pictures for the newspapers. The pale pink roses, anxiously tended by Patterson at Blackwood, had reached their peak at exactly the right moment, though by the time the wedding breakfast was over and Miranda and Lionel were ready to leave they were beginning to wilt. When Miranda (with uncharacteristic whimsy) tossed her bouquet, it sailed through the air in a shower of petals.

Going back into the house after the couple had departed for their honeymoon, Selina found herself beside Rupert.

'You didn't catch the bouquet.'

'Oh – no.' She hadn't even tried. 'I'd forgotten about that tradition. Why on earth do brides do it?'

'I couldn't say. I believe whoever catches it is supposed to be the next one to get married.'

Selina smothered a smile. So that was why Margot had dived so inelegantly to intercept it. 'Oh dear. Well, of course if I'd known that I would have tried harder.'

She wondered if he had picked up the note of sarcasm in her voice. She had got through the interminable luncheon and speeches by discreetly drinking Margot's champagne as well as her own, and was a little too tipsy to trust herself in conversation with Rupert. They stopped at the top of the stairs. She wanted to carry on, up the next flight to her bedroom, to tear off her coronet of roses and put on lipstick (forbidden by Mama for the wedding, of course) and rush outside to hail a taxicab to Marchmont Street. To see Lawrence and say thank you.

Thank you for being there amongst the other photographers, like he said he would be. Thank you for mouthing '*you're beautiful*' as she'd emerged from the house that morning, and for pointing his camera at her as well as Miranda.

For making her blush and tingle when he lowered the camera and just looked at her.

'A few of us are going out for dinner tonight – Margot and Pips Broughton and that sort of crowd. I wondered if you might like to join us?'

'Oh—'

That sensation of coming back to earth with a bump. For a second she floundered, even though she had a perfectly respectable excuse. 'I'm so sorry ... I'm – I mean, I didn't expect – I'm meeting friends – Flick Fanshawe and Theo Osborne – one last evening before we go our separate ways for the summer. They're dying to hear all about the wedding, and then of course we're going on to The Embassy. It's Thursday,' she finished lamely.

'Of course. Another time.' His face was shuttered as he stepped away, and she couldn't tell whether the invitation had been motivated by duty or a genuine desire for her company. 'I gather that you'll be in Scotland for the twelfth?'

'Yes.' The 'glorious' twelfth of August, when the shooting season began. Glorious for the men perhaps, but anything but for bored women and doomed grouse. 'Staying with the Rutherfords at Inverosse.'

'I'm with the Blair-Fergussons at Braedoun. It's less than an hour away, by motor. Perhaps we might see each other.' He stated it blandly, making it hard to tell whether it was an observation or invitation.

'Yes! Lovely!' The attempt at enthusiasm tipped over into insincerity. She winced as she turned to walk quickly away, but by the time she had reached her bedroom on the next floor, by the time she had shut the door and kicked off her shoes her thoughts were already racing ahead to Marchmont Street, and Rupert Carew had entirely vanished from her mind.

What am I doing? she asked the glitter-eyed girl in the mirror.

Once, at Blackwood, just before the war, she had been allowed to join the hunt. At nine she had been considered too young really, but one of the grooms had been ordered to ride alongside, to keep an eye on her. She had lost him almost immediately, and vividly remembered the mixture of terror and exhilaration as her pony had fought for his head and galloped with the rest of the field, out of control, caught up in something primal and unstoppable.

It was like that now, she thought, pulling pins from her hair with shaking hands. Frightening. Exciting. There was nothing to do but hold on tight and enjoy the ride, like she had that sparkling winter day with the wind whipping her cheeks and the drum of hoofbeats in her ears.

And to try to forget how it had ended. With the frenzied baying of the hounds, a scarlet trail of blood in the frost.

In the faint, residual light he hadn't quite been able to shut out of his makeshift darkroom, Lawrence watched the images slowly emerge.

It was one of the things he loved most about photography, this magical moment of revelation. Alchemy. Beneath the water Selina's features appeared on the wet paper, taking shape, gathering clarity. Smiling at him.

That smile.

It had been far more dazzling than the diamonds her sister wore. She had come out of the house just ahead of the bride, flawless in pale green silk, but he could tell from the stiffness of her shoulders and the way her eyes kept darting to the huddle of pressmen that she was tense and on edge. He had dodged his way past the sharp elbows of the seasoned hacks, whistling Offenbach's Can-Can tune to catch her attention and as she saw him her rigid posture relaxed and her face lit up. That was the moment he had caught.

The first of many, throughout the day. Once she and the other bridesmaid had left in the huge black Daimler, he had hailed a taxi and followed on, without bothering to wait for the bride to appear. This had given him a head start over some of the other photographers, though there were plenty outside the Westminster chapel already, and an excited crowd of onlookers, members of the public who pored over the illustrated weekly papers and followed the antics of the Bright Young People, those who had a wistful fascination with the gilded lives of the aristocracy, or people who were simply passing by and couldn't resist stopping for the spectacle of a society wedding on a bright summer's day.

Peering into the developing tray balanced on the stovetop, he let out a breath he hadn't been aware of holding. The photographs were better than he'd dared hope and he murmured a 'thank you' to Sam, who had managed to get hold of an up-to-the-minute compact camera to lend him for the day. It was a Leica, the latest design from Germany, and used rolled film in place of the cumbersome plates Lawrence was used to working with, enabling him to shoot twice the number of frames with a fraction of the fuss. He had been suspicious of its simplicity, but the clarity of the images was remarkable, not just for such a small camera, but for any camera at all. The fast shutter speed had meant that even when Selina had turned her head it had somehow captured the motion, instead of just producing a blur of movement.

Looking at that last photograph he felt a sudden lurch, the sensation of missing a step in the dark. The moment when he had taken it came rushing back. It was after the service, when the wedding party had come out of the church. The bride and groom were in the foreground, of course, but he had framed the shot so that Selina was at the centre. He had begun whistling again just as he had taken it, and she had swung round towards the sound, knowing it was him. The camera had captured that second of recognition.

It was like a love letter.

He let out another breath, a sigh this time. How had it happened? How had he got to this place, with a girl like her? Sometimes, lying in bed in his stuffy room, the sound of other people's breathing filtering through the thin walls, he thought of her and was certain he'd imagined it all. Imagined sharing a cigarette with her in the undergrowth. Imagined running away from the party and kissing her on a rainy street. Imagined dinner and candlelight and shared confidences.

Here was the evidence that it was real.

And yet it was still impossible. A chance meeting that had led to an impulsive, illicit evening, that was all. A rash promise made and now fulfilled. It was their differences that attracted them to each other; the fascinating, magnetic pull of opposites, but those differences were too great to sustain anything more than a few spontaneous moments, secretly snatched. He had no place in her world, amongst her people, and no more did she belong in his. After today he wasn't even sure he'd see her again. She would be leaving London for the summer, like they all did; going back to the country estate she had talked about. Their paths, which had come together so unexpectedly, would diverge again, and revert to their rightful course.

Which was for the best.

As he lifted dripping sheets of photographic paper out of the developing fluid, dropping them into the stop bath (on the draining board) and then into the fixing solution (in the sink) he could feel the sweat dampening the hair at the back of his neck. He'd shut the skylight when he'd pinned the black crepe over it, and the landing was hot and airless, filled with the sulphurous smell of the developing chemicals. At any other time he might leave the photographs in the fixing solution and go outside for a cigarette, breathing in comforting nicotine and fresh air while the chemicals did their work, but there was no time for that now. If he was going to sell the photographs to one of the illustrated magazines, where he would get the best price, Sam had told him he needed to have them by seven o'clock at the latest.

When the process was finally finished he climbed up onto a chair and yanked away the black fabric, pushing up the glass and wincing in the sudden flood of evening light. Her face looked up at him from the images, laid out to dry on newspaper on the floor. He looked down at her – all the versions of her that he had captured that day, pinned like butterflies. In spite of the uncomfortable heat and his weariness, his stomach twisted with want.

It might be over, but it felt unfinished.

Stupid bastard, he said to himself, peeling off his sweat-soaked shirt and going out onto the landing, to the bathroom he and Sam shared with Mr Kaminiski and the Hicksons on the floor below. As if it ever could be *finished*. She wasn't Hannah from the fairground, with her knowing eyes and quick, grasping hands. She wasn't one of the girls who haunted the artists' lofts in Paris and Bloomsbury, drifting from couch to couch, bed to bed, not much caring who they sat for or slept with as long as they were provided with food and booze and kept warm when posing nude. He splashed his face with water, again and again. Straightening up he looked at his reflection in the small square of mirror and dragged a hand over his jaw. He needed a shave, and a haircut. He looked like a gypsy, or a bare-knuckle fighter in one of the less salubrious pubs around Smithfield Market.

His father's voice came back to him. *Your trouble is you've got ideas above your station, boy. You need to know your place.*

He turned away, sickened by the contrast between his own appearance and the men he had observed that day; seal-sleek, as well-groomed as race horses. He had found himself watching Rupert Carew in particular, and was taken aback by the loathing he felt for him; for his haughty self-assurance, his bland, superior face and plummy voice, clipped to the point of unintelligibility. He knew that none of these things were the real reason for his antipathy, though. He was a cold bastard. The idea of him with Selina was obscene.

Whereas the idea of you with Selina . . . ? A little voice inside his head mocked.

Back in his room he found a clean shirt hanging on the back of the door and felt a moment of grudging gratitude for Sam's insistence on paying Mrs Hickson to char for them and do the laundry. He didn't know what time it was, but could tell by the mauve sky that day was tipping into evening. Hurriedly he gathered up the photos and shoved them in a folder, slamming the door behind him and clattering down the stairs.

Outside the air was cool against his damp skin. He walked quickly, heading towards Russell Square where he was likely to find taxicabs coming and going from the smart hotels. It was a comfortable walk to Sam's office – a little under half an hour – but it was half an hour he couldn't afford to waste. More so than the money for the taxi.

As he turned into Bernard Street he saw one, but its 'for hire' flag wasn't displayed, so he kept walking. A few moments later he heard a shout behind him; someone calling his name in a voice that was unmistakable.

He turned.

The taxi had come to a halt at the side of the road and Selina was coming towards him – running – the breeze flattening the thin silk of her bridesmaid's dress against her body. His heart crashed.

'I was coming to see you.'

She was breathless, glitter-eyed, unsmiling. He wanted to take her in his arms and kiss her, right there on the street. It was out of the question, but the spectre of it – of them, embracing – seemed to hang in front of him. He didn't dare touch her, though their gazes locked.

'I'm going out,' he said, unnecessarily, holding up the folder. 'I need to hurry. I'm taking the photographs to Sam – he'll find the best buyer for them. If that's all right with you?'

She laughed shortly. 'Well, that depends on how awful I look . . .'

'You're beautiful. You're always beautiful, but today you were . . .' He shook his head, reaching for a word that didn't sound trite or insincere or trivial. Finding nothing.

'Can I see them?'

He thought quickly, his eyes leaving hers to dart to the taxicab still waiting at the kerb behind her. 'Can I appropriate your taxi and show you on the way? Sam needs to have them by seven o'clock. Once I've delivered them we could . . . go somewhere . . . ?'

As he said it he knew how desperate it sounded, and how unlikely. She was still wearing the dress she had worn for her sister's high profile society wedding. She could hardly risk being seen out drinking in the sort of places he frequented, and it would take more than a clean shirt for him to fit in at The Savoy.

'I can't.' They were standing a careful distance apart, but her eyes were still fixed on his, unblinking and urgent. 'I have a dinner arrangement.'

Of course she did. Disappointment knifed him in the guts. He gestured to the taxi. 'Can we share it?'

She nodded, and they hurried back to where it waited. He gave the address of Sam's office to the driver (who stared at him with such open curiosity that he might as well have come out and said 'What's a geezer like you doing with a fancy bird like her?') and climbed in beside her, handing her the folder.

'I'm sorry,' she said, keeping her voice low so that the driver couldn't hear through the glass. 'About dinner. Everyone's leaving town tomorrow, so it's the last time we'll see each other all summer. I can't cry off. But I wanted to come and say thank you, for being there today.'

'You haven't seen the photographs yet.'

She slid them out of the folder, but didn't look at them straight away.

'I don't have to see them to be grateful. Just you being there ... We spoke about it so briefly, but you understood, and remembered ...'

That almost made him laugh. As if he would forget.

The taxi was speeding down Gray's Inn Road. At this time of the evening the carts and drays and delivery vans had mostly finished their business; in spite of the time pressure he found himself wishing there was more traffic to hold them up. Beside him she had begun to look down at the photographs, slowly studying each one in turn, her hair falling forwards and obscuring her face with a veil of gold. He looked out of the window, waiting for her to say something, wondering if she was disappointed.

The seconds ticked by, marked by the click of the taxi's meter. The driver swung into Fleet Street, and Lawrence noticed an ornate clock with embellished gold hands suspended over the doorway of a building. Ten minutes to seven.

'We're nearly there.' His voice was hoarse. 'If you don't like them – if you don't want me to give them to Sam, say now.'

'They're wonderful.' She gathered the photographs together and slid them back into the folder. '*You're* wonderful. And I want every editor in London to know it.' Handing it back to him she leaned across to cup his cheek, and kissed him.

It was swift and fierce, over in a heartbeat. If the taxi driver had looked in his mirror he would have seen nothing too untoward, nothing to shock or shatter a reputation, but Lawrence felt the urgency in the press of her mouth; the longing and regret. When she pulled away her aquamarine eyes had a brilliant glitter and her cheeks were flushed.

'Thank you.'

The taxi turned into a narrow street between tall, serious-looking buildings. The low evening sun was visible through the gap between them at the far end, its rosy beams giving everything a sense of finality. His mouth throbbed. Frustration tightened his jaw, his chest.

He took her hand and lifted it to his lips; an old-fashioned gesture, dressed up as courtesy but masking so much more. Turning it over he pressed a kiss into her palm and folded her fingers around it.

'Will I see you again?'

Her voice held a note of despair that echoed his own.

'I . . . don't know.'

Except he did. He knew that the chance of their worlds colliding again was vanishingly remote.

'I want to,' she whispered fiercely.

Hope burned like brandy in his throat. The taxi was slowing down, bumping over cobbles. The squat, square building that housed Sam's offices was visible ahead, the windows of its upper floors thrown open against the warm evening. His thoughts jumped around, chaotic and impossible to grasp.

'Can you stay? In London, when your parents go to back to—?'

She shook her head rapidly, cutting him off. 'The house will be closed up. It's not possible.'

Their hands remained clasped, fingers twisting together on the seat, out of sight of the driver. In a few seconds they would be there. The journey would be over.

'Come to Blackwood.'

'*What?*'

He thought he'd misheard. Or misunderstood. An image

swam into his head: himself, seated at an endless dining table laid with silver and damask, beneath the glacial stares of her parents. 'What about your family?'

She gave a gasp of laughter. 'They won't be there. They're going to Scotland. I'm supposed to be going too, but I'll make an excuse – say I'm ill or something. The servants have a fortnight off, so the house will be empty. We can camp out and fend for ourselves, like gypsies.'

'Are you serious?'

He needed to know. The moment of parting was almost upon them. He could feel resistance slipping away, common sense dissolving, like it did on boozy nights in smoky bars when he just kept drinking, even though he knew he would pay the price in the morning.

'I think I am . . .' Her eyes had a feverish glitter as they searched his. 'Serious and possibly quite mad and maybe the slightest bit sloshed too, but I don't care. It's summer and we're young and alive and I don't want to waste any of those things. I don't want to waste endless beautiful days making polite conversation with people I don't care for. I know it's wicked to lie, but it's more wicked to wish away precious time, isn't it? A week. Just one week off from duty and responsibility, for fun and adventure and pure selfish hedonism. A week of living, instead of just existing.' She laughed, a little wildly, as the taxi juddered to a halt outside Sam's building. 'Please, Lawrence – say you'll come.'

And so he did.

Of course he did.

Hill View
Club Road
Maymyo
Burma

12th April 1936

Dearest Darling Alice,

I'm sitting on the verandah of our new (temporary) home
and thinking of you. It's Easter Sunday and I believe that
Aunt Miranda, Uncle Lionel and Cousin Archie have come to
stay at Blackwood. I do hope you're having a nice time and
are not feeling too overwhelmed by 'Athertonness'. They do
mean well, of course ... but I am sending you strength and
support across the miles — I hope you can sense that, and
know how much I long to be with you.

It's been the oddest time. We arrived in Mandalay last
week, and I must admit I felt rather wretched — still
getting over the Rangoon fever, I expect. After a sticky
two days in an hotel beside the old fort (the less said
about *that* the better!) Papa managed to secure a sweet
little bungalow here in Maymyo, which is a hill station
about an hour's drive away from the city.

It feels curiously English. Not just because it's where
all the Europeans come to escape the heat (which is at its
peak just now) but because it's green and lush and shaded by
pine forests, and the resiny scent is wafted on the delicious
breeze. The streets of the little town all have English names
and it feels very odd to see signs saying 'Downing Street'
and 'The Mall' in a place that looks more like a Wiltshire
village than London, but is actually on the other side of the
world from both. Even the clock in the town centre chimes
like Big Ben!

Our house is perfectly darling, and from the outside looks
just like something one might stumble across on a country
walk in Sussex or somewhere seasidey. We have three servants;
Ba Nayar is the cook and Thant and Lwin look after the house,
and they are all marvellously kind and friendly. The owner,
an Englishman, is currently in Ceylon, but he works for the
Motoring Association and has a little study room at the back
of the house where I found this typewriter! I thought it
would be rather fun to see if I could get the hang of it, so
I've set it up on a card table out here. I hope you don't mind
me practising on you!

There is a very established British community here, with
golf courses and polo grounds, all of which is useful to
Papa. In the evenings he likes to go up to the Club to talk
with the other men whose business has brought them out here.
I prefer to stay here, unless he needs me. The evenings are
heaven, with the sunset turning the sky into a kaleidoscope
of pink and orange and crimson and the green parakeets

settling themselves in the trees and the noise of the jungle just audible above the music of the gramophone. I always intend to read, but I'm so terribly lazy that I usually just sit, watching the first stars appear and thinking of you.

I miss you, darling. But I hope and pray and truly believe that soon this will be over and we'll be back together again.

Until then, my best and fondest love

Mama

xxxxx

13

Mr Patterson

May 1936

Arthur Patterson was not much of a drinking man. He had seen too many fall foul of the habit – his own father, for one – and had to deal with green-faced boys unfit for work too often not to be wary of overindulgence. Sometimes, when Mary had been alive, they would share a bottle or two of stout on a Saturday evening, or a small sherry on a Sunday before lunch, and he missed those days. Missed her. The gardener's cottage at Blackwood was large, as these things went, reflecting the significance of the gardens in which it sat and the status of the man in charge of them, and its emptiness oppressed him now. It wasn't the beer that drew him out to the Blackwood Arms on a Thursday evening, but the company. (And the surprisingly fierce competition in the dominoes league.)

His work was governed by the seasons, and looking out for the tiny changes they brought was second nature to him, as instinctive as breathing. The weekly walk through the park into the village was part of the pleasure of the evening. He liked to vary the route he took – sometimes walking through the woods to the west of the lake, sometimes taking the weed-choked avenue that wound its way through the neglected garden – according to the weather and his mood. The way through the garden was quicker, but on summer evenings when the setting sun glinted through the leathery leaves of rhododendron and azalea and blue shadows gathered on the overgrown pathways, it was all too easy to fancy he saw things: pale figures flitting at the edge of his vision, pushing wheelbarrows, clipping at hedges. Names came back to him then – names he hadn't spoken for years, which were now carved in stone on the memorial by the village pump. Before going into the public bar at the Blackwood Arms he would make a point of looking across the street and tipping his hat to it. To them, because they were not forgotten.

Regardless of the route he had taken to get there, he always came back the same way, sticking to the road that led to the main gates of the park and walking along the carriage drive towards the house. The parkland was too uneven to traverse safely in the dark, when a foot caught in a rabbit hole would result in a slow and painful limp home, and it gave him the opportunity to keep an eye on the ancient horse chestnut trees along the drive and make sure their dipping branches needed no work. Those trees were as much a part of Blackwood as the stones of the house itself, it seemed to him. He loved them through all the seasons, but never more so than in late May when their candle-like blooms glowed palely in the dusk, lighting the way.

Last week they hadn't quite been open. As he walked back, between hedgerows that frothed white with May blossom (filling the evening with a scent that reminded him of the Yardley soap he used to buy for Mary at Christmas) he savoured the anticipation of witnessing one of the year's most pleasurable milestones. He whistled softly, warmed inside by two pints of ale and a long-awaited dominoes victory over Eric Goodwin. A three-quarter moon sailed serenely above the dark outline of the woods, giving enough light to cast shadows like spilled ink on the road's uneven surface, silvering the hawthorn.

From somewhere in the distance he heard a faint, plaintive cry, and stopped whistling to listen. An owl perhaps? Not the sound he recognized, but at this time of year they'd have babies, which made everything different. He smiled fondly to himself as he walked on, his thoughts drifting back to when Paul was born. Mary had changed overnight from a girl to a woman; it was the thing that had struck him most forcefully (well, that and a great sledgehammer of love) when he was finally allowed upstairs to see her, holding the swaddled form of their newborn son. He had been in awe of her.

The sound came again, slicing into his thoughts. Not

bird nor animal, he realized, but human. A voice, calling for help.

He quickened his pace, not quite breaking into a run. Sciatica had made that unwise, and he felt a certain resignation – a reluctance, if he was honest. Almost twenty years after the war and you still came across them from time to time, sleeping in outbuildings, slumped in hedgerows, the worse for drink: the lost ones, who'd never quite managed to come back properly. Rounding a bend in the lane the gatehouse came into view and he heard another cry.

There was a figure on the ground: a huddle of black, that made him think of an injured crow. Beside it, a little distance away, a bicycle lay on its side.

The governess. She had come back after Easter with a bicycle – he knew that because he had been asked to collect her suitcase from the station master's office in the motor – which she used to get to evening meetings of some organization she belonged to (not the WI, which had always been good enough for Mary). He supposed she must have been returning from one and taken the turning into the gates too sharply. She was sitting up, bent over her outstretched leg.

'Mr Patterson! Oh, thank heavens!'

She was a good deal more enthusiastic to see him than usual, he noted, going towards her. The thin moonlight picked out the white oval of her face, hovering between a peculiar pancake-like hat and a black shirt, buttoned to the neck. A silver badge glinted there.

'Are you all right?'

'I fear not. The wretched contraption quite went from beneath me. My foot got caught in the pedal.' Her voice wavered. 'It's almost certainly broken. The pain is quite indescribable.'

'Can you walk back up to the house?'

'Of course not! If I could, do you think I would be sitting here like this?'

He went over to the bicycle, which seemed more approachable than its rider. The contents of the basket – a sturdy handbag and several copies of a flimsy newspaper – had spilled out onto the gravel. He replaced them and picked up the bicycle, pushing it backwards and forwards experimentally.

'She seems to be in one piece . . . How about I ride up to the house and get someone to phone for Dr Pembridge? I'll send Jimmy down with the motor.'

'And leave me here alone?' The governess gave a tremulous moan. 'Oh – very well, but do hurry up. I'm chilled to the bone, and it's pitch dark.'

What rubbish, Patterson thought, shrugging off his jacket to put around her shoulders. It wasn't dark at all, not with a moon like that – the parish lantern, his mother used to call it – which gave enough light to read the newspaper in the bicycle basket. *The Blackshirt*, it was called: *The Patriotic Worker's Paper. Onwards to Fascist Revolution!* declared the headline. That sounded like a lot of rubbish too.

He reassured her he'd be as quick as he could, and set off

up the drive. He didn't quite keep his word though. The sight of the avenue of horse chestnut trees, their candles luminous in the gentle twilight, distracted him from the governess's calamity, and was too magical to hurry.

Alice discovered Miss Lovelock's misfortune the following morning.

Polly pulled back the curtains and she opened her eyes to bright sunlight and her breakfast porridge on a tray.

'Thought I'd let you sleep in a bit today,' Polly said, coming to sit down. 'No lessons for you this morning. Miss Lovelock's gone and broken her ankle, falling off that bicycle of hers. Luckily it happened just by the gate and Mr Patterson found her on his way back from dominoes night at the pub. Dr Pembridge came out and bandaged it up. She's resting today, though I suppose she'll be able to start your lessons again on Monday. No afternoon walks for a while, though . . .'

It was a lot to take in, especially alongside the special treat of breakfast in bed and the fact that it was accompanied by a lot of other instructions and information, because Polly was leaving to catch the half past nine train to London, to visit a friend who was poorly. She bustled around, distracted and a little flustered, laying out Alice's clothes and telling her to make sure Ellen brought up her tea later. 'Don't you be shy about ringing the bell or going down to find her if it doesn't appear – she's got a head like a sieve, that one. Not that I imagine she'll have much time for daydreaming today.

Miss Lovelock's had her up and down like a fiddler's elbow already this morning, fetching tea and toast and hot water cans and whatnot.'

'What shall I do? If there's no lessons, and no walk?'

The question seemed to take Polly by surprise. She paused for a moment, shaking the creases out of a cotton dress.

'Why don't you go out to the garden and find Mr Patterson? See if he needs any help. There's always plenty that wants doing at this time of year – I'm sure he'll be glad of an extra pair of hands.'

The lawn mowing machine was a temperamental beast. Patterson took personal charge of its care and maintenance, not trusting its delicate mechanism to Jimmy's careless hands, but even so, it coughed and wheezed its way across Blackwood's lawns, frequently coming to a spluttering standstill and having to be gently coaxed back into action.

It had been a state of the art machine in its time, but that time had been in 1904 (according to the faded sales leaflet, still pinned up on the board in the gardeners' bothy) and the years had taken their toll. Patterson knew that feeling. Usually at the start of the summer he looked out for advertisements in *Horticulture Week* for the lighter, more efficient machines now on the market, to show to Lady Lennox, but no purchase was ever forthcoming. This year he would be keeping his opinion about whether the Atco was superior to the Qualcast to himself. The state of the lawns was the least of Lady Lennox's troubles, by his reckoning.

With a petrol-reeking belch the lawn mower shuddered to a halt. Sighing, Patterson went round to crouch beside it, and out of the corner of his eye caught a flicker of movement. He turned his head. Not one of the lost lads this time, but a real person, flesh and blood; Miss Selina's girl. She must have come through the passage from the kitchen yard and was hesitating in the doorway. He raised his hand in brief welcome then returned to his task, not wanting to scare her off.

Shy little thing, she was – nothing like her mother in that respect. He smiled to remember Miss Selina at that age, tearing across the lawn swinging a cricket bat and begging the under-gardeners to bowl for her, or hiding up in the branches of the big cedar of Lebanon and firing arrows from her brother's bow at them as they worked, her laughter echoing down. Little monkey. His smile subsided. Looking up he saw that Alice was coming hesitantly towards him.

'Now then . . . I wonder if that might be the problem . . . ?'

Speaking as if to himself, he bent to adjust the valve behind the petrol tank. 'Funny old girl, this one. You know, when I started my first job they had donkeys to pull the mowers. Cussed creatures they could be, but I reckon none of them were as tricky as this old lady here. If she doesn't feel like working, it seems there's not much I can do to make her work.'

'Donkeys?'

'That's right. Tiny hooves, they have, like teacups, which don't make a mark on the grass.' He gave the valve a final tweak and took a rag from his pocket to wipe his fingers. 'How's that governess of yours?'

'Resting. She's broken her ankle.'

'Broken, is it? I thought it might be.'

'And Polly's gone to visit a friend who's poorly.'

'Has she now? So you've been left on your own?'

She nodded, making those dark curls bounce. It wasn't just her temperament that was unlike her mother's, it was her appearance too. Unlike any of them, as those in the Blackwood Arms had been quick to point out. Blond as Vikings, the Lennoxes were – everyone used to remark on it, when the three youngsters stood together by the Christmas tree for the servants' boxes or appeared at the village fête; blue-eyed as angels. Carew was a fair chap, too (in colouring, at least). 'Been taken from the gypsies, that one,' old Joshua Vetch had said, with a sly look over his pint pot. Patterson had turned his back on the old curmudgeon and said nothing.

But he remembered that summer.

She had always been one to push the boundaries, Miss Selina had, especially after Master Howard died. That carefree nature he remembered in the child had turned into something more reckless, more dangerous. Mary had doted on the little girl and kept a jar of barley sugar on the kitchen shelf especially for her. He'd always thought it a blessing that she hadn't lived to see the things they said about young Miss Selina in the newspapers. The photographs they printed. Drinking. Dancing. Nightclubs. Mary would have disapproved.

He supposed he did too, though it wasn't his place. He made a point of skimming over the society columns when he sat down with his morning brew, but he used the old newspapers for potting on seedlings and it was harder to ignore what was right there under his nose as he worked.

Like that summer, the one before Miss Selina got married.

He had tried to avoid them as much as he could. He'd tried not to notice, but it was impossible not to see them sometimes as they wandered through the gardens together holding hands, or ran down to the boathouse. One evening, walking down to the Blackwood Arms, he had heard gramophone music, sweet and soaring, drifting across the lake from the Chinese Tea House. He had seen them dancing together on its wooden deck, bodies close, heads touching, fair against dark.

He'd been very dark-haired, that lad.

He blinked and cleared his throat, dragging himself back to the present. To the little girl in front of him.

'Well then. Looks like I've got myself a new under-gardener.' He smiled. 'That's grand. If you're going to be working here, I reckon you can spend your first morning the same way all my apprentices do. So, are you ready for a tour of the gardens?'

It was a magical kingdom: Sleeping Beauty's garden before the handsome prince hacked his way through the thorny forest to wake her with a kiss.

She followed Mr Patterson past towering hedges – sprawling

now, though they used to be sharply clipped into the shapes of chess pieces, he told her – along overgrown paths, through gates that creaked on rusty hinges and led to moss-covered fountains and shaded pools where the water was green and thick with leaves. He pulled back curtains of ivy to reveal statues and benches, where the Lennoxes of a hundred years ago would have stopped to rest and admire their elegant pleasure grounds. That was what they called the gardens, Mr Patterson said – pleasure grounds – and they had employed twenty gardeners to maintain them. They picked their way carefully over banks of brambles that rampaged over borders and she followed him through a forest of shrubbery, which blocked out the sunlight but blazed with gaudy flowers in crimson and purple. Emerging again she saw an expanse of water, mottled green with water lily leaves. A wooden bridge, delicately arched, stretched across it to a little wooded island in the centre.

'Oh – a house!'

It was half hidden by foliage and tattered blossom, but its roof was visible, sweeping down steeply and then flicking up at the eaves, like an exotic hat. Its walls had been painted turquoise blue, its windows scarlet, but the colours were faded now, the paint peeling and mossy.

'It's called the Chinese Tea House,' Patterson said, with satisfaction. 'I thought you'd like it.'

'What is it for?'

'Well, decoration as much as anything, I suppose. But also to show visitors how fashionable the family were, and how well-travelled. The ladies would have come down here for tea on summer afternoons. It's designed to catch the afternoon sun on the front – see? – but you could draw the blinds to keep the inside cool and shady in the hotter weather. Imagine that ... a procession of maids coming all the way from the house with cups and saucers – special Chinese-style ones – and a spirit kettle and all the plates of sandwiches and cakes ...'

'Did my Mama used to have tea here?'

Mr Patterson looked away, fishing in his pocket for his handkerchief, and she wondered what she had said to embarrass him. 'Well now, maybe when she was very young. Before the war. There wasn't the staff afterwards for all that fetching and carrying, see. That's when it all fell into disrepair. I don't think anyone's used it since then, really ...'

He trailed off, burying his face in his handkerchief as he blew his nose loudly. Alice turned back to the little house. 'Can I look inside?'

'I daresay you can look, but the door's kept locked and I don't have the key. If the blinds are down I don't suppose you'll be able to see much.'

But she was already going towards the wooden bridge, the long grass whipping her bare legs as she ran. She was aware of Mr Patterson following, but at a distance. He called to her as she reached the bridge: 'Mind yourself, now ... That wood might be rotten. Watch your step!'

It didn't look rotten. It was dry and sun-bleached, warm

beneath her hand. A sweet, cloying smell hung over the little island, coming, she realized, from the remaining cup-shaped blossoms on the tree beside the house, and the petals that had fallen onto the earth beneath it, their waxy whiteness creased with brown.

At the front of the house there was a wooden platform that extended out to jut over the water. The cream-coloured blinds at the windows were shut, just as Mr Patterson had said, giving the impression of closed eyes, as if the little house was sleeping with the sun on its face. She tried the door, but he was right about that too. Wistfully she traced her finger over the square brass keyhole, then moved across to press her face against the glass, trying to peer through the narrow gap at the side of the blind.

A glimpse. A sliver: enticing and exasperating. Jade green walls. A glimmer of gold, or brass – a gramophone horn? She went to the other window to see if she could see any more, but it was similarly frustrating. Cobwebs laced the glass, studded with dead flies.

'I can't see anything.'

Reluctantly she turned away. Mr Patterson was standing at the other side of the bridge, and she just caught an expression of great sadness on his face before his smile brushed it away.

'Well, I don't suppose there's that much to see. And by my reckoning it's way past lunchtime. Do you like cheese sandwiches?'

*

They ate on upturned apple crates outside the gardener's bothy. The cheese sandwiches Mr Patterson cut in his little cottage kitchen were a different breed altogether from the crustless fingers Alice was used to: thick wedges of bread spread with butter from Polly's father's farm and crumbling slices of cheese, brought out on a seedling tray with lemon barley water and a slice of fruitcake. The day was ripe with the promise of summer. The main gardens (*pleasure grounds*) were so overgrown that they kept out the warmth and brightness of the sun, but the kitchen garden embraced it within its rosy walls. That's what it was designed to do, Mr Patterson told her, sipping his glass of barley water. The walls kept out the wind and were heated by the sun, so it was always warmer there than anywhere else.

It looked completely different from the last time she had been in there, in the winter with Miss Lovelock. The beds that had been bare and brown were now frilled with green. Mr Patterson pointed out currant bushes, tiny pea and bean plants and lines of lacy carrot leaves. Papery poppies in sweetshop colours bloomed by the fence around the cottage.

'Still no lilies, mind,' Mr Patterson remarked with a smile.

Alice thought back to that cold, bleak day. It seemed like years ago. She felt a sudden stab of homesickness at the renewed realization of how long Mama had been away. 'I needed to find them to solve a puzzle.'

'A puzzle?'

'A clue.' A robin had kept them company as they ate, hopping from the top of a glass frame to a spade handle to the edge of a plant pot as his boldness grew. 'In a treasure hunt. Mama was doing one for me, but I didn't tell Miss Lovelock. That's why I couldn't say.'

'I see. A treasure hunt sounds grand. Did you find the treasure?'

'No.' She frowned, picking a currant from her cake and dropping it for the robin. 'I don't think it's that sort of treasure hunt. It's not the sort where one clue leads you to the next one – she wanted to make it last longer, you see. She's telling me a story, about before I was born, but so far there's only been two clues. I know that she must be very busy and there won't be much time for writing, but I think . . . I think she might have forgotten.'

Mama's letters still came, but the lengthy gaps between them seemed to mirror the distance between Blackwood and Burma. The last one had not been written in Mama's usual turquoise ink, but on a typewriter she'd found in the house they were renting. Alice didn't blame her for wanting to use it (she would, too) but it made the letter seem a little more impersonal somehow. And there had been no mention of the treasure hunt. No clue.

Mr Patterson had finished his fruitcake. For long moments he said nothing as he took the pipe from his pocket and began the unhurried ritual of packing it with tobacco from a worn leather pouch. At length, he nodded in the direction of the glass frames, like miniature greenhouses, that were lined up alongside the path, their lids propped up to show the pots inside.

'See those there?' He pointed his pipe at the small shoots poking their way through the soil in the pots. 'Those are tomatoes – or will be soon enough. I was planting those seeds that day you came by, with Miss Whatshername.' He paused to light the pipe, his moustache bristling as he puffed. 'Checked them every day since, I have. Nothing to see for weeks, just bare soil, for so long that you might believe that they would never grow, never mind produce anything you could have in a nice salad.'

He sucked on the pipe, until a thin column of smoke twisted up into the air and dissolved.

'Every year it's the same, but I knew they'd appear eventually. When they were ready. We can't see it, but there's plenty going on under that soil. We don't know what, exactly, but we don't have to, see? All we have to do is wait and have faith. Everything happens in its own time.'

Alice thought of the map on the schoolroom wall, the stretches of ocean Mama had crossed, the thin blue squiggle of river she had sailed up to Mandalay. It looked so simple on the map, but of course it wasn't like that really. The distance was incomprehensible, the journey Mama's letters had to make was complicated. But another one would come.

All Alice had to do was wait, and have faith. Sitting with the warm sun on her face and breathing in the woody, comforting scent of Mr Patterson's pipe it seemed easier, somehow.

At the end of the afternoon he delivered Alice back to the servants' door, with a basket of little new potatoes and an early lettuce from the glasshouse. 'I was about to send out a search party,' Ellen grumbled, taking Alice's grimy hand and recoiling sharply. 'Saints alive! Didn't you have a spade she could use for digging, Mr Patterson?'

The old gardener gave Alice a wink. 'You tell her, Alice. Honest hard work, that is.'

Alice held up the basket. 'I dug these up. Is Polly back yet?'

Ellen glanced back along the servants' passageway. 'No. Not yet. You can leave those potatoes with me and run along upstairs to get those hands scrubbed. I'll bring your tea up in a minute.'

Alice thanked Mr Patterson and did as she was told, though not at a run. The house felt stale and airless as she trailed up the back stairs; the light muted, sound hushed compared to outside. She paused at her favourite place on the stairway's bend, listening. She could just make out the sound of Ellen's voice talking to Mr Patterson. A burst of faint music reached her from Miss Lovelock's wireless, and then, from downstairs, another sound. Like muffled weeping.

Alice's grimy fingers tightened on the banister. The air stirred a little as Ellen shut the outside door. Her footsteps echoed along the passageway, and a moment later the kitchen door clicked firmly closed, shutting off all further sound.

The day had been an unexpected treat, full of surprises, but as the sun slid down towards the tops of the trees, filling the nursery with mellow gold light, the happiness ebbed away to leave a strange, empty feeling. Alice ate the fish cakes that Ellen brought up, but without enthusiasm. The pain in her tummy was back, and the tightness in her throat that made it hard to swallow. She left half of her food, and braced herself to be scolded, but Ellen took the plate without comment when she came up, and went along the corridor to run the bath. Alice shrank inside at the thought of undressing in front of her, and felt a rush of relief when she came back a few minutes later to take the tray away.

'I've put a towel on the rail. Mind you leave the door open a crack. Don't want you drowning while I'm in charge.'

There wasn't much chance of that. Ellen had only run a few inches of water into the bath, whereas Polly always let her have it nice and deep. Alice sat, trickling rivulets from the sponge over her raised knees and thinking about the garden. It was strange to realize that it had been there all this time, just a few hundred yards away, but closed up and hidden, like a secret. Strange to think that it was there now, being reclaimed by the shadows and the silence they had left in their wake, closing in on itself once more.

She rested her chin on her knees, picturing it as it must have been sixty years ago, when Grandfather was a little boy. Had he played hide and seek with his brothers and sisters along the paths and between the bushes? Had their nanny taken them down to the Chinese House for tea sometimes? Had Mama's? She decided that she would write, that evening before bed, and tell Mama about Miss Lovelock's accident and what she had done in place of lessons. She would ask if Mama remembered the tea house; if she had spent summer afternoons there when she was younger. Alice didn't think the lack of servants would stop her from being in such a magical place. She wouldn't have gone there to be served afternoon tea anyway – that wasn't what Mama was like. She would have gone to be alone, to read or doze in the sun, or – she remembered the glimpse of brass she'd caught at the edge of the window – to listen to music.

And quite suddenly she thought of the box she had found in Mama's wardrobe, with its hoard of mysterious treasures. A jolt went through her, as if she had accidentally touched the hot tap, making ripples spread across the surface of the water. Hurriedly she clambered out of the bath, splashing water onto the floor as she grabbed the towel and wrapped it around herself, running on wet tiptoes along the corridor to the night nursery.

She slid the box out from under the bed and lifted the lid, sifting through the contents to find the brass key. Finding it, she held it up to the fading light, rubbing her thumb over the embossed pattern – a pattern she recognized now as Chinese. A shiver of excitement spread goosebumps over her damp skin.

That night, after she'd written to Mama, she switched off the light and lay down in the summer dark, aware of the huge sleeping house around her, and beyond it, the garden. Reaching out she picked up the key she had left on her nightstand. It was cool against her palm. Comforting. A proper excuse to find Mr Patterson again tomorrow and ask to go back to the Chinese House.

She fell asleep holding it, like a talisman.

*

She woke in a pulse of panic, tugged sharply from sleep like a hooked fish. A figure loomed over her. Fingers touched her hair. Fear catapulted her into a sitting position.

'Shhh, love . . . It's all right. I didn't mean to wake you.'

Polly's voice.

The nursery was pearly with early morning light. Polly was nothing more than a shadow, her face impossible to make out as she stroked Alice's hair. Even though it was only Polly, the sluice of alarm hadn't quite abated. Alice groped for the key.

'What's happened?'

'Nothing. Nothing's happened, love. You go back to sleep. Here – shall I take that . . . ?'

She was looking at Alice's hand. Alice held the key more tightly.

'Is it morning?'

'It is, but it's very early. Not time for you to be awake yet.'

'But I am awake. Is it Mama? Has something happened?'

Flashes of fear were exploding in her head, each one illuminating a different disaster. Bandits. A tropical storm. Fire.

With a resigned sigh, Polly lowered herself to sit on the edge of the bed. 'Oh Alice . . . You've caught me out good and proper. I'd never make much of a criminal, would I?' She pulled an envelope from the pocket of her apron. 'I have heard from your Mama, as a matter of fact, but nothing bad. I'm trying to do this blessed treasure hunt, that's all.' She laughed softly. 'You don't make it easy, you know. I was looking for that.' She nodded to the key. 'It was supposed to be in the box with the other things.'

'It was. I took it out last night. It's for the Chinese Tea House, isn't it? Mr Patterson showed it to me.'

Polly laughed again, throwing up her hands. 'Well, that's that then! I give up. I'll have to tell your Mama that you got this one without even reading the clue!'

Alice wriggled down under the sheet again, a sudden flood of relief and happiness making her shivery. 'Can I read it anyway?'

The fold of paper in the envelope was torn at the edges, and heavily creased. Opening it up, Alice found a sketchily drawn map, with faint, spidery words written underneath.

Take the map
And the key
And follow me

'She asked me to put the key in the envelope, see? But first I needed it to put the clue in the Chinese House.' Polly shook her head sadly. 'I should have waited until later, but I wanted you to have it when you woke up. I had no idea you'd be clutching the blasted thing. Gone and ruined this one, haven't I?'

'You haven't.' Alice looked at the map, working out its features: the walled kitchen garden where she'd eaten her sandwiches yesterday, the iron gate into the main garden and the tunnel of tall yews. She recognized the Italian garden with the pool at its centre, the goddess statue Mr Patterson had revealed from behind curtains of ivy and the big banks of gaudy-flowered bushes by the lake. Mama had drawn the little bridge and marked the island with a large, shaky cross. 'Have you got the treasure letter here? I *do* want to go to the Chinese Tea House, but would it be cheating to read it now?'

Polly slid another envelope from her pocket. 'I don't suppose so. And it would certainly save me a long walk. Here—' She held it out to Alice. 'You can read it while I go and make a pot of tea. I'm good for nothing until I've had two cups.'

Alice shoved the pillow into a wedge behind her and opened the letter. It was typewritten, but her brief prick of disappointment was forgotten as she began to read.

Darling Alice,

I know you've been dying to explore the gardens so I thought you might enjoy looking for this clue — and I know you'll adore the Chinese Tea House. Isn't it perfect? I believe it was built in my grandparents' day, when the fashion for all things Eastern began. They made the lake by widening the river (cleverly leaving that little island) and made the sweet house as a backdrop for the lovely blossoming trees. I'm cursing myself for having been so hopelessly slow with my clues, because I have a feeling that the blossom will mostly be over by now, which is such a shame. Out here I've lost track of the lovely English seasons.

Anyway, like all fashionable things, the Chinese Tea House

fell out of favour once the novelty had worn off and when I was a little girl it was hardly ever used for the purpose for which it had been intended (which was, I suppose, taking tea). Howard and his friends used to go down there after dinner to play cards and be riotous without disturbing The Grands, which is how the gramophone came to be down there (I suppose no one could quite bear to take it away after he died).

I had rather forgotten about it until that summer before you were born, when I came to spend some time on my own at Blackwood. I was supposed to go to Scotland with my parents, as I always did, to stay with the Rutherfords at Inverosse. I always dreaded it. There were very few young people there and they were not my sort at all — hearty, outdoor types who relished the chance to stride out in all weathers across the grouse moors and slaughter as much wildlife as possible. Usually Aunt Miranda was there too, which was at least someone to talk to (it was the only time we were remotely glad of each other's company) but that summer she had left for her honeymoon and was enjoying the sights and the warmth of Italy.

Perhaps that played a part in my decision to cry off. I resented the fact that she should be seeing Rome and Florence and Venice while I was stuck swatting at midges in Scotland again. My friends were doing far more thrilling things. Flick had a glamorous godmother who had escaped some scandal or other and taken up residence in Cap Ferrat, and she went to spend the summer with her. Theo, as a man, was able to go

wherever he pleased, without need of consent or chaperone —
another thing I resented. As London emptied at the end of
July I felt that life was slipping through my fingers and that
if I didn't catch hold of it I would regret it for ever.

And so I did something terribly wicked. The evening before
we were due to leave for Scotland I said I felt unwell and
excused myself halfway through dinner — a shameful lie. The
following morning, I got Polly to tell my mother that I had
been terribly ill through the night — ptomaine poisoning —
and wouldn't be able to travel. Darling Polly. As you know,
she's as honest as the day is long and hated being part
of a deception. I hated involving her, but the annual trip
to Scotland was the time when the house was closed up and
the servants given a fortnight off, and I knew The Grands
wouldn't consider leaving me behind unless she was there to
look after me.

Of course, my mother made the most frightful fuss, but she
couldn't bear anything to do with sickness so only came as
far as the bedroom door to peer at me reproachfully with a
handkerchief over her mouth. There was much talk of calling
Dr Pembridge, and then further argument about delaying their
departure for a few days until I was well enough to go with
them, but luckily Grandfather was far too fond of shooting
to consider losing a moment, and Grandmama simply hated
travelling without him. And so finally it was agreed that
they would go, as planned, leaving me in Polly's more than
capable hands.

At long last I watched the Daimler make its way up the

drive, bearing Grandmama and Grandfather away to Salisbury
to catch the first of several trains to Scotland. Lying in bed
I listened to the servants moving through the house, closing
shutters and draping dustsheets over furniture. One by one,
they left too — to go back to their families or, in Denham's
case, to a bed and breakfast by the sea, where he could be
looked after for a change — until by the evening all was
still and quiet and only Polly remained.

She's such an angel, and so unused to dishonesty that
she had begun to believe she was staying with me. I had to
convince her that I would be perfectly fine on my own, and
that it was what I wanted, but I don't think I could have
persuaded her to go if she had been going any further than
her parents' farm on the other side of the park. Eventually
she left, promising to come up regularly with supplies of
milk and bread, and I stood on the front steps and watched
her walk down the drive with her basket on her arm until
she'd disappeared from view. And then I went inside, shut the
door and stood in the great big empty hallway of the great
big empty house. Entirely, deliciously, illicitly alone.

14

A String of Golden Days

August 1925

The summer, until then so damp and disappointing, produced a sudden spell of glorious weather. The timing was perfect, almost as if it was intended especially for them, as a personal blessing. When she looked back later (as she sometimes did, no matter how hard she tried not to) Selina would see that time at Blackwood as sealed off from reality, subject to a sort of enchantment. A time of awakening and startling discovery.

They had made their plans by stealth, in letters, but his arrival – a day early, just after Polly had left – took her by surprise. He had been in Guildford, delivering a painting, and arriving at the station to return to London had heard an announcement for the train to Salisbury. He had boarded it on impulse, changing to the branch line to Hindbury as she'd instructed and walking across the park in the lilac dusk. Selina had been in the bath, blotting out the eerie silence of the empty house with the gramophone, and had not heard the distant jangle of the bell down in the basement. It was only when the music slowed into silence that she heard the echo of footsteps in the hall below and realized she wasn't alone.

Her mind instantly conjured scenes from her darkest nightmares, and the extent of her isolation had come crashing into her consciousness. There was no one to come to her aid, no one to hear her scream. Snatching a silk kimono she had pinched from Miranda's room and shrugging it onto her wet body she crept out into the corridor, hiding behind a pillar to peer over the balustrade and down the sweep of the staircase. He was standing at the bottom, his white shirt pale in the dim blue light and as she looked down, his voice drifted up, audible over the frantic hammer of her heart.

Hello?

Terror gave way to relief. Joy. With a cry she rushed down the stairs to throw herself into his arms, and they kissed and laughed and tried to speak.

'I'm a day early—'

'I thought you were an intruder.'

'Sorry. I tried to telephone from the station. But—' Holding her face in his hands he kissed her fiercely. 'I *could* have been an intruder. The door downstairs was unlocked.'

She gave a groan. As she was leaving Polly had told her to

250

bolt it, but she'd forgotten. The responsibility of managing the house was strange to her.

'I'm so glad you're here.'

'Thank God for that. I didn't know whether to come. I didn't know if you were alone.'

'I'm alone.'

She hadn't been able to imagine him there. Since she had left him in the taxi that day, after Miranda's wedding, she had been torn between excitement and horror at the thought of what she'd done, inviting him to Blackwood. Even when she'd been writing to him, giving him the date of her parents' departure, the details of train times and the station name, there had been a part of her that didn't believe he would come. That didn't want him to. She feared that what had been exciting in London might collapse into awkwardness at Blackwood; that the words that had tumbled out of them would dry up in the oppressive silence of aloneness and the magic would turn out to be an illusion, but as he cupped her face and kissed her again she knew that she had worried for nothing. The rightness of him being there made her blood sing.

'Come on, come upstairs.' She pulled him forwards. 'Where are your things?'

'I don't have any. Just my camera, and a few supplies I bought in Salisbury.'

'Supplies?'

'A toothbrush and—'

He broke off and stopped, just below her on the stairs. In

the fading light his eyes were dark and liquid as they took in what she was wearing. Or wasn't wearing. She heard his sharply indrawn breath.

'*Jesus . . .*'

She laughed, but there was an edge to it. 'Sorry. I was in the bath.' She wrapped the flimsy, fluttering silk kimono more tightly around her, though she wasn't sure if that made it worse or better. Three steps below she saw the movement of his throat as he swallowed.

'It's me who should apologize.' His voice was hoarse. He looked away, a muscle flickering in his cheek, above his clenched jaw. 'I didn't mean to—' He swallowed again, and shook his head. 'I'm sorry. I should wait downstairs until you're dressed—'

He was clinging desperately to the last shattered fragments of propriety, she realized, for her sake, and the idea was touching and strangely empowering. The air between them buzzed with some invisible charge and her blood ran hot in her veins as she went to him, stopping on the step above, where their eyes were level. She took his hand, put it on her waist, beneath the open kimono and, in the second before she kissed him, murmured, 'Don't you dare.'

Later they went down to the servants' basement in search of food. In the enormous kitchen Lawrence took charge, bringing in kindling and coal from the store outside to light the range while Selina went down to raid the cellar for champagne, which they drank from plain china teacups from the huge dresser. They talked softly, quietly, even though there was no one to hear them, afraid of breaking the bubble of shimmering intimacy.

He cooked scrambled eggs and they ate them sitting at one end of the table, knees touching, gazes tangling and then darting apart. There was a new shyness between them, in spite of the barrier they had crossed. Because of it. She felt dazed and full of wonder, as if she'd just discovered an astonishing secret or stumbled across some priceless treasure. She couldn't stop looking at him; at his bare chest and his hands.

'I never thought it would be like that,' she murmured eventually, when curiosity overcame her shyness. 'I didn't know what it would be like, to be honest, but I didn't expect it to be so . . . heavenly. No one tells girls anything except that it's not nice. A duty, to be endured rather than enjoyed.'

He took her hand and lifted it to his mouth to kiss her fingers. 'Since the continuation of the human race depends on it, it really needs to be enjoyable, for both parties.'

'That's the other thing I was wondering . . .'

'What?'

She looked down, heat flooding her cheeks at her own ignorance. 'The bit about the continuation of the human race. How do I know I won't have a baby?'

'Don't worry. I'll take care of that.'

'But how?'

It was his turn to blush. 'I went to a chemist's shop. There are things you can buy.'

Her eyes widened. 'What things?'

'I didn't use one this time.'

'Why not?'

'We didn't need to. I didn't want to rush you, or hurt you, or do anything to compromise you ...' His eyes were very dark as he looked at her, reflecting the gold points of the electric lights, high up, and his smile was grave. 'If your father came bursting in with a shotgun right now you could claim quite honestly to be unspoiled for your husband on your wedding night.'

She hesitated, trying to make sense of this, then gave a gasp of astonished laughter.

'Do you mean ... that we didn't actually do it?'

'Technically, no. But there's more to it than just ... well, the basic act. I believe for women that alone can be a bit ... disappointing.' She saw the flash of his smile as he pressed a kiss into her palm. 'Someone once told me that a woman's body is like a piano. It's up to the man whether he chooses to pick out a nursery rhyme with one finger, or learn how to play a symphony. I suppose that was the first movement ...'

Selina's breathing was ragged in the quiet kitchen as his lips brushed the inside of her wrist. She wondered absently who had told him that, who had taught him, but his mouth was spreading shivering warmth up her arm and there were more urgent things on her mind.

'I'm terribly ignorant about culture,' she whispered. 'Remind me – how many movements are there in a symphony?'

His dark gaze found hers and made goosebumps rise at the nape of her neck.

'Four.'

Blackwood was beautiful in the summer.

She had forgotten that, or stopped noticing it a long time ago. Since Howard died it had become a sort of mausoleum of memories, a place of exile, where time hung heavy and there were no distractions from her thoughts. But in those long, golden days and warm nights as she led him through its empty, elegant rooms she saw it through Lawrence's eyes, and she began to love it again.

The first day set the pattern for the ones that followed. They dozed away the morning, waking early to make love when the pink light of the rising sun made the lilies on the bedroom curtains blush. Then they slept again and woke, ravenous, to run down to the kitchen and breakfast on whatever they had to hand. Most mornings they found supplies in the scullery, brought up from the farm by Polly: a jug of milk, a loaf of bread, a basket of eggs – sometimes a fruit cake or a waxed paper parcel of bacon – and they picnicked on these delicacies as Lawrence waged his own personal battle with the kitchen range, determined to get it up to a good heat and keep it going. Selina's gratitude to Polly was laced with guilt, but she pushed it to the back of her mind, not wanting anything to break the spell of their perfect solitude.

On that first day she took him through the house, opening

doors to rooms she hadn't looked inside for years, where the furniture was draped in dust-sheets, the chandeliers wrapped in Holland, and unfaded squares on the wallpaper showed where paintings had been sold to pay debts and fund Miranda's wedding. There was one door she didn't open, one room she didn't show him. The drawing room remained shuttered and closed, Howard's portrait gazing impassively through the gloom over the shrouded furniture. She couldn't quite bring herself to share it, because that would mean confronting the obscenity of Howard's loss all over again.

Death had no place in their selfish, stolen idyll. Her whole body, awoken by Lawrence, thrummed with life. She felt strong, quick, hungry, beautiful: miraculously invincible. By keeping the drawing room shuttered and sealed she had made death her prisoner, preventing it from slipping out to follow her along the corridors and wait for her around corners, or lie between her and Lawrence at night, tarnishing her joy.

They explored outside too, wandering in the afternoon heat through the neglected garden. They avoided the walled garden, where Patterson (the only servant never to take advantage of the annual fortnight of leave) pottered amongst the raspberry canes and rows of beans, roaming instead through the wilderness, discovering overgrown follies and features, once fashionable, now forgotten.

Lawrence carried his camera with him all the time, but never photographed anything just as it was, for itself alone, as other people did. She came to understand that he saw things in terms of shadow and shape, texture and contrast. Light. Instead of taking a picture of the Botticelli pool in the old orangery (so called because of its shell-shaped bowl) he made her trail her hand in the water and photographed the sunlight captured in the droplets that fell from her fingers. Instead of recording the exotic plants that rampaged untended up the orangery's wall and pressed against its grimy glass, he framed the shadow of their leaves on her bare midriff as she lay on the tiled floor. And then she gently took the camera from his hands and watched the detached, focused expression on his face change as he looked at her without the filter of the lens.

In many ways it was like she had gone back in time as she rediscovered the places that had formed the outposts of her nursery-centred world. They hacked a path through the overgrown garden to the lake with the Chinese Tea House in its centre. She was amazed to discover the key was still in its old hiding place on a ledge beneath the sweeping eaves, and the gramophone was still inside, records stacked untidily beside it. Its brass horn was tarnished to match the green of the walls, and mice had nibbled the corners of the striped cushions on the low settee bench that ran along the back wall, but it didn't take long to tidy up, and they set up camp there, whiling away the languid afternoon of that first magical day, draped lazily together on the couch, taking it in turns to wind up the gramophone and let music fill the drowsy air.

The next day they returned, taking a picnic of bread and cheese and a bottle of Montrachet, and an old fishing rod discovered by Lawrence in the gun room. His seaside childhood had made him a confident fisherman and, using dead flies from the cobwebbed window as bait, he stood on the wooden deck and cast his line. Selina lay on the sunwarmed boards and watched him, mesmerized by the sunlight on the water and the movement of the muscles beneath the gleaming skin on his back.

Bach's Goldberg Variations (selected by Lawrence) poured from the gramophone, the sound faded and scratched but still searingly sweet. She rolled onto her back and closed her eyes, watching colours burst in the darkness behind her closed lids. It was like being permanently in that glorious, fleeting state at the start of the evening – the glittering hour, Flick called it – when the first swiftly downed cocktail drove away the demons; when her blood was warm and her limbs loose and everything shimmered with promise. She was intoxicated by him. Beneath his hands the clamour inside her had quietened and the endless questions – half formed, never spoken – that had nagged at her for years had been answered. Or simply scattered like dandelion seeds in a breath of wind.

Sex. It was the feral beast that slunk through the ballrooms of Belgravia, fascinating and dangerous. It was the sharp tang of bodies beneath the waft of Turkish tobacco and French perfume, and the frantic rhythm of a jazz band; the sense of something just out of sight, beyond her reach. What little she knew about it had been pieced together from the slivers of information reluctantly imparted by governesses (asking forthright questions about it had been one of her favourite ways of tormenting them) and debutantes' gossip. One thing she was sure of was that it was wrong to want it. Nice girls absolutely didn't. (She had learned that lesson early from Nanny Cole; the punishment for *touching* had been more severe than for lying even, or elbows on the table.) She had thought that there was something wrong with her for being curious. Something unnatural.

How fabulously absurd that seemed now.

Her uneducated, unfocused imagination had pictured something that was business-like, but noble – some sort of perfunctory courtship ritual from which she would emerge feeling womanly and complete. Instead she felt undone. The sharp-edged fragments of herself, her armour against the world, had been dismantled, piece by piece. She had been prepared for discomfort, awkwardness, embarrassment: to feel acutely self-conscious, like she had at her first proper dances when she didn't know anyone and wasn't quite sure what to do or how to behave but, wrapped in the darkness of his gaze as his fingertips traced delicate patterns of pleasure on her skin, she simply *was* . . . More profoundly herself than she'd ever been before. And the damaged world felt perfect again.

That night, to her delight and astonishment, there was fish for dinner. Perch, Lawrence thought; golden green and delicately striped. Selina was so impressed by his skill and practicality that it galvanized her into making her own contribution to the menu. She waited until she knew Patterson would have retreated to his cottage before slipping into the kitchen garden to gather handfuls of French beans and emerald green pea pods, and unearth waxy little potatoes. The strawberries were nearly over, but raspberries still hung from the canes and there were peaches – as big and warm and pink as the sinking sun – on the glasshouse wall. She took one, breathing in the heady sweetness of its warm skin as she went back up to the house.

After the makeshift picnics of the past couple of days, it felt like a feast, worthy of celebration. While Lawrence expertly gutted and filleted the fish in the shallow scullery sink Selina went down to the cellars to bring up more champagne (carefully amending the number Denham chalked above the rack, to leave no discrepancy) and left it to cool in a bucket of water while she laid the table in the dining room.

It was like playing house. No grown-ups. No rules. She didn't bother with the handpainted Dresden dinner service, or the stiff damask napkins (she had no intention of taking the time to wash them afterwards) and brought up plain white china from the servants' hall instead. She placed the silver rococo candelabra in the centre of the table, and went out to collect whatever she could find in the garden to put in the elaborate Sevres centrepiece.

Walking back to the house in the rosy gold evening she thought suddenly of Flick and Theo. She could picture them vividly – Flick in the South of France, Theo in Italy – preparing for the evening ahead; a cocktail while dressing ('a little sharpener' she could hear Theo saying) followed by dinner in the right restaurant, a party perhaps, with the other smart people who flocked to Cap Ferrat and Florence. Had Selina been in Scotland, the vision would have driven arrows of envy into her heart, but there in the silent garden with the shadows deepening around her, the soft air shimmering, she knew that there was nowhere on earth she'd rather be. The evening stretched ahead of her, as sweet and delicious as the stolen peach; a pathway into another exquisite night.

And there she stopped herself. Thinking ahead was strictly forbidden. Live for the moment – that was the creed by which she lived, and it was more important now than ever. She didn't want to count the dwindling days or confront the fact that separation waited on the other side of this spell of perfection, just as surely as the real world lay beyond Blackwood's sleeping parkland. She wanted to forget that their paradise was a fool's one, and all this bliss only borrowed.

In the kitchen Lawrence stoked a shower of sparks from the range, pausing to admire its fierce glow for a moment before shutting the iron door. After three days he had finally got to grips with its moods and idiosyncrasies and managed to keep it alight, which would make cooking significantly easier and the results considerably better. He felt a beat of satisfaction.

He'd never thought of himself as much of a cook, had never been very interested in food before, beyond the basic requirement of fending off hunger, but everything was different here. The shafts of evening light filtering through the high-up windows (positioned so the kitchen staff wouldn't be distracted by the view, he supposed) onto the clean, worn wood of the table turned the produce into a still life from the Dutch School: pearly potatoes with the earth still clinging to their skins, peas spilling like jewels from their tight pods, the peach ... Everything was beautiful. Sensual. He photographed them, glad that he had used the money from the wedding photographs (an amount he would have had to paint three portraits to earn) to buy a second-hand roll-film camera, cursing the fact that he'd only got two spare reels of photographic film. It had been all he could afford that evening in Salisbury, but was woefully inadequate in this place of aesthetic wonder. He would have pawned something to buy more if he'd realized what awaited him.

But how could he have known? How could a boy who'd grown up in a few ramshackle rooms where everything was cheap and shabby and worn and mended have anticipated this? Not just the grandeur of the house itself – the marble columned hallway and wide staircase; the ornamented ceilings in the state rooms and the formidable array of paintings and statuary – but the abundance of light that flooded in through high, clean windows and reflected off gilded mirrors, turning everything into a subject, a still life, a study. All his life he had been instinctively drawn to beauty, like a plant is drawn to the sun, but it was only now that he realized how little he'd learned to survive on. The sheen of rain on rooftiles, the jewelled shadow cast by a wine bottle on a windowsill, a bucket of yellow roses outside a florist's shop, those had been the crumbs that sustained him. This was a different world.

And at the centre of it all was Selina, whose own beauty was both reflected and enhanced by the house. She was like a chameleon who adapted to her surroundings. In London she was glossy and sharp and sophisticated, with her painted lips and mascara'd, kohl-smudged eyes, and he had found her explosively attractive like that. But this other version of her – bare-faced, bare-footed and golden – was another thing entirely. He was fascinated by her: captivated by the velvet texture of her skin, the glints in her hair, the delicious contours of her body and her fluid movements. He felt like touching her should be forbidden, like when his mother had taken him into a country church and held his hand tightly as he'd stood, awe-struck, before an Arts and Crafts sculpture of the Virgin Mary. *Don't touch, Laurie. Just look. Isn't she beautiful?*

He was still that small, undernourished boy. Still awe-struck by beauty, still hungry for it, still desperate to escape the meanness of the life into which he'd been born. And here he was . . . He lifted a handful of beans out of the water he'd been washing them in, tossing them into a colander in a shower of droplets, noticing the resonance of their intense green against the copper. He was a beggar at the feast, gorging himself, but a part of him was aware that more famine lay ahead. This was just a brief spell of plenty. How could it be anything else?

Out in the passageway a bell rang. He froze for a moment, his heart ricocheting off his ribs. It was too late for visitors. Had someone seen lights and come to check if the house had been broken into? Cautiously, wiping his hands on a cloth, he went out into the servants' corridor and was wondering if it would make more trouble if he answered the door himself when the bell rang again.

He looked behind him, in the direction from which the sound came, and saw a row of bells high up on the wall. One still shivered with silvery sound.

He expelled a breath of relief as understanding dawned, and felt a smile begin to pull at his mouth as desire uncurled in the pit of his stomach. Without hesitation he headed for the servants' stairs, taking them two at a time in his haste to answer her summons to the Blue Bathroom.

Selina had intended that they would dress for dinner. As part of the game, she had imagined putting on one of the silk and chiffon dresses Polly had carefully unpacked and steamed when they'd returned from London – the sea green one, perhaps, with the tiny glass bugle beads that would glitter in the candlelight – and had thought that he could choose one of the dinner jackets and evening shirts that still hung in Howard's dressing room.

But in the end it didn't turn out like that. When the

bathwater had cooled around their sated bodies and the bottle of champagne they'd shared was empty it seemed silly to go to the trouble of dressing. And so they went downstairs barefoot; Lawrence in a clean shirt (not just without a tie, but collarless too – Mama would faint) and Selina in nothing but Miranda's silk kimono and a smudge of red lipstick. She lit the candles and uncorked wine in the dining room while Lawrence went down to the kitchen to boil the potatoes and fry the fish.

The day had faded into dusk. Selina folded back the shutters and left the curtains open so the long windows glittered with reflected candlelight. They sat opposite each other, on either side of the table, not at its ends, though it still seemed too far apart. As they ate she found herself watching his hands, mesmerized by the movement of his long and beautiful fingers as he picked up his wineglass or pushed back the heavy lock of hair that fell over his forehead.

The perch were white-fleshed and delicately flavoured, surprisingly good. When her plate was empty she picked little potatoes from the bowl between them, licking the butter off her fingers, abandoning herself to the pleasure of eating in a way that would once have made her feel guilty and ashamed. Their gazes held across the expanse of polished mahogany and he smiled that slow, lopsided smile.

'Your mother is looking at me.'

She glanced sideways, to where the Sargent portrait of Lady Lennox in her Coming Out diamonds hung beside the chimneypiece.

'How do you know that's my mother?'

'I can feel her disapproval.'

She laughed. 'I'm not surprised. Mama is of the white tie for dinner generation. The modern fashion for black tie is enough of an assault on propriety to her; poor dear must be positively apoplectic at the sight of a young man in her dining room in no tie at all, and servants' hall china on the table.'

'Do those things really matter so much to them?'

'Oh God, yes.' Picking a slender French bean from the serving bowl she trailed it through the melted butter on her plate. 'They matter more than anything.'

'Not more than you do, surely? Your happiness.'

She looked up at him in surprise, wondering if he was being sarcastic, and deciding from his unsmiling face that he wasn't. 'Of course they do. Those things are the foundations on which their world is built – solid, important things that support the entire social structure. My happiness is infinitesimally small and insignificant by comparison. They distrust strong emotions of any kind. I'm sure they'd rather I was happy than unhappy, but they'd really rather not be troubled by my feelings at all. Or anyone's.' She took a mouthful of wine. 'Much better if we're all just sensible about things. No fuss.'

His face was shuttered and inscrutable, but a muscle was flickering above his jaw. 'Do you agree with that?'

She pictured Howard's portrait in the darkened drawing room, and made an effort to keep her tone light. 'I certainly don't disagree. Other people's emotions are always rather tiresome, don't you think? In fact, come to think of it, so are one's own . . .'

They were in danger of becoming serious; straying perilously close to the line she had drawn in her mind and the barriers she had built around her heart. Getting to her feet she picked up the wine bottle and splashed some into her glass then reached across the table to fill his. 'Which is why it's best not to think about them. And also why cocktails were invented, and jazz and dancing. And sex . . .'

'Sex isn't a new invention.'

He was leaning back in his chair, outwardly at ease. Only the hoarseness of his voice gave him away, and the dark gleam of his eyes. Warmth unfurled like smoke in the pit of her stomach. In one fluid, impulsive movement she pushed her plate aside and got up onto the table, stepping between serving bowls and silver in her bare feet, snatching the billow of her silk robe away from the candle flames as she lowered herself onto the table-edge in front of him.

'It might as well be as far as I'm concerned.'

Her feet were in his lap. She watched his eyelids flicker and his jaw tense as she flexed her toes. 'If we do it here, on the dining table, will we be responsible for the collapse of the civilized world?'

Her laugh was throaty as she leaned down to kiss him. 'Let's try it and find out . . .'

15

Distant Thunder

The house was full of shadows and whispers. Footsteps echoed along the corridors, as rapid as the hammer-thud of Lawrence's heart. His own rasping breath was loud in his ears, but he could hear Selina's too, and the murmur of her laughter drifting back along the narrow passageways. Every now and again he caught a glimpse of her – the flash of her smile, a ripple of silk – before she disappeared around the next corner. He tried to call out to her, but his voice cracked in his throat and no words came out. He tried to run faster, to catch up with her, but his legs were leaden and the air dragged at him, as if he was under water. As the thought occurred to him he felt his chest squeeze and burn, and suddenly the air wasn't air any more and his lungs were full and he was drowning. Through the greenish depths faces stared down at him from portraits on the walls with cold, superior eyes, and the submerged corridors stretched ahead and behind and in all directions, leading nowhere.

He woke with a strangled gasp, heart ricocheting off his ribs, skin clammy with sweat. For long seconds he lay still, breathing heavily as the room reassembled itself around him and the shapes of furniture and objects solidified in the pre-dawn light.

A dream. Just a dream.

They never bothered to fold across the shutters or close the curtains, and he could see the moon's face, as pale and serene as a Renaissance Madonna, drifting above milky layers of mist over the park. Almost reluctantly he adjusted his focus to look at Selina, lying beside him. Her hand was curled as sweetly as a child's against her cheek, her lips slightly parted. The melting light stole the colour from her face, turning her into a living photograph. She looked secretive and self-contained as she moved through places where he couldn't follow her, just like in the dream. His heart gave a painful lurch as it came back to him; that feeling of helplessness as she slipped away, forever just beyond his reach.

It wasn't just a dream. It was how things were between them. How they would always be. Their store of stolen days was almost used up. A telegram had arrived from Selina's mother, pointedly asking if she was better and reminding her that her presence was expected at some dinner party on Friday. She would take the train to Scotland and he would return to London, to the squalor of Marchmont Street and the studio, the tedium of commissions. And when the summer was over he would still be doing that, while she resumed her round of house parties, cocktail parties, costume parties, and he read about them in newspapers that were as disposable as he was.

His breathing had slowed, his heartbeat steadied, but the feeling of despair remained. The moon looked down on him with infinite pity.

They woke to heavy skies massed with pewter grey clouds, and an odd yellow light that tarnished the gold stubble in the fields. The sun had disappeared but the air was hot and heavy, as if the world was holding its breath, waiting for something.

It was their last full day together; the knowledge was as oppressive as the sultry air. The conversation that had flowed so easily, so naturally between them seemed to have dried up, leaving silences weighted with things they couldn't say. That afternoon they crossed the ha-ha at the front of the house and walked through the long grass to the lake where the water was deeper for swimming. There was a boathouse there, and an old rowing boat, its rotting hull filled with six inches of green slime. She showed him the rope swing that her brother had made, and told him how he'd taught her to swing out over the lake and jump in. They went on it together, as she'd once done with Howard, clinging to the rope and to each other, then letting go and plunging down into the water.

The dream came back to him as he kicked up through the

depths, glimpsing the glimmer of her pale limbs just above him. The ache in his chest when he surfaced wasn't entirely from the temporary lack of oxygen. He swam to the deck that jutted out from the boathouse and hauled himself onto it, to avoid having to wade through the mud and reeds at the water's edge. She was still swimming, floating on her back a little way out, her thin chemise turned transparent, her breasts just breaking the surface. She looked like a water nymph in a pre-Raphaelite painting, or a particularly erotic Ophelia. The light was leaden, but shaking the water from his hands he reached for his camera and managed to take a shot before she flipped over, mermaid like, and disappeared beneath the water.

Ripples spread over the surface of the lake. Above the trees the inky clouds boiled, and thunder echoed faintly on the still air. He lay down and stared up at the dull sky. Perhaps it was the change in the weather that made everything feel different; the brewing storm that gave the day its unsettling end-of-the-world atmosphere. Closing his eyes he heard the splash of water as she surfaced and climbed out, felt a shower of droplets as she came over. In the darkness behind his closed lids he pictured the clinging silk against her wet skin and swallowed, not trusting himself to look. This morning's lovemaking had had a ferocity that had left him feeling drained and hollowed out. There was a little pause, and then the rasp of a match, the smell of singed paper and good Turkish tobacco, and he felt her lower herself onto the deck beside him.

Her fingertips brushed his lips as she offered him the cigarette. He opened his eyes a crack to see her looking at him.

'You're miles away,' she murmured. 'What are you thinking?'

'I was actually thinking how far away the rest of the world seems. It could have ceased to exist for all we know.'

She laughed, and lay back on the wooden boards, her arm touching his. 'How wonderful if it had. If there had been some kind of giant catastrophe that had wiped out all of civilization in an instant, and we were the only survivors. We could live here for ever, like this. It would be heaven.'

He took a drag on the cigarette and blew out a long column of smoke. 'You'd get bored eventually, without the parties and the dancing and your London friends.'

'I wouldn't. We could have parties here, just the two of us. Why would I want to dance anywhere else, with anyone else, when I could dance here, with you?'

'Because I'm a terrible dancer.'

'I'd teach you. I'd teach you to dance like you've taught me to make love. I'm sure the principles are very similar.' She took back the cigarette. 'I daresay you'd get bored though. You'd miss the city. The variety. You'd run out of things to photograph.'

They were teasing, but testing each other too. Dangerous undercurrents swirled just beneath the playful words, threatening to drag them down. Far above, the treetops shivered and whispered in some sudden breeze, too high up to disturb the still air where they lay.

He rolled onto his side, propping himself up on one elbow to look at her. 'I'd photograph you. Every day. The changes in your moods, your face, your body.'

'You'd long for me to get old and ugly to make your photographs more interesting.'

'I'd be waiting until doomsday. You'll never be old and ugly.'

There was a little silence as she sucked smoke into her lungs and exhaled it again. When she spoke the teasing note had evaporated from her voice and she sounded subdued. Resigned.

'Time catches up with us all in the end. We can't run away from reality for ever.'

And there it was; the truth they had been trying to ignore. A direct acknowledgement that the adventure they had plunged into so recklessly was coming to an end. His chest felt like it had a stone pressing on it. The air was too thick to breathe.

'Why not?' he said hoarsely. 'You're not that little girl hiding behind the milk churns anymore. You can run away to wherever you like now. No one's going to haul you out and send you home.'

'And where would I go?'

'Wherever you wanted. Paris. Provence. America. Anywhere.'

'With you?'

'If you wanted to.'

He wasn't sure if they were still teasing. He suspected

that she was, but he knew that he was serious and that he would go anywhere with her, if she said the word. To the ends of the earth. He sat up, pushing his damp hair back from his forehead.

'What would we do for money?' Her voice, from behind him, was soft and sleepy. She was inviting him to tell her a story, he realized; to conjure a fairy tale with a happy-ever-after, like the ones he used to make up for Cassie. With a sigh he rested his elbows on his raised knees.

'I'd paint. We could go to Cornwall . . . Edith has a house in St Ives. There's quite a community of artists down there and some of them are beginning to make a name for themselves. We could live cheaply enough, and I know I can sell enough paintings for us not to starve—'

'But it's not what you want to do. You don't want to paint.'

He almost laughed. As if that mattered. As if he'd let a stupid, abstract preference like that stop him from being with her.

'I'd still take photographs. The light there is purer than anywhere. And there's the sea – I might even be able to sell more.'

'Have you been there?'

'Once, last year. Edith put me in touch with a family near Penzance who had lost two sons; they wanted a portrait incorporating both of them. They were a well-off family . . . lots of photographs, which they were reluctant to part with for long. I spent a week in St Ives doing sketches to work out a final composition for them to approve.'

It was like remembering something that had happened to someone else, in a lifetime when he didn't know her. He had liked it there. He had liked the emptiness of the streets when the wind blew salt spray off the sea, the dark cave-like pubs where the landlords turned a blind eye to licensing hours. The smell of sea and fish and tar had reminded him of home, of Hastings, in a way that was peaceful rather than painful, which it always was when he went back. He had photographed the clouds and the cobbles glistening like the silver scales of a fish in a sudden shaft of afternoon sunlight, and an old woman sitting in the window of a house on the quay, her face creased like an old map.

He described Edith's house on a narrow street between the town's two stretches of sand, its whitewashed bedroom with the sagging brass bed overlooking the church on the hill, the studio Edith had created in the attic, where the precious light flooded in. And as he talked, he envied the person he had been then, ignorant and untroubled and self-reliant, before he'd laid his heart in the hands of another.

The thunder's growl was closer now. No breath of wind disturbed the glassy surface of the lake, but the highest branches of the trees writhed in silent agitation.

'It sounds perfect. I'd love to go there.'

Her note of regret was like a death knell. He felt a sudden wrench of anger, and understood that he hadn't been telling her a story but offering her a choice. A chance.

'You could. If you wanted to.'

'It's not that simple.'

'I thought you wanted freedom? Independence?'

'I do. I'd swap places with those Cornish fishermen any day, if I could. Or with your fairground people.'

'But that's a fantasy.' Exasperation crackled through his words. 'You don't need to swap places with anyone. You can be yourself and still be independent.'

She gave a short laugh. 'No – *that's* a fantasy.' She sat up. 'Do you think if I waltzed off to live in a fisherman's cottage in Cornwall with an artist that my parents wouldn't cut me off without a penny? That I wouldn't be instantly excommunicated from the social circles in which we move? As far as everyone I know is concerned it would be as if I'd died, only slightly more embarrassing.'

'Wouldn't your friends understand?'

'How could they when I'd be giving them up too?'

He stood up and moved away from her, frustration beating a hot tattoo through his veins. Going to the edge of the jetty he looked across the lake. Its surface reflected the angry sky, giving the impression of swirling currents in its depths.

'So what can you do?'

He said *you*, but as he waited for her reply he knew his future rested on it too. His happiness.

'I can play the game, like a good girl.' She spoke in a tone of careful reason. 'I can obey the rules, outwardly at least. I can get married to the right sort of man, and have a home of my own and an income and ten times the freedom that I have now, with my parents and the rest of the world watching every move. I've thought about it from all angles, and I believe it's my best chance. On my own I'm nothing. I *have* nothing – no money, no status, no power. As a wife I'll be in a position to make choices. To have some control—'

Marry me, then, he wanted to say, but managed to stop himself. He knew that wasn't what she meant. Bitterness seeped into his laugh.

'Selina, are you serious? *Control?*' He turned to face her. 'You'd just be exchanging one gilded cage for another. Bigger perhaps, furnished according to your taste, but still a cage.'

'Lawrence, don't . . .'

The first drops of rain had begun to fall, shattering the glassy smoothness of the lake, but neither of them moved.

'Don't what?' He didn't want to say the things that were seething in his mind, but somewhere they had passed a point of no return and it was too late to stop. 'Don't make you face up to the truth? That isn't independence Selina. It's cowardice. Being married to a rich man you don't love isn't being free, it's being too afraid to live properly.'

He saw her stiffen and go still, then she drew herself upright, lifting her chin and meeting his gaze unflinchingly. In the odd brooding light her eyes had a dazzling, dangerous glitter.

'Don't say that.' Her voice shook with fury. 'You know nothing, Lawrence. *Nothing*. You're a *man* – you go where you like, you sleep with whom you like and no one bats an eyelid. You please yourself, and you have no idea what it's like to have no autonomy and to be scrutinized and judged every day – on your clothes, your body, your friends, your face.' She crossed the wooden deck to scoop up the linen dress she had stripped off in such a different mood an hour ago. 'Oh, don't worry – I'm quite used to being told that I'm too silly, too brazen, too fat, too wild. Too disrespectful of my brother and all the boys like him who died. I must admit, being called a coward is new, but it doesn't hurt any more than all the things I've heard a thousand times before.'

'Selina, wait—'

Her anger had lanced the boil of his own frustration. He felt stricken and contrite, ashamed of the impulse that had driven him to push her for a reaction. But it was too late to say sorry. She had turned and was walking up the jetty with quick, angry strides that made the boards shake beneath him. She didn't look round when he called her, and he was left standing there as the rain began to fall in earnest, filling the air with the silvery rush of water, the smell of wet earth, the feeling that summer had ended, and with it something far more precious that wouldn't come again.

The light in the drawing room was murky in the sudden downpour. Howard's face was shadowy in the gloom. She sloshed brandy into a glass and raised it to her lips, closing her eyes as she felt its burn down the back of her throat.

She had run back from the boathouse. Her body fizzed and pulsed with unspent energy and her lungs felt scorched. Going straight up to her room she had stripped off her wet chemise and pulled old clothes from her drawer – an ancient cricket sweater of Howard's and a pair of his prep school pyjama trousers, the striped flannelette soft and faded. In the mirror above the fireplace she caught sight of her reflection now and felt a stab of perverse satisfaction at its unattractive oddness. She swallowed the brandy and poured more.

He had made her feel beautiful. He had made her feel fearless and powerful, but the truth was she was none of those things. It was right that he should see her as she was now he'd realized the truth.

The only sounds were the murmur of the rain outside and the unsteady rasp of her breath. The house was quiet enough for her to hear the door close downstairs in the servants' passage, still enough for her to feel the air stir as the baize door swung open. His bare feet made no noise on the marble floor, but she was aware of a flicker of movement in the mirror's silvery surface. He was standing in the doorway. The silence stretched, and then he expelled a long, shaky breath.

'Selina, I'm sorry.'

She sipped her brandy, holding the glass very close to her lips.

'I was wrong. I shouldn't have said those things – I was stupid and I had no right. I shouldn't have fallen in love with you – I had no right to do that either.' He sighed again, sweeping his hair back with a weary hand, making droplets of water shower the Aubusson roses beneath his feet. 'Look, I'll go. I'll get my things and—'

'What did you say?'

Her voice was small. A shivering breath in the rain-dark room.

'I'll leave. Now. I don't know if there's a train, but it doesn't matter. I'll—'

'Not that. The other bit.'

'About falling in love with you?'

'Yes.'

'I didn't want to.' He gave a hollow laugh. 'This was supposed to be fun . . . an adventure, but I couldn't help it. You're astonishing, Selina. How could I not fall hopelessly in love with you? If I'm honest, I knew it would happen, but I never intended to tell you.' His mouth twisted in a bitter parody of a smile as he echoed her words from days before. 'I never wanted to burden you with my tiresome emotions. Forget I said it.'

Very carefully, she put her glass down.

'Stay. Please stay.'

PART II

Hill View
Club Road
Maymyo
Burma

August 1st 1936

Darling Alice,

So, here we are at the start of another month. Every time
that happens I hope it will be the last before Papa and I set
sail for home again and our separation draws to a close. This
time, perhaps. I feel confident and hopeful. This time.

Papa's business is going well and he is satisfied that he
can achieve a successful outcome. I think I mentioned in my
last letter that he was to have a series of meetings with
an important government chap from the Mogok region, where
the mines are? He was pleased with how these went and their
discussions were useful. I dined with them one night at the
Club, and when that seemed to go down well, invited the chap
(a Glaswegian called Mr Melville) for dinner here. I was
pleased to be of some use to Papa at last (it was why I came,
after all) and it was actually rather fun to have something
to plan and prepare for. Ba Nayar was a marvellous sport and

283

made a good attempt at a Scottish-themed menu. He couldn't get haggis here, obviously, and though he sweetly offered to attempt his own I thought it was best not to try, but he made a very creditable Cranachan for pudding, and I believe Mr Melville enjoyed it. I feel sure I almost saw him smile.

Papa has been away a lot lately, trying to complete all his work as quickly as possible. It's the rainy season here (did I tell you that last time? I'm sure I must have. Silly me, repeating things) so none of the wives tend to venture out much, to meet up for afternoon tea or bridge or sewing circles, as they usually do. It's an enormous relief to me, as I'm sure you can imagine — I'd far rather be here on my own than having to force an interest in bridge and gossip, to fit in for Papa's sake. I like the solitude. It gives me time to think, about the future and how it will be when I finally leave this place, the bliss of being with you again, doing perfectly ordinary things. I'm quite sure you must have grown a foot at least while I've been away and will need an entire new wardrobe of clothing. We will have a shopping trip of epic proportions, broken up by luncheon in Harrods and tea in Lyons or Liberty, or wherever you choose. We will buy a bag of toffees and go to the picture house and watch the film around twice. We will go away to the seaside and walk on the beach, which will be quiet after the summer crowds. We will go to the zoo as well. You can draw the animals with your coloured pencils.

As well as thinking of all those things, I find myself dwelling on the past a lot too, in these solitary hours. Time

is a funny thing. Eleven years have passed in the blink of
an eye, and yet these few months that we've been apart have
dragged like centuries. All the days here merge into one, so
I find it difficult to remember what happened last Tuesday, and
yet I can remember moments and conversations from years ago
as vividly as if they had just taken place. As if the person
who spoke has just left the room.

I feel terribly guilty about the treasure hunt, darling.
It's been ages since I sent you a clue. I haven't forgotten,
but I suppose I have been putting it off. It's getting to the
difficult part of the story, you see, but that's no excuse.
I've begun now, and I need to see it through. I want to. It's
your story too, and I want you to know it. The moment I've
finished this letter I'll write the next part, and send it to
Polly with the clue.

Thank you for your letters, my darling. You have no idea
how precious they are to me here, and how much I treasure
every line. I love to think of you in that lovely old
neglected garden, exploring it and enjoying it. I love to
think of you at the Chinese Tea House, tidying it up and
caring for it again. I'm happy to think of you in the kitchen
garden with Patterson, digging up potatoes and picking
peaches. Your words bring tastes and scents and memories
rushing back.

I love you darling. More than I can ever say.

Mama

Xxxxx

16

Polly

September 1936

The woollen vests had been bought from Harrods; eight of them, enough to last between laundry van visits, with one to spare. Kneeling in front of the open drawer in the nursery Polly held one up and examined it. They were lovely quality, no doubt about that; beautiful soft wool with plenty more wear left in them ... Which would be all well and good if Alice hadn't grown so much.

With a sigh Polly re-folded the vest and put it on the pile on the floor. Who would have thought a child could grow so quickly? She must be two inches taller now than she had been when she'd arrived at Blackwood.

Her brisk hands stilled at the realization that it had been eight months, give or take, since that bleak January Sunday. The earth had nearly completed its cycle through the seasons;

of course the child was going to have grown. It might feel like time was suspended, like they were all stopped and waiting, but the world kept turning, just as it always had. She shook her head sadly. Funny how it often took a child to remind you of how things were. That life went on.

Blinking hard she reached for her list and wrote '*vests, wool. Size 28"*', then shut the drawer and opened the one below it. Luckily most of Alice's skirts were the kilt variety, which allowed for a bit more growing room. She'd need a couple of new jerseys for the coming winter, and ideally a new best dress for Sundays, though Polly suspected Lady Lennox would rather turn a blind eye to the two inch gap that had appeared between knee and hem than pay for a new one. Resentment twisted like a knife beneath her ribs. Miss Selina had made sure money was available for things like that, but Polly was prepared to bet that it would be easier to get blood from a stone. The old witch didn't bother to hide her lack of warmth to the child. Even now.

Blushing with guilt at this private dissidence she shut the drawer with unnecessary force and picked up the pile of out-grown clothes. It was best to strike while the iron was hot and catch Lady Lennox in the Morning Room before Alice finished her lessons. As she went out into the corridor Polly could hear the governess's voice – reciting poetry, by the sound of it. Poor Alice. Once old Sergeant Major Lovelock's ankle had healed she had been granted three weeks' leave for a trip to Europe (it was all right for some) and, freed from the schoolroom, Alice had been as happy as Polly had seen her. Thankfully, since the governess's return, the ritual of the afternoon walk had been dropped and Alice was allowed to continue helping Patterson in the kitchen garden, which was something. No wonder she'd shot up; a summer of fresh air and useful activity. It had done her good; kept her occupied and put colour in her cheeks. It would do Miss Selina's heart good to see her.

The breath caught in Polly's throat. Her hand tightened on the banister.

If only.

She paused outside the Morning Room, balancing the pile of clothing as she straightened her skirt and smoothed her hair. After all these years Lady Lennox still made her feel like the plump fourteen-year-old who had trailed up the drive after her mother, wearing her Sunday dress and a borrowed hat. The balance of power had shifted these days, she reminded herself firmly. She no longer had to be grateful to Her Ladyship for offering her a place. If anything the boot was firmly on the other foot, though Polly hadn't come back to Blackwood for Lady Lennox's sake, that was for sure. It was Miss Selina who had asked her, and for Miss Selina that she had agreed.

It hadn't occurred to her for a second to refuse.

The bond between them was unusual; impossible for anyone else to understand. 'She takes advantage,' Polly's mother had said that long-ago summer, lips compressed with disapproval because she listened to the village gossip, gleaned from newspapers, about the drinking and the dancing, the skinny dipping in the Serpentine and kissing Prince Albert. But her Mam didn't know about the other things. The vulnerability that lay behind Miss Selina's apparent confidence. The kindness. The late night conversations, when Miss Selina would invite Polly to climb onto the bed beside her to share the petits fours she'd smuggled out from dinner in her handbag, the times she let Polly use the bathwater once she'd finished, topping it up with more hot and telling her to take as much time as she wanted, to use her Floris talcum powder afterwards and not to feel in the slightest bit guilty that the other maids only got one meagre bath a week. The shared confidences and complaints, the petty grievances that often turned into amusing anecdotes in the lamplit bedroom. The laughter. The knowledge that Miss Selina was on her side (like the time Polly broke a valuable china figurine and Miss Selina told Lady Lennox she had done it herself) and the certainty that she was on Miss Selina's. That they would be there for each other, no matter what.

All those years ago Polly had never imagined what that might mean.

She took a breath and knocked. Entering the room she saw Lady Lennox seated at her writing desk in front of the window. She didn't raise her head, but carried on writing while Polly stood there, determined not to be cowed.

She looked at the woman in front of her. Diamonds flashed dully on her fingers as her hand moved across the page, but the rings were too loose now. Years of monitoring every mouthful, watching her figure, Polly thought, and she'd ended up frail enough to snap. Deep grooves were scored on either side of her mouth, giving her a permanently sour expression. Polly felt a sudden flash of pity. All that wealth, all that privilege, but what happiness had it brought her? Her life was bound by strict rules rather than emotions. She was like a plant, tightly staked and rigidly clipped, whose roots had withered in dry soil.

'Well?'

Polly started, and her pity evaporated under Lady Lennox's chilly gaze. She held up the bundle of clothing.

'Sorry to bother you, ma'am, but I was just sorting through Alice's clothing, what with the seasons changing. She'll be needing some new things, I'm afraid – she's grown that much. I'll see what I can do about turning hems down, but all these vests are no good now. I was wondering if I might pass them to my mother, for the WI jumble sale? And I could go into Salisbury on my half day and buy some replacements from Draycott's, along with a few other bits—'

'No, I don't think so.'

Lady Lennox was looking down at the letter she had been writing. Picking up her pen she crossed something out and moved the top sheet aside to scan the one beneath. Polly stood, open-mouthed, feeling both foolish and quietly furious. Lady Lennox screwed the cap onto the fountain pen and laid it down again.

'I've been meaning to tell you.' Her tone was offhand. 'We've made arrangements for Alice to go to school – Carlton Hall, in Yorkshire – so she must manage with the clothing she has for the time being. I have a uniform list, so when new things are purchased it will be with reference to that, and from the correct supplier and so on. But thank you for your concern.'

'*Boarding* school, ma'am?'

'Yes, Polly, boarding school. I'm sure you can appreciate that Yorkshire is too far to travel each day. The new term starts next week, which is unfortunate timing. We took the decision that it was too soon for Alice to start now, with everything being rather ... uncertain.' It was as if she was referring to rain at a picnic. 'The Headmistress has been most understanding. Alice will be able to start at a time to suit her. To suit ... the circumstances.'

Lady Lennox's voice trailed away into silence.

'Does she know?'

She didn't need to ask. It wasn't something Alice would have kept to herself if she'd known about it. Polly didn't know whether to be angry that the poor child was being kept in the dark while everyone decided what to do with her, or grateful that she was being spared the worry. But there was only so much sparing that could be done. Sooner or later she would have to be told the truth.

Anguish squeezed at her insides.

'No.' Lady Lennox folded the sheets of paper and slotted them into an envelope. 'It's not the right time to tell her yet. It's in the child's best interests to keep things ... normal ... for as long as possible. I think you'd agree she seems happy enough?'

'Yes, ma'am.' She swallowed. 'Does Miss Selina know? About the school? It's just she always said—'

'Selina wants what's best for Alice.' There was an edge of steel in Lady Lennox's tone and it cut cleanly through Polly's protest. 'We all do. Now, I'm sure you have things to be getting on with . . . ?'

'Have you heard anything?' Polly couldn't stop herself from blurting it out, even though she knew it wasn't her place to ask. 'Has there been any news?'

Lady Lennox's face twitched with disapproval. Almost imperceptibly she shook her head. 'You will be kept informed. For the time being we must carry on.' Her chilly smile faltered. 'For the child's sake.'

Polly retreated, still clutching the bundle of clothing. Going back up the servants' stairs to the nursery she had to stop to catch her breath, and it was only then that she realized she was crying.

The afternoon sun slanted through the trees and fell onto the face of the Chinese House. Alice could feel it on her back too, warm and luxurious. It was gentler now than it had been a few weeks ago; lower in the sky, Patterson said, now autumn was coming on. Alice had found that fascinating. To her the sun was always just *there*, but Patterson showed her how it tracked across the sky, so you could tell by looking up when it was time to stop for milk and a biscuit, and when Polly would be expecting her back at the kitchen door. Journeyman gardeners didn't have fancy watches, Patterson said.

He had shown her all sorts of other things too, signs that the season was changing. The bright green, spiked horse chestnut cases on the trees along the drive were swelling and beginning to fall, and birds (swifts, Patterson told her) circled high up in the sky, getting ready to fly south for the winter. Around the lake the bulrushes had grown fluffy white heads that turned them into sticks of fairground candy floss, and in the kitchen garden everything was ripe and ready, so there was always tomatoes to pick and a basket of beans, peas, apples and plums to take back to the house.

Patterson said that she was a champion helper and he didn't know how he'd managed without her. Jimmy was useful for heavy work like pruning and digging, he said, but small hands were best for picking fruit and planting seedlings. Alice loved being given jobs to do, but today she had been excused from work and allowed to come down to the Chinese House with paper and her precious tin of pencils, which Polly had defiantly reclaimed after Cousin Archie's visit. It was Mama's birthday soon, and Alice wanted to send her a picture. She had mentioned, in the letter that Polly was supposed to have put in the Chinese House, that she had come down here often during the happy week she'd spent alone at Blackwood, so it made an obvious subject.

Alice narrowed her eyes to study the fancy pattern of bars on the windows, then bent her head to reproduce it on the paper. She thought of Mama's letter – the last clue – and in her mind an image formed as she drew, of another summer's day in a time before she existed; young Mama stretched out on the wooden boards and music from the gramophone drifting out across the water. *It felt like the rest of the world was very far away,* Mama had written; *we caught fish in the lake and cooked them for dinner one night . . .* The word 'we' had jarred in Alice's head like a stone thrown into water, breaking up the clear reflections that had formed on its surface. Polly must have been there some of the time, she supposed. She must remember to ask her.

Mama's letters came less often now. It was the post, Polly said. The place where they were was very remote, and it was the rainy season of course, which Polly said might slow things down more. In her last letter Mama had sounded hopeful that Papa's business would soon be finished, and then they could begin the journey home. Her optimism had cheered Alice up immensely.

It couldn't be long now. The summer was almost over and autumn was here, drawing the year's circle closer to its close. It was Alice's birthday in November.

Mama would be back by then, she felt sure.

In the quiet of the afternoon when Alice had gone out to the garden and Ivy and Ellen sat in the servants' hall poring over the autumn fashion feature in *Peg's Paper*, Polly went to her room.

It wasn't the same one she'd had when she'd worked at Blackwood before. Ivy and Ellen shared that one now, and Polly had one to herself at the end of the corridor, with damp-blistered plaster and a high-up window that held nothing but a square of sky. (All the rooms were half below ground level in the servants' basement.) She'd had a position as under-housekeeper in a modern house just outside Winchester when Miss Selina's letter had arrived last December. Sometimes she thought wistfully of the attic room she had given up, which not only had a proper view over the garden, but also a carpet and a central heating radiator and a bathroom across the landing. It was little wonder that no one wanted to work in the big houses anymore. Blackwood felt like the workhouse in comparison to Meadowcroft Villa. Her mother had made her a rag rug for the tiled floor and given her an old patchwork quilt from the farmhouse to keep off the worst of the chill, but it was still like sleeping in a game larder. It hadn't been too bad during the summer, but winter was a different matter.

She'd hoped she wouldn't be there for another one.

Puffing out a breath she stooped down to drag a squat black case out from beneath the narrow bed (the legs of which were placed in jam jars of water, to catch the cockroaches. Not that there were many, but the precaution made Polly sleep easier). She lifted the case onto a rickety old table behind the door and opened the lid to reveal a typewriter, with the words *Remington Portable* picked out in gold above the keys.

She breathed in the metallic smell of oil and ink, running her fingers tentatively across the keys and making the little hammers ripple, like a dog's hackles rising. That seemed to sum up the mutual mistrust that persisted between her and the machine. It was – apparently – supposed to offer a more efficient method of writing, though Polly failed to see how when it took her a full minute to locate each letter, and the 'c' key didn't work properly. Tucked into the lid of the case was a box of writing paper (expensive, bought from Bond Street) and a ruled exercise book (cheap, bought from Woolworths) and an envelope with Alice's name on the front in turquoise ink. She took out a sheet of paper and fed it into the Remington's roller.

The flimsy chair creaked in protest as she sank down onto it, shoulders sagging. Everything she needed was in the notebook. All she had to do was decipher the handwriting and type out what was written, but every time it seemed to get harder, and feel more wrong. For the last week she had been aware of putting it off, hiding behind the flimsiest of excuses (going through Alice's clothes had been one of them) to avoid having to confront the deepening deception in which she was so enmeshed.

It wasn't the first time she'd got caught up in a lie for Miss Selina. Typing the last letter to Alice – the clue that she had botched so badly – had brought back the sweaty, palm-prickling torment of that morning eleven years ago, telling Lady Lennox that Miss Selina had been taken badly in the night and wouldn't be able to travel to Scotland. She'd felt herself going as red as a beetroot and been sure that God would strike her down right there and then, on Lady Lennox's bedroom carpet. Never again, she'd told herself afterwards. *Never again*.

And yet here she was.

But what choice did she have? She remembered the little girl who had arrived at Blackwood in the winter, who had been too homesick to utter a word for virtually a whole week. She thought of the evenings when she'd gone up to turn out the light and heard the child sobbing quietly, trying to muffle the sound in the pillow. She thought of her pale little face, pinched with misery, her dark eyes full of anguish, and remembered how helpless she had felt in the face of such distress. Little duck. The truth was Polly would have sworn on the Bible that the moon was made of cheese if it would have made her happier. She hadn't hesitated before agreeing to go along with Miss Selina's deception.

Her gaze was drawn reluctantly down to the exercise book. It was all in there; the last bit of the story, waiting to be told, though she couldn't quite bring herself to open it. Instead she got up and went over to the cheap little chest of drawers by the bed. Her hands shook a little as she pulled open the bottom drawer, moving aside a neatly folded nightdress, a slip and a couple of spare aprons to find what she was looking for.

A little square box of black leather, embossed with gold, and beneath it, an illustrated newspaper. The *Sphere*, it was called. News, descriptions of political goings-on in foreign places whose names Polly couldn't pronounce, reviews of London theatre productions; not a publication she would ever purchase herself. She had almost left it lying on the seat in the train back from London, and had only picked it up to avoid having to talk to the creepy-looking man with the waxed moustache who had sat down opposite her.

Everything happens for a reason. That was what her mother always said.

She sat down on the edge of the bed, turning the pages. Amongst all the dull news stories, it had been the photographs that caught her eye: faces that she recognized from the pictures at the Gaumont, but photographed in a way that made her look twice because they'd looked like ordinary people. Beautiful of course, but human. Like friends.

Her interest piqued, she'd read the article. A new film studio was opening, just outside London. Pinewood, it was called – the name similar enough to Hollywood to show that it was going to be as good – and the photographs showed various stages of its construction, and different stars looking around its sets and facilities. There was a lovely one of Anna Neagle, all laughing and relaxed, and Maurice Chevalier standing in the middle of a huge, empty studio. She had decided to take the magazine home for Ellen and Ivy before she noticed the name of the photographer.

Lawrence Weston.

She held the little box tightly in her hand for a moment, then tucked it back into the corner of the drawer to return to later. The magazine she took over to the table. She had kept it, brought it home, but something had stopped her handing it over to Ellen. She hadn't been sure what she would do with it, or if she would do anything at all, but this morning's conversation with Lady Lennox had made her mind up.

She knew that Selina would never have agreed to boarding school in Yorkshire if there had been any other option. Polly would never forgive herself if she didn't find out if there was.

But first, the treasure hunt. She couldn't put it off any longer. Miss Selina had written her story in the notebook for Polly to copy on the typewriter, but she was on her own now when it came to thinking up the clues. She wasn't good with words, not like Miss Selina, but Alice wasn't likely to notice if they weren't as clever as the earlier ones, and there were only two envelopes left to hide. She would apply her mind to that later. Straightening her shoulders she opened the exercise book and steeled herself to flick through the pages of spidery handwriting until she found the right place. With one finger, she began laboriously to type out the shaky words.

My Darling Al-i-c-e . . .

17

Things Left Unsaid

September 1925

There wasn't an empty table to be seen in Claridge's Grand Foyer. The summer was over and the wealthy and fashionable had drifted back from continental villas and country houses to visit dressmakers and hair salons and place orders at Harrods and Dickens and Jones. The space was filled with drawling, well-bred voices above the clink of china and restrained piano music.

Theo had already been at the table when Selina arrived. He had stood up to wish her a happy birthday when she was still halfway across the room, prompting the pianist to launch into the jaunty little tune and everyone to look round, much to Selina's embarrassment. It was mid-September but Theo still had the remains of his Italian suntan. He had an enticingly wrapped box with him – a birthday present for Selina – but since it was from him and Flick jointly he couldn't give it to her until Flick arrived.

'Twenty-two,' he said wistfully, dropping a lump of sugar into his teacup. 'Do you feel terribly old?'

'Not old so much as grown-up, I suppose. Much more so than I did on my last birthday, even though that's supposed to be the milestone.'

'Grown-up?' Theo dropped the sugar tongs with a clatter. 'My dear, how frightful. Don't tell me you'll be taking up embroidery and good causes like your sister? I shall have to disown you.'

'Darling, I'll disown myself if I ever become like my sister. I feel that the time has come to take more control of my life, that's all. I can't live by my parents' draconian rules for ever – or on their meagre allowance for that matter.'

Theo glanced at her sharply. 'I predict an upturn in interest in the ruby magnate may be on the cards. I don't believe you ever really told us what happened in Scotland. In fact, I recall you being distinctly evasive when the subject was brought up . . .'

She shrugged, not quite meeting his eye. 'Not at all. There's really nothing to say. It was all very yawn-making – I only saw Rupert twice and it rained incessantly.'

'Really?' Theo's elegant eyebrows rose a fraction. 'I bumped into Clarence Seaton at my tailor's last week – the poor boy's nose was still as pink as that carnation. He spent most of August at Buffy Campbell's lodge and said the weather had been scorching.'

'Well, yes . . .' Selina felt her cheeks going the same colour as Clarence's sunburned nose. If there had been a moment to confide in Flick and Theo about Lawrence and their stolen week it had long since passed. 'I suppose it was rather warm at the beginning, but after the third day of relentless rain one quite forgets that the sun has ever shone, don't you think?'

Theo leaned back, crossing his legs in their extravagant Oxford bags and brushing a crumb off one knee. 'Only twice in two weeks,' he said musingly. 'Carew's a cool customer, one must admit. I thought he might take full advantage of your inability to escape and beat a path through the heather to your door.'

'I imagine the guns wanted to make the most of the weather while it was so good. He and his parents came over for dinner at the end of the first week and of course, Ruthie seated us together.' Selina pulled a face. 'He suggested we ride out to see some screamingly dull Celtic monument, but thankfully I was spared by the rain. Not from him coming back, but from the monument at least.'

They had sat in the library together and she had tried to keep her mind from straying constantly to Lawrence. Lawrence, shirtless, making scrambled eggs in the kitchen at Blackwood. Lawrence on the deck at the Chinese Tea House, a cigarette dangling from his mouth as he'd fished for the perch. Lawrence across the dining table in the candlelight, his eyes like pools of ink. Everyone believed that it had been illness that had delayed her arrival, so she had used

302

that as a shield to hide behind. An excuse for her detachment and distance.

'A lucky escape,' Theo drawled. 'Dear God, I do hope he hasn't mistaken you for a sturdy country type. What did you talk about?'

'Burma mostly. It was the only thing I could think of to ask him about.'

Rupert had talked, and she had listened, with a growing interest that surprised her. With the Highland mountains cloaked in mist and the rattle of rain against the window it had been rather soothing to let her imagination wander to the places he described – the damp heat of the jungle, the extravagant gold temples and endless rice fields and the little hill station where the streets were all given English names. He outlined the problems that were endemic in the management of the ruby mines: an isolated and inaccessible location, intractable workers, the difficulty of importing supplies. As he spoke she turned these difficulties over in her mind. Following their complicated strands gave her temporary respite from the monotony of her own thoughts. *Lawrence. Lawrence. Lawrence.*

'Good show,' Theo said faintly, sipping his tea. 'Commendably grown-up.'

Beneath his wholesome suntan he looked tired, she noticed, and wondered if things had disintegrated further with Andrei. He had confessed that their Italian idyll had been marred by petty arguments and sulky silences. Andrei's artistic temperament, which had formed a large part of his attraction in London, had manifested itself in jealous rages when they were abroad, and Theo had been unable to catch the eye of a waiter in a restaurant without it sparking a quarrel that would simmer for days. She was about to ask him how things were between them now when he looked pointedly towards the door and twitched his cuff back irritably.

'The idea of fashionable lateness is one of several things Lady Felicity is taking just a tiny bit too far these days,' he said acidly. 'I even told her we were meeting half an hour earlier than was the case. Really, one doesn't want to be a dreadful old fusspot – that's what Aunt Constant Killjoy is for – but since she got back from Cap Ferrat she's been worse than ever. Have you noticed? Too terribly *distrait*.'

'Flick is always *distrait*. It's why we adore her.'

'Of course, but I can't help noticing it's worse of late. My dear, one doesn't want to be a gossip, but she *forgets* things. Last week—'

'Oh look – here she is now!'

Selina cut him off as she saw Flick emerge from the revolving doors – looking as marvellous as ever, she noted with relief. Under the stylish influence of her Godless-mother she had taken full advantage of the boutiques and couture studios during her stay on the Riviera and was wearing a coat Selina hadn't seen before, in ivy green velvet with a tawny fur collar that framed her elfin face. Shoes in rich brown leather, the colour of conkers, clitter-clattered across the marble floor as she hurried towards them, bringing the scent of autumn air and coal soot from outside. Her cheeks were pink and her eyes shone.

'Am I unforgivably late? So silly – I just lay down for the tiniest nap after luncheon, and the next thing I knew it was four o'clock. Isn't that too funny? Darlings, I haven't kept you waiting, have I?'

'The teeniest bit,' Theo snapped. 'I didn't think I ought to give Selina her present until you arrived.'

'Present? Oh – your *birthday* present! Of course—' Flick leaned across the table to kiss Selina's cheek, misjudging the distance slightly so that Selina had to grab her arm to stop her from falling. 'Many happy returns, angel. I've quite lost track of the days, because they're all so damp and miserable. I feel like I'm suffering from a permanent chill and Nanny will start threatening to rub my chest with goose fat. It's not at all like darling France, where it's warm all the time, even in the evenings, and one can wear pretty clothes and take siestas and have marvellous fun in the casino.'

A waiter appeared to take her coat. She shrugged it off carelessly, swiping one silky fur cuff through the cream on the top of a Tarte Parisienne, and revealing a fabulously up-to-the minute dress beneath; drop-waisted and knife-pleated. Compared to what Selina was wearing – one of Miranda's blouses from last year, with a skirt that Polly had taken up to this year's length – her clothes were excessively pretty.

'Tea, madam?' the waiter asked.

Flick pulled a face as she looked around the table. 'Is that what we're having? I rather hoped it might be cocktail time.'

Theo took the cigarette case from his pocket and flipped it open before offering it to Selina. 'It's a quarter to five.' His voice was clipped.

'How dreary. In Cap Ferrat it's *always* cocktail time, and there are always fascinating people just falling over themselves to buy them for one. Oh, but wait – it's your *birthday*!' She brightened visibly, clapping her hands. 'We should have champagne! Do let's!'

The waiter bent and murmured something discreet about licensing hours. Flick's face fell. 'Too unutterably tiresome. Bring a bottle over the very second we can drink it without being swooped upon by officers of the law. Now—' she turned to Selina. 'Do open your present, darling.'

There was something slightly frantic about her. Her eyes didn't shine so much as glitter, and the hand she cupped around her cigarette as Theo lit it fluttered like a leaf in a breeze. Squashing down her unease, Selina took the ribbon-tied box Theo held out to her and smiled broadly at them both.

'How exciting! You *are* lovely.' She touched the glossy ribbon. 'It's too pretty to open.'

'Don't be silly, and do hurry up – I'm dying to see your face. Theo found it in Florence. Or was it Venice? Anyway – simply *too* clever of him . . .'

Selina undid the ribbon and lifted the lid of the box, folding back layers of crisp tissue paper to reveal a lustrous tortoiseshell trinket box, edged and inlaid with delicate silver filigree patterns. In the centre, in swirling silver inlay, were the entwined letters S and L.

Her heart faltered. For a heady second she wondered how they knew, when they'd discovered her secret, before realising that as far as her friends were concerned the letters were her initials, nothing more. Laughing, she blinked back tears.

'Isn't it simply perfect?' Flick said triumphantly. 'Terribly old apparently, but it could have been made just for you. Isn't Theo clever to have spotted it?'

'Lucky, really,' Theo said modestly. 'It was in the window of a jeweller's shop in Venice – I only noticed it because Andrei was in one of his moods and had flounced off, and I was in no hurry to catch up. And not quite perfect. I believe that it actually says *S&L* on the top, but even so. I like to think it was meant to be.'

'It was.' Selina's voice cracked. She wanted to tell them that the '*&*' made it even more special, but she didn't know where to start. 'Absolutely meant to be, and absolutely perfect. Thank you. Thank you both so much. I adore it.'

After that the waiter brought the champagne and they toasted and drank and Flick talked again about Cap Ferrat, scattering exotic names and improbable titles over the table like ash from the cigarette she waved about. 'Next year you must come with me, Selina darling. No argument. I simply cannot think why you still agree to go to a dreary old castle for shooting with your mama and papa – it's too absurd at your age.'

Selina didn't bother reminding her that she didn't have the financial independence to do anything else and seized her moment. 'I rather agree. In fact, the less time I spend with my mama and papa the better, which brings me back to what we were saying the other night – do you remember?'

Flick's glass was empty and she was looking round for the waiter. 'The other night? Which one?'

'Monday, after the KitKat, when we couldn't find a taxi. We talked about getting a set of rooms together. Somewhere small but central – a sort of base.'

'Darling, I thought it was one of your outlandish schemes,' Flick said, giving up on the waiter and refilling her glass herself. 'Were you serious?'

'Why not? Wouldn't it be marvellous to have somewhere lovely and central that was all our own? No one to make a fuss about us coming in late, or the noise of the gramophone and the number of empty bottles.'

'Oh gosh, yes . . .' Flick said, with feeling. 'Aunt Constance has been worse than ever since I got back from France – watching me like a hawk, instructing Harris and dear old Simpson to spy. She's even started to mark the levels on the decanters in the drawing room.'

Across the table Theo's expression was oddly blank, but one elegantly manicured finger tapped against the stem of his glass. Selina sensed his disapproval without understanding it; it wasn't like him to be a dog in the manger. 'You have to admit, it would be heaven . . . Our own place to get ready before going out, and to go back to after the bars have closed. Our own fire to toast crumpets on with no one to be cross because it's too early or too late or the servants are busy.'

'It's a topping idea,' Flick beamed. 'We should start looking straight away. Well, not straight away because it must be
time to think about dressing for dinner – where on earth did
the day go? What are we doing this evening? Did Aggie say
she was having an At Home, or is that tomorrow?'

'Angel, it was Tuesday.' There was an edge to Theo's tone.
'We went, remember?'

'Oh yes – silly me.' Flick laughed, a sound like the tinkle
of the piano, but a little off key. 'It's Thursday today, isn't
it? So that means The Embassy. Dinner at the Eiffel first?'

'I can't.' Guiltily, Selina drained her glass and began to gather
up her belongings. 'I promised Mama I'd be home for a birthday
dinner – Miranda and Lionel are back from their honeymoon
and desperate to show off reams of tedious photographs.'

'Oh *Selina*!' Flick wailed. 'That's too bad! It's *your* birthday, you should be allowed to have fun. You can come later,
can't you? To The Embassy. You simply *must.*'

'I'll try,' she lied. 'And I'll buy an evening paper on the
way home and look in the advertisements for lodgings. The
sooner we can make our escape the better.'

She said her goodbyes, and repeated her thanks for the
present, in a flurry of kisses, uneasily aware of Theo's slight
froideur and Flick's disappointment. As she made her way
through the tables and across the foyer she could feel their
eyes on her, tiny needles of reproach pricking at the back of
her neck. Or maybe she was being paranoid. Maybe it was
just her own guilty conscience, rightly punishing her for her
dishonesty and disloyalty.

The cold air hit her as the revolving door spat her onto the street. The light was bleeding out from the day and the headlamps of motorcars made ribbons of gold on the wet road. A gust of wind whipped leaves around her ankles and she pulled her coat more tightly around her. The doorman stepped forward.

'Taxi, miss?'

She should decline the offer and take the underground train, which would be so much cheaper. But it would be slower too, and impatience pulsed through her veins. Another time she would brave the discomfort and inconvenience of public transport, but not now. Not today, when he was waiting for her. When they would be properly alone together for the first time in over a month.

She nodded. 'To Bloomsbury. Marchmont Street.'

At five o'clock, when there was still almost an hour of usable light left, Lawrence dropped his brush into a marmalade jar of turpentine and wiped his fingers on a stained rag. Edith looked round in surprise.

'Finished?'

'For today.'

He had been painting like a demon for weeks, working harder than he ever had. Against the studio walls, interspersed with numerous vast and energetic seascapes Edith had painted during a summer in St Ives, were several completed portrait commissions, waiting for the paint to harden sufficiently to be parcelled up and delivered. The portrait on the easel – Lance Corporal Douglas Mackay, Royal Highlanders Division – would join them tomorrow.

'Splendid!' Edith beamed. 'Am I finally going to be able to tempt you out for a drink?'

He usually worked until well after she had downed tools (literally – since returning from St Ives she had begun experimenting with woodcuts, and acquired a collection of alarming sharp implements) and flung on her old coachman's cloak to take herself off to the Marlborough Arms, where a new influx of Slade students waited to be dazzled by her bohemian glamour and buy her drinks. She was always trying to persuade him to accompany her and he always refused. He felt guilty to be doing it again.

'Sorry. I'm afraid I've got to be off.'

'Ah. Special occasion?' Edith's tone was one of casual enquiry, but he sensed a challenge in the way she was looking at him. 'Or is it just the girl that's special?'

'Both,' he admitted. Going over to the velvet-draped divan in the corner he picked up his jacket from amongst the clutter and checked that the little square box was still in the pocket. He had collected it this morning from a jeweller's shop in Holborn, which was conveniently situated next to a barber's. The package he had picked up from there was in the other pocket. He still had to go to La Normandie to collect the *pot au feu* Madame had agreed to sell him, to heat up on the stove at Marchmont Street for dinner.

Luck was on his side; Selina's birthday, and Sam had gone away for a few days. (To Northumberland, to write a piece about a pit disaster that had taken the lives of thirty-eight miners. Not so lucky for them.) Since Selina's return to London the frustration of snatched, unsatisfactory meetings in public places was getting to them both. Separation had almost been easier to bear than being together and not being able to touch, of having to carry his camera with him like a shield, so that anyone who recognized either of them would presume that the meeting was professional. The opportunity to be alone together was rare and precious, and he wanted it to be perfect.

Edith's eyes were still on him. 'Do I know her?'

'*Of* her, yes.'

'Ah.' Edith sighed. 'I feared as much. I suppose you were never going to fall in love with anyone ordinary, but you could have chosen a slightly more realistic object for your affections than Selina Lennox.'

He paused, his jacket half-on. 'How did you know it was her?'

Her smile was rueful, a little sad. 'Dear boy, I'm not nearly as dippy as I make out. I saw those photographs in *The Sketch* – the ones that were supposedly of her sister's wedding. And I never quite believed that you left the Napier girls' party early because you were tired.'

It was always difficult to fool Edith. He didn't bother trying to deny it.

'I never said anything about falling in love with her.'

Edith gave him a pitying look.

'You didn't have to.'

18

The Watchers On The Walls

It was strange, being back where it all began.

He opened the door and pulled her into the hallway where she'd first seen him. They fell together against the worn Lincrusta, grinning and kissing, clumsy with delight, bumping against the table (where the sickly potted aspidistra still clung to life) before he seized her hand and led her up the stairs.

She followed him to the top of the house, past the closed doors to other people's lives. Raised voices and the smell of burnt toast came from behind one, the strains of a violin from another. The windows on each landing were large and dirty, looking out onto the black-brick backs of other houses, pressed up close. She had an impression of crowded humanity, as if she could hear hearts beating, strangers breathing through the thin walls. It only heightened the excitement, the audacity of their aloneness, as if they were hiding in plain sight.

At the top of the house they stumbled through a half-open door onto a small landing. There was a makeshift sort of a kitchen – an enamel sink with a single tap, a two-ring gas stove – beneath a skylight showing a patch of dusk. He broke off from kissing her long enough to nod to an iron pot on the stove.

'Dinner. Are you hungry?'

'Always, remember?' Already she was tugging his shirt free from his trousers. 'But let's eat later.'

With a groan he led her down to the room at the end, kicking the door shut behind them, pushing her against it and sliding his hands into her hair as their kisses grew more urgent. She slipped off her shoes and wriggled out of her coat, letting it fall to the floor with her handbag and the box Theo and Flick had given her, then pushed his braces over his shoulders and fumbled for the buttons of his shirt. He pulled away to yank it over his head, and it was then that she noticed the faces around the walls.

The light outside was dying. Numerous pairs of eyes gazed through the gathering dusk from hundreds of photographs, pinned haphazardly around the room. She wanted to look more closely, to study the expressions and emotions of the people they showed, but he was unfastening the tiny pearl buttons at the neck of her blouse and pulling it aside, bending his head to press his lips to her shoulder ... her breast.

She closed her eyes, and there was only darkness, and him.

*

There was a streetlamp outside the window. Its yellow light filtered through the grime, past the undrawn curtains, and striped the pictures on the walls. Selina lay in Lawrence's arms, drowsy and content, and let her eyes wander unhurriedly over them.

They were like nothing she'd ever seen before. Many of them were close-up shots of faces, but they hadn't been taken to flatter or to celebrate a particular event – a party, a day at the races – like the kind of photographs she knew. These people were unsmiling. They were, for the most part, dirty and dishevelled. They were miners with coal-blackened faces and veterans with missing limbs, toothless tramps and shoeless urchins. Selina felt uncomfortable, looking at them, but she couldn't look away.

Downstairs the violinist was still playing. At some point between their heart-thumping dash up the stairs and the moment when they had fallen together onto the bed the unseen musician had changed from scales and arpeggios to practising a soaring, complicated piece, which had given a sweet poignancy to their passion. Selina didn't recognize it, but she knew that she would never forget it.

Lawrence's breath was warm on her neck, his arm deliciously heavy across her ribs. Looking down she could see his hand, resting between her breasts, his beautiful fingers relaxed. She took them in hers, straightening them out gently, marvelling at their length and elegance. Working hands, stained with paint. Hands that could build a fire and gut a fish. Hands that could capture a moment with a camera and bring a face to life on canvas. Hands that could make her quiver and tense and take her breath away.

He stirred and sighed, and she felt the delicate graze of his stubble against the back of her neck as he kissed her nape.

'Happy birthday. I don't think I said it, did I?'

She smiled. 'Deeds not words, as the marvellous Mrs Pankhurst used to say.'

'I'm glad you think she'd approve.'

Selina raised her head briefly to look down at their entwined limbs. 'I think approval might be going a bit far . . .'

Kissing her shoulder he got up, lighting an oil lamp beside the bed and pulling on trousers. 'In that case I'll go and heat up dinner, to prove I'm an ally to the cause of female emancipation.'

The leaping light animated the faces on the walls, casting different shadows, bringing them to life. She reached for a depleted pack of Woodbines on the nightstand and lit one, leaning back against the pillows to look at them. Amongst the portraits of anger and hopelessness there were different kinds of photographs, she realized now. Jealousy curdled in her stomach as she noticed one of a naked girl lying on a velvet-covered couch. She had her back to the camera and her sharp shoulder blades looked like little wings. In another, a girl (the same one?) lay on her back holding a cigarette aloft between languid fingers. The pale wreaths of smoke, and their darker shadow on the wall, were at the centre of the image, but Selina found herself studying the girl's hand and the curve of her wrist. How was it possible for such an innocuous thing to appear so sensual?

He came back carrying a bottle of red wine and two glasses. She wanted to ask him about the girl – who she was, and whether he had really just made love to her, as the photograph suggested – but knew she had no right. And that the answers might very well be ones she didn't want to hear.

'It's like being at the very best kind of private view,' she said, taking the glass of wine he poured her. 'More generous drinks and better music than most I've been to.'

'That's Mr Kaminski. He's second violinist for the Queen's Hall Orchestra. They're rehearsing for a new programme.'

'I like it. What is it?'

'Vaughan Williams.' He slipped into bed beside her. 'That piece was *The Lark Ascending*.'

The rich, delicious smell of cooking began to drift across the landing. They lay there, sipping wine, sharing the cigarette, listening to the soar and dip of the strings through the floorboards until the piece came to its shivering end.

It had been foolish, Selina later acknowledged, to have suggested spending her birthday with him. Unlike any other day of the year, it would never slip into the stream of ordinary, unremarkable dates and be lost amongst them. It would never be forgotten. For ever afterwards, as long as she lived, she knew that every year, every birthday, she would remember this one. And that none of the ones that followed would ever quite match up.

*

They ate with spoons from mismatched bowls, sitting crosslegged on the bed. The *pot au feu* was perfect; every bit as mouth-watering heated up on the battered old stove as it had been straight from Arnaud's kitchen. Better for being just the two of them, in a tumble of crumpled sheets and soft voices and the faint music of Mr Kaminski's violin.

They finished the first bottle of wine and he opened another. She told him, hesitantly, about the conversation she'd had with her friend, their intention to get a flat together, and hope stole through him like the warmth of the wine as he listened.

'I had lots of time to think in Scotland, and I know you were right. For so long I've yearned for independence, but without really thinking through the implications. What I'd have to give up to gain it.' She threw him a swift, self-deprecating smile. 'Polly, mainly. She's been with me for years. I'd trust her with my life.'

'Would she stay with you? On different terms, maybe?'

'I couldn't ask her. She loathes London. And anyway, I couldn't afford her. My allowance is tiny. I'll have to rely on Flick for the deposit on a flat as it is, and I'll need to get a job, to manage the rent. My parents will hate the idea, of course . . .' She was pleating the corner of the sheet nervously as she spoke, her lashes casting black shadows on her cheeks. 'But it's not uncommon these days for girls to work, and live independently. Look at Nancy Mitford, and Georgie Stanhope. Elizabeth Ponsonby has worked in most of the boutiques on Bond Street – one never knows where she's going to appear next.'

He reached across to stroke back the lock of hair that had fallen across her face, beginning to understand the significance of the step she was taking. 'Do they know about ... us? Your friends?'

She shook her head. 'Polly's the only one who knows. I couldn't keep it from her, after Blackwood, and she'd guessed anyway. I almost told Flick and Theo today. They gave me this, for my birthday—' She unfolded her legs and went across to get the parcel she'd dropped when she came in: a tortoiseshell box with silver letters on the top. Their initials, together. 'Theo was sorry about the "and" in the middle, but I said it was perfect, and I wanted to tell them why, but ...' Her eyes met his. 'How can I explain? It sounds like ... insanity. Girls like me have been put into asylums for less.'

He understood what she was referring to. Girls from good families who let themselves be seduced by the gardener, the chauffeur. Girls who were disobedient. Who would be called 'wanton' and deemed to be out of control because they fell for the wrong sort of boy. The common sort.

The hope evaporated a little.

'I'll tell them, of course. Soon.' She was crisp again as she swathed the tortoiseshell box back in its tissue layers, and he remembered the dining room at Blackwood, the candlelight glittering in her eyes. *Other people's emotions are always rather tiresome ... In fact, come to think of it, so are one's own ...*

He got up. Going over to where his jacket hung on a hook behind the door he took out the little jeweller's box and took it back to the bed in its circle of lamplight. The lamp was behind her, turning her hair into a halo of gold, leaving her face in shadow. He resisted the temptation to reach for his camera and held out the box instead.

'What's this?'

'Your birthday present.'

'Lawrence . . . ?' Her voice was wary. 'You didn't have to. I wasn't expecting anything. I just wanted to be with you this evening.'

'And I just wanted to give you something. It's not diamonds or rubies.' He couldn't quite keep the sarcasm from his tone. 'And don't worry – it's not a ring. I'm not going to embarrass you by asking you to marry me.'

She took it then, her hair falling over her face again as she bent to open the box. Mr Kaminski had finished practising and it was very quiet; quiet enough for him to hear her low inhalation.

'Lawrence . . . it's *beautiful*.'

Reverently she lifted the stone from its bed of ivory satin, holding it up by the chain so it glittered in the light. It was a large aquamarine; facet-cut and perfectly translucent, once the fob of a gentleman's old-fashioned pocket watch, but now suspended from a fine gold chain as a pendant. The Holborn jeweller had spent a long time telling him about its history – Georgian, apparently – the exceptional quality of the stone and the superiority of the swivel mount, none of which had any bearing on why he wanted it.

'I bought it,' he said gruffly, 'because it's the exact same colour as your eyes. Here—'

He took it from her and slipped it over her head. The chain was long enough for her to wear it beneath her clothes, unseen. He'd made sure of that. It rested between her breasts.

'Thank you.' She leaned across to take his face in her hands and kiss his mouth. 'I love it. I love you.'

'I love you too.'

'I'm scared, Lawrence.' Her forehead rested against his and her voice dropped to a whisper. 'Sometimes I feel like I'm ... walking a tightrope, across some bottomless abyss, and I'm scared that I'll slip and fall. And there'll be nothing there to catch me.'

'You won't fall. I've got you.'

'Don't let go.'

He rocked her gently, so that the bedsprings creaked a gentle lullaby.

'I won't.'

Hill View
Club Road
Maymyo
Burma

12th September 1936

Darling Alice,
    And so it goes on. Another month, and still we wait.
I try to stay cheerful and optimistic but it's so hard. In
my darker moments I have to confess I struggle to believe
I'll ever come home, ever see you again, and I ask myself
whether I was entirely wrong to begin all of this. I did it for
you, my darling, please understand that. There are times
when I think the truth, however awful, would have been
~~easier to~~ better for both of us. I don't know. Better for me,
certainly. Perhaps I'm being selfish. ~~I just want to~~

19

Selina

September 1936

She thought her eyes were open but it was so dark she couldn't be sure. Was she still asleep? Still dreaming?

The steady beat of pain in her head suggested not.

She lay very still, hoping that might ease it, knowing that it wouldn't. She tried to think around it, to grasp hold of something to anchor her, something comforting. She could hear rain on the window, steady and silvery. Was it still the rainy season? Her lips were dry but her skin was sticky with sweat, and with an effort she turned her head to see if the ceiling fan was turning, but her eyes burned and the tent of darkness above her was too thick to penetrate.

She should call someone. Ring the bell for Polly. Even as the thought formed in her head she knew it was wrong and that Polly wasn't there. For Lwin, or Than, then? Or Rupert. Would Rupert come?

A pale rectangle emerged from the gloom, close at hand. Memory stirred. Her birthday. Alice had sent a picture. Another pain joined the throb in her head, sharp and sudden, like a knife in her chest. She drew her legs up, curling around the emptiness like she had in the nursing home on the night that Alice was born. Such *love*, blossoming and bleeding inside her, expanding into the void of her misery. *Alice.* She wanted to pick up the picture, to look at it again, but the pale outline of it shimmered and shifted, beyond her reach. Instead she went to clasp the aquamarine pendant around her neck, warm and heavy between her breasts, her touchstone and talisman through all these years.

She heard her own cry of anguish.

Gone. *All gone.*

Footsteps outside. Voices and hands. A light switched on, making the pain bounce wildly around her head. A stinging pinch on her arm and then warmth, spreading upwards. Relief as the light dimmed again and quiet darkness returned.

She felt herself slipping back into numbness, and didn't resist. Someone was standing at the foot of the bed, watching, and she felt comforted by that. Not Polly. Not Lwin or Than or Rupert. A nurse. She opened her eyes a crack to see which one and felt a flash of delighted surprise.

'*Flick . . . !*'

'I've been waiting for you, darling,' she said, and laughed. 'Doesn't that make quite a change?'

20

The Fall

October 1925

As usual, Flick was late.

Selina stood beneath a leafless plane tree and peered out from under her umbrella, along Bayswater Road. It was going dark already and raindrops shimmered in the headlamps of the motorcars and buses swishing past. Every now and then a tram rattled along, its bright windows fogged, reducing the occupants to an impressionistic blur.

The advertisement for the flat in the *Evening Standard* had sounded promising, although after almost three weeks of flat-hunting she knew not to get her hopes up. *Close proximity to Hyde Park,* it had reassuringly stated: *all modern improvements and constant hot water.* The first blow to her optimism had been delivered on the telephone, when an overly elocuted female voice had informed her of the flat's address, thereby revealing that while it might be close to Hyde Park, it was on very much the wrong side of it.

It had taken much persuasion and two very strong Sidecars to convince Flick that Bayswater wasn't such a bad address, and they should at least look at the flat. Even after two weeks of disappointment Flick refused to accept that compromise was going to be necessary, and that the kind of accommodation she had in mind (which, so far as Selina could make out, was something with the space, comfort and staff of her father's house in Eaton Place but without the oppressive presence of Aunt Constance) was simply beyond their budget.

Money was another problem. Selina's search for a job had proved no more fruitful than the quest for a flat. Less so, in some ways, since everyone to whom she mentioned it seemed to think it was a huge joke. Everything was so much more difficult than Selina had anticipated.

It was the time of year, she thought wearily, struggling to hold her umbrella while pushing the cuff of her coat up and the top of her glove down to peer at her wristwatch. Autumn was always a trial. The Americans called it 'fall' which always struck her as wonderfully appropriate, describing as it did the season's effect on her spirits.

When she was little she'd adored it. She'd loved the majesty of the trees at Blackwood, the crisp morning walks with Nanny when the first frosts made the red-gold carpet of leaves crunch underfoot; the glossy conkers and jewel-like blackberries; sweet chestnuts that she was allowed to stuff into her pockets and bring back to roast on the nursery fire. On rare trips to London she loved the crackle of energy that arrived with the cold, carrying the first whisper of Christmas. She had never really noticed the rain, or the way the colour drained from the world as the leaves fell and the skies turned from summer blue to gunmetal grey. Until Howard died.

The news had come on a chilly morning in late October. No one told her at first, but she had known something was wrong because the maids were wide-eyed and silent and her governess had allowed her to play jacks while she left the schoolroom to talk with Nanny. She hadn't played, of course; she had listened at the door, and that was when she had heard it first. A word like the rustle of silk, so pretty she had kept hold of it. *Passchendaele.*

And then the next autumn had brought the Armistice; the leaden, exhausted relief that it was over tainted with bitterness that it was *too late.* And every autumn since, the attention of the whole nation had turned to its collective loss, with flag days and the Cenotaph and the building of village memorials, and the craze for wearing a paper poppy to signify remembrance.

As if one could forget.

She shivered and tugged up the collar of her coat. A taxi turned the corner at the end of the road and came towards her, its windscreen wiper waving cheerily. Maybe this would be Flick. She squashed down her irritation and stepped forward, summoning a smile. No doubt Flick would complain that she was late because Bayswater was such a terribly long way out, practically in the wilds of nowhere ... Hastily Selina went over the arguments in its favour. Proximity to the park, of course, and the darling coffee stand where they all congregated at the end of evenings out, and Whiteleys Department Store, which was almost as good as Harrods, really ... She briefly considered adding the tram route on Bayswater Road and Queensway underground station, but thought that mentioning public transport was more likely to put Flick off than anything.

The taxi sailed past, spraying her with water.

She gasped, and gaped down at her feet. In the gathering darkness she could see that her ivory stockings were now splattered with black, like the milkman's piebald pony. She gritted her teeth and gripped her umbrella more tightly, fighting back a shameful urge to cry.

Flick obviously wasn't coming, which was hardly surprising. Since the summer her habitual vagueness had reached record levels. Selina hesitated, wondering whether to give up and hail the next taxi that passed, or go on alone. A dray horse plodded towards her, head down, mane dripping. Behind it she could just make out a taxi. She thought of Chester Square, and tea by the drawing room fire, but even as she thought of those things her hand went to her chest, to clasp the stone that lay warm and heavy against her heart.

You won't fall. I've got you.

She turned and began to walk down Queensborough

Terrace, to find number seventeen, with its modern improvements and constant hot water.

It was late when she got back to Chester Square. She had braved the underground, starting as she meant to go on in her new life as an independent working girl, but it had been choked with people making their way home and the journey had been more complicated than she'd realized, with a change of line at Notting Hill Gate. It had taken over an hour, and by the time she reached Chester Square her shoes had rubbed her wet skin raw.

As Fenton ushered her in she tried not to compare the accommodation she had just viewed with her present surroundings. Her mother's taste was still firmly rooted in the Edwardian style and Selina had always been disdainful of the heavy furniture and richly patterned wallpapers and curtains. Tonight she only noticed that it was deliciously warm and smelled of pot pourri and polish, and had an indefinable atmosphere of stability. The flat in Queensborough Terrace had been dark and clammily cold, and had smelled like the potting sheds at Blackwood – of leaf mould and mushrooms. Its fittings had been flimsy, with newspaper stuffed into the window frames and handles missing from the doors. It was just as well Flick hadn't seen it. She would have fainted on the bald linoleum.

She shrugged off her coat and handed it to Fenton. 'Could you leave that out for Polly to take care of? I got splashed by a beastly taxi and I'm sure the oily water will stain.'

'Very good, miss.' Fenton was usually rather chipper, but tonight his tone was almost as sepulchral as Denham's. 'Sir Robert and Lady Lennox are waiting for you in the drawing room. Mr and Mrs Atherton are with them.'

Selina was so preoccupied with the idea of going upstairs and sinking into the deepest, warmest bath that for a moment she couldn't think who Mr and Mrs Atherton were, and it was something of a relief to realize it was only Miranda and Lionel. 'I'm afraid they'll just have to wait a bit longer,' she said going towards the stairs. 'I simply must go up and change.'

She was about to risk Fenton's further disapproval by asking him to get Polly to bring up a large medicinal whisky when the drawing room door opened and Miranda appeared.

'Selina darling . . .'

She was smiling, which was unusual in itself, but there was something about the smile that set off a dull drumbeat of alarm in Selina's chest. It contained neither triumph nor scorn. Only pity. The solid marble floor tilted beneath her.

'What's happened?'

'Come into the drawing room where it's warm.'

'Miranda, what's wrong?'

'We can hardly talk out here. Do come in and sit down . . .'

'I don't want to sit down. Tell me now.'

'Selina . . .'

Who knows how long the stalemate might have lasted if Lionel hadn't appeared. He wore the same smile as Miranda, and suddenly she remembered where she had seen it before. At Blackwood, on another October evening when she was fourteen years old.

'I'm terribly sorry, old girl ...' Lionel's hand was on her arm. She looked down at it and thought how pale and soft it was. Not like Lawrence's. 'I heard this afternoon, at my club. Details are a bit sketchy at present, but we thought you should know as soon as possible ...'

'Know what?' Her voice sounded as if it was coming from the end of a long tunnel.

'It's Flick. I'm afraid – Dash it all, Selina, I'm so sorry ...'

The rest of what he said was swallowed up in the booming echoes inside her head. It felt like she had slipped underwater: everything was muffled and slow. She opened her mouth to argue – to tell Lionel not to be ridiculous; Flick was always doing outrageous things, causing them to worry, but she wouldn't do anything as foolish as *dying* – but found she couldn't draw in breath. Miranda's blurred face hung in front of her, stretching and contracting. 'Catch her, Lionel – she's going to faint.'

The black and white tiled floor was in the wrong place. How annoying, Selina thought; Miranda was right – she should have sat down.

Lawrence read about the death of Lady Felicity Fanshawe in the *Evening Standard*, which appeared in the studio two days after the event, wrapped around a bunch of dahlias Edith had bought.

He had heard about it already, from Sam, in the kind of scurrilous, speculative detail that newspapers were forbidden from going into. Especially respectable newspapers like the *Standard*, which had simply stated that twenty-one-year-old Lady Felicity had been discovered by her maid in the bath, and the cause of death was drowning. A bland mention of the fact that she was part of the group referred to as 'The Bright Young People', famed for their 'extravagant parties and lavish lifestyle' was the closest it came to mentioning the combination of drink and drugs that, according to Sam, had brought about her end.

Lawrence would never have imagined that the premature death of a society girl he had never met would have an impact on him. But it did. Selina had spoken about her so much, with such affection, and he knew that her death would be a huge and terrible blow. He desperately wanted to comfort her and willed her to appear at the studio, as she sometimes did in the evenings after Edith had left. Day after day he waited, and compassion tipped into concern, then slipped towards despair.

Why didn't she come?

The worst thing was his helplessness. Or, more specifically, the painful truth it brought home, which was that the threads that connected them were gossamer-fine and easily broken. Since Selina's birthday he had allowed himself to start believing that it might just be possible for them to be together, somehow; that they could find a way. But the tragedy of Flick Fanshawe's death was like an explosion in the

No Man's Land between them, and in its aftermath he felt like he was left on the opposite edge of an immense crater with no way of reaching her, or knowing if she was all right.

In desperation, he wrote to her. The letter took him most of the night, and his screwed up, discarded attempts kept the fire burning into the small hours, which was some bleak, ironic comfort. He couldn't find the words to pin down the thoughts he wanted to express. The feelings. He didn't want to intrude on her grief, but he wanted her to know that he was there, waiting to offer her comfort and to listen and to hold her . . . Jesus, that was the problem. He just wanted to hold her and not say anything at all. But she wasn't there and words were all he had.

In the morning, sleepless and dishevelled in yesterday's clothes, he took the first tube to Victoria and walked to Chester Square through streets that were stirring with the subdued industry of maids and delivery boys. The house was cream-stuccoed, immaculate, imposing. Standing outside, he had an urge to hammer on the glossy door, to shove past whoever answered it and storm up the stairs shouting her name, pushing open doors until he found her. He had to remind himself that she wasn't being held captive, against her will. She didn't need to be rescued. She had closed herself off from him by choice.

When he got back to Marchmont Street Sam was frying bread and black pudding on the landing. 'That funeral's this afternoon,' he remarked casually through a miasma of acrid smoke. 'Chelsea Old Church; not very grand, but I'll bet it'll be quite a spectacle. Get along there with that camera of yours and you could earn a pretty penny . . .'

Lawrence turned away in disgust.

The worst thing was, he thought about it. Not taking his camera, of course, but just going there. The idea of standing at a discreet distance to see her and reassure himself that she still lived and breathed held a horrible attraction.

In his second year at the Slade, when they'd been allowed to move on from the endless anatomical studies of skeleton and muscle, they'd done sketches of various organs. The tutor had unwrapped scarlet-stained newspaper packages from the butchers and the room had filled with the smell of the charnel house as the day wore on and the sun had poured its warmth through the huge windows.

He thought back now, remembering the heart; a bloody fist, purplish and trailing tubes. At the time he had been struck by the absurdity of this misshapen lump of raw flesh being the symbol of love. Now he understood it better. Love wasn't neat or pretty.

It was messy, raw and brutal.

21

Going On

The single thin note of the church bell echoed through the frozen air. It had turned suddenly colder, and though clouds massed above the river, there was no rain. It was as if the sky, like Selina, was too shocked to shed its tears.

Other people were arriving; black-clad figures stepping out of chauffeur-driven cars and taxicabs, materializing through the gloom. Selina kept her eyes downcast. Miranda's fingers dug into the flesh at the top of her arm as she steered her towards the church door.

No one spoke. The only sound, beneath the relentless tolling of the bell, was expensively shod feet on the frozen pavement and the faint, sepulchral swell of organ music from inside the church, but just as Selina reached the porch she heard the muffled click of a camera shutter. Her head snapped up in time to see a thickset, florid-faced man standing on the other side of the street lower his camera and turn

335

quickly away. The hot flash of hope was replaced by icy loathing; for the callous photographer, who couldn't leave Flick alone even now, but just as much for herself, unable to stop thinking of Lawrence when that had played such a large hand in Flick's tragedy.

'I tried to tell you,' Theo had said, unable to stop bitterness seeping into his voice. He had come to the house, and seeing him in her mother's domain, amongst the Sèvres china and needlepoint cushions, only added to the surreal nightmare atmosphere of the days following Flick's death. 'I noticed things were different when she came back from the continent. I recognized some of the names she mentioned . . .' He had shuddered then, sloshing tea over the rim of his cup. 'European royalty? There's not a drop of blue blood in the whole bogus crowd.'

Selina had tried to get her numb brain to take in what he was saying, and to go back over the last few weeks and pick up the clues she had been too caught up in herself to notice. They hadn't seen as much of each other as they might usually have, but autumn was an odd time of year when half of their crowd was in the country and parties were few and far between. She remembered the times when they had arranged to meet and Flick had arrived late, her eyes shining a little too brightly and her words spilling out a little too quickly, her insistence that it was drinks time, whatever the hour. She had talked about people that Selina didn't know, unfamiliar names and exotic titles littering her conversation like the autumn leaves on the pavements outside, but Selina hadn't minded that she had new friends and a part of her life that she didn't share.

Because so did she.

A waft of Mitsouko heralded Lally's arrival. She was dramatically swathed in a squashy dark fur coat with a black turban hat, faultlessly stylish even in grief. 'Darling,' she murmured as she kissed Selina's cheek. And then, because there was nothing else to say, she took out her cigarette case and offered it around. Miranda, standing tight-lipped at Selina's side, gave a curt shake of her head, but Selina took one. Dutifully, Lionel offered his lighter. As she leaned into the flame Lally's eyes slid past Selina's shoulder. She blew smoke into the frosty air.

'Poor Theo. He's aged twenty years in a week.'

Selina turned. Theo had just got out of a taxi, and was leaning on Clarence Seaton's arm while Harry Lonsdale paid the driver. Lally was right. Theo's face was milk-white against his dark suit and tie, his eyes swollen and red-rimmed. As he began to walk towards them he appeared as frail and shaky as an old man.

'I must say, I've been to better parties,' he joked weakly as he joined them. Fumbling for Selina's hand he gripped it tightly as they embraced. For a moment they clung together, and she could feel the heave of his thin chest against her still, cold, empty one. He pulled away, hastily scrubbing his eyes with a silk handkerchief, standing back to look at her sternly. 'Dear God, child, what are you wearing? Did you borrow it from a diminutive parlourmaid?'

He was braver, better at keeping up the pretence of normality than she was. It cost her everything to muster a wan smile. 'It's my pale blue. Polly dyed it, but we only realized when I put it on today that it's shrunk.'

Thank God for Polly. Her calm, steady, practical presence had been as comforting as the glow of a candle in endless, impenetrable darkness. She had looked after Selina as tenderly as a child, keeping the fire stoked in her room, ordering milk puddings from the cook to tempt her vanished appetite, staying with her through the long nights. Miranda, in her new superior status as a married woman, was making a great effort to be kind and supportive, but Selina would have welcomed her old animosity. Her sister's spiteful asides would have given her own anger an outlet; an excuse to unleash the rage that whirled inside her like a destructive tornado.

'Look at us.' Theo's voice was bitter and his eyes filled with tears again as he glanced around their forlorn little group. 'The Bright Young People. No wonder the newspapers have sent photographers to document our downfall. The editors must be positively gleeful that the gilded bubble has burst and we've got our comeuppance—'

'Flick's here,' Harry cut him off, and for a split second Selina's heart leapt with wild relief. And then she saw the large black motorcar pulling up at the kerb and reality knocked the air from her lungs again.

As sombre-faced men in top hats opened the doors of the hearse and slid out a flower-decked coffin, an elderly man emerged from a second motorcar, his narrow shoulders stooped, his face creased with age and grief. Flick's father, Selina realized, who usually shunned society completely, but had been forced from the sanctuary of his library and the company of his books and microscopes for this saddest of gatherings. He had Flick's slight build, the same faintly childlike air of puzzlement as he held his hand out to help his sister from the car. Aunt Constance was exactly as Selina remembered her from the days of their Coming Out. Her face was pinched with suspicion, her thin lips pursed in disapproval, as if she expected to be confronted with a Negro jazz band and a troop of chorus girls in sequins and feathers.

'Poor old Constant Killjoy,' Theo said. 'I'm sorry for being so cruel about her now. She was only trying to do what was best for Flick. To keep her safe.'

Safe. The word beat like butterfly wings inside Selina's head as they joined the slow, shuffling procession behind the coffin. She kept her eyes averted from it, instead looking up at the pewter-grey sky, the church steps, the glowing electric lights suspended above the aisle.

Aunt Constance's vigilance hadn't kept Flick safe. Flick had been too set on her own course, in pursuit of novelty and fun, to brighten up a merciless world. In her head Selina saw the trapeze artist, swinging high and wide and fast across the big top, fear and frailty hidden behind a dazzling smile.

'I am the resurrection and the life . . .' the vicar intoned.

Selina's heart jolted. For a dizzying moment she was no longer in the polish-scented church but a dark garden in

Bloomsbury, listening not to the vicar but to Lawrence. *Something about us coming into the world with nothing, and leaving with nothing? And a bit about the resurrection and the life. He who believeth in me will live, even though he dies.*

In a panic, she tried to force her thoughts away from him, stumbling a little as Miranda steered her into a pew. The ground beneath her felt like it was dissolving, slipping away like sand.

Oh God . . .

She had looked down. Halfway across the tightrope she had allowed herself to become too bold, too self-assured, and now she looked down and saw the yawning void below. Emptiness. A dark vortex, waiting to swallow her, like it had swallowed Howard and now Flick, and there was nothing to stop her from falling.

Lawrence had told her that he wouldn't let her fall. She had allowed herself to believe him; she had desperately wanted to. He had made her feel safe, but it had been an illusion. A lie.

He had written. A letter had arrived that morning, the absence of a stamp indicating that he had delivered it himself. The idea of him coming to the house, being so close without her knowing, was both absurd and unbearable; she had briefly felt irrationally angry with him for not trying to see her, though she knew how ridiculous that was.

The letter was long. Beautiful. Reading it was like listening to his voice. *I am here,* he had written. *I will be waiting for you, whenever you are ready. Day or night, whether it takes a week or a month or a year. I love you.* She hadn't been able to read any further. Hadn't let herself go back there, to that time when she believed that all would be well if she just wished it so, and that loving and being loved made her invincible.

It didn't. It made her foolish and wild and irrational. Like too many cocktails, or the powder Flick kept in her compact. It was dangerous. Destructive.

The cloying scent from the lilies massed on top of the coffin was making her feel sick. She pictured the light filtering through the curtains in her room at Blackwood and remembered lying beside him, *beneath him*, imprinting every white throated bloom with the glow of her bliss. Staring at the waxy petals now, she wondered how she could have forgotten that they were funeral flowers.

'*Lord, let me know mine end,*' the vicar was saying tonelessly, '*and the number of my days, that I may be certified how long I have to live . . . Oh spare me a little that I may recover my strength, before I go hence and be no more seen . . .*' She needed air. In desperation she turned round, and met the cool gaze of Rupert Carew.

He was sitting right at the back of the church, on his own, and was the last person she expected to see; he hadn't known Flick or exchanged more than the briefest and most cursory of social pleasantries with her. For a moment his eyes held hers, and then he smiled faintly. Approvingly.

'Let us pray.'

Dazed, she turned back to the vicar again and bowed her head.

*

There was no opportunity for a proper goodbye.

When they left the church the coffin was carried back to the hearse, to be driven to Suffolk where Flick's body would be laid to rest alongside her mother.

Selina had no right to feel resentful. The Chelsea service had been a concession; a belated acknowledgement from Flick's father and aunt of the friends they had found so hard to accept during her life. She could understand their wish to take Flick home and say a private farewell to their lost girl but, as the hearse doors were shut, she felt a wrench of agonizing anguish.

Twisting her arm from Miranda's grip she went forwards, pushing through the huddles of mourners. She heard Theo say her name, his voice cutting jaggedly through the dull winter afternoon, but she didn't turn round. *It was too soon.* She had spent the whole church service trying not to look at the coffin, but now she couldn't bear to let it out of her sight. Because that would mean Flick really was gone.

She wasn't sure exactly what she had intended to do. Afterwards she wondered if she would have pulled open the hearse's doors or battered her fists against its windows – had she been that unhinged? She would never know, because, just before she reached it, Rupert Carew appeared in front of her, blocking her way.

He took hold of her shoulders, bending smoothly to kiss her cheek. To an observer, who couldn't feel the iron strength of his grip, it would look like the most correct of greetings. Selina thought about struggling but let herself go limp.

'Good girl.'

The engines of the motorcars spluttered and throbbed. Doors slammed. From behind her Selina heard the sound of muffled sobbing as the hearse began to move away. Her own eyes were dry and her throat felt swollen and sore, as if she had swallowed something that had stuck there. She watched, unblinking, as the hearse and its beloved cargo was gradually lost from sight in the traffic of an ordinary London day.

It was only then that she realized that Rupert was still holding on to her. Holding her up. Gently, he let her go.

She stepped back, brushing invisible dust from her coat, pulling it closed to hide her shrunken dress.

'I didn't expect to see you here.' Her voice seemed to come from far away, as if someone else was speaking for her. 'I wasn't aware that you knew Flick.'

'I didn't. I came for you, to support you. These things are never easy. One just has to . . . go on.'

His reply surprised her. She glanced up, and saw that his face was as expressionless as ever. 'Yes, I suppose one does.' She looked away again. 'The trouble is, I'm not quite sure how.'

'There's a concert tonight, at the Queen's Hall. A modern programme, I think – not particularly my taste, but the orchestra is excellent. Perhaps you would join me?'

She almost laughed. Sitting through a programme of modern music beside Rupert Carew was just about the last thing she wanted to do, but then she didn't want to do anything. Except flag down the next taxi and hammer on

Lawrence's door until he came down and took her in his arms. Took her into his bed and enclosed her in the private world they had made their own, where no one else existed and nothing else mattered. Where there was no death or danger. Where lies seemed like promises and ugly reality had no place.

Her battered heart ached. She couldn't find her way back to that place now, because it had never been real. Her throat burned. She tipped up her chin and forced a small, tight smile for Rupert Carew and his dull invitation.

'Thank you. What time shall I be ready?'

SS Illyria
Rangoon

My Darling Alice,

We are finally on our way home — can you believe it?! I
didn't want to say anything until now, until I was absolutely
sure it was going to happen, but Papa has booked us onto the
most marvellous, modern ship and the voyage should be lovely
and quick. We'll be home in time for your birthday!

Oh darling, how I long to see you again. And hold you
in my arms, and fill you in properly on everything that's
happened these past few months. I know how horrid it's been
for you at Blackwood, and how marvellously brave you've
been. It's been terrible for me too. Unbearable, at times,
and the thought of you has been the only thing that has
kept me going.

Anyway, enough of that now. (But how much I have to
tell you!)

I'll see you soon. SOON!

All my love

Mama xxxx

22

Rupert

October 1936

The letter had been left on the nightstand, ready for posting to Polly at Blackwood Park. Rupert glanced at the sleeping face of his wife before slipping it out of its envelope and reading it. Then he carefully refolded it and put it into the pocket of his jacket.

Beneath the letter there was a drawing, done by Alice, of one of the follies in the garden at Blackwood. It had been folded in half to form a flimsy birthday card and inside, in writing that would suggest an author half her age, it said *I love you more than anything in the hole world.*

Rupert flinched.

As he went to replace it, he noticed the book it had been resting on: a rather battered leather-bound journal. Almost reluctantly he picked it up, running a hand thoughtfully over its cover, down its gilded edge, steeling himself to open it.

He knew what it was and where it had come from. He had bought it himself, at Smythson's on Bond Street, just before Christmas eleven years ago. One of the first presents he had given to Selina (if one didn't count the ruby engagement ring) when he had still believed there was hope. Not of a great romance – he had never expected that, nor wanted it – but he had thought that they might make a success of things. He had made a promise to Howard, in the filth and fear of that shell hole at Passchendaele, that he would look after her, and he had been prepared to overlook her waywardness to keep his word. He had known her since she was a child and believed that, given time and a firm hand, she would settle down and make a good wife.

But of course, it turned out that he hadn't known her at all.

He opened the journal in the middle and flicked back through the pages. Her turquoise handwriting galloped across them, slightly out of control. Like her. On the front page, in the top right hand corner was her name – *Selina Lennox Carew* (how typical of her to retain the 'Lennox'). Lower down, in the centre of the page was written

Trip to Burma,
   February 1926.

Their honeymoon.

It had been a vindication of his decision to ask for her

hand: a woman who would agree to a trip like that as a honeymoon – involving not only arduous travel in basic conditions, but an element of business too – was exactly the sort of wife he needed. In fact, she hadn't just agreed to it, but suggested it. She had wanted to get away from London, she'd said. So many reminders.

He'd thought she'd meant of Flick Fanshawe.

The journal had been a gift for her to record the trip. He had thought it would provide her with something to do while he was occupied with work, and make an interesting souvenir for their children, their children's children. In a rare moment of sentimental self-indulgence he remembered imagining some future Carew taking it down from a shelf in the library at Blackwood to be charmed and fascinated by descriptions of a time that would then seem old-fashioned, and places that might have changed beyond recognition. A piece of family history.

Selina had used it for a different purpose. He had looked forward to reading her jottings, but she had kept the journal private and hidden it for years. It was only recently that it had come to light again, and he had read it here, as she slept in her hospital bed. Bits of it, anyway. *I am ill with longing,* she had written, *with missing him.* That was somewhat fanciful. The sickness that had racked her on the trip had turned out to have a simple biological explanation.

A discreet cough from the doorway made him shut the book sharply.

'Mr Carew? Sorry to disturb you.'

It was the nurse with the red hair – he couldn't remember her name. 'Professor Tyler would like to see you,' she said, in the gentle voice they all used now. 'He's in his office, if you're ready.'

She was holding a bouquet of flowers. As he passed her in the doorway he paused to remove the card that protruded from the top. She spoke again, a little uncertainly.

'I typed the letter for Mrs Carew last night. Did you find it?'

All love and constant thoughts, Theo

Rupert's lip curled as he replaced the card. At least Osborne was at a safe distance, in Florence, and they were spared his extravagant emotions at close quarters.

'Yes. Thank you. I'll see to it.'

Tyler's office was at the end of the corridor. Rupert was familiar with it now, having had cause to visit several times over the last few months. Unlike the professor's rooms in nearby Harley Street, which had the reassuring air of a gentleman's club, this space was unmistakably institutional, although small concessions had been made to comfort. Tyler came round the desk and extended a hand as Rupert entered.

'Carew. Please – sit down. Drink?'

The Beaumont Nursing Home in Marylebone was the best in London, and Professor Gilbert Tyler was the most eminent man in his field. The days of performing surgery in front of rows of students and spectators might be over, but there was something theatrical about him, something of the dandy in the silk handkerchief in his top pocket and his thin

349

moustache. He poured whisky into two glasses with steady surgeon's hands and held one out to Rupert.

'You've seen Mrs Carew?'

'Yes. She's asleep.'

Professor Tyler smiled. 'Morphine. Marvellous stuff.'

Rupert remembered. The bliss of oblivion. 'The x-ray results. Have you had them?'

Tyler took a mouthful of his drink and set the glass down thoughtfully. 'Ah. Yes.' He reached unhurriedly for a buff-coloured folder and opened it. 'Not good news, I'm afraid. As I feared. I performed the second, more radical surgery in ... let me see, July? The scars have healed well, which was encouraging, but the cough and those nasty headaches have been a cause of concern, as you know. Rightly so, as the x-rays explain.'

He held up a sheet of celluloid. An incomprehensible pattern in shades of grey and white was visible against the glossy black. It looked like something one might come across on the walls of the Royal Academy under the guise of modern art. Tyler tapped a pale area with his fountain pen.

'This is the plate of the lungs. The mass here confirms what I suspected. An educated guess says that there is a similar picture in the brain.'

Rupert shifted slightly in his seat. As an officer in the war he had learned to shut down his personal responses and to focus his attention entirely on facts and details. Practicalities. He did that now. The letter in his pocket crackled faintly.

'Is there anything you can do?'

'Keep her comfortable. Manage the pain. Nothing more.'

'She seems to think that she's getting better.' He thought of what she'd written to Alice. 'Going home.'

'Yes.' Tyler put the x-ray back into the folder. 'Experience has taught me that honesty isn't always the best policy in these matters. It's a kindness to give hope, even where there is none. *Especially* where there is none.'

Rupert paused for a moment to allow this to sink in. To make sure he had understood correctly.

'You told her that the operation had been a success?'

His voice was toneless. By contrast Tyler's held an edge of impatience.

'Mr Carew, I am a specialist in diseases of the breast. That gives me, by default, a measure of expertise in the fairer sex. Women's minds aren't as rational as ours, as I'm sure you're aware. Their responses are more . . . emotional. It's nature, I'm afraid.'

'But sooner or later . . .'

'Of course. When it becomes unavoidable she'll have to be told. By then she may well have understood the situation for herself. A natural realization, one might call it.'

'She has a child.'

Dimly he registered what he had said. Her child. Not his.

'Yes. How much does the girl know about her mother's illness?'

Rupert had been holding his whisky glass, watching the surface of the liquid shiver with the shake of his hand. He lifted it now, and took a large mouthful.

'Nothing.'

Tyler's eyebrows appeared above the rim of his spectacles. 'At all?'

'They're very close. An only child, you see, and my wife—' He took another mouthful of whisky to stop himself saying too much. 'My wife has indulged her. She's a sensitive child. At the beginning, when it seemed like the first operation would sort things out she thought she might never have to know. A few weeks in hospital, a few more at home to recover . . .'

He thought of the journal beside Selina's bed and a pulse of anger flickered in his temple, setting up an echo of pain in his jaw. He rubbed it, hard. How stupid Selina's plan seemed now. Yet another of the outlandish schemes and childish games she dreamed up – letting Alice miss school to go to the zoo or the seaside or do a scavenger hunt (no wonder she was barely literate) – which disrupted everyone's routine and kept the child unhealthily dependent.

He should have put his foot down at the beginning, when she'd first told him about the fantasy she intended to spin. He'd agreed, with great relief, that Alice should go to Blackwood to stay with her grandparents; it was much more appropriate than her remaining under his care at Onslow Square. (Not directly under his care, of course, but Selina had dismissed the last nanny two years ago and it was unfair to expect Mrs Winton or the kitchen girls to take on the extra responsibility.) If he was honest, he was glad to be let off the hook so easily. The lie that Selina was accompanying him on foreign business freed him from the duty to visit Blackwood, and the child he had never been able to accept as his own.

He was conscious of the professor's eyes on him. The unpleasant sensation of being under a microscope.

'Well, I'm afraid you must think about how to tell your daughter. Might I suggest Mrs Carew's sister performs the unenviable task of breaking the news? I know she's been a regular visitor here. Better coming from a woman, I always think. When it comes to these tricky things they're far more capable than us chaps. More empathy.'

Rupert nodded, and tried to imagine Miranda being empathetic. The conversation had taken on an unreal quality. Dreamlike. He took a mouthful of whisky to jolt him back to full consciousness.

'Do you . . .' He cleared his throat. 'Would it be recommended that Alice sees her mother? Before . . .'

'To say goodbye?' Tyler leaned back, inhaling deeply, creating a theatrical pause. 'Sometimes. It depends on the child. You said she was sensitive? And very attached to her mother? In which case I'd suggest not. It would cause unnecessary distress all round, and we like to keep things as calm as possible at this stage. We're keeping Mrs Carew well sedated. She won't be terribly aware of what's going on. I suggest Mrs Atherton goes to visit the child at her grandparents soon and apprises her of the situation. The fact that she's been there for so long already is a great advantage; I'm sure she'll take the news far better than you fear. Children are surprisingly resilient. And easily distracted – I prescribe a trip to Hamleys first to buy her something nice. A doll or what have you.' He smiled. 'Doctor's orders.'

Rupert got to his feet and picked up his hat. He hadn't removed his overcoat when he came in and he suddenly realized how stuffy it was. He wanted to get outside as soon as possible, where the autumn air was laced with frost. The professor stood up, reaching across the desk to shake his hand again. He held on to it for a second longer than necessary.

'A difficult time, Carew. You have my great sympathy. And support, naturally. Anything I can do to make things easier will be done, you can be assured of that.'

'Yes.' He stopped short of thanking him. Professor Tyler's 'support' came at a premium price.

'And if you have any questions, you know where to find me.'

Rupert paused. Miranda had said something, months ago – at the beginning of all this – that had been playing on his mind increasingly in recent weeks.

'There was something.' Looking down at his hands gripping his hat, he saw white bone through the skin. 'Would it be correct to say that a disease like this can be brought on by . . . certain types of behaviour?'

He had expected Tyler to ask him to elaborate, but he didn't.

'Interesting question.' He sat down again, steepling his fingers. 'The suffragettes might have won their battle for the vote, but it's my belief that they opened something of a Pandora's Box with their demand for equality and independence. Women may be free to drink alcohol like men, but at what price? They're free to follow daring fashion, but with what effect? One of my colleagues – an obstetrician – reports a dramatic rise in female fertility difficulties, which *could* be unrelated to the fact that high-heeled shoes tilt the uterus out of position . . .' His expression conveyed his scepticism. 'In my own field, I think back to the "flappers"' (Rupert could hear the inverted commas he placed around the word) 'drinking cocktails, binding their breasts, performing those outrageous dances, and somehow the increase in my workload doesn't seem so surprising. I'm speaking in the most general terms, of course,' he concluded with a disarming smile. 'I'm not suggesting for a moment this is true in Mrs Carew's case.'

'No. No, of course not,' Rupert said, blandly.

He thought about what the professor had said as he walked back along the corridor and went down the echoing stairs. It supported what Miranda had read in the magazine at her hairdresser's about the fast living of the flapper generation having 'all sorts of unpleasant consequences', as Miranda had put it. *One doesn't want to talk about blame, but at the same time it doesn't do to be an ostrich about these things. Of course she wasn't to know, but we did try to tell her to be more sensible . . .*

He stood at the top of the steps to the street and applied himself to the ritual of lighting a cigar. One could never tell Selina anything. It was a relief, in a way, to discover that her persistent lack of compliance wasn't just disrespectful to him, but a danger to herself. He had always suspected as much, and the professor had as good as confirmed that her illness was a direct result of her own imprudence.

He breathed in, lungs warming; expanding as they filled with the comforting smoke. Of course, it brought him no pleasure, and it certainly left him with a lot of problems to resolve. The child, for one. Emilia Lennox had found a school that would take her, in Yorkshire, for which he assumed he would be expected to pay. Being a gentleman, he wouldn't challenge that assumption. That he had never, in all of the last ten years, alluded to his wife's flagrant betrayal was a matter of some pride. He had never brought up the subject of Alice's dark curls and brown eyes, or disputed the face-saving myth that the sole child of their union was a honeymoon baby, because he had understood that doing so would achieve nothing and cause further damage to an already blighted marriage. There was no point in drawing attention to it now. He would maintain his dignity. His decency.

He would have to go to Blackwood, he supposed, to pass on what Tyler had just told him. An unpleasant task. Remembering the letter, he took it out of his pocket and looked at the typewritten address for a moment. And then he tore it in half, and in half again, until it was nothing more than confetti in his fingers.

Going down the steps he scattered the pieces over a metal grille on the pavement, where they fell down to join drifts of rubbish and dead leaves in a coal chute. He looked at his watch. There was time for a visit to Maida Vale before performing his onerous duty. He had bought a flat there some years ago, and installed in it a very obliging widow called Maud Hampson, who, if she had any opinions, was sensible enough to keep them to herself.

Alice sat on the servants' stairs, just beyond the point where the dim light from the passageway melted into shadow. She was in her nightdress, which she had pulled down over her raised knees to make a sort of tent into which she could tuck her icy feet. She had left her slippers off to make her footsteps soundless.

Downstairs in the servants' hall the wireless was playing. The programme was called *Songs from the Shows*, which she liked, but the music meant she couldn't make out much of what Ivy and Ellen, Polly and Mrs Rutter were saying. The low note of their voices, and the fact that Mrs Rutter was there at all and not in her comfortable little parlour, suggested it was something serious. To do with Miss Lovelock, perhaps? The governess had departed for a trip to London last weekend and failed to return, as expected, on Sunday evening, eventually cycling unsteadily up the drive on Monday afternoon with one wrist bandaged and her beret pulled down over a puffy black eye. Alice had been with Mr Patterson in the glasshouse when Ellen had appeared, bursting with the drama of it all, to say he was needed to take the governess and all her possessions to the station.

Alice had only been given the blandest of explanations, of course, but later that night she had crouched on the stairs and heard Mrs Rutter reading out a newspaper article about violent clashes in London's East End. Alice had struggled to make sense of it. It was hard to imagine Miss Lovelock as a soldier, yet it seemed she had fought in a battle called Cable Street. 'I always knew she was creepy,' Ellen said darkly. 'But I never thought she'd turn out to be violent. Thank God Lady Lennox sent her packing.'

The days had felt untethered since then, without the rigid routine to which Alice had become so accustomed. So far there had been no mention of a replacement governess, which she hoped meant that Mama would soon be home, though no mention had been made of that either. As she strained to catch hold of words beneath the music her hand went to her neck, to the heavy pendant on the chain that hung there. She closed her fingers around the aquamarine, squeezing tightly so that the gold edges of the stone's mount pressed into her palm.

The treasure hunt was over. The final clue (not a riddle, but a drawing of a dear little tortoise with Mama's initials on his shell) had led her to the box on Mama's dressing table where, to her astonishment, she had found the aquamarine pendant: Mama's most precious thing. For as long as Alice could remember Mama had worn it: every day, with every outfit, hidden beneath her clothes if it didn't look right over the top, and finding it gave Alice hope that she would be home very soon, because she knew she wouldn't want to be without it for long. In the meantime, she was awed with the privilege of having it for herself. *You can look after it for me,* Mama had said in the letter that had been folded in the box alongside it.

The band on the wireless struck up a new tune, which Alice recognized. It was called 'Someday I'll Find You' and Mama often played it at home on the gramophone. She laid her cheek on her knee and hummed along softly in the dark, sliding the pendant backwards and forwards along its chain. She had always assumed that the necklace had been a gift from Papa, though now she wondered why she had ever thought that. Papa gave her rubies; dark and lustrous like drops of blood dripping from her earlobes or glistening at her throat. The necklace was the clear blue-green of the water in the pool in the orangery; the very same colour as Mama's eyes. *It was given to me for my twenty-second birthday, by someone incredibly special,* the letter said. *Someone I loved very much. He was called Lawrence Weston and he taught me more than anyone else has ever done. Until you came along, my darling*

The song on the wireless came to an end, and in the momentary lull Alice heard a sniffling sound, as if someone was crying. It had been the sound of a motor engine earlier that had piqued her curiosity and brought her to sit on the stairs: she guessed that Dr Pembridge had been called to attend to Grandfather, who had a chest cold, which (Polly said) could be very serious at his age. Alice wondered if, somewhere in the vast house, Grandfather was dying. The idea was intriguing rather than distressing, and she felt mild surprise that anyone downstairs would shed tears for such a cold and distant figure.

Perhaps it wasn't Grandfather himself that they were sad about, but the future of Blackwood and their own positions. Alice knew that his death would bring changes, but it was as if the house knew it too. It felt different lately. She was used to it now; she was attuned to its moods and heard its whispered voices, and she sensed the tension that vibrated through the still air. The servants moved through the rooms more quietly, their voices subdued. Polly always told the truth – *she's as honest as the day is long*, Mama had said in one of her letters – but Alice sensed that she was keeping something back now. Secrets and half-truths seemed to swirl through the corridors on icy currents of air.

Deep inside her the old familiar pain tugged again, like a kite pulling on a string. It had been absent for most of the summer, but as the days shortened and turned colder and Mama didn't come home it returned to jab her with its bony fingers. She pulled her knees up tighter to her chest.

Suddenly one of the bells in the servants' passageway jangled loudly, making her jump. Chairs scraped in the servants' hall and the music got louder as the door opened. From her vantage point Alice could see a square of tiled floor at the doorway and Polly's feet as she came out to check which bell had rung.

'Morning room.' That was where Grandmama sat in the evenings now, because it was smaller and easier to keep warm than the drawing room.

'That'll be him leaving,' Ellen said, moving past Polly. 'Wait a mo while I fetch Mr Denham . . .'

Alice got to her feet and scampered back up the stairs. She didn't mind Polly finding her there – she rather wanted her to – but Denham was a different matter. In his way he was as terrifying as Grandfather.

Her heart bounced around her chest and her blood felt hot and stinging inside her veins, like iodine on a cut. Back in the nursery she went over to the window, folding back the shutter a couple of inches and peering out.

The darkness was thick and enveloping. Looking upwards she could just make out a pale smudge, like a chalky fingerprint on a blackboard, where the moon hid behind the clouds. There were no stars. From far below she heard the faint sound of a motor engine starting up and a moment later headlamps sliced the blackness. The beams swung round as the car began to move.

It seemed bigger than Dr Pembridge's car, and smarter, just like the car Beechcroft drove them around in at home. Shivering, she pushed the shutter closed again and went back to bed. The sheets felt chilled and slightly damp. She curled herself into a ball, as small and tight as possible around the jab of pain in her tummy. Holding the stone around her neck she listened into the darkness, wishing for the sound of Polly's feet on the stairs.

It was the right decision to have given Beechcroft the night off and driven himself, Rupert thought. He found motoring surprisingly relaxing and, as he bumped the Bentley up the uneven drive, he was glad to be alone.

The visit had been less unpleasant than he'd feared. Not easy, of course, but Robert, suffering from yet another chest cold, had remained upstairs (which meant that Rupert hadn't had to bellow the difficult news, to accommodate his deafness) and Emilia had taken it with admirable calm. They had spoken of practical matters: how to manage the coming weeks and what would happen afterwards. Interment in the little chapel at Blackwood would seem obvious were it not for the fact that the future of the house – or specifically, the Lennox tenure in it – was in itself uncertain. Young Archie Atherton was set to inherit, but with the entire estate requiring substantial investment Lionel was making noises about selling. They had discussed it during a visit at Easter, apparently.

This was the only point at which Rupert had detected tears in his mother-in-law's eyes, but she had not allowed them to fall. He remembered the stoicism she had shown after Howard's death, when he had been home on leave and made the trip to Blackwood to offer his condolences. She had asked him about Howard's last moments, and he had given her a much-sanitized version, though there was no way of making bleeding out into a mud-filled shell hole sound like the kind of peaceful end a mother would wish for her son. But she had thanked him. For staying with Howard and being there to ease him to his end. To Rupert's eternal shame it had been he who had wept, with relief and gratitude that she didn't blame him for not doing more.

He slowed down to ease the Bentley over the cattle grid where the drive forked to Home Farm. Emilia Lennox had thanked him again tonight, and he wondered if she too heard the echo of that previous conversation. This time he felt no guilty anguish, no thankfulness for her absolution. He had never quite forgiven himself for not being able to save Howard, but his conscience was clear when it came to his marriage. He had done all he could to keep that alive, at least.

The fact was, it had been ill-fated from the start, he could see that now. Occasionally, over the years, he had retraced the chain of events that had led to it, identifying each point at which a path had been taken and a link forged. There was his promise to Howard, of course, and his guilt at the fact that he was still living while his friend was not. Timing too; his return from Burma when pressure was mounting on Selina to settle down, but he had come to the conclusion that none of these things would have precipitated a proposal had it not been for Flick Fanshawe's death.

That had been the turning point. Seeing Selina's suffering had unleashed in him some spring of protectiveness that he thought the war had dried up for ever. When he'd collected her from Chester Square on the evening of the funeral he remembered being struck by how lovely she was, her face bare of the dreadful paint she usually wore, her blonde hair gleaming against a sober black silk evening dress. She had held herself very stiffly, rigidly polite and self-contained, until halfway through Part II of the concert programme when, during Vaughan Williams's *Lark Ascending* he became aware that she was sobbing, quietly and uncontrollably, beside him.

Immediately he had ushered her out, shielding her from prying eyes, straight into his waiting car. He'd intended to take her straight home but, emboldened, instructed his driver to go to Simpsons in the Strand instead. There he had waved away the offer of his usual table and requested one of the secluded booths at the back. He had never thought of himself as a romantic, but that evening as they talked and he coaxed her to eat, he felt something shift inside him. The burden of guilt, perhaps. If he could look after her, make her happy, he believed it might make his own mind easier.

Bloody fool that he was.

At the gatehouse he stopped and looked in the rearview mirror, but the old house was lost to the darkness. He pulled out into the road and accelerated away, his thoughts travelling ahead, across the dark fields and sleeping towns, to London. Not to the hospital bed where his wife lay or the Maida Vale room where he had spent the afternoon, but to the mansion flat in the ugly red brick block behind Harrods where Margot Atherton lived. He sometimes called there for a drink on the way home from the office, especially if he'd had a trying day; Margot was an extremely good listener. If he gave the Bentley its head he might just make it in time for a nightcap.

Ten years ago that urge to look after Selina had seemed so noble, but he had quickly come to see it as being ridiculously naïve; he had never understood her or been able to make her happy. It occurred to him now that a far more reliable formula for fulfilment would have been to marry someone who would look after him. And that person had been under his nose all along.

23

Survivors

November 1925

The ruby engagement ring that Rupert had commissioned from Aspreys was far too big. He had it altered to fit her finger, but that only solved half the problem. Nothing could reduce the size of the stone, which felt as heavy as an anchor on her hand and kept twisting around, catching on things. In the early weeks of her engagement it served as a constant reminder of the strange new reality in which she so suddenly found herself, and the rather incredible fact that she was Rupert's fiancée.

She stumbled through the days like a sleepwalker, going through the motions of normality, reciting lines that sounded correct in a voice that was carefully controlled. In an attempt to economize, Sir Robert had decided to close up the house on Chester Square for the winter, but Miranda had allowed Selina to stay with her and Lionel in their new house in Egerton Crescent, and for that she was grateful. She couldn't have borne to be at Blackwood; to sleep every night in the bed she had shared with Lawrence and watch the dawn break through the lily-strewn curtains, to dine every evening at the table on which she had lain back amongst the servants' hall crockery and scattered roses.

But being in London brought its own kind of torment, especially at this, the darkest time of year, when the earth seemed to spin less steadily on its axis and the sodden earth beneath her feet felt less solid. Sitting in Miranda's freshly decorated drawing room on her hard, new sofa, Selina wondered how she might stop herself from going mad. Usually she got through the late autumn days by packing her diary with lunches and shopping trips and cocktails and the theatre, so the time passed in a champagne haze and the lights of Mayfair's bars and clubs kept the darkness at bay. Usually she had Flick, to take her hand and pull her onto dancefloors, to order a succession of extravagant drinks, to make her smile with her spontaneity and irreverence (last year she had bought twenty paper poppies from a street seller outside Knightsbridge tube station and fashioned them into an eye-catching headpiece which she had worn to the theatre on the eve of Armistice Day) and to remind her airily that life went on.

Except when it didn't.

The room was brightly lit, but she could feel the darkness encroaching. Already it had swallowed the branches of the trees in the square and was creeping, like fog, up the steps of the house. She should get up and ring the bell to get Jean to come and draw the complicated swagged curtains, but somehow it seemed safer to stay where she had sat all afternoon, and try to ignore the ice stealing through her limbs and the darkness pressing against the windows and the vortex beneath the tightrope.

She felt like a fox that had managed to outrun the snarling hounds and had gone to earth, crouched in the cold, cramped darkness, sensing it was safe so long as it didn't move a muscle. The journey to Bloomsbury, to apologize and try somehow to explain, was impossible to contemplate. How could she find the strength to face Lawrence, when she couldn't even cope with Miranda's housemaid? The girl always looked at Selina with sly curiosity, as if she couldn't quite believe she was the same person whose picture she had seen in the newspapers, dancing at the Café de Paris, or piled into a motorcar on one of the original treasure hunts.

Perhaps she was right. Perhaps Selina wasn't that person anymore.

The clock ticked on. Somewhere a door opened and shut again, and a faint current of air sighed through the house. Footsteps tapped on tiles. Voices murmured and then died away. The fire hissed and subsided into ash and the twilight deepened. At length the drawing room door opened, making her start.

'Oh – here you are!'

Miranda came in, still wearing her fur stole and hat. She sounded surprised and a little irritated, as if she'd expected Selina to be out drinking cocktails or shopping for gloves. (It was funny – when she had done those things it had irritated Miranda too.) 'Goodness – why are the curtains still wide open? It's quite dark outside – Jean should have closed them when she brought in the tea.' Going over to ring the bell she looked around for the tray. 'You have had tea, haven't you?'

'No.'

Miranda gave an exasperated click of her tongue. It seemed that her stores of kindness and patience were finite, and having Selina under the same roof was rapidly depleting them. Standing at the fireplace she flicked through the sheaf of envelopes she had picked up from the hall table, pulling off her gloves to tear one open.

'I hope you returned Rupert's telephone call ... Is he taking you out for dinner tonight?'

'No.'

Miranda pulled a face at the card in her hand. 'Ugh – Monica Fitzpatrick *At Home*.' She shoved the card to the back of the sheaf and looked at Selina with a frown. 'No, you didn't return the call, or no you're not going out to dinner?'

'Both.'

She wondered what Miranda would say if she told her that she had forgotten all about the telephone call, which had apparently come this morning when Selina was still in bed. How convenient it would be if Rupert slipped into her thoughts as often, as effortlessly and insistently as Lawrence did.

She saw Rupert every few days, and when they were together he was as polite and distant as ever. His proposal had been unexpected, but also understated; offered in the spirit of a solution to some practical problem. He had told her to think about it, but she had known that if she did all the good, solid reasons for accepting would be dissolved by the simple truth that she didn't love him. As it was, she said yes with only the smallest hesitation, the briefest pang of regret for the life she might have had.

She didn't want that life now. She didn't want the uncertainty that had once seemed so exciting, or the wild extremes of emotion that had made her blood rush and her senses reel. She didn't want that savage, exhilarating, annihilating craving for another human being ... Not when human beings were so fallible. So fragile.

Life with Rupert would be safer. More settled. She felt nothing for him but a sort of detached admiration, a distant affection, and that was a relief; like stepping into cool shade after the burn and dazzle of the midday sun. His emotions, if he had them, were safely contained behind an impenetrable façade of correctness. In his world, a cushioned safety net of wealth and status and authority lay between her and the void. Once she had striven to *live*. Now she just wanted to survive.

Miranda was looking at her narrowly, her hand on her hip. 'I do hope you're not having second thoughts.'

'No,' Selina said again, this time with more conviction. 'Not at all.'

Sam Evans was not a man much given to worrying.

If he felt concern it tended to be in a general, rather than a personal sense: for families in Welsh pit villages struggling to send their children to school with shoes on their feet and food in their stomachs, or the poor bastards who were heroes in wartime and embarrassing inconveniences when peace came. But this morning the unease that had been gnawing intermittently at the back of his mind for several days had got acute enough to drive him from his bed half an hour early and take a detour from his usual route to work via the studio on Gower Street.

As far as he could tell Lawrence hadn't crossed the threshold at Marchmont Street for the best part of a week; since Sam had shown him the Lennox girl's engagement announcement in *The Times*, in fact. He hadn't known for sure that there was something going on there, but Lawrence's subsequent disappearance put it pretty much beyond reasonable doubt. As for the daft bugger's current whereabouts, Sam had narrowed it down to three possibilities. He would either be at the studio, working like a madman in an attempt to forget her; in a cheap hotel somewhere, having persuaded her to run away with him; or face down in a gutter in Soho, mired in drink and self-pity. The first was preferable, especially as the boy owed him three weeks' rent. The last was most likely.

It was a hard, cold morning, with a white sky and a weak sun that promised warmth but didn't deliver. Sam paused by the railings on Russell Square to fill his pipe, then strolled on, merging with the students in flapping Oxford bags and mufflers hurrying along Gower Street. He knocked on the door of a house that must have once been distinguished, but had sunk into shabby disrepute since being divided into flats for students at the nearby university and the Slade. Leaning easily against the railings he waited, sucking on his pipe.

It was a recent thing, the pipe, and he wasn't quite used to it yet. He'd taken it up in the hope that it would prove to be economical, and also because he thought it gave him an air of intellectual gravitas. In newspaper offices, cigarettes were for hacks. If he wanted to be taken seriously as a social and political commentator he had to look the part.

He knocked again, more loudly this time, and gave the door handle an optimistic shake. Locked. He checked his watch. He'd give it another five minutes, but he couldn't wait much longer than that. The vague concern solidified a little, its edges sharpening with irritation. Bloody temperamental artists, he thought. Give me a straightforward working man who says what he thinks and eats, sleeps and drinks at normal times. Who beds a few women, finds one he wants to marry, then spends the rest of his life eating and sleeping with her and drinking in the pub with the boys. None of this exhausting grand passion. None of the bloody melodrama.

A brewers' dray lumbered past, the harnesses of the horses

clinking. Sam watched the students in idle fascination. A smug, self-absorbed bunch, for the most part, still wet behind the ears and not one amongst them that looked like he could do a day's labour. He caught snatches of their conversations as they passed, their public school voices carrying on the cold air. For all their learning, their minds were as narrow as their ridiculous trousers were wide. Glancing back down towards Russell Square a figure amongst them caught his eye and made him look again.

The same voluminous tweed trousers, the same flannel blazer and striped school scarf, but topped off with a turban fashioned from a green paisley scarf. Recognizing Lawrence's friend Edith, Sam levered himself upright and straightened his corduroy jacket, shoving his pipe into the pocket. He watched her face change as she saw him, registering first recognition and then alarm.

'Mr Evans, isn't it? Is something wrong?'

'No – at least, I hope not. I came to ask the same question. Haven't seen young Weston for a week, so I thought I'd check if he's here before I telephone Scotland Yard.'

Young Weston? What the hell had made him say that? He sounded like Lawrence's ridiculous old uncle. Edith Linde moved past him to open the door with a sympathetic (pitying?) smile. 'Yes, don't bother the detectives just yet. I imagine he's here. He usually is . . .' Sam followed her into the hallway and up a scruffy staircase. She sniffed the air. 'I'd say he's been working.'

'Painting?'

Sam would have said he wasn't a fan of women in trousers, but he'd never followed one closely up a steep flight of stairs before. There was something rather magnificent about Edith's tweed-clad behind. He wondered fleetingly if she was a Sapphist, and tried to remember if Lawrence had ever mentioned anything about it.

'No,' she said, reaching the landing at the top. 'Finished his last portrait commission weeks ago and hasn't taken any more on, even though I could get him five by lunchtime, for certain. He's not interested. He's suffering the agonies of unrequited love, so he's not interested in anything; just wanders the streets with that blasted camera of his, and then works all night developing the photographs.' She wrinkled her nose. 'Doesn't it smell evil?'

'Tell me about it. He usually uses the sink at the flat. So . . . taken it badly, has he? The Lennox girl's engagement?'

Edith pushed the door open. 'See for yourself . . .'

The vinegary chemical smell was stronger in here, mingling with the reek of stale alcohol. Clear winter light poured through the skylights onto the chaos below, but Sam didn't notice the mess. His attention was grabbed by the string that stretched from one window to the next, like a washing line, and the photographs that had been pegged on it to dry.

Edith sighed and muttered something as she went over to the Belfast sink and filled the kettle, then lit the stove. Sam was aware of her tidying up behind him, stacking plates and gathering cups, tipping landslides of cigarette ends into the dustbin, talking all the time. Finally, when he'd made his way along the line of photographs, he turned to face her.

'Sorry?'

She gave him a withering look. 'I said, I've tried everything. Stern lectures. Praise and encouragement. Dragging him to the pub and dangling pretty young things in front of him – they might as well be my elderly maiden aunts for all the interest he shows. As this is an *artists'* studio I've even threatened to evict him unless he starts painting again, but I'm afraid he knows I don't mean it.' She paused for a moment, an empty wine bottle in her hand, and looked wistfully towards the divan in the corner. 'I'm afraid I'm far too fond of him.'

Sam followed her gaze. The subject of their discussion was just about visible, lying face down under a faded green velvet curtain, a half-empty bottle of brandy beside him. His hair – which Sam was always bellowing at him to get cut – was inky black against the white pillow he was clutching, and his bare shoulders, rising and falling gently as he breathed, were as pale and hard as sculpted marble. Bastard, Sam thought with fleeting envy. If he'd been discovered sleeping off a heavy night you could bet he'd be lying on his back snoring like a walrus with his mouth open. Trust Weston to look like some bloody Pre-Raphaelite painting.

The kettle hissed on the stove. Edith went over to the sink and began rinsing cups. She had taken off her blazer and was wearing a white shirt and a sleeveless Fairisle jumper. Splendid bosom as well as a magnificent bottom, Sam noticed. He made an effort to look away, turning back to the photographs and rubbing a hand across his beard.

'You're right to be tough on him. That's what he needs – a kick up the backside. He's too soft for his own good. Romantic ideals are all very nice but they don't put food in your belly or a roof over your head. How long since he's paid you rent?'

'I don't mind about that. I've told him it doesn't matter. He always pays when he's got work—'

'Then we'll just have to get him some.'

Briskly, Sam began unpegging the photographs from the line. Some had been taken on the Embankment, by the look of it, others beneath cavernous railway arches somewhere. All of them exposed the city's secret shame: men in ragged layers of clothing sleeping rough on newspaper beds, limbless veterans on winter pavements being passed by smart shoes. Lawrence must have carried a lantern with him to light the night shots adequately without resorting to the glare of a flashbulb. In some the men had their faces tipped up towards the light so that it shone in their blank eyes and on the hollows hunger had carved in their unshaven cheeks. In some it glinted off the medals pinned incongruously to their tattered coats. Sam was the least sentimental person imaginable (when sober, anyway) but even raw, uncropped and unedited the images brought a lump to his throat.

Edith's voice was sharp. 'What do you think you're doing, Mr Evans?'

'I'll tell you exactly what I'm doing, Miss Linde . . .' He continued unpegging until he'd gathered all the photographs, then turned to her with a bland smile. 'I'm doing Lawrence Weston a very large favour, though there's a chance he won't see it that way at first. What's the date today?'

'Gosh – I don't know – the third of November? Something like that.'

'Exactly that. Which means that in just over a week it'll be the eleventh of November, and the newspapers and illustrated magazines will be falling over themselves to pay tribute to our Glorious Dead.' He held up the sheaf of photographs. 'I'm going to see if I can sell them the idea of remembering our Inglorious Living as well.'

She was impressed, he could tell. And rightly so, because anyone could see it was a ruddy good idea. 'Shouldn't you ask him first? They're not yours to sell.'

'And have him come out with a string of excuses? Not bloody likely. And in a way they are mine. Boyo over there owes me three weeks' rent. I'm taking goods to the value of, instead.'

'I'm not sure that I approve, but I'm not going to argue.' She dried a cup with a square of paint-stained linen. 'Coffee?'

He felt a pang of regret. 'I must be off. I'm late as it is.'

'Ah. You're leaving me to do the explaining when he wakes up.'

'Tell him he can take it up with me – if he ever comes back to the flat.' Tucking the sheaf of photographs into his document folder Sam went over to the stairs. 'I know he won't believe it, but I'm doing it for his own good. I actually care about him, the daft sod.'

'So do I,' Edith said sadly.

Buggeration, thought Sam as he thudded down the stairs a moment later. So there was his answer. The good news was that Edith Linde wasn't a lesbian. The bad news was she was carrying a bloody great torch for Lawrence Weston.

As soon as Selina saw the photographs in *The Bystander* she knew they were his. It wasn't just the subject that gave them away as Lawrence's, but his perspective on it; the emphasis on small, significant details, the unexpected angles and the way he used the light. It jolted her, like a step missed in the dark.

It was the afternoon of Armistice Day, a day of striking clocks and muffling silence; a damp, dripping day at the dying of the year, so much worse this time than any of the awful ones that had come before. Lady Lennox, in town to collect some things from Chester Square, had called for tea. While she and Miranda discussed a dinner party Miranda was to host, a seating plan dilemma, Selina absently turned the pages of the magazine. Until she reached the feature entitled *Our Forgotten Heroes.*

In an instant she was catapulted back to the night of her birthday and the room with the faces around the walls. Warmth spread through her body, radiating out from her poor, battered heart, and she ran her fingers over the pages, the faces of the men in them, because they felt like a part of him. She didn't realize she was crying until a tear splashed onto a ragged chest of medals. Miranda stopped talking and looked at her in alarm, then reached over to remove the magazine from her hands. 'Such a dreadful article – one expects better from *The Bystander*. As if seeing all those people begging on the streets wasn't depressing enough. One doesn't want to be confronted with them in one's own drawing room as well. Here – look at *The Tatler* instead. There are photographs of Lettice Wilton's wedding. Her dress was a bit Hail Caesar, don't you think? Unfortunate.'

The photographs shifted something inside of her, jolting her out of her numbness. She hadn't seen him, hadn't even written to explain, though she had intended to. As the blank days passed she had found it was safest not to think about him, not to think about anything at all, but suddenly it seemed incredible that she had cut herself off so brutally. She wondered if he was waiting for her, understanding that she needed time, or if he was angry. She wondered if he had heard of her engagement, and felt her heart shrivel with guilty anguish.

Tomorrow, she resolved, closing her fist around the aquamarine pendant.

Tomorrow she would go. And then maybe she would be able to put it behind her and get on with the rest of her life.

She left Egerton Crescent while the maids were still opening shutters and laying fires (causing a flurry of alarm; no one expected her up before luncheon). She couldn't face the prospect of encountering the terrifying Edith at the studio in Gower Street, so she wanted to catch Lawrence before he left the flat. If she had to wait until he returned in the evening she suspected she might lose her nerve.

It was a drab morning. As the taxi made its way along Piccadilly she wondered why the streets were so busy and leaned forward to tap on the glass and ask the driver if there was some public event that she was unaware of. It was just the time of day, he told her with a shrug. People on their way to work in shops and offices, delivery men doing their morning rounds. A harassed-looking policeman directed traffic at Piccadilly Circus, trying to make order out of chaos, his white sleeves flashing in the November gloom.

An ordinary day, she thought, looking out of the window. Ordinary people. Ordinary lives. No outward sign of pain or passion. Did they experience it? Had the woman hurrying down the steps of the motorbus on Shaftesbury Avenue known what it was to be undone with need? Had the policeman laid himself bare before someone, body and soul? Had it brought him happiness, or destroyed him? Had he ever broken someone's heart?

She thought of Lawrence's photographs. Everyone knew about those whose lives had been shattered by war, but what about love? No medals for them. Their wounds were hidden, but no less devastating.

The taxi set her down in the usual place at the end of Marchmont Street. As she paid the driver her hands were shaking so much that coins slipped between her gloved fingers and rolled into the gutter. She couldn't bring herself to scrabble around in the dirt to pick them up. There was a dustcart outside the Marquis Cornwallis pub, and men whistling as they hauled dustbins. The cold air was filled with the reek of rubbish and rang with the clang of iron. The ordered tranquillity of Egerton Crescent felt like a continent away.

As she approached number twenty-three the door opened and an elderly man emerged, carrying a violin case. He looked at her in surprise as she slipped past him and went into the hall. She remembered the silvery ribbons of sound that had shimmered through the walls.

Her chest burned as she climbed the stairs. Lawrence's world was attics and stairs and skylights, a view of chimneypots and rooftops. It was bare floorboards and thin walls and unmade beds, rough red wine and Woodbines. It was inconvenient and insubstantial, not solid enough to hold back the great nothingness beyond. Resolve gathered inside her. He would see that she couldn't live like that, surely? He would understand what she had done.

There was a clutch of empty bottles, like skittles, outside the door at the top of the stairs. She looked at them as she knocked. The landing smelled like the blast of air one breathed in when one passed a public bar. She waited a moment then knocked again, harder. A muffled shout came from inside.

'For Christ's sake – it's *open*!'

Hearing his voice almost made her knees buckle. She

went in. Her head still felt empty, like it was floating, but her heart was beating so hard she was sure it must be echoing through the whole building. The corridor was gloomy, striped with bands of pale light that came through open doorways. At its end a shadow moved across the door of Lawrence's room. For the first time the thought occurred to her that he might not be alone. She felt sick.

'Lawrence?'

Her voice was a croak. The word died away into silence. The shadow moved and he appeared in the doorway, holding on to it for support.

He was naked to the waist, barefoot, wearing trousers with the braces hanging loosely down. In the dirty light his skin was so pale it looked almost bloodless. He was thinner than when she'd last seen him, and than in those ripe days of August when the sun had burnished his skin and the ridges of his ribs and the hollows in his cheeks had been less pronounced. In a second he was in front of her, pulling her roughly into his arms. It took every ounce of strength she possessed to resist.

'No – please, Lawrence – I can't! I didn't come here for that!'

He stepped back, his chest rising and falling rapidly. His eyes glittered darkly, as if with a fever. For a moment he gazed at her, then he turned away abruptly, his whole body taut.

'What then? What did you come here for? To ask me to take photographs at your wedding?'

'You saw the announcement,' she said, shakily.

'Of course I bloody saw it.' He walked down the corridor, into the bedroom. 'Did you think I wouldn't? This is Bloomsbury, not Outer Mongolia. We do get *The Times* here.'

Hesitantly she followed him, her eyes automatically drawn to the faces on the walls. She had known it would be hard. She had been prepared for him to be hurt, frustrated perhaps ... Not bitter. Not cold. She had allowed herself to imagine that he might hold her and tell her he understood, and that he would always love her. Would always be there, if she needed him. She hadn't realized until that moment how much she had been relying on hearing that.

'Lawrence, please—'

He rounded on her. 'Do you love him?'

'You know I don't.'

'Then *why? Why* are you doing this?'

His anger sparked her own. 'Because I *don't* love him – that's why! I don't feel very much for him at all, and do you know what? It's a *relief*. I can't do it, Lawrence! I can't live like that – like we did; everything heightened and intense – so intense it hurts. It's dangerous, love like that. It's an addiction, just like the drugs and drink that killed Flick. It feels marvellous at the time, of course – that first hit, when you're glittering and invincible – but it doesn't last. It *can't*. You have to know when to stop, or it'll destroy you.'

'And that's what you've done, is it? Decided to stop loving?' He was incredulous. Scornful. 'What a genius idea – just like signing the temperance pledge! You're going to marry a man who treats you like one of his possessions and live the rest of your life with your heart buried in stone? You're going to pretend love is just another one of those *tiresome emotions* –' his lip curled as he threw her own words back at her '– and become as cold and hard as your mother. Is that it?'

'No!' The dart hit home, more painful than she could have imagined. With great effort she schooled her tone into one of careful reason, squashing her anguish into a tight hard ball. 'Please – try to understand. I can't trust myself, that's all. I love too much. First Howard, then Flick – I can't put my heart on the line again, Lawrence; I'm simply not strong enough, or brave enough to take the risk.' She broke off with a sudden, painful laugh. 'How ridiculous. Taking risks is the thing I've always done best. All the years I fooled myself and everyone else into believing I was fearless by doing foolish stunts and breaking silly rules, and now I'm too scared to leave the house.' She took in a shuddering breath. 'I want certainty, Lawrence. Stability. Permanence.'

'*Permanence?* I give it a year before you're climbing your silk-lined walls with boredom and drinking too much sherry at lunchtime. Two years and you'll have made a discreet arrangement with some obliging chap to help pass the long afternoons until the husband you don't love comes home.' His laugh was harsh. 'Perhaps I could offer myself for the position? It would be just like old times, but with more expensive sheets and a maid to make them afterwards.'

'You make it sound sordid.' A tear slipped down her cheek. She was too ashamed to admit that he had voiced her secret hope; one that she had scarcely dared admit to herself. That somehow, this wasn't the end.

'It would be. Sordid and wrong.'

'Because I'd be someone else's wife?'

'I've slept with married women before. I didn't give a fuck about their husbands and I don't see why yours would be any different.'

She felt herself flinch. Her jaw ached with the effort of not crying out.

'Then why?'

He went over to the table beside the bed to pick up a packet of cigarettes. She watched the movement of the muscles beneath his skin as he bent his head and hunched his shoulders to light one. How well she remembered the feel of his back beneath the palms of her hands, those constellations of freckles. Once he would have lit one cigarette for them to share and passed it to her, easy and intimate, but now he held the packet out. She shook her head dumbly.

'Because it would be a betrayal of the girl I fell in love with.' He tossed the spent match into a saucer of others. 'I wouldn't stain her memory by going to bed with her ghost. I wouldn't humiliate myself by becoming the occasional amusement of a rich man's bored wife.'

'It wouldn't be like that—'

'Yes, it *would*.' His fury was contained beneath a thin veneer of controlled exasperation. '*Jesus*, Sclina – can't you see the irony of what you're doing? You're so scared of death that you're meeting it halfway. That's not keeping yourself safe from what you fear, it's giving yourself up to it. You want certainty? I can give you that. Not in diamonds and rubies and grand houses, but in waking up every day and knowing beyond doubt that you are loved more than you can comprehend—' He broke off, thrusting his fingers into his untidy hair, stricken and helpless. 'We're all going to die sometime – that's a fact. And the only thing we can do to cheat death is to live properly. Bravely. Love wholly. *Living, instead of just existing* – you said that, remember?'

'That was before,' she sobbed. Before the obscenity of Flick's death. Before she fell in love with him, when it was still a silly, shallow game of dare. 'Grand houses and rubies can't be snatched away in an instant, but people can. Love doesn't protect you from hurt, it makes you more vulnerable to it.'

He slumped back against the wall as the fight suddenly went out of him. 'Don't do this, Selina. Don't marry him. Please.'

This weary defeat was even harder to bear than his anger. She shook her head. 'It's too late.'

'It's *not*. Not yet.'

She thought of the announcement in *The Times*, Miranda's list of instructions about guest lists and menus, the engagement dinner Rupert's parents had held for them at The Dorchester. Could all of that be wished away? Undone? He was just a foot away from her. A single step and she would be in his arms. For a fragment of a second she allowed herself to imagine it. Kissing him. Tasting him and breathing him in and feeling the silken tangle of his hair in her fingers . . .

'It's better this way. For both of us,' she whispered. 'Even if it doesn't feel like that now.'

'In that case, go. There's nothing more to say.'

They gazed at each other, wide-eyed, from opposite sides of the chasm that had opened up between them. Dazed with disbelief, she turned and forced herself towards the door, out into the passageway.

A sense of unreality carried her forwards. With every step she waited for his voice calling her back, or his footsteps behind her and his hands, pulling her against him, not letting her go. But there was silence at her back and emptiness ahead of her. She walked towards it and closed the door with quiet finality.

The breath of air that gusted through the rooms carried the faint trace of her scent. Leaning against the wall Lawrence remained perfectly still, listening to the crash of his desperate heart and her footsteps fading on the stairs. In the saucer on the desk the cigarette he had lit was burning itself into ash. His own words echoed in his head: *it's not too late.*

He could go after her – she was still under the same roof, still within reach . . .

He raised his hands to his head and closed his eyes, surrendering to the painful realization that that wasn't true. She was far beyond his reach, and always had been. She might still be in the same building but she belonged to a different world.

When Lawrence had woken up that morning he'd thought that nothing could hurt more than his hangover. He'd been wrong. In a few hours the pain in his head would start to ebb as the alcohol gradually left his bloodstream. He knew he would spend the rest of his life recovering from falling in love with Selina Lennox.

THE BEAUMONT NURSING HOME
BEAUMONT STREET
LONDON W1

Darling Alice,
    I don't know how to write this. I don't know where to
start to tell you the truth. ~~I wish I had done it earlier.~~ I
wish I didn't have to do it at all but it seems

24

Lawrence

October 1936

The London Lawrence returned to was grimy, damp and cold, a world away from the golden city he remembered. Time and distance had made him sentimental, he supposed, and memory was unreliable. During the eleven years he had spent in America, when he had thought of England it had been as it was that summer, before he left.

He hadn't allowed himself to think of it very often.

But it was impossible not to now, as he walked down Oxford Street towards Marble Arch, pausing outside Selfridges to look in the window as they had done on that rainy July night. There was a display of winter coats now, artfully staged against a backdrop of bare branches, but he saw the Ascot fashions of 1925 with a vividness that made the world tilt and rush. It seemed as though, if he peered closely enough at the glass he might see the reflection of a glorious blonde girl in a stolen frock coat and a scruffy, half-naked artist, holding hands and passing a bottle of champagne between them. Perhaps if he searched in the litter of dead leaves and discarded cigarette ends at the edge of the pavement he might discover the remains of his heart still lying there. It was probably somewhere around here that he lost it.

He walked on. These days he could easily afford a taxi, but it was pleasant to be out in the chill air after two hours in the editor's office at the *Spectator,* where the air was opaque with cigarette smoke and the smell of deadline pressure. He had deliberately extricated himself with plenty of time to spare before he was due to meet with Polly Davies, to allow a little thinking space. Once the time and place for this meeting had been arranged, an instinct for self-preservation had made him put it from his mind. With some reluctance he turned his thoughts to it now, and felt a sense of unease.

Her initial letter, forwarded on to him by the editor of the *Sphere*, had been vague. *I used to work for the Lennox family at Blackwood Park,* she had written in a schoolgirlish hand. *I left their employment following Miss Selina's marriage but due to unfortunate sircumstanse I have returned to Blackwood recently to look after Miss Selina's daughter.*

Seeing Selina's name on paper after all these years had made his heart turn over. The lines that followed had chilled it.

I know a little of what you and Miss Selina were to each other before her marriage and there are matters that I would like to discuss with you, should you still hold any regard for her.

He combed his memory for what he knew about Polly, searching for clues. He had never met her, but he must have come very close that summer at Blackwood. She had been the invisible presence who had left the supplies for their glorious makeshift picnics (sometimes, dining in an upmarket restaurant, he would suddenly recall the scrambled eggs he had made in the kitchen on that first night and lose all appetite for the elaborate dish in front of him), their secret accomplice and Selina's trusted ally. Had something happened between them to change this? He couldn't imagine what 'matters' Polly Davies might wish to discuss, but instinct told him the conversation wasn't going to leave him with a warm glow. 'Blackmail' was a melodramatic word, but his best guess was that Polly had hit hard times and discovered somehow that the second-rate artist her mistress had had a secret dalliance with over a decade ago was now worth tapping for some cash.

Maybe he was too cynical. Even so ... even though his head had told him not to respond, his heart hadn't been able to resist. Selina's name was a siren call that he was compelled to answer. Even after all this time.

He hadn't told Edith about the meeting with Selina Lennox's erstwhile maid, only warning her that his appointment with the *Spectator* editor might extend into the evening, and not to expect him home for dinner.

When he had first returned to London he had stayed in

a suite at The Langham, which Edith had declared a vulgar signal of his new wealth and an insult to their old friendship, and insisted he come and stay with her instead. She had got married – quite suddenly and unexpectedly – a year after Lawrence left England, to a distinguished naturalist fifteen years her senior, called Peregrine Hesketh. They lived, with their wild brood of children (two boys, two girls, not always possible to tell which was which) in a gothic folly of a house on the edge of Regent's Park, close to the zoo, where Hesketh held a senior position. In many ways Lawrence would have preferred the freedom and tranquillity of the hotel to the eccentric chaos of the Hesketh household, but he appreciated Edith's kindness as much as he had ever done. And it was only temporary. He just needed to finalize plans for his next project and he would be off again, to Spain, where simmering unrest had lurched into civil war. These plans had dominated the conversation in the *Spectator* editor's office.

Outside Maison Lyons a pack of grubby children tussled with each other around the grotesque figure of a bonfire guy slumped on the pavement; a parody of the veterans he'd once photographed on these streets. They were early – bonfire night was still three weeks away – but he had to admire their enterprise in getting ahead of the competition and their shameless exploitation of the season's earning potential. At any other time he would have slipped the compact camera from his pocket and taken a series of shots, but today he flipped a sixpence at them and went into the restaurant.

He had suggested this place because of its ubiquity. He knew that it was likely to be busy, but there was a certain safe anonymity in that. He was enveloped by a humid fug of steam and humanity as the door swung shut behind him; the mixed aromas of coffee, stale smoke, fried eggs and damp tweed. A pianist was fighting a losing battle to be heard above the clamour of conversation.

A waitress in a cap that had almost slid down over her eyes directed him to the restaurant on the second floor, where tea was being served. It was quieter up there, which meant the piano music was almost too invasive. He asked to be seated as far away from it as possible, and was shown to a table half hidden by a marble pillar. He chose the seat that gave him a view of the stairs.

He wondered if he would recognize her. In his head he pictured someone quick and dark and slight, though he had no idea why. The mental image was strong enough that he didn't register the woman weaving her way through the tables until she was a few feet away.

'Mr Weston?'

He got hastily to his feet, caught off-guard. She was as plump and rosy as a Renoir, with a fringe of wheat-coloured hair visible beneath her rather severe hat. She had also, very obviously, been crying.

'Miss Davies.'

She nodded and pulled out the chair opposite, depositing her belongings (a battered handbag and umbrella) on the floor and scrabbling in the pocket of her coat for a handkerchief. He watched helplessly, unsure how to go about comforting a weeping woman he'd only just met. His mind raced and his eyes moved down to the buttons of her coat, as the blackmail theory reasserted itself. Surely Selina would help her old friend if she found herself in that sort of trouble though? Polly scrubbed at her nose with the handkerchief and gave him a watery smile.

'Sorry, sir. What must you think of me?'

The smile encouraged him. Ignoring the question, he took his own clean handkerchief from his pocket and handed it to her, recalling another time, another handkerchief, another woman.

'Please, call me Lawrence. Or Mr Weston if you prefer. I've spent the last eleven years in America and been called sir so much that I've almost forgotten my own name.'

He caught the eye of a passing waitress, who diverted her course through the tables to take their order. He sensed Polly's hesitancy and guessed that she was thinking about the expense, so asked for a selection of cakes to be brought over. (If his suspicion was correct he imagined she'd be hungry.) By the time all this had been done and the waitress had retreated she seemed a little more composed.

'So . . .' A mixture of curiosity and impatience made him keen to get straight to the point. 'You were very clever to find me. I haven't been back in England for long.'

'It was luck, really.' She spoke haltingly, and her accent conjured images of Blackwood in summer; lush parkland, grazing cows, and the cool, creamy milk she used to leave on the slate in the scullery. 'I'd come to London on the train one day, and on the way home someone had left a copy of that magazine, the *Sphere*, on the seat. I picked it up to pass the time. The photographs of that new picture studio caught my eye and I thought to take it with me to show to Ellen and Ivy – the maids, at Blackwood. It was only then that I noticed the name at the end of the article.' Colour crept into her cheeks. 'I thought there couldn't be too many Lawrence Westons around, especially not taking photographs, and – well, it just seemed like a sign.'

'A sign?'

It took him by surprise. The woman sitting opposite seemed practical and level-headed, not one for signs and superstitions and magic.

'Yes.' She took a breath in, and straightened her shoulders, reinforcing the impression. 'You see the reason I'd been in London was to visit Miss Selina. In hospital.'

The waitress was making her way towards them, carrying a tray of tea things. Behind her, another trundled a trolley displaying an array of cakes and pastries. The room was suddenly very hot. The piano music was jangling and jarring. He fought the urge to stand up and shout for it to stop, to tell the waitresses to push off and not interrupt until he'd cleared this up.

Hospital?

Girls like me have been put in asylums for less.

In a painful pantomime of politeness the waitresses set the tea things on the table and invited them to choose from the trolley. Polly pointed apparently at random to a Madeira cake, stammering her thanks. Lawrence dismissed them with a curt shake of his head.

'Selina – is she unwell?'

Perhaps the piano masked the tremor in his voice. If that bastard Carew had beaten her down ... If he'd broken her beautiful, brave spirit and pulled strings with his eminent, influential medical friends and had her locked up in some god-forsaken institution ...

Polly held herself very still, very stiff, and closed her eyes for a moment. When she opened them again fresh tears wobbled on her lower lashes.

'Yes. That's why I had to get in touch. I'm afraid she is.'

Lying in her narrow bed in the night nursery, Alice watched the sky change from school uniform grey to paper white, and back again. If she stayed very still the pain in her tummy was easier. She had begun to think of it as a savage animal that must not be woken.

The hours dragged. Polly, she had been told, had left Blackwood early to spend another day in London, visiting her poorly friend. Hearing this from Ellen when she came to wake her up made Alice burst into tears. She was tired from another night of fitful sleep and had decided, in the long hours of darkness, that she would have to tell Polly about the tummy ache. 'I'm poorly too,' she had blurted out to a bewildered Ellen, and then cried harder with embarrassment and fury – at Polly for not being there, and herself for being such a baby.

At least the secret was out now, she thought, watching a ragged black bird flap across the blank sky. Ellen was the last person Alice would have chosen to tell, but she had been surprisingly kind, ordering her to get back under the covers while she went down to get a hot water bottle and see Grandmama. Alice had begged her not to do the latter, but Ellen had been firm. 'I can't telephone for Dr Pembridge without her say so, can I? Now, get back into bed and keep warm. Cold feet make a fever worse, you know.'

Alice was sure she didn't have a fever. She had had measles when she was six and remembered the cycle of burning and shivering, the sense of being adrift from reality, as if her soul was a balloon, tugging at the string that tied it to her body on the bed. She felt nothing like that now. Reality was all too . . . real. The day crept by, made up of minutes that were ten times longer than usual. Ellen brought her some soup at lunchtime and said that Dr Pembridge would call when he could, though he was attending a lying in so who knew when that might be? (Alice didn't know what a lying in was so couldn't begin to guess the answer to that.)

In the afternoon the beast in her tummy slumbered, lulled by the warmth of the hot water bottle and Mrs Rutter's chicken soup. Alice would have liked to slip down to her usual place on the back stairs and listen to the goings on in the kitchen, but she didn't dare. Ellen would be cross if she found her there, and think she had been making it up about feeling poorly. Instead she slid the Maison D'Or box out from beneath the bed and lifted the lid.

She had kept all Mama's letters in there, and all the clues from the treasure hunt. She got them out now and spread them across the candlewick cover, in the order in which she had received them. Seeing them like that, the contrast between the handwritten ones of the early months and the more recent black type was very marked.

The beast stirred and stretched its claws.

The last letter had arrived over a month ago. It had made Alice happy to read that it looked like Papa's business was finally coming to an end and that he would soon be making arrangements for their return voyage. *I had almost given up believing that this time would come,* Mama had written — or rather, typed, *but I'm keeping my fingers crossed that we'll be back together in Onslow Square soon. The moment I find out when that might be, I'll write and let you know.*

But no more letters had arrived. Alice knew what Mama meant about giving up believing.

Dark things scuttled and scratched at the edges of her thoughts, like the beetles that hid under the pots in the kitchen garden, darting away when they were exposed to the light. She tried to follow them, determined to clear away the confusion and evasion and find the truth. Like solving a clue without knowing what it was.

The letters were of two types, and she began to separate them now, putting the ones Mama had written on the journey to Burma and from the house in Maymyo in one pile, and all the treasure hunt clues in another. Those ones, when pieced together, told the story Mama had mentioned at the beginning, in one of her earliest letters ... *the story of how you came to be,* she had called it, with *the happiest ending of all.*

Inside her, the beast snarled. Alice tried to ignore it and focus on grasping at the threads of information that kept slipping through her fingers. She hated the small, spoiled part of her that felt cheated; Mama was usually brilliant at telling stories, but this one seemed unfinished and full of holes. She knew there would be no more instalments because she had found the 'treasure' – Mama's beloved aquamarine pendant – and while it was lovely to have it, she felt cross and resentful. She hadn't found out how she came to be at all, and there had been no happy ending. Only that bit about Alice teaching Mama how to love properly, or whatever it had said.

She picked out the last letter from the treasure hunt pile and pulled it from the envelope.

Darling Alice,

So here it is, the final clue and the last bit of the story. How clever you are to have found them all, and the 'treasure'! I'm sure you'll have no trouble recognizing this pendant, but you perhaps don't know that it was given to me for my twenty-second birthday, by someone incredibly special — someone I loved very much.

It was the happiest of birthdays. I met Theo and Flick for tea at Claridge's and they gave me the beautiful tortoiseshell box, which clever Theo had spotted in an

antique shop in Venice during his Italian summer. (He lives
in Italy all the time now, as you might remember. A few years
ago he sent me that little porcelain cherub that sits on the
chimneypiece in my bedroom from the very same shop. Dear
Theo — I do miss him.) The pendant was given to me later that
evening, by someone else I miss very much. He was called
Lawrence Weston and he taught me more than anyone else had
ever done. Until you came along, my darling.

Life is full of upsets that feel like endings, and that
autumn of 1925 was one of those times. It was the end of
the summer, and the end of my carefree youth, because not
long after that lovely birthday tea at Claridge's my darling
friend Flick died very suddenly and everything changed.

It felt then as if I'd never be happy again. I truly
believed it. Everything felt horribly dark and frightening,
like a nightmare that kept going on. I couldn't believe that
Flick — who was so sweet and funny and full of mischief —
was gone because it seemed so absurd, like God had made a
terrible mistake. I was furious at the injustice and the lack
of sense, and terrified that it would happen again. I had lost
my beloved brother and my best friend and I didn't think I
could bear losing another person I loved. And so I decided
that it was safest not to love anyone very much. Isn't that
an awful thing to admit?

And that is where you saved me, you see. You taught me how
to love deeply and unstintingly, and how to embrace the
fear and pain that goes with it. I had been too afraid
before. I wanted to protect myself from being hurt. I

wanted a life that was comfortable and safe. I refused to
believe then that such a thing is no life at all and I
told myself —

Alice suddenly became aware of voices, getting louder.
Grandmama was talking to someone as she came up the
stairs and along the corridor. In a panic she swept all the
letters back into the box and shoved it under the bed.

'Unfortunate that Polly isn't here,' she heard Grandmama
say as she came into the day nursery next door. 'She would
be able to answer your questions more easily than I.'

Alice collapsed back onto the pillows and hauled the
blankets over her. Her heart was galloping and sweat prick-
led under her arms. The nursery floorboards creaked and a
second later Dr Pembridge appeared.

He was tall and angular, and the overwhelming impression Alice got of him at close quarters was of some large,
ungainly bird; a heron, perhaps, like the one she used to see
on her miserable walks with Miss Lovelock. He put his bag
down on the chair and came forward, rubbing his hands
together heartily.

'So, young lady. Your grandmother tells me you're not
quite the ticket. Feeling a bit off colour. Pain in that tummy,
eh?'

Alice nodded, wishing she could pull the covers over her
head and hide. For ages she had longed to tell Dr Pembridge
about the pain, but now he was here she just wanted him to
go away. He loomed over the bed, blocking out the light,

slipping a thermometer under her tongue. He smelled of disinfectant. As he removed the thermometer and examined it she saw grey bristles on the lower half of his face.

'Let's have a little feel, shall we? You tell me where it hurts.'

There was a smudge of blood on the front of his shirt. She kept her eyes fixed on it as he folded down the blanket and pulled up her nightdress. She stiffened with shame. His fingers were cold and hard, but the pain darted away from his touch, always elusive. As he probed he asked questions about Alice's appetite and awful, embarrassing things about the lavatory, which made her want to hide even more. He pressed his fingertips hard down beside her tummy button and looked at her expectantly, as if she were a teddy bear and he was anticipating a growl. She kept silent. Eventually he tugged down her nightdress and stood up.

'Well, that all seems to be as it should be. Nothing to alarm there, and nothing to keep you in bed. Best to get up and keep busy, I say – read a good book or play with some of those splendid toys in the nursery, eh? Too much time to mope never did anyone any good.'

He thought she was making it up, she could tell. Before she could find the words to explain he had retrieved his bag and gone back through to the day nursery, with the cheery advice that once she was up and about she'd be feeling better in no time. With tears burning at the back of her eyes Alice scrambled out of bed, not wanting to let the chance she had waited for slip away. Going into the day nursery she was just in time to see Dr Pembridge's tweed shoulders disappearing through the doorway.

'No sign of appendicitis,' she heard him say. 'She doesn't have a fever and everything appears normal.'

'I'm sorry for wasting your time, Doctor.'

'Not at all. I believe the pain is quite genuine. As a matter of fact I was reading an interesting paper on this just last week. Psychosomatic illness, it's called – symptoms that have a hysterical cause rather than a physiological one. Children are particularly susceptible apparently. Especially those of a sensitive disposition.' A pause. A discreet clearing of the throat. 'Have you told her about her mother?'

'No.'

Alice stood perfectly still at the nursery door, listening with every atom of her being.

'I'd hazard that she may have picked up that things aren't quite as they seem,' Dr Pembridge was saying. 'She might have overheard something – servants' gossip, perhaps.'

'They were given strict instructions to be careful. She thinks her mother is abroad with her father on a business trip. Selina was most insistent she shouldn't know about—'

There was a rushing in Alice's head, and a surge of fiery heat, all through her body. The floor felt like it was turning to quicksand beneath her feet as she staggered out into the corridor. Grandmama and Dr Pembridge looked round with identical expressions of alarm as she started to scream.

'No! No, no, *no!*'

*

'I say, are you all right?'

Lawrence straightened up and opened his eyes, to meet those of a stranger in the mirror. He nodded mutely, noticing that his face was the same shade of green as the ceramic tiles around the walls. He cupped his palms together and splashed it with cold water again, then moved across to the stiff roller towel to scrub it dry. When he turned round the stranger was gone and the cloakroom was empty.

He wasn't all right at all.

He fumbled for a cigarette (Murad these days, not Woodbines) and lit it with an unsteady hand. He had seen Polly off already, flagging down a taxi and paying the driver way over the likely fare to get her to Waterloo in time for her train. Before she'd got in they had clasped hands tightly and looked at each other in helpless despair. Thankfully he had managed to get himself back inside Maison Lyons and find his way to the gentlemen's cloakroom before he fainted or threw up or wept out there on the street.

He smoked the cigarette in rapid, desperate drags, leaning against the tiled wall, head reeling. The door swung open and someone else came in, so he stumbled out and made his way back through the restaurant, a different person to the one he'd been an hour ago.

A father.

Christ. He couldn't take it in, any of it. He was dazed and nauseous — numb, for the moment, though he knew that wouldn't last. Outside the restaurant the children with the guy were trying to organize themselves to get home, squabbling and scuffling as they loaded their cumbersome creation onto a set of pram wheels. Lawrence stared at them, wondering how old they were. She was nine, his girl. *Alice.* Dark eyes, dark curls – the image of him, Polly said; it was quite uncanny.

One of the older girls scowled at him and put her arm roughly around a smaller one, who gave a squawk of protest and wriggled free. Lawrence backed away, cannoning into a woman carrying a large carpet bag. He stuttered an apology and walked on, the image of his unknown daughter evaporating, leaving only Selina.

He quickened his pace. The blood was pulsing loud and hard through his body, making him too hot in spite of the chill of the afternoon. The pavements of Oxford Street were crowded with people at this going-home hour of the day and he loathed and resented them all for being unhurried and unaware. For being well enough to walk down Oxford Street when the glorious girl who had danced through puddles with him on this very pavement was in a hospital bed that she wouldn't now leave.

Jesus.

His eyes stung and his throat was raw. He stepped out into the road, holding up his hand to halt a furious delivery boy on a bicycle and dodging in front of a motorbus, to a cacophony of horn-blasts. The hospital was in Marylebone, Polly said. Beaumont Street – not far. It had taken her a quarter hour to walk.

He started to run.

25

The Beginning of The End

In the aftermath of her storm of weeping Alice felt empty. Exhausted.

Dr Pembridge had given her some bitter-tasting medicine, and Ellen had been called to help hold her as he forced it into her mouth. As she had fought and howled a distant part of Alice's mind remained detached and floating above herself, appalled. Now, tucked tightly into bed, she thought of how she had behaved and felt nothing.

The curtains were pulled shut again and the pillow was cool against her cheek. The lamp was lit and Grandmama's shadow loomed on the nursery wall. It seemed odd that she was there: Alice had never known her to cross the nursery threshold before. She didn't want to look at her, sitting at the end of the bed. She lay on her side, facing the wall while Grandmama talked in a low voice, telling her the truth that everyone had hidden for all this time.

Mama was not in Burma. She never had been – at least, not since her honeymoon. All the things that she had written about – the voyage on the *Eastern Star*, the journey up the blood-red Irawaddy river, staying in the little house at the hill station – had happened *ten years ago*, before Alice was born. She had kept a journal, Grandmama said. That's how she was able to describe it in such vivid detail in her letters.

Alice wondered how long Grandmama had known about the letters. She'd thought they were secret.

She'd thought a lot of things that had turned out to be wrong.

'Your mother wanted to protect you,' Grandmama said. 'She knew that she had some very difficult and unpleasant times ahead and she didn't want you to be worried. Your Papa made sure she had the very best doctor, and we all thought that once the operation was over and she had had a chance to recover, everything would be perfectly all right again.'

Grandmama's voice faltered a little. Alice felt mild surprise at this, but did not turn her head. Her eyes stayed fixed to Grandmama's dark shape on the wall. 'Of course, none of us knew that it would take so long . . .'

Or that it wouldn't be all right, Alice thought. Not at all. Not ever.

Grandmama stopped talking. Alice thought she heard her take a little in-out breath, but her shadow stayed perfectly still.

'She had to have another operation,' Grandmama went

on. 'On her chest. Even so, it seems that her illness has got worse. It's very . . . unlucky. Very unexpected.'

Grandmama always held herself very upright, but the shadow that stretched across the wall was stooped, as if she was suddenly as old and frail as Grandfather.

'Will she die?' Alice asked, in a voice that didn't sound like her own.

'Yes,' Grandmama said coolly. 'Yes, I'm afraid so.'

Alice gripped the aquamarine tightly. She felt as if the spiky kernel that had been lodged in her tummy since Mama went away had split open, and the pain had spread to every part of her, like poison.

'Can I see her?'

The stooped shadow shoulders stiffened.

'No. No, I don't think that's wise. Not now. Your mama is very weak, you see, and very tired. The doctor thinks it would place too much strain on her and be too upsetting. For you both. You must be very brave and wait for news.'

The aquamarine pressed hard into Alice's fingers. Poison burned in her throat.

'Is there anything else you'd like to ask?' Grandmama said.

'No.'

'Very well.' Grandmama hesitated, and then Alice felt the movement of the mattress as she stood up. The shadow reared across the wall with sudden menace, like a monster from a nightmare. Not real, Mama would murmur, stroking her forehead, just a bad dream. Except it wasn't.

'Goodnight, Alice.'

Grandmama's voice was softer than usual, but the face of the shadow figure remained black and empty as it retreated to the door.

Alice didn't reply.

Lawrence had expected resistance. Arriving at the smart nursing home sweating and out of breath he had expected to be challenged at the very least, and had been ready to fight.

He hadn't got as far as working out what that might mean and the lengths to which he would go to see Selina, but in the end it wasn't necessary. By some stroke of luck his arrival was perfectly timed. The doctors who would have disapproved of him being there had gone home for the day and the night nurse who had just reported for duty seemed to know exactly who this dishevelled stranger was. She led him quickly down the corridor and, outside Selina's door, she squeezed his arm and told him she was glad that he was there. And then she took him into the room where the girl he loved – still, after all these years – lay sleeping.

The nurse checked the chart at the foot of her bed, smoothed the sheet and adjusted the angle of the dim lamp, then retreated. There was a chair against the wall on the other side of the room, and Lawrence brought it across (what was it doing over there anyway? Did her bloody husband not sit beside her?) then he sank down into it and gazed at her as tears coursed down his face.

She was so thin. Her skin was almost translucent, showing the blue veins beneath. He wanted to gather her up into his arms and breathe life back into her, kiss warmth into her pale, dry lips. The blankets lay flat across her chest and he remembered the break in Polly's voice when she'd described the surgery she'd had. The doctors called it 'radical', apparently. Polly's word had been 'brutal'.

God, how he ached for her. He had been on the verge of getting up and leaving the room so he could find somewhere to go and howl out his rage and sorrow when she had opened her eyes and seen him.

They cried together, then. Silently, between kisses, and her tears had run over his hands as he stroked her hair.

There was so much to say, so many years to catch up on, but her breathing was laboured and he could see how much the effort of speaking exhausted her. And so he squashed down his questions and talked to her instead, telling her about Polly's letter and their meeting at Maison Lyons.

'She said . . . She said you have a daughter . . . ?'

'Alice.'

Her eyes had gone to the nightstand then, and a child's drawing that was propped against a jug of water. His heart turned over as he picked it up.

'The Chinese Tea House.'

'Yes.'

His eyes blurred. For eleven years it had been a place that existed only in his dreams and his memory and in a sheaf of old photographs, but now the October evening fell away and he was back there, at Blackwood that summer, dazzled by the beauty of it all. Overwhelmed and stupefied with first love.

Only love, as it turned out.

'It's good.' He cleared his throat. 'She's quite an artist.'

Nine years old, Polly had said, but her penwork was precise and clever. Surely most children didn't draw like that?

'I wonder where she gets that from?'

Selina's voice was a cracked whisper, but her eyes glittered brilliantly and there was a smile on her milk-pale lips. 'A ... honeymoon baby, everyone assumed. I did too, until ... I saw her. And then I knew ...'

Her breath had spent itself and she spluttered to a halt in a gasping cough.

'Ours?' he asked gently. 'That night ...'

She nodded. Her eyes closed, and it felt like a light going out. Anguish gripped him. He had to stiffen himself against the urge to hold her then, and his fingers tingled with the effort of not squeezing her fragile ones too hard. His jaw was set as his eyes darted wildly around the room, furiously willing himself not to let her down by crying. He thought she was asleep, but at length she murmured, 'Do you remember it?'

He leaned forward and kissed her gently on the mouth. 'Every moment.'

*

February 1926

The cold numbed Lawrence's fingers as he unpinned the photographs from the walls of his room in Marchmont Street. Outside, a steel-edged wind blew mean flakes of snow around the dirty sky while, in the flat below, Mr Kaminski's violin scratched out scales.

He didn't have much to pack. A few clothes (Edith had insisted he buy a dinner suit and some decent shirts; apparently Americans set a lot of store by smartness) and his camera. Not much to show for his life so far. Not much to start a new one.

He collected together the images of miners, the shots of smoky streets and backyards and grimy-faced children and put them in a pile for Sam. He had been going to dispose of the others (he had the negatives, after all) but Edith had denounced this as artistic sacrilege and insisted that she would keep them at the studio. He hesitated as he took down a picture of Selina in the orangery at Blackwood, then set it ruthlessly aside.

He didn't need photographs to remember. And anyway, the whole point was that he needed to forget.

America had been Sam's idea. A brighter, better, more progressive place than England, he said; he'd be off like a shot himself if there wasn't so much to fight for still in the Welsh Valleys and the pit villages of Nottingham and the North East. But Lawrence had nothing to keep him in

England, no work, and seemingly little interest in finding any. The suggestion that he book his passage and make a fresh start had come at the end of a lengthy lecture in which the words 'self-indulgent', 'pissed-up waster' and 'fucking pathetic' had also been used.

The fact that Lawrence had been too hungover to mount any defence rather proved Sam's point.

Weeks had passed since that November morning when Selina had come to say goodbye. He had told her that it wasn't too late to change her mind but as each short day blurred into the next that possibility began to seem increasingly remote, until it felt laughably embarrassing that he had ever allowed himself to believe it. (Or fucking pathetic, as Sam so succinctly put it.) He longed to see her – craved it, in fact – and he gave up wandering the seedier parts of the city with his camera, instead spending his evenings haunting its smart streets, huddling in the shadows opposite The Embassy, the KitKat Club, the Eiffel Tower and The Ritz in the hope of seeing her. His efforts were hardly ever rewarded. New stars glittered in the firmament of the Bright Young Things now; new clubs replaced the old favourites, new dances, new cocktails, new games and names and crazes. Sometimes he saw Theo Osborne, rake-thin, dramatically swathed in furs, but Selina was never with him. On the rare occasions when he did see her she was with Rupert and he barely caught a glimpse of her bright hair as she stepped from motorcar to doorway. Those were the nights when he drank to oblivion. It was just as well it didn't happen often.

It was Edith, predictably, who took him in hand. He had grown used to her kindness and took her unconditional support for granted, so having it abruptly withdrawn came as a shock. 'This can't go on,' she'd snapped after one of those nights. 'You're not the first person to suffer a broken heart and you won't be the last. You need to pull yourself together before you lose everything.' When Lawrence told her he already had, she gave him a withering look. 'Don't be silly. You still have friends, talent and a shred of dignity. *Just.*'

Christmas came. In despair he went home to Hastings and spent a sober, largely silent festival with his father and brother. Returning to London in the dead days at the close of the year he went to the Thomas Cook offices in Ludgate Circus and booked a third class ticket to New York, simply because he didn't know what else to do. The sailing date, at the start of February, had meant nothing to him then. It was only last week that Sam had pointed out that it was the day of Selina Lennox's wedding.

He turned to look back around the stripped walls. The room had already ceased to feel like his, or like home. It was blank and ready for a new occupant – an earnest trainee reporter Sam knew from his socialist meetings. Only one photograph remained. Lawrence looked at it for a long time before unpinning it with trembling fingers.

It was his favourite one, taken by the Chinese Tea House at Blackwood in the aftermath of languid lovemaking, when she had the sun in her eyes and a drowsy, dreamy smile on her lips. He remembered that moment of ripe contentment, and as he looked at it he could almost feel her touch on his skin and hear the sweet echo of Bach above Mr Kaminski's laborious scales. He wondered if he would ever know happiness like that again.

He wondered if she would.

The pen he had borrowed from Sam to label his bag still lay on the table. He picked it up and, without stopping to think, turned the photograph over and began to write.

'Good heavens, it's bitter.' Miranda cast her eyes to the leaden heavens as she got out of the car in Egerton Crescent. 'I can hardly think of worse weather for a wedding. Now perhaps you might see that you should have waited until spring . . .'

Selina said nothing as she followed her up the path. She had been cold for months, cold right through to the marrow of her bones, and the spiteful little flurries of snow made little difference. It might not be traditional wedding weather, but to her it seemed fitting enough for the spirit of this particular occasion.

It had been unanimously agreed that a small wedding would be best. Both bride and groom had suffered the loss of friends – Selina more recently, but Rupert in greater numbers – and a lavish celebration felt inappropriate. (Sir Robert, who had sold a Canaletto and farm with seventy-five acres to pay for Miranda's wedding, couldn't conceal his relief.) Rupert, faced with continuing difficulties with the ruby mines, had intended to travel to Burma immediately after New Year and return in time for a June wedding, but Selina had known that wouldn't work. If she was left to cool her heels for that long it was likely that she would lose her nerve and there would be no wedding at all. And so she had suggested accompanying him to Burma, as an extended honeymoon. Surely her longing for Lawrence would begin to abate with half a world's distance between them?

The door was opened by Jean the housemaid, who reverently relieved Miranda of her fur whilst appearing not to notice Selina. 'There's a good fire in the drawing room, madam,' she said. 'Will you be wanting tea?'

'Yes, that might be rather nice. We've just had tea in Fortnums, but it's so cold I think we could do with some more to warm us up. Just tea though – tell Mrs Robins not to send up any cake. Although you barely touched a crumb.' She glanced accusingly at Selina. 'I rather think you're taking the slimming a little too far these days.'

'We're dining at The Ritz tonight. You don't need to worry about me starving.'

Jean's eyes moved over Selina. 'A letter came for you, Miss Lennox,' she said, her gaze settling somewhere around Selina's chest. 'In the last post. Well, when I say letter . . . it's larger than that. An invitation, perhaps. Or a catalogue . . .'

'Yes, thank you, Jean,' Miranda said crisply. 'I'm sure Miss Lennox doesn't need you to tell her what her letter contains.'

No, Selina thought dazedly, picking up the envelope from the salver on the table and blinking at the writing she recognized so well. She was suddenly boiling hot, though her face in the hall mirror was as white as the paper in her hands. Her pulse beat loud in her ears.

'I'll just – I need to—'

'But, miss, your coat . . .' she heard Jean protesting as she hurried up the stairs.

In her room she shut the door and leaned back against it while she fumbled with the envelope. In her haste she had forgotten to remove her gloves, which made her fingers clumsy and useless. She tore them off and threw them aside, then slid a finger beneath the envelope's seal and pulled out the contents.

She found herself looking into the half-closed eyes of a girl she barely recognized. A girl with tousled hair and plump cheeks and a sleepy smile, who seemed to be about to take her hand and pull her back into last summer. The feeling made her dizzy. That's what she had done to him, she remembered, in the second after he had taken that photograph outside the Chinese House. She had taken his hand and pulled him towards her, and they had fallen together on the sun-warmed boards where they had just made love and she had lain with her head on his chest as the echoes of pleasure reverberated through her, keeping time with the beat of his heart.

I want you to have this, he had written on the back. *I want you to remember this incredible girl, who was brave and beautiful and happy. I will never forget her.*

I once told you that I wouldn't share you and I couldn't accept half measures, but that was before I'd tried to live without you. I wouldn't have the strength or the arrogance to say it now. Knowing you are in the same city, that I might come across your photograph in the newspaper or see you in the street is a temptation and a torment I can no longer endure.

Tomorrow I travel to Southampton, and from there sail to America. When the ship pulls away from the dock perhaps I'll finally accept that it's over and maybe then I'll be able to work out what to do with the rest of my life. I'd like to say that I'll be able to stop loving you, but I don't think that will be possible. No matter how much easier it would be.

I hope he makes you happy. I hope he makes you feel safe. I hope he tells you every day that you're the most beautiful woman in the world. Because, as you can see from this photograph, you truly are.

She was crying when she finished reading: silent, helpless tears streaming down her cheeks. But then her breath caught and she stopped. Gulping and sniffing she scanned the lines again, this time concentrating on the message that lay between them.

Tomorrow he was leaving and she would be married.

But it wasn't tomorrow yet.

She dressed for him with infinite care, using the silk underwear and expensive scent that had been bought for her honeymoon, putting kohl around her eyes and painting her mouth. Polly said nothing when Selina asked her to unpack the tissue-wrapped treasures from her trousseau, but her eyes were full of questions and anguish.

Lady Lennox had insisted on arranging a pre-wedding dinner at The Ritz for Rupert's parents. On the way there Selina told Miranda that she would be going on to meet Theo at The Embassy afterwards (and prayed that they wouldn't bump into him in the dining room). Miranda's lips tightened with disapproval, but Selina had deliberately waited until they were almost there and there was no time for argument.

If anyone noticed that she barely touched the food that was put before her no one remarked on it. Pre-wedding nerves, they perhaps assumed, which might also account for the slight tremor of her hands and her distraction: twice Miranda had to kick her beneath the table to get her attention when Rupert's mother addressed a remark to her. She drank the champagne that was poured to toast the joining of their two families, but otherwise her wineglass remained full. She wanted to be clear-headed. For every detail of the hours ahead to remain sharp.

Dinner seemed to last for an eternity – how unfair that seemed when she knew that the night that followed would slip away from her so quickly – but finally her mother was laying aside her napkin, rising from her seat. Selina gritted her teeth through the expansive goodbyes in the foyer, her smile a painful rictus as she tilted her cheek up to accept Rupert's kiss. Outside she gulped the icy air and looked around for a taxi as Lionel handed Miranda and her parents into their waiting car. 'What on earth is she doing?' she heard her mother ask sharply in the moment before the chauffeur shut the door. She didn't hear Miranda's answer, or care what it was, because the doorman had hailed a cab which was pulling up at the kerb.

In the years afterwards she would come to think how strange it was that she could recall almost nothing about her wedding day – just a blurred impression of cold satin, the cruel spikes of hairpins in her scalp, the fragrance of lilies – but every detail of the night before it remained etched on her memory. She remembered speeding through the dark streets to Bloomsbury and letting herself into the familiar hallway. She remembered the little jolt of surprise as she saw the candle burning on the windowsill, the slow spread of wonder as she realized he'd placed them all the way up the stairs – quivering flames in glasses and jars and cocoa tins – little pots of gold, leading to his door. She remembered knocking and him letting her in without speaking and how she'd followed him down the corridor to his room.

Candlelight flickered over bare walls. He'd taken down the photographs and packed his possessions. A battered canvas kitbag was on the floor beneath the window and there was a bottle of red wine on the table. From downstairs the spiralling, swooping strains of the violin.

She remembered particularly, with shivering clarity, the expression on his face as she'd stood in front of him in her peacock blue chiffon dress, her gold shoes. Helpless. Wistful. Tender. She had slipped her shoes off and they had danced together, to the borrowed music, breathing in unison, holding each other as if they were made of something fragile, touching as if they were afraid of breaking the spell, bursting the shimmering bubble of candlelight. They spoke little, in low voices, even though Sam was away and they had the flat to themselves. There was nothing more to say.

They drank the wine slowly, eking out the last drops, tasting it on each other's lips so that for ever after she couldn't drink claret without a tremor of sensory recollection. She undressed unhurriedly, as if they had all the time in the world, and he lay back on the bed, watching her with dark, liquid eyes. She remembered the rattling hiss as her dress, heavy with beads, slithered off her shoulders onto the bare wooden floor.

She remembered every touch. Every kiss. Every sigh.

They didn't sleep. At some time in the dark hours, when the candles had burned out, he made coffee and she leaned against his chest in the circle of his arms to drink it. She remembered watching the light gather and wash the bare walls. She remembered turning to him again, wanting to imprint him on every cell in her body.

Had that been the moment that Alice had been created?

She remembered their goodbye. Lawrence, barefoot and bare-chested in the hallway where they'd first met, kissing on and on as the tears streamed down their cheeks. She remembered walking out into the frozen morning, bruised-lipped in her thin silk dress.

That was the bit she remembered best about her wedding day. His mouth on hers as he said *I love you* for the last time.

*

October 1936

Lawrence heard her breathing hitch. He was holding her hand and felt her fingers suddenly tighten around his. She opened her eyes with a little cry.

'Shhh – it's all right. Sweetheart, it's all right.'

For a moment she stared at him, as if trying to remember who he was, and then she went limp against the pillows again. Her eyes closed and a tear slid down her cheek.

'I was ... dreaming. About when we said goodbye. I thought ... I'd imagined you were ever here.'

He kissed her forehead, then rested his cheek against it, breathing in the scent of her hair, still discernibly hers beneath the hospital smell.

'I'm here.'

The air rattled through her lungs. He felt her whole body move and sensed the effort it took.

'Sometimes, when I wake up I see Flick here, or Howard, and I know ... they're waiting for me. Last night ... when I saw you there ... I thought that it was time. I thought that you had gone before and ... come back to take me with you.'

His heart tripped painfully.

'I wish I had,' he whispered hoarsely. 'If it meant we wouldn't have to say goodbye again.'

'That morning ... I thought it was the end. Of everything. I thought I'd never be happy again. Never love again.'

'You didn't want to,' he reminded her, gently teasing.

'No . . .' A smile. 'But then there was Alice. She showed me that you were right. The only way to cheat death is to love . . . wholly.' She took a breath. 'From the start I loved her so much it . . . *terrified* me . . . But I didn't run away. Not like I did from you. I learned that there was . . . a special kind of joy in that fear. I realized that love is . . . always painful. But in the end . . . it's all that matters.'

He had to pause before answering, to control the sob in his voice. 'It's not the end. It wasn't then and it isn't now.'

He waited until her eyes closed and her rasping breath steadied before letting go of her hand and laying it down on the blankets, wincing at the bruises on her papery skin. He stood up and flexed his stiff shoulders. Everything in him resisted the thought of leaving her, but he knew what he had to do.

He just hoped he would have time.

26

Alice Again

Alice had thought it through carefully. Made plans.

She had made no conscious decision to go to London, but from the moment she understood the situation she knew that was what she had to do. Instead of dwelling on the thing that Grandmama had told her, she occupied her mind with practicalities. She had worked out that the best time to leave was after lunch, when Polly thought she was going out to join Mr Patterson in the garden. Dressing that morning, she had put on an extra vest and her warmest jersey and tucked the half crown Uncle Lionel had given her at Easter into her pocket. (That was the only thing she was uncertain about – would half a crown be enough to buy a railway ticket to London, even in third class?) Last night she had packed her old school satchel with Mama's letters, the tin of coloured pencils and the precious things from the box under the bed as well as gloves, a spare pair of socks and two apples smuggled from the store by the garden bothy. She had crept down the back stairs to hide it in the boot room, behind the layers of ancient coats that hung there. She believed she had thought of everything.

Mr Patterson had once told her that the quickest way to the village was through the garden, but she didn't dare take that route. She knew that Jimmy had been working there recently, cutting dead branches from the trees before the winter winds tore them down, and so she took the path she used to walk with Miss Lovelock. Instead of following it around the lake she turned down the narrower track into the woods. She walked quickly, her back prickling with unease at the thought that she might be being watched from the house, resisting the temptation to look.

She felt guilty too, about Polly and Mr Patterson. She pictured the old gardener in the glasshouse, peering out through the misted panes to look for her. She had originally intended to go and see him before she left, to make an excuse about helping Mrs Rutter or wanting to do some drawing, but she couldn't quite bring herself to fib to someone who had been so very kind to her. She had a feeling that he might see through her excuses anyway, with that way he had of listening and saying little and working out what was what. She trudged unhappily on, reassuring herself that she could explain everything later, when she got to London and was with Mama again. Surely they would understand?

The embers of her anger glowed again then. She was only doing this because there was no one else she could trust.

Everyone had lied. Everyone had known that Mama was poorly and everyone had kept it from her and that was why she had to go to see for herself. Grandmama said Mama was too weak for visitors, but Alice wouldn't believe that until she saw it with her own eyes. At the back of her mind she nurtured a spark of hope that she would get to the hospital (in Marylebone, she had managed to find out – hopefully there was only one) and find that Grandmama had been wrong, or exaggerating and Mama would open her arms and laugh and say that she was getting better every day and everything was going to be fine.

The woods were gloomy and rank with the decaying smell of wet earth. Alice was walking so fast that she was far too hot in the extra layers she had put on. Her mind travelled ahead, mapping out the journey. When she came out of the woods she had to cross a field, then turn right when she reached the road and follow it – ignoring the turning to the village – until she eventually came to the station. She knew there was a train in the late afternoon and, ignoring the sweat cooling on the back of her neck, she walked faster as she emerged from the thicket of trees.

Ahead of her was the gate to the field she had to cross and, on the other side of it, a dark huddle of cows. She faltered, senses prickling with unease. The animals were pressed together, staring at her with black, unblinking eyes in which it was impossible not to read menace. Tentatively she approached the gate, but when she put her foot on the bottom rung to climb it the cows began to jostle together in obvious agitation. One of them let out an alarming bellow, which startled both Alice and the other cows. Stumbling away from the gate she ran back into the shelter of the woods. She would just have to find another way to the road.

Her cheeks were hot with anger and shame at her own cowardice. She retraced her steps to a place where the path branched off into a narrower trail, choked up with brambles and goosegrass, overgrown with branches. She tried not to notice the sound of snapping twigs and rustling leaves and the darkness that was thickening between the trees. She kept her eyes fixed on her feet, focusing on the flash of her socks in the gloom, the rhythm of her steps. After a little way the path all but disappeared, and she had to scramble over fallen trees and pick her way around banks of tangled plants. She kept going, doggedly, pausing only to rub at the nettle stings on her knees, and was surprised to find that she was crying.

There was nothing to do but go on. She didn't know what time it was, but far above the rooks had begun their circling and screeching prelude to roosting, which told her that the afternoon would soon be waning. She thought wistfully of the warm glasshouse and ginger cake and the hum of the wireless and wondered if anyone had discovered yet that she had gone.

It was raining when she eventually emerged from the trees. Not hard, but in a fine mist that clung to the rough wool of her coat like the tiny glass beads on the dresses in Mama's wardrobe. Gritting her teeth, she hitched the satchel higher on her shoulder. She wasn't allowed to think about

Mama until she got to London; that was the bargain she had made with herself. She had assumed that she would be there before the end of the day but, glancing anxiously at the great grey blanket of sky above her, she felt a lurch of fear. It was already going dark and she hadn't even got to the station. When did the last train go?

There was a gate in the hedgerow ahead of her and she directed herself towards it. Her legs were tired now, the damp skin above her socks chilled and chafed, stippled with white welts from the nettles. The ache in her tummy that Dr Pembridge said was caused by worrying was so familiar that she had almost stopped noticing it, but it stabbed at her again as she climbed the gate.

She stood for a moment, perched on the top, looking around. Behind, over the tops of the trees she had walked through, a long row of chimneys was silhouetted against the pale remnants of the dying day. Surely that couldn't be Blackwood? Her mind gaped. How could she have walked for so long and still be so close? She gave a whimper at the realization that she had come in a wide circle, and that the road on the other side of the gate would take her straight back to Blackwood's tree-lined drive.

And then, echoing eerily across the drab fields, she heard the distant whistle of the train.

Edith's motorcar was a yellow Wolseley Hornet with a badly fitting hood that let in icy draughts and drips of rainwater. To Lawrence, who had learned to drive in America, it felt like a child's tin car that had broken loose from a carousel, and he wondered if the name 'Hornet' had been chosen because its six-cylinder engine sounded like the buzz of a persistent insect. He was grateful, however, for the use of it, and for Edith's unquestioning support. 'Of course you must go,' she had said staunchly, after listening to the whole story. And then she had asked the cook to cut sandwiches and prepare a Thermos of coffee for him while she showed him how best to manage the Hornet's tricky second gear.

The challenges of the gearbox and navigating his way through London's unfamiliar suburbs provided a welcome distraction during the first half of the journey. He stopped in a little town called Basingstoke to buy a motoring map and gulp the lukewarm coffee, but as he motored onwards, along straight roads once marched by Roman legions, exhaustion swamped him. Throwing open the windows, he tried to remember when he'd last slept and found that time had somehow lost its meaning: there was simply before he had seen Selina again, and now. Thinking of her, remembering the purple shadows beneath her eyes and the bruises that bloomed on her arms where the needles had been, sent a surge of adrenaline crashing through him, more effective than all the coffee and fresh air in the world.

The short day faded. The Hornet's headlamps wavered over the miles of empty roads, occasionally picking out a fox or a pheasant strutting to safety. His shoulders were rigid and his head ringing by the time he passed a fingerpost sign to Hindbury village, and he was catapulted back to the summer evening eleven years ago when he had alighted from the train to walk across the fields to Blackwood.

And there were the gates he had been too intimidated to go through last time. He swung the Hornet between them, slowing down and blinking through the winter twilight to look around. He remembered the avenue of trees – soaked in autumn now, but as blowsy and billowing as a flotilla of galleons that green August – and knew that the lake in which they had swum that day when thunder thickened the air lay somewhere to the right. His heart ached suddenly for the girl Selina had been then – strong and quick and certain – and the foolish boy who was too blinkered by inferiority, too preoccupied with his own insecurity to be able to make her feel safe. It had taken him ten years in America to see that Edith was right, and that the only reward for knowing your place was staying in it. By then he'd thought it was too late.

It almost was.

Blackwood loomed as he emerged from the trees, shuttered and forbidding, nothing like the golden treasure house of his memory. The Hornet's feeble headlamps picked out the weeds that choked the gravel and sprouted from the steps to the front door, the paint that peeled from the windowframes.

Last time he had stolen round to the servants' yard, terrified of feeling a hand on his shoulder and a voice ordering him to leave, but now, going up the steps to the front door, the only thing he was afraid of was losing his temper. Letting Selina down.

He felt for the bell-pull in the darkness. Its distant jangle echoed back across the years. He felt like he'd stepped out of time as he waited, insulated from the cold and sleety rain by the heat of adrenaline. Despite the long, empty hours of the journey he hadn't thought ahead to his arrival, or what kind of reception he might get; the shadowy figure from their daughter's past. The stain on their family's honour.

Even if he'd thought about nothing else all the way he still wouldn't have anticipated what happened next. Hurried footsteps. The door thrown open. A young woman, white-faced in the winter gloom, standing back to admit him as if he were expected. And welcome.

'Thank goodness. Come in, officer. If you wouldn't mind waiting here, I'll fetch Lady Lennox.'

He went forwards into the hallway he remembered so well. A single lamp burned on a side table, so that the marble columns stretched up into shadow and the mirrors reflected back on themselves. For a moment he was distracted from the confusion as the past hauled him back to the lilac dusk of an August evening when he had stood here and looked around in awe, and then, heart crashing, had gone to the foot of the stairs and called up, and she had appeared in a silk kimono . . .

He turned to look there now. Another figure was coming down the stairs, stiff and upright, gripping the ornate banister. The ghosts of his youth dissolved.

He cleared his throat. 'Lady Lennox.'

'Thank you for coming, officer . . . ?'

Questions rushed back, spiked with alarm. He thought he'd misheard when the maid said it before. Impatience made him abrupt. 'I'm afraid not. My name is Lawrence Weston. I'm a friend of Selina's, from a long time ago. I've just come from the hospital—'

Lady Lennox had reached the foot of the stairs now and as she stepped into the circle of light cast by the lamp he saw the face from the portrait in the dining room. Aged of course, but recognizable by the expression of chilly disapproval he recalled so clearly. Her eyes swept over him slowly as she came towards him.

'I see.' A pause, as they faced each other, and then, 'You've come for Alice, I suppose.'

At that moment the baize door to the servants' basement swung open. Lawrence felt a flash of irrational surprise at seeing the woman who had sat across the table from him in Maison Lyons appear, in a black dress and white apron. The last time he saw her she had been tearful, but now she looked terrified; almost unhinged. 'We've searched all the bedrooms,' she said, barely stifling a sob, 'and turned Miss Selina's out – looked under the bed, in the wardrobe—' She stopped when she recognized Lawrence. 'Oh!'

Lady Lennox's composure was in stark contrast to Polly's palpable panic, but through his own mounting agitation Lawrence was grateful for it. 'Thank you, Polly,' she said firmly, then turned back to Lawrence. 'Now is not the time to discuss your claim on my granddaughter. As you can see, you have arrived during something of a crisis.'

'Where is she?'

'That's rather the question. It appears that the child has run away.'

Alice crouched in the dark. Her hands, in the gloves she had packed, were balled into fists and she pressed them to her eyes until the endless blackness was filled with angry orange stars.

Her confidence that she had thought of everything seemed stupid now; stupid and embarrassing. Apples and spare socks were little comfort against the cold of an October night, and if she truly had planned properly she wouldn't be in her current predicament. She would have looked at the stained old estate map on the garden bothy wall and made sure she knew how to get to the station, and how long it would take. She would be in London by now, with Mama.

At least there was one thing she had done right, though it was by luck rather than careful preparation. The key to the Chinese House had been amongst the treasures she had packed into her satchel, and she had remembered it as she sat on the gate in the rapidly gathering dusk. She had stopped crying then, as the answer to her dilemma presented itself. The thought of being out in the woods when it got properly dark was terrifying, but she couldn't bear to go back to the house either. Everyone would be angry, but they would hide that behind relief that she was back and make a great fuss. They would watch her more closely from now on. She wouldn't get another chance.

And so she had made her way wearily back to the garden, tripping over thorny bramble ropes and snagging her coat on branches as darkness closed in. A misshapen moon slid between banks of cloud, lending some light and then snatching it away again. The wind in the trees sounded like the sigh of breath at her back and every so often the cry of a pheasant or a fox had made Alice's blood turn cold. Her whole body throbbed with fear as she came to the passage between the tall bushes and she had run then, but when she emerged on the other side the moon had turned the lake to silver and the Chinese House was in front of her.

In her mind it was a place of safety and comfort; a place where she would feel close to Mama. The reality was rather different. Perhaps it was the damp that made it feel colder in here than outside. Curled up in the dark she was aware of a rank, animal smell which she hadn't noticed in the daylight, and pictured spiders emerging from gaps and cracks to crouch in the cobwebbed corners above her head. Her mind recoiled from these imagined horrors and all of her senses felt stretched to breaking point. She wondered what time it was, and how she was going to get through the night.

But then she thought of Mama, and she knew she had no choice. Just a few hours, and as soon as it began to get light she would set off again and get the milk train to London. In a sudden burst of desperate energy she stood up, staggering the few paces over to the window on stiff legs. The gramophone's horn gleamed dully in the fitful moonlight. She turned the handle and moved the needle across with a shaking hand. It skidded and screeched, but after a moment the hostile dark was filled with music.

It was better when she couldn't hear the night's noises. She went back to the couch, clenching her chattering teeth together, hugging her satchel and its precious contents. Mama had once told her that if one listened carefully, one could hear pictures in music. She squeezed her eyes shut and saw sunlight and blue sky and Mama dancing.

It had started to rain again.

A police officer from Hindbury village had arrived shortly after Lawrence, wobbling up the drive on his bicycle under the cover of a great oilskin cape. Lawrence, however, had no intention of standing idly by while he asked irrelevant questions and made ponderous notes in a tiny book. Polly led him down the familiar stone steps to the servants' basement, where the gardener had joined the other servants to wait for news or instruction. After the briefest of introductions and no explanation, torches were found and Lawrence and Patterson set off into the streaming night to search.

'Looked everywhere I can think of already,' Patterson mumbled as they crossed the stableyard, arcing their lights around the empty stalls. 'Kicking myself for not starting earlier. I thought it was odd when she didn't show up – it's a rare day when I don't see her down in the kitchen garden, but I didn't like to pester. Stands to reason that she might not feel like it since she found out about . . .'

'We'll look again,' Lawrence said tersely. 'Cover each

area together, but split up to work more quickly.' A wave of hot nausea swept over him as he thought of the lake, lying somewhere in the darkness on the other side of the house. 'Have you checked the boathouse?'

'First thing I did when I found out she was missing. No sign that she'd been anywhere near.'

That was something at least. They went through the passageway into the kitchen garden, and from there took separate paths. Lawrence was aware of the other man's torch-light flashing across walls and into bothies and glasshouses and heard him calling Alice's name, his voice deliberately cheerful, as if they were playing a game of hide and seek. He felt unable to shout, like it wasn't his place. He was a stranger to her, and the knowledge was a spear in his side.

He moved faster and reached the gate to the main garden first. Too keyed up to wait, he went through it, down the tunnel of towering yews, and out into the garden, ready to tear the night apart to find this little girl. It was raining softly and steadily and the moon's light was watery, but even now he knew the way. He swung his torch sideways, picking out the landmarks from his memory, now forlorn and forgotten. Heart bursting with adrenaline, he shone his torch over stagnant pools and into mountains of shrubbery, not knowing what he expected to find. Patterson must be some way behind now, but in spite of his own advice to stay together, the spectre of the lake beyond the banks of rhododendrons drove him on. Alice had drawn the Chinese House for Selina; what if she'd gone back there to do another picture and slipped in the mud at the edge of the water? Lady Lennox had said that she had run away, but what if that wasn't true and she'd met with some sickening accident instead?

Suddenly his mind was alive with terrors. He started to run. The beam of his torch bounced wildly and weakly over dense leaves and tangled branches; the paradise he remembered was well and truly lost. Ducking out from the shrubbery he saw the shimmer of the lake ahead, the island in its centre. The pointed roof of the Chinese House glistened beneath the moon.

He stopped, breathing hard, staring at it. For a moment the memories were so vivid that he swore he heard music: Bach's Goldberg Variations drifting across the years.

And then he understood.

'*Patterson!*'

His voice rang with urgency. The gardener's answering shout came almost immediately but indistinctly, revealing that he was still some way behind. Lawrence was torn between the primitive need to get to Alice and an awareness that she might be scared by a stranger, but his feet made the decision before his head and he was crossing the bridge, trying to control his galloping heart.

He slowed as he approached the Chinese House. His hand was white in the beam of the torch as he lifted it to the handle, distantly surprised at its steadiness. He turned it, and the music swelled as it opened.

'Alice?'

At first he thought he had been wrong and the place was empty, of everything except ghosts and memories. And then he saw the little figure pressed against the wall in the furthest corner, as if to make herself invisible. He shone the torch into the space beside her, not wanting to dazzle her, and the air rushed from his lungs.

Cassie. Cassie's hair, but shorter. Cassie's eyes, Cassie's face. Jesus, *his* face, from the polished tin mirror on his parents' bedroom wall. The shock of its familiarity spread through him, a muted explosion.

She shrank further into the corner. He gathered his reeling thoughts, moving the light away from her and onto himself, so that she could see he meant no harm.

'It's all right, Alice. It's all right. My name is Lawrence. I'm a friend of your Mama's, from London—'

He had thought that this would reassure her, but instead it had the opposite effect. She gave a sort of snarl and pressed her hands to her ears as her whole body went rigid. 'No!' she shouted. 'No, no, no—'

He put the torch down beside the gramophone and went towards her, but she flinched away, ducking down and darting past him in the dark. Instinct took over and he went after her, catching up with her easily on the bridge and stooping to block her way with his arm. Her strength took him by surprise. He had to gather her against him to muffle the blows of her small fists, but they kept coming, on his shoulder and back as dry sobs racked her skinny body.

His chest was torn open with love. He loosened his grip

and let her strike him, soothing and steadying until the blows grew weaker and her fury burned out into the misery of a frightened child.

'I–i–is she . . . dead?'

'*No*. No, she's not.' The music had wound down into silence now and there was just the soft hiss of the rain. Gently he took the handkerchief she was clutching to wipe her eyes and nose. It was dark blue and spotted, faintly familiar. 'She's alive, and she very much wants to see you.'

By the time Patterson came upon them they had been back to collect her satchel from the Chinese House, and she had allowed Lawrence to take her hand. As they made their way through the dripping darkness it felt small and fragile in his, and impossibly, infinitely precious.

27

The House by the Park

When Lawrence had gone Selina thought again about that morning, waking up on her wedding day in the room in Marchmont Street. She remembered watching the dawn creep across the walls, making the edges of things grow more definite: the chair and the desk, the coffee cups and wine glasses. The kitbag, packed for America.

The opposite was happening now.

The light was fading and the world was sliding out of focus, until there was only voices and memories and feelings. Pain, of course; her constant shadow. But mostly overwhelming love.

Sometimes that hurt more.

'Is she sleeping?'

'Yes. But I think she knows you're here. I think she can hear you. Talk to her – she'd like that.'

'I don't know what to say . . .'

'You've got lots to tell her. About coming to London with Polly on the train. And about Edith's house, and the children and their strange pets. Tell her about the nursery—'

'And Mrs Hesketh's studio?'

'Yes. All of that.'

'All right.'

The Heskeths' house was directly opposite Regent's Park and it looked like a miniature castle. Alice had noticed it before, when she'd visited the zoo with Mama because, with its arched windows and grey stone gables and rows of chimneys, it was the kind of house you couldn't help noticing, and wondering who lived there.

The answer was an eccentric family who perfectly fitted their unusual home. Mr Hesketh was an ancient naturalist who had travelled to all corners of the globe in his younger years before a late marriage and the arrival, in rapid succession, of his four children. The eldest of these – Perseus, or Percy for short – was a year or so younger than Alice, but he had an easy confidence that made him seem older. All of them were perfectly sanguine about the addition to their chaotic nursery, treating Alice with the same benevolent curiosity as the injured jackdaw Percy was nursing back to health.

Polly had brought Alice to London on the train, the day after she had tried to make the journey on her own. Without Alice to look after at Blackwood there was no need for Polly to return, so Lawrence took a room for her in a boarding house in the next street to the hospital, so she could be on hand for Mama. Alice was glad to have her there, but she found she liked the Heskeths' house, with its cheerful nursery and shelves full of gloriously illustrated books. She had been given her own tiny bedroom, with a velvet patchwork counterpane and gold stars painted on the ceiling, but the part of the house she loved best was Mrs Hesketh's studio. (She had been instructed numerous times to call her Aunt Edith, but shyness had so far prevented her.)

Mrs Hesketh was an artist, and while her children roamed the park across the road or conducted alarming experiments in the scullery downstairs she retreated to an airy turret room stuffed with treasures – fragments of stained glass, a broken violin, the battered plaster head of a statue – to paint. She must have understood that Alice, still in shock and struggling to come to terms with Mama's illness, was overwhelmed by her children's exuberance at times, and she cleared a table in one corner for her to use, supplied with paper and charcoal and watercolours. Passing behind her one afternoon she bent over to look more closely at the sketch Alice was doing, of a feather she had found on the walk home from the hospital.

'Extraordinary,' Mrs Hesketh muttered, leaning over to pick up the paper. 'Exceptional. You have your father's talent, young lady, that's for sure.'

Alice was surprised.

'Do you know Papa?' She had never suspected that stern, upright Rupert Carew had an ounce of artistic ability.

Beneath her gypsy headscarf Mrs Hesketh's face flooded with red. She put the drawing down quickly.

'Oh – from years back. A whole lifetime ago. Good heavens – is that the time? Let's go and see what's for tea before those savages devour it all.'

'Alice?'

'She's gone. Back to Edith's.'

'Of course.' Through the cracks of her eyelids and the haze of pain, Selina could see that the curtains were drawn shut. 'Is it late?'

'Not so very late. She's probably having tea in the nursery about now, toasting muffins on the fire with the others.'

'She likes it there.'

'Yes, and the other children like having her. She and Percy have forged quite a bond over his collection of fossils.'

'She'll want . . . to draw them . . .'

'She does. She's brilliant. I thought that maybe I was biased, but Edith says it too. She can't get over how good she is.'

Selina let her eyes close again, counting in her head until the pain passed. It came in waves and there was no point in trying to fight them anymore. The only thing to do was let them take her, drag her down, and hope that she would resurface. She counted her breaths and tried to concentrate on Lawrence's voice. His words. After Rupert's cool indifference, his pride in Alice was like a candleglow in the darkness. The glimmer of sunlight on the surface of the water above her head. She focused on it now, and willed herself back to it.

'Shall I get the nurse?'

She shook her head. 'We need to talk ... About Alice. Afterwards.'

'Yes.'

She loved him for not pretending. She loved him for understanding that she didn't have the energy to cut through meaningless reassurance and lies.

'Will you take care of her?'

'Of course I will.' There was a break in his voice. 'I don't know her very well yet, but I love her. I'll do whatever's best for her. And for you.'

Another wave was surging inside her; she knew that in a moment she would be sinking. 'You ... were going to Spain ... The war ...'

'There'll be other wars. I'm not going anywhere.'

She gave herself up to the swell.

If time had gone slowly at Blackwood, it flowed by quickly in London. Too quickly. Like water draining out of the bath, Alice knew that it would soon be gone, and she dreaded it.

She saw Mama every day. She was at her best in the late mornings, when the doctor had done his rounds and the medicine the nurses gave her (not on a spoon, but by injection) had had a chance to work. When she arrived Mama was usually awake, her eyes shining with pleasure to see them, but after an hour she would be tired out, drifting in and out of sleep. Sometimes it was obvious that Mama was in great pain. She would close her eyes and her whole body would go stiff, and Alice couldn't look at her then because the suffering on her face was too hard to bear.

But in between those times they talked. There was always news to report from the Hesketh nursery, of the jackdaw (called Jackson, of course) and his increasing appetite now he was recovering, which meant Percy was forever in the garden digging for worms. Mama said he must be a good person to go to such lengths for an injured bird. Alice remembered the cat she had written about in the first clue in the treasure hunt – the one that her friend had hit with his car, and she had buried in the garden square with the kind stranger. She wanted to ask Mama about it, but she was far away again, beyond Alice's reach, battling a savage enemy no one else could see.

Sometimes Mama talked. Alice would lie beside her on the bed (carefully – oh, so carefully) and Mama would talk about when she was a little girl, playing games with Uncle Howard and tricks on her governesses, running around, half wild in the great gardens at Blackwood. Mr Patterson had been her friend too, she said, and all the gardener's boys – in the days when there had been gardener's boys. She had gone quiet after that, and the hand stroking Alice's hair had stilled.

'Mama?' Alice whispered.

Mama had lifted her hand then, and kissed Alice's head. 'It's all right, darling. I was just remembering, that's all. Wishing I could go back.'

'Can she?' she asked Lawrence later, when Mama had slipped away again and he was taking her back to Regent's Park; walking, because it wasn't far, and they both liked the sting of the cold air and the chance to breathe and think and talk. 'Can she go back to Blackwood? If I was poorly like that I'd far rather be at home, with familiar things all around. Polly could look after her, and maybe the nice nurse could come too, to do the injections and things. And I think Grandmama should spend more time with her, because she'll be sad later if she doesn't. If Mama was at Blackwood she could look out over the gardens and it would make her feel better. Maybe she might even be well enough to go out there sometime . . .'

She stopped then, because she knew it wasn't possible. Not just that Mama would be able to walk outside again, but that she would be well enough to make the journey to Blackwood at all.

'I don't think . . .' Lawrence said slowly.

'It's all right. I know it can't happen.'

They walked on for a few paces. He was holding her hand, which was another thing she liked because it was a perfectly normal thing to do out on the street, but it felt special. He gave it a squeeze.

'Maybe not, but you've given me an idea.'

*

The swell of the wave was more powerful now. It had dragged her far from the shore and rolled her round and round. Just when she thought its strength might be ebbing it gathered again and she was helpless. She cried out. She knew how hopeless it was, but she couldn't stop. On and on, begging for mercy, though her voice was lost in the roar.

The nurses came. Hands on her, faces mouthing words she couldn't hear. Polly was there, her hands cool and her voice immeasurably comforting. She stopped fighting after that, stopped trying to get back to the light and air and gave herself up to the great sucking ocean of pain.

When she surfaced again the light had changed. The wave had receded and her body felt insubstantial, as if it was already dissolving. Opening her eyes a crack she saw the Chinese House at Blackwood, the sun slanting across the wooden boards of the deck. She saw the orangery, with the fountain at its centre. She saw herself, aged twenty-one, lying on the tiled floor with her eyes closed and bars of shadow making patterns on her skin.

The images flickered across her exhausted mind, filling the black, blank spaces. Colour seeped into them, and sound and sensation. The sun on her face. The touch of his fingertips on her bare midriff. The taste of buttery new potatoes. When she closed her eyes she was there again, walking through the shadows between the yew hedges, and Lawrence was behind her, close by, carrying the gramophone down to the Chinese House.

She heard the music. Even when the surging waters closed

over her, she heard the haunting soar of strings, and it carried her through.

The pain in Alice's tummy had mostly gone now. It was only in the mornings, emerging slowly from sleep, that it came back, but it was no longer the sharp, insistent jab that it had been. It was harder, blunter, like a punch to the stomach or a weight being dropped on her. The weight of reality.

On the morning of her birthday it was worse than usual. The date had always held a kind of magic, but the very fact of it rolling round as if everything was normal felt like a mockery. The only thing that made her feel better was the thought that most people didn't know about it, and those that did had probably forgotten.

But it didn't turn out like that. Going down to breakfast she discovered that the chair in which she usually sat had been decorated with paper streamers and Christmas tinsel, and a large parcel had been left on the table in her place. 'Many happy returns, my dear,' Mr Hesketh said with great kindness, peering at her over the tops of his spectacles. 'It might not be the happiest of birthdays, but achieving double figures is a milestone. We must try to make it one on which you look back fondly in years to come.'

The parcel contained a book – *The Illustrated Encyclopaedia of British Birds and Mammals.* It was one she had discovered upstairs on the shelves in the nursery and to which she returned often, turning the pages slowly and marvelling at the watercolour plates inside.

'Your very own copy,' Percy said cheerfully. 'Look – it says so in the front.'

For Alice, she read. *'Art does not reproduce what we see; rather, it makes us see.' With love on your birthday from us all.* Six signatures, of varying degrees of flamboyance, were scrawled beneath.

'Thank you,' she managed to croak.

'Oh gosh, don't blub – you'll set us all off,' Percy said. 'Quick, help yourself to sausages. We only have them for special breakfasts, so it would be an awful waste to weep all over them.'

Mrs Hesketh told her that Lawrence had left the house early, so she would take Alice to the hospital to see Mama. She parked her car (the yellow one in which Lawrence had come to Blackwood) outside the main door and insisted on coming in to deliver her safely. Alice tried to tell her that there was no need and she knew the way up to Mama's room well enough by now, but she was very glad that Edith hadn't listened when they bumped into Papa on the stairs.

Alice felt herself going very red. If Mrs Hesketh hadn't been there she thought she might have turned and run away, though she wasn't quite sure why. In case Papa was angry with her, perhaps. In case he made her go back to Onslow Square with him. She hadn't realized until that moment how much she didn't want that. How, without Mama, their comfortable house in Onslow Square was just that – a house. No longer home.

Papa seemed to falter as he noticed her, which made Alice

go even redder; she had never seen him anything less than perfectly assured before, utterly composed. He removed his hat and nodded curtly to Edith, then his gaze moved down to Alice. 'I'm just on my way out, as you can see. Your mother is asleep. If she wakes up, tell her I was here.'

He said nothing to Mrs Hesketh, and gave no sign that he knew her. From years back, Mrs Hesketh had said, but still, Alice was surprised. Papa was very correct when it came to manners, and she wasn't the kind of person one would forget.

Before she even went into Mama's room she could see that it was different. There were photographs – big black and white photographs, five times the size of ordinary snapshots – stuck to the walls around the bed. On the table at its foot, beside a huge bouquet of lilies, there was a gramophone.

Mama was sleeping, propped up against a bank of pillows. She was wearing a beautiful grey silk bed jacket and her hair was brushed to spun gold over her shoulders. Letting go of Edith's hand Alice went forward, gazing around at the photographs.

'It's Blackwood!' She kept her voice to a whisper. 'That's the orangery, with the fountain in the middle. And there's the Chinese House. Who took them?'

Sunlight slanted across the pictures and the leaves were lush and blowsy with summer. And Mama ... Mama was young and strong and golden.

'Lawrence did, a long time ago,' Edith said softly.

'Alice?'

They both turned. Mama's eyelids had lifted a little. Her eyes seemed unusually dark.

'Yes, Mama. I'm here.'

'Happy birthday, my darling. Are you alone?'

'No. Mrs Hesketh is here. She brought me, in her car.'

'Edith . . . ?'

'That's right.' Edith went forward, closer to the bed. She looked very large in her big blue coachman's cape, but her voice was very gentle, very kind. Mama's pale lips softened into a smile.

'We almost met . . . years ago. At a party.'

'The Napiers. Grosvenor Square.'

'You had . . . painted . . .'

'Their portrait,' Edith finished for her. 'That's right.'

Mama's eyes closed. The smile widened. 'Lawrence's chest.'

Alice's head felt very full of jagged, disjointed thoughts, like pieces of a puzzle that didn't fit together. Or maybe did fit, but to make a picture that was completely different from the one she was expecting. The letter in the dressing up box had mentioned a boy with his whole chest painted with Van Gogh stars. Mama had run away from the party with him and they had had dinner late at night in a tiny French restaurant.

Mrs Hesketh was holding Mama's hand, which looked as thin and frail as Jackson the jackdaw's claw in her strong, square one. 'You have my word,' Alice heard her say softly. 'One mother to another.' She turned away, staring hard at the arrangement of lilies on the table at the foot of the bed, not wanting to know what they were talking about. Or knowing, but not wanting to admit it.

'Ah – and talk of the devil,' Mrs Hesketh said with sudden, forced cheerfulness. 'I'm just on my way, dear boy. I'll leave you in peace.'

Alice was aware of a sense of relief at seeing Lawrence. Release, like something tight inside her relaxing a little. He was holding a large, square box and he came over to where Alice stood, shoving aside the flower arrangement and the gramophone on the table to put it down. He ruffled Alice's hair and wished her happy birthday, then went over to Mama, bending to kiss her in a way that Papa never had.

'You got it?'

'I did.'

Mama tried to raise herself up and he helped her, cradling her against him as he banked up the pillows for her to rest on. She was so frail. So terribly delicate. Alice had given her back the aquamarine pendant, and it rested against her hollow chest, catching the light and glittering with each rapid breath. Her face was tense and shuttered, but as Lawrence settled her back against the pillows she cried out and her hand grasped at his arm, clutching his sleeve so hard that her knuckles gleamed like pearls beneath the thin skin.

Alice turned away as Lawrence held her and soothed and stroked. She wanted to cry out too – wanted to scream and snatch at Mama's shoulders and shake her until this brittle, unrecognizable shell dissolved and the old Mama came back – but she knew it wouldn't work. Nothing would work now. Her hands were curled into painful fists and the pain stabbed at her tummy. She held her breath until her ears rang, trying to squash down the sobs that she was afraid would escape with it.

And then, through the boom and roar of her fury she heard a sound that made her stop. And breathe. A plaintive little sound that came from the box on the table.

Lawrence laughed shakily. 'I think you'd better open your present.'

The box was lined with straw. The tiny kitten had obviously been asleep in it, but it was awake now, looking up at her with wide round eyes. He was entirely black, so that when he opened his mouth to make a sound his tongue looked startlingly pink. Alice gasped.

'Is he really mine?'

'All yours.'

Tentatively she picked him up. Cupping him between her hands, she held his tiny body against her chest, carried him closer to where Mama lay, and crouched down. 'Feel, Mama. He's so tiny, and so soft . . .'

Mama lifted her hand and, as her fingertips brushed the downy fur she smiled, properly and delightedly, so that for a moment it was possible to glimpse her as she used to be. Beautiful and alive.

'What are you going to call him?' Lawrence said.

'I don't know.'

'Cartwright . . .' Mama murmured, and she turned her

head towards Lawrence, though her eyes didn't seem to focus.

He took hold of her hand and cradled it as tenderly as Alice was holding the kitten. His voice was calm but his face reminded Alice of a painting she had seen of Jesus on the cross.

'Perfect.'

That night, as the kitten purred loudly on the quilt beside her, Alice unearthed the satchel she had hidden in the bottom of the wardrobe and took out the stash of letters.

She picked up the last one again. It was the only one in which Mama had written Lawrence's name, but Alice understood now that it was the final clue. The missing piece. She hadn't mentioned him by name in the earlier letters, but Alice understood now that he was on every page. In every part of Mama's story.

The story of how Alice came to be.

28

Selina

There was a tree outside the window of Selina's room. Its branches cast shadows over the bed and the rain plastered its fallen leaves against the glass.

November again.

Time had slipped away from her and become meaningless, but through the liminal veils in her mind she registered the season and felt a grudging satisfaction. The pain was relentless now; in her head mostly, but it radiated outwards until it was everywhere. Everything. As the afternoon slipped into evening and the day nurse handed over charge to the night sister she saw Howard standing in the doorway. He was dressed in his uniform and was checking his wristwatch.

I know, she told him. *Just a little longer.*

The days were shortening rapidly. When tea was over it was too dark to go across to the park and look for conkers or dig for Jackson's worms in the garden, and so the children would go into the parlour where the fire was lit and listen to Mr Hesketh reading the *Just So Stories* in his deep, slow voice.

Artemis and Hebe vied for the honour of sitting on his knee and being allowed to turn the pages. Alice hung back beside Percy, feigning indifference but wishing that Lawrence was there. He spent most of his time at the hospital now, and though Alice tried to stay awake until she heard the slam of the front door and his tread on the stairs, last night she hadn't been able to.

She knew this meant there wasn't much time left, but she didn't want to think about it. Instead she concentrated on buttering the muffins Percy toasted on the fire and listening to how the elephant got his trunk.

'Howard?'

'No, it's Lawrence.'

Thank goodness. His hand, warm against her cheek, his touch gentle, familiar, beloved.

'Lawrence, I . . .'

She had opened her eyes, but it was still dark. She wanted to ask if it was night time, if the light was off, but she was afraid the answer might be no. The pain had been unbearable earlier – excruciating – and the nurses had whispered urgently amongst themselves. Whatever they had injected her with had taken effect now and driven it back, but it was hard to concentrate.

In the shadows at the foot of the bed a little girl with dark tangled hair and a slightly grubby face watched her. Gripping Lawrence's hand she took another breath.

'Do you remember . . . the night we met . . . we talked . . . about the afterlife?'

'Yes.'

'We said we didn't . . . believe.'

'Yes.'

The little girl's eyes were as dark as sloes, like Lawrence's. Like Alice's. Her cheeks dimpled as she smiled shyly.

'I believe now. And I'm not afraid.'

Alice woke to a world of smoky mist and soft edges on the morning of Bonfire Night. The trees in the park opposite her room had lost most of their leaves now but a few clung on, tattered pennants, bravely scarlet in the milk-white air.

At breakfast Percy and Hebe were discussing the fireworks that would be set off in the garden later, and arguing good-naturedly over who was going to be in charge of making parkin, when Alice heard the front door and the sound of voices in the hall. She slipped down from her seat, her whole body prickling with dread as she went to the door.

'You can't be there all the time, anyway, Lawrence.' Mrs Hesketh was saying. 'Look at you—'

'I don't care. All that matters is what Selina wants, not her fucking *sister*—'

He broke off abruptly when he saw Alice, and rubbed a

hand over his hollow eyes. He looked like one of the poor men who sat in the mouth of the underground station, unshaven and desolate.

'Sorry, sweetheart.'

Icy fingers closed around Alice's heart. 'Is Mama . . . ?'

He shook his head. 'She's sleeping. She's peaceful – in no pain. Your Aunt Miranda came.' He attempted a smile. 'And your grandmother. I thought it was best if I left.'

Edith came forward and put her hand on Alice's shoulder. 'It might be nice for you to all be together with your mama. If you'd like to see them, I'm very happy to take you.' She spoke firmly. 'Your father needs to sleep now.'

'I don't want to see them.' She would have to sometime she supposed, but she didn't want that time to be today. 'I want to be with Mama. Can we go later, after they've gone?'

Lawrence stooped and dropped a kiss on the top of her head.

'Of course.'

None of them noticed Edith's slip of the tongue. Or if they did, they didn't remark on it, or try to explain. There was no need now. And anyway, they were all too busy hoping it wouldn't be too late.

She was floating. Adrift on a wide, dark sea.

The savage storm had passed now and the waves had not swallowed her, but they had carried her far from the shore. She couldn't get back.

Everything felt very far away. She heard voices – Mama,

Miranda, Rupert, even Lionel at one point – and they were clear, but seemed to come from a great distance away. Echoes from another room.

'Music?' (Lionel; fussy, disapproving.) 'Is that quite the thing?'

'She seems to like it,' Mama said.

Mama's fingers touched her forehead, stroking back her hair. Selina could smell her scent. It took her back to the nursery, when Mama would come up to say goodnight to them before she went down to dinner. Not to kiss them. Mama had never been one for kisses.

'At least it's not jazz. Can you imagine?' There was a tremor in Miranda's voice. 'I rather think she'd appreciate it though. She always loved dancing.'

I'm too tired now, Selina wanted to say. *Too tired to dance.*

The music soothed her. She could smell bonfires. Wet leaves. Lilies, sent by Theo – funeral flowers, ironically appropriate. Rupert's pipe.

'Where's the child?' Lionel asked.

A pause.

'With her father, one assumes,' Rupert replied gruffly, and in that moment Selina loved him more than she ever had during their ill-advised marriage.

I ought to say goodbye, she thought. *Very bad form not to,* but the effort of opening her eyes was immense. And they were only shadows anyway; dark shapes, dissolving at the edges, losing definition. Except for Flick, sitting on the edge of the bed.

The Glittering Hour

'Ready, darling?'
Not quite.

It was a perfect night for fireworks; clear and sharp and cold. A full moon hung low in the sky, close enough to see the marbled shadows on its surface. It looked like a face, looking down on the world with a sort of sorrowful serenity.

Alice felt calm. She had cried earlier, face down on her bed, gasping and heaving, but the exhaustion that followed had been welcome. Cartwright, apparently sensing her distress, had clambered onto her back as she lay there, settling between her shoulder blades and purring his motor-engine purr against her neck. Percy had come up and knocked softly, bringing her the first square of parkin to try, warm from the tin, and a glass of milk.

The hospital was quiet in the evenings. As she and Lawrence walked together along the corridor the echo of their footsteps reminded Alice of being in church. The nurse at the desk smiled at them, kindly. Visitors weren't really supposed to come so late, Alice knew that. She also understood why it was all right for them to be there. Why the rules didn't matter so much now. Mama was sleeping. Peacefully, as Lawrence had said. The aquamarine was no longer around her neck but in her hand, the chain slipping through her loosely curled fingers. Her eyes seemed sunken in and there were blue shadows beneath them. Her breathing was very slow now. It felt like she had retreated to a place where Alice could no longer reach her.

Lawrence brought the chair across again, to the place where he always put it. And then he went over to the gramophone and looked through the records that were stacked beside it. He slid one from its paper case and put it on the turntable. The needle crackled as it started to rotate and a violin's thin, clear note emerged from the horn, spiralling upwards.

He pulled her onto his knee and they sat together, close to Mama, listening to the music, looking at the photographs dissolving into the encroaching dusk.

'Have I told you that I had a little sister?' His voice was soft and low. 'She was called Cassie. You remind me of her very much. The same dark eyes.'

'What happened to her?'

'She died when she was eight, of the flu just after the war.'

The photographs on the walls shimmered and blurred. 'That's sad.'

'Yes. And my mother died too, at the same time. But I think of them often – Cassie in particular. Especially since I've met you. It's like having a bit of her back, in a way. It makes me realize that the people you love don't leave you. You carry them inside your head and your heart, but also in yourself too. Cassie is in your eyes. Your mama is in your beautiful smile and your hands—' he took one, and spread it across his own. 'She's in your voice and your spirit and your courage. And she'll always be in those things, and beside you. Your whole life through.'

The tears spilled. She didn't bother to wipe them. They

ran down her face as the music rose and swooped through light and shadow and subsided again into the bittersweet song of a single violin. It faded into silence, leaving only the hiss of the gramophone and the slow rasp of Mama's breath.

Lawrence's chest shuddered beneath her cheek. He rubbed a hand over his face. Leaning forward, he stroked Mama's hair with a tenderness that made Alice look away.

'Darling, it's time to go,' he said softly. Alice wasn't sure which one of them he was talking to.

A tear splashed on her cheek. She felt the brush of her daughter's lips and heard her voice.

I love you, Mama. I love you.

A flicker of life quickened her tired heart. A pulse of love.

Lawrence was beside her. She could sense him, even before he cupped her cheek with his hand, stroking his thumb gently across it.

Was she crying too?

The little girl emerged from the shadows at the foot of the bed, losing her shyness now. Selina wanted to tell him she was there, but the words were scattering, leaves on the wind. There wasn't enough breath.

He let go. She felt them move away.

And then a hand was slipping into hers and tugging her after them, out into the glittering night.

Epilogue

May 1937

In the clean, clear sunshine of early summer the garden looked almost as it had in its glory days as the small procession made its way down to the Chinese House. Patterson had worked tirelessly, through winter frosts and early spring downpours, clearing paths, clipping hedges, cutting paths, to make it the very best it could be for this day, and the weather had not let him down. The sky was forget-me-not blue, and the brisk breeze was perfumed with green sap and blossom.

Alice led the way, neat in her new school uniform. Langley House was the school that Hebe Hesketh went to, but she, three years younger, still had to wear a smock, whereas Alice had a gymslip. Its navy and green tartan pleats swished pleasingly against her legs (three inches longer now, Polly swore) as she walked. She had chosen to wear it because she liked it and wished Mama could have seen her in it, and because it was smart without being sombre. She and Lawrence had agreed that today wasn't to be a sad occasion.

He walked beside her, carrying the box. Alice had never heard the word *cremation* before Mama died, but Percy told her that it had been practised by great civilizations throughout history for their most revered people – great Viking warriors and members of the best Roman Imperial families. It had fallen out of fashion but was gaining popularity again now, Percy said, and Alice knew that Mama would like the idea of being part of a new Thing. When Grandfather had died in January and Alice had seen for herself the damp, cramped vault beneath the chapel floor she was immensely glad that Mama had not been left there.

The brightness of the day was suddenly lost as they reached the rhododendron tunnel. Lawrence took her hand then and together they emerged from the shadows to see the lake glittering in front of them, the Chinese House almost hidden behind clouds of blossom.

'Ready?'

She looked back. Grandmama was a little way behind, with Polly and Patterson (almost unrecognizable in his dark Sunday suit) behind her, then Ellen, Ivy and Mrs Rutter. Denham was last, as slow and formal as ever, with a white cloth over his arm and a champagne bottle in his hand. It had been Grandmama's idea. Mama would have insisted upon it, she said.

She nodded and held a little tighter to Lawrence's hand. 'Ready.'

She had thought that Grandmama would come onto the island with them, but as they crossed the little wooden bridge she went to stand on the edge of the lake. The others assembled alongside her, so when Alice and Lawrence reached the island and looked back they were standing in a line, looking over to the Chinese House. The brisk wind caught at Ivy and Ellen's aprons, making them flutter like white flags.

A sob rose in her throat.

In spite of their resolution, Lawrence was struggling too. Putting the box down he went into the Chinese House and Alice heard him winding up the gramophone. She took the spotted handkerchief from her pocket and hastily scrubbed at her eyes. The first notes of the violin spiralled out of the open doorway.

The music from the hospital on the night that Mama died. The music she sometimes heard on nights when she couldn't sleep, coming from the gramophone downstairs in the little house Lawrence had taken in Primrose Hill. Nights when Polly (who had decided that London wasn't so bad after all) would make her warm milk and let her sit for a while in the cosy basement kitchen and talk about Mama.

Lawrence came to stand beside her. The violin's notes soared up into the wide blue sky, like the lark. Across on the bank, Polly turned her head away to wipe her eyes discreetly. Lawrence's throat moved as he swallowed.

'I suppose it's time . . .'

Alice picked up the box. It was lighter than she expected, and the miscalculation made her clumsy. The hinged lid fell open.

'Oh!'

Lawrence moved to help her, to hold it, his hands covering hers on the box, but it was too late.

A gust of wind. A flurry of blossom petals caught and carried, a haze of grey, clouding the figures on the bank. In the second before it cleared Alice saw a small figure – a dark-haired girl in an old-fashioned dress – standing a little distance from Grandmama. She was looking upwards, laughing in delight in a shower of swirling petals. The wind snatched at a lock of Alice's hair, blowing it across her eyes. She shook it away impatiently.

'Oh, she's gone—'

Lawrence was staring out across the lake, as if desperately searching for something that was just out of sight. Agony was etched onto his face.

'I think she's still with us.' There was a break in his voice. 'Don't you?'

On the bank Patterson put his arm around Polly's shoulders. Grandmama bowed her head. There was no sign of the little girl.

Alice felt calm as she took Lawrence's hand.

'Yes,' she said.

Acknowledgements

Before I wrote *The Glittering Hour* I started, and set aside, three other books – an experience I hope never to repeat! I'm so grateful to the friends and family members who listened, sympathized, advised and encouraged during that time, especially Jenny Ashcroft, who has been there to talk through many a thorny plot issue, and ace group-therapy team Abby Green, Heidi Rice, Susan Wilson and Fiona Harper for their twenty-four-hour email counselling service. And to writer friends old and new, who provide the lifeline of genuine understanding and joyous get-togethers; who celebrate the highs and commiserate during the lows, and whose company is always inspiring. (Kerry Fisher, Amanda Jennings, the historical lunch gals, Liz Fenwick, Andy Jones and Rebecca Mascull, I'm looking at you all!)

A special thank you to Rebecca Ritchie, the most patient and supportive agent imaginable, to Deborah Schneider for her positivity and wisdom, and the amazing teams at Simon and Schuster UK and St Martin's Press, for giving me time and space to discover the story I wanted to write. To the dedicated book champions – the readers and reviewers and bloggers – I met in person and online, following the publication of my first book, and who have buoyed me up and made me smile as I battled to bring the second one into the world, sincere and slightly tearful thanks. Your support means more than I can possibly say.

I'm indebted, as always, to my family, but particularly so with this book, which was inspired by my grandmother's experience, eloquently (if illegibly) written by my mother and typed up for permanent record by my eldest daughter. Selina's story, as it appears here, bears little outward resemblance to that of my academic, determined grandmother, who went to university at a time when it was rare for women to do so, who qualified as a doctor and defied convention by continuing to work after she married and became a mother (but who was still denied any agency during her final illness, when fellow medics deferred to her estranged husband and lied to her about her prognosis). I cherish the thread that connects us all, four generations, which her premature death, twenty years before I was born, couldn't quite sever.

I'm immensely thankful for the boundless support of my husband John, who knows when to bring tea, when to pour wine, when to listen to my plot-related ramblings and existential panic, and when to intervene with a cleverly framed question or insightful observation (and who also does my tax return – surely the most underrated expression of love in the modern age.)

Writing is a fairly lonely business and I'd like to say a final and heartfelt thank you to Ruby the cat, who has been my constant companion since I took the first tentative steps on the road to writing an actual book in 2004. She has been there ever since, appearing at my elbow to remind me when it's lunchtime, distracting me with her tractor-engine purr, walking across the keyboard and filling the day's blank pages with enviable ease (and also getting a cameo role in my previous book, *Letters to the Lost*). As I write this on a blustery November afternoon, she is dozing on the sofa and hasn't got the energy to jump onto the desk to make up improbable words. Her silky fur is getting duller by the day and she's moving more stiffly and, though she can still rouse herself at the sound of a tuna can being opened, I know that by the time this book hits the shelves in the springtime and another one is underway she'll be gone.

But still with us, of course.

Questions for Discussion

1. Lady Lennox is very detached from her granddaughter. What are the reasons for this? Does her attitude change throughout the course of the book and, if so, why?

2. Can you see any similarities between the world of the Bright Young Things in the 1920s and celebrity culture in the present day? Any differences?

3. How does the legacy of the First World War make itself felt in the story?

4. Selina and Lawrence come from very different backgrounds and, on the surface, have little in common. What is it about Lawrence that Selina finds so attractive? And what draws Lawrence to Selina?

5. Why do you think Rupert asked Selina to marry him? Was he thinking primarily of her, or himself? Why do

you think she gave him the answer she did, and was it a good decision?

6. What do you think would have happened if Selina had chosen to stay with Lawrence?

7. How did attitudes to illness differ in the 1930s from the present day?

8. In the 1936 strand, Polly and Rupert both express their regret about the deception they have become caught up in. Did you understand Selina's reasons for beginning it? Do you think she should have done things differently?

9. How might the story have played out in the present day? Which aspects would be different, which the same?

10. What do you think happens in the years that follow the end?

Enjoyed *The Glittering Hour*?

Read on for an extract from Iona Grey's
bestselling novel, and winner of the RNA award,

Letters to the Lost

Prologue

Maine, February 2011

The house is at its most beautiful in the mornings.

He designed it to be that way, with wide, wide windows which stretch from floor to ceiling, to bring in the sand and the ocean and the wide, wide sky. In the mornings the beach is empty and clean, a page on which the day is yet to be written. And the sunrise over the Atlantic is a daily miracle he always feels honoured to witness.

He never forgets how different it could have been.

There are no curtains in the house, nothing to shut out the view. The walls are white and they take on the tint of the light; pearly pale, or pink as the inside of a seashell, or the rich, warm gold of maple syrup. He sleeps little these days and mostly he is awake to see the slow spread of dawn on the horizon. Sometimes he comes to suddenly, feeling that familiar touch on his shoulder.

Lieutenant, it's 4.30 a.m. and you're flying today . . .

A circle is closing. The finger tracing it on the misted glass is slowly coming around to the top again, to the point where it all began. The memories are with him almost constantly now, their colours fresh, voices vivid. Dawns of long ago. The smell of oil and hot metal. The plaintive, primitive thrum of engines on the flight line and a red ribbon on a map.

Today gentlemen, your target is . . .

It is such a long time ago. Almost a lifetime. It is the past, but it doesn't feel like it's over. The ribbon is stretching across the ocean outside his window, beyond the distant horizon, to England.

The letter lies amid the bottles of pills and sterile needle packs on the nightstand beside him, its familiar address as evocative as a poem. A love song. He has waited too long to write it. For years he has tried to reconcile himself to how things are and to forget how they should have been, but as the days dwindle and the strength ebbs out of him he sees that this is impossible.

The things that are left behind are the things that matter, like rocks exposed by the retreating tide. And so he has written, and now he is impatient for the letter to begin its journey, into the past.

1

London, February 2011

It was a nice part of London. Respectable. Affluent. The shops that lined the street in the villagey centre were closed and shuttered but you could tell they were posh, and there were restaurants – so many restaurants – their windows lit up like wide-screen TVs showing the people inside. People who were too well-mannered to turn and gawp at the girl running past on the street outside.

Not running for fitness, wearing lycra and headphones and a focused expression, but messily, desperately, with her short skirt riding up to her knickers and her unshod feet splashing through the greasy puddles on the pavement. She'd kicked off her stupid shoes as she left the pub, knowing she wouldn't get far wearing them. Platform stilettos; the twenty-first-century equivalent of a ball and chain.

At the corner she hesitated, chest heaving. Across the road was a row of shops with an alleyway at the side; behind, the pounding echo of feet. She ran again, seeking out the dark. There was a backyard with bins. A security light exploded above her, glittering on broken glass and ragged bushes beyond a high wooden gate. She let herself through, wincing and whimpering as the ground beneath her feet changed from hard tarmac to oozing earth that seeped through her sodden tights. Up ahead there was the glimmer of a streetlight. It gave her something to head towards; she pushed aside branches and emerged into a narrow lane.

It was flanked on one side by garages and the backs of houses, and by a row of plain terraced cottages on the other. She swung round, her heart battering against her ribs. If he followed her down here there would be nowhere to hide. No one to see. The windows of the houses glowed behind closed curtains, like slumbering eyes. Briefly she considered knocking on the door of one of the small cottages and throwing herself on the mercy of the people inside, but realizing how she must look in her clinging dress and stage make-up she dismissed the idea and stumbled on.

The last house in the little terrace was in darkness. As she got closer she could see that its front garden was overgrown and neglected, with weeds growing halfway up the peeling front door and a forest of shrubbery encroaching upon it from the side. The windows were blank and black. They swallowed up her reflection in their filth-furred glass.

She heard it again, the beat of running feet, coming closer. What if he'd got the others to look for her too? What if they came from the opposite direction, surrounding her and leaving no escape? For a moment she froze, and then adrenaline squirted, hot and stinging, galvanizing her into movement. With nowhere else to go she slipped along the side of the end house, between the wall and the tangle of foliage. Panic made her push forward, tripping over branches, gagging on the feral, unfamiliar stink. Something shot out from beneath the hedge at her feet, so close that she felt rough fur brush briefly against her shin. Recoiling, she tripped. Her ankle was wrenched round and a hot shaft of pain shot up her leg.

She sat on the damp ground and gripped her ankle hard, as if she could squash the pain back in to where it had come from. Tears sprang to her eyes, but at that moment she heard footsteps and a single angry shout from the front of the house. She clenched her teeth, picturing Dodge beneath the streetlamp, hands on his hips as he swung around searching for her, his face wearing that particular belligerent expression jaw jutting, eyes narrowed – that it did when he was thwarted.

Holding her breath she strained to listen. The seconds stretched and quivered with tension, until at last she picked up the sound of his receding feet. The air rushed from her lungs and she collapsed forward, limp with relief.

The money crackled inside her pocket. Fifty pounds – she'd only taken her share, not what was due to the rest of the band, but he wouldn't like it: he made the bookings, he took the money. She slid a hand into her pocket to touch the waxy, well-used notes, and a tiny ember of triumph glowed in her heart.

booksandthecity.co.uk

the home of female fiction